TRAITOR'S HOPE

CHRONICLES OF GENSOKAI
BOOK II

VIRGINIA McCLAIN

Copyright © 2017 Virginia McClain

All rights reserved.

This is a work of fiction. Any and all resemblance to actual people, places, or events is purely coincidental.

ISBN: 1974135934
ISBN-13: 978-1974135936

To Corey, for being a true partner.
To my parents, for teaching me about all kinds of strength.
To Cedar, for letting me ignore you long enough to write a book.

A Map of Gensokai

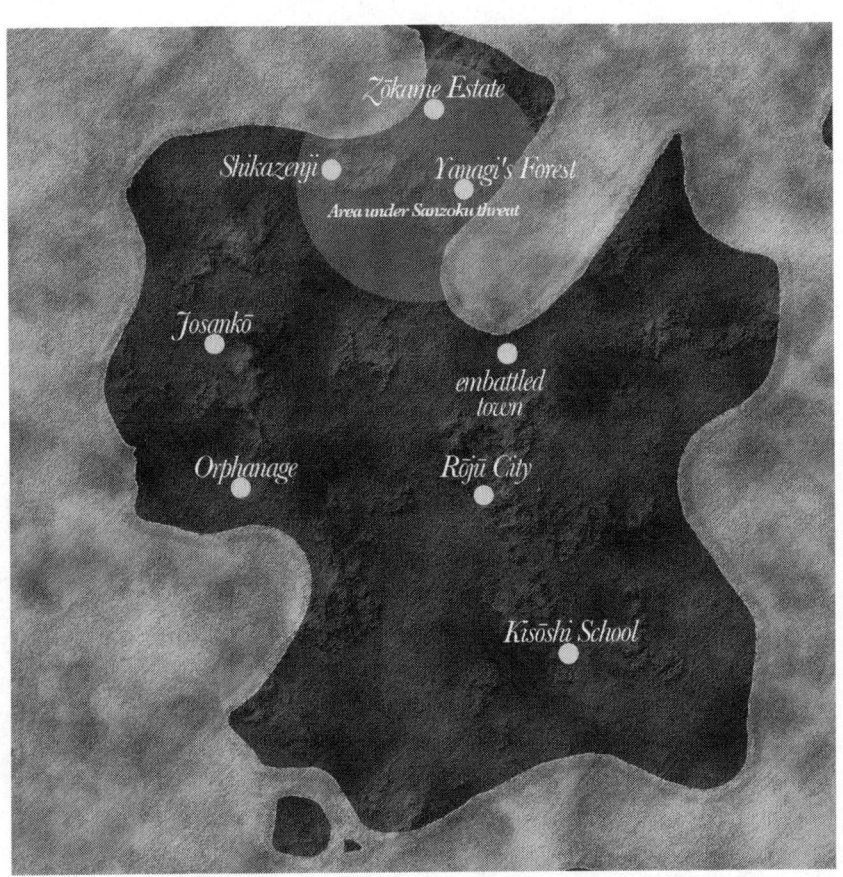

Glossary of Terms

Some of the following terms are actual Japanese words, however, most of them are fabricated words made strictly for the purpose of this fictional work. Some are based in Japanese roots, while others are simply English terms made to apply to things in the book. While Gensokai is its own world and is not actually based on Japan, lots of the vocabulary for the book is taken from Japanese to help give it the feel of the feudal Japanese culture that the book was inspired by.

Please note that Japanese plurals are not denoted with an s, so you will see things such as: "three kimono" or "a hundred sanzoku" throughout the book.

cycle - *see seasoncycle
chawan - bowl or cup used to serve tea (an actual Japanese term)
eihei - the elite guard of the Rōjū (an actual Japanese term meaning elite guard)
fuchi - the well of one's ki (taken from the actual Japanese word for abyss)
Gensokai - the name of the island realm in which our adventure takes place (taken from the Japanese words for element and world)
ha - the actual Japanese word for the sharp edge of a blade
hakama - the pants worn by Kisōshi (actual Japanese term for divided skirts that men wear on formal occasions or for certain martial arts)
hebi-dan - this is a made-up term containing the actual Japanese word for snake (hebi) and the actual Japanese word for level or rank (dan). In the context of the book, Hebi-dan is the lowest rank for a Kisōshi (it is the first rank they achieve through testing) whereas the highest is Ryū-dan.
hishi - the elite assassins used by the Rōjū (taken from the Japanese word for secret history)
izakaya - a tavern-like place where people go for drinks and food, most often consisting of private rooms for friends to meet and talk (taken from the actual Japanese word)
Josankō - the school where all josanpu are trained (taken from the Japanese words for midwifery and school)
josanpu - a woman trained in the arts of birthing and care for women's health (the actual Japanese word for midwife)

Kami/kami - this word is taken from the actual Japanese for spirit or deity. For the purposes of this book the capitalized Kami means deity and the lowercase kami means spirit.
katana - the long, curved blade used by all Kisōshi (the actual Japanese word for a single edged sword)
ki - a person's spirit or energy (actual Japanese word for spirit/essence)
kimono - traditional clothing worn by men and women throughout Gensokai (the Japanese word for clothing–especially traditional Japanese clothing)
kisaki - the point of a blade (actual Japanese word for the point of a blade)
kisō - energy manipulation (taken from the Japanese words for energy and manipulation–note that the actual Japanese definition differs from this made up usage)
kisōseki - a rare person who, due to an overlap in elemental powers, is able to track using kisō (word fabricated from a combination of energy manipulation and tracking)
Kisōshi - elite warriors trained in fighting who possess an innate ability to manipulate one element (word taken from Japanese for "energy manipulation person")
mooncycle (moon) - three tendays in Gensokai. Most common usage is "moon"
mune - the blunt back edge of a blade (actual Japanese word)
obi - the wide decorative belt worn with kimono (actual Japanese word)
oni - demons or bad spirits
raiko - a rare Kisōshi who can call on both water and wind (taken from Japanese roots for storm and caller)
Rōjū - the ruling council of elder Kisōshi in charge of making all decisions for Gensokai (using the actual Japanese word for the Shogun's council of Elders)
ryokan - a traditional inn (actual Japanese word)
ryū-dan - see "hebi-dan"
sanzoku - a mountain bandit (actual Japanese word for mountain bandit)
saya - a scabbard (actual Japanese word)
seiza - a seating position with legs folded at the knees and one's seat resting on one's feet (actual Japanese word)
senkisō - a Kisōshi with elemental ties to fire or air and thus to battle (taken from the Japanese words for energy manipulation and war/battle)

seasoncycle (cycle) - the term for a year in Gensokai, most commonly referred to as a "cycle"

shoji - sliding screen door or window (actual Japanese word)

shinogi - the widest part of a katana, the part between the mune and the hasami (actual Japanese word)

shuriken - a small sharpened disk used as a weapon by the hishi, often coated in poison (actual Japanese word for "throwing star")

tatami - a mat made of dried woven grass and straw typically used as flooring, also a standard measure of length: approximately one meter by two meters in size (actual Japanese word)

tenday - a period of ten days (taking the place of weeks in this world)

tsuka - the hilt of a katana

uwagi - the jacket worn by all Kisōshi (taken from the Japanese word for a traditional jacket)

wa - harmony (taken from the actual Japanese)

wakizashi - the short sword worn by Kisōshi to accompany a katana.

yukisō - a Kisōshi with elemental ties to earth or water and thus to healing (taken from the Japanese words for energy manipulation and healing/medicine)

Yūwaku - the all-female ruling power in Gensokai before the Rōjū took power

zantō - an ally of the Rōjū after they were deposed (taken from the actual Japanese)

17日 1月 老中 1102年

17ᵗʰ Day, 1ˢᵗ Moon, Cycle 1102 of the Rōjū Council

⁓ Prologue ⁓

"SHE HAS ENOUGH kisō to be Kisōshi," Yuki said, as she wiped the blood from the baby's tiny mewling face. The tiny creature's cries filled the small room, along with the tang of blood and afterbirth.

Suzumi nodded. "And a fire kisō at that."

"I hate this," Yuki whispered. "The mother dead from blood loss, no one to mourn her loss, and now this?"

Suzumi slapped the younger josanpu and took the baby from her.

"I'm not risking my life just because you've grown wistful," she said, as she stepped toward the basin with the newborn.

Yuki grimaced, but didn't move to stop the older woman.

"I wasn't suggesting anything... only... it's so sad."

Suzumi grunted.

"Sad? Sad would be what anyone will do to us if they hear you talking like that. And in the middle of Rōjū City no less. Now let's get this over with and be gone from here. Ieda-san is likely to give birth at any moment and I want to go check on her. She, at least, is unlikely to spawn anything that I'll be forced to drown. The woman hasn't an ounce of kisō in her body."

Suzumi paused when she noticed the silence behind her. Yuki normally took any excuse to laugh at Ieda-san. When she turned she felt a hand clamp over her mouth and cold steel press against her throat.

"Careful now. Don't drop her," the man before her, covered in grey and almost invisible in the dimly lit room, whispered as he carefully uncovered her mouth. "No screaming," he added, as he moved his hand to support the tiny infant that Suzumi had been about to submerge.

Suzumi was surprised by the care with which he handled the child. It contrasted strangely with the collapsed form of Yuki that she could see behind him. The young woman's throat was slashed, her blood cooling on the floor. That scene instead matched the pressure of the knife held to her own throat and the chilling hatred she could see reflected in the man's eyes.

"The babe's mother lies dead beyond those curtains, and you plan to drown my only child.... Hasn't there been enough death for one night?" he asked, as he cradled the newborn against his chest.

Suzumi whispered, afraid that a full speaking voice might break whatever compulsion had kept the man from killing her until now.

"They won't let her live, Dono," she whispered. "The Rōjū will never let her live. Death is the only way out."

"I suppose you are right," the man said. And Suzumi felt the blade slide across her throat before she felt her life's blood spill out and leave her.

The last thing she heard before blackness took her was the sound of a man's voice over the soft crying of a new babe.

"I will never let them take you, my darling Kusuko-chan."

1日 1月 新議 1年
1st Day, 1st Moon, Cycle 1 of the New Council

～Kusuko～

THE BACKHAND CAUGHT Kusuko by surprise and the sting alone brought tears to her eyes. She blinked, and the open, sparsely decorated room regained some of its focus. She wondered if the dizziness was more to do with the slap, or with the injuries she hadn't quite recovered from fully.

She stared at the large wooden beams that spanned the ceiling above Mamushi-san's head, ignoring his sharp features, greying hair, and dark brown eyes, and tried to dismiss the tears before they could raise his ire.

"That," Mamushi-san said, calmly folding his hands over his midsection so the sleeves of his kimono lay neatly atop one another, "is for drawing a sword against the first Rōjū without orders to do so."

The second backhand wasn't a surprise, and Kusuko took it stoically.

"And that," he continued, "is for almost getting yourself killed for your troubles. If that female Kisōshi had not saved you with her incredible display of power, you would be dead along with everyone else caught in that blast of wind. That is unacceptable."

"I am sorry Mamushi-san," Kusuko replied, keeping her chestnut eyes downcast. She would have to adjust her face paints after this meeting, but for now it was better not to remind Mamushi-san that he'd been 'forced' to hit her. "I did not attack the first Rōjū. It was that hifu. She was drawn to the freedom offered by Kuma-sensei and his allies. She was drawn to their bravery as well."

"That may be, but if the skins you adopt for your various assignments cannot follow orders then they have lost their usefulness."

"Is it not useful to you now that the Rōjū are deposed?"

"Hmph... as if you could have known the outcome of that battle."

"I did not. My hifu at that time seemed to think the outcome was inevitable, however."

"Luckily for you she was right. I can still make use of you even though the Rōjū no longer trust you."

"Do you still serve them?" Kusuko asked before she could stop herself. Luckily, Mamushi decided not to hit her again, he merely glared as he answered.

"They still see fit to pay me. They seem to think that they can regain power given enough time and information."

"And what do you think?"

"I think that you would serve me best by serving your new allies."

"They are not my allies, Mamushi-san. You are my only ally. They are the allies of my hifu and nothing more."

"As you say. You will do well to remember that." Kusuko didn't flinch the next time that Mamushi-san reached for her, but this time it was a light caress of her cheek. Kusuko glowed at the rare show of affection.

"You will be of great use to me still, little one, if you can continue your guise with Tsuku-san and her allies. Though the New Council purports to have no interest in dealing with spies and assassins, I believe Yasuhiko-san and his wife are more practical than that. They may even maintain my former contract."

"What are my instructions, then?"

"For now, simply learn as much as you can and gain their trust."

Kusuko nodded and Mamushi-san stood and crossed to the far side of the room.

"In time, depending on what the first Rōjū plans, and the information I receive, I will send along further instructions."

Kusuko rose to take her leave, sensing her dismissal.

"And Kusuko-san," Mamushi said, just as she reached for the shoji that would allow her egress into the hallway. "Take care."

"Yes, father," Kusuko whispered, as she opened the shoji and left the room.

17日 2月 新議 1年

17th Day, 2nd Moon, Cycle 1 of the New Council

~ Mishi ~

AS THEY ROUNDED the corner that opened onto the view of Rōjū City, Mishi's skin felt as though a thousand snakes were writhing across it. The view was breathtaking, certainly, a hundred tall buildings with intricate roofs joined by dozens of bridges that crossed over gorges, rivers, and canals, all shrouded in mist and nestled in the cradle of two large mountains. But that wasn't why she found it difficult to draw air into her lungs. No, that was caused by the icy claws of memory that grappled with her now, tearing at her body as well as her mind, forcing her to remember the last time that she had been in this place, all the violence done to her and, worst of all, by her.

She closed her eyes against the memories that flooded her, but it did nothing to stop them. The sound of steel ringing against steel was almost drowned out by the cries of men as they were cut down before her. The smell of blood mixed with smoke filled her nostrils, replacing the cool scent of pine that had pervaded only moments before. Mishi reminded herself that it wasn't real, but that didn't stop the visions from coming. It never did.

Suddenly, she was surrounded by the rush of battle, men fought on all sides of her, she could hear the screams of the dying and she held her katana at the ready as yet another Kisōshi allied with the Rōjū Council charged her. She cut the man down, and only as her blade slid through his shoulder did she realize she was on horseback. Why was she on horseback? She dismounted and prepared for the next attacker. Did she have room to use her fire kisō without hurting her friends? Better not to risk it. She kept her hands on her katana, but when she shifted her grip she found her katana was no longer there.

Someone grabbed her shoulders and she shifted and threw him to the ground. She didn't need a weapon to kill a man. She lunged for his throat as he lay on the ground, planning to crush his windpipe and be ready for the next attacker. She had to get back to Taka and the others. They were too far away from her current position. She couldn't protect them from here.

Just as she reached for the man on the ground she thought she heard a voice call her name, and then a hand grabbed her neck and darkness overtook her.

~~~

A gentle hand shook her awake. She saw treetops and mountain peaks behind a familiar face.

"Mishi-san?"

Taka's voice was calm and quiet, but her face was pale and she appeared to be shaking. Mishi looked once more at the trees and mountains. There were no buildings nearby, and it didn't feel like cobblestones beneath her feet. They weren't in Rōjū City.

It had been moons since the battle at Rōjū City.

She tried taking a deep breath, and found the smell of pines and horses filled her nostrils once more. They weren't in battle, they were on their way to Rōjū City to see Tsuku-san and the New Council.

"Mishi-san, what happened?" Taka asked.

Mishi didn't like how pale Taka looked.

"Are you all right, Taka-san?" she asked, though she was almost afraid of the answer. "Where is Mitsu-san?"

Mishi felt her own blood leave her face as she considered what she might have done to Taka or Mitsu.

Mitsu appeared beside Taka. He looked ragged, and battered...as though he'd been fighting.

"Do you remember what happened, Mishi-chan?" Taka asked.

Mishi shook her head.

"I saw Rōjū City in the distance and then...I had another waking nightmare."

"Another?" Taka asked. "This isn't the first time?"

"No," Mishi replied. "There have been others. Ever since..."

Her voice trailed off as she looked at Mitsu again and she realized who he must have been fighting.

"Did I hurt you?"

Mitsu said nothing.

"Mitsu-san, did I hurt you?"

Mitsu hesitated.

"No..." he began to speak, but Mishi could sense the lie. The kisō that ran through her body shivered, as though a ghost had touched it.

"How bad is it?" she asked, her body beginning to shake as her eyes frantically searched Mitsu for signs of injury.

"Not bad," Taka replied. "I was able to put you to sleep before you could do too much damage."

Mishi's eyes snapped to her lifelong friend. She sensed no lie.

"I already checked him," Taka continued. "Bruises, perhaps a cracked rib. Nothing that won't heal quickly, especially with my help."

Mishi nodded, although she could already feel the emotion making her throat tight. She had hurt Mitsu-san.

"And you, Taka-chan?" she asked again, her stomach tight with dread.

Taka held up her wrist. A patch of black and blue that would match the shape of Mishi's hand spread up her forearm. Mishi stared at it, horrified at how much damage she must have done if Taka—Gensokai's greatest healer—hadn't managed to undo the injury before it could bruise.

"I will be fine too," Taka said, her voice calm.

"What have I done?" Mishi felt her stomach turn. She had attacked her friends. She had attacked Taka.

She had to get away from them. They weren't safe with her. Panic tried to fill her, but she took deep breaths to keep it at bay.

She couldn't simply ride away from them now, they would only follow her. They were clearly worried about her, and she knew Taka well enough to know she would allow that worry to get her killed. Taka and Mitsu's horses were just as fast as the mount Mishi had ridden to get here, and Mitsu was an excellent tracker. She wouldn't be able to protect either of them if she tried to run from them now. The city would be safer. There would be more trained warriors to intervene should she turn on them again, and hopefully it wouldn't take long for her to find a chance to escape them.

Taka knew Mishi too well for her to be able to hide her intentions for very long. Taka would expect her to run. So instead, Mishi swallowed down the bile that had risen in her throat, stood up, and brushed herself off, hoping the move would be unexpected enough to distract both of her companions.

An apology could never make up for what she had done, so she didn't bother with one.

"We've made good time," she said, once more looking at the city that lay below them. "Tsuku-san will be pleased to see us so soon."

Taka's eyes widened with shock and lingered on Mishi's face longer than Mishi would have liked, but eventually her friend seemed convinced that Mishi wasn't planning to bolt right away.

"Indeed," Taka said. "If things are as dire as her summons made it sound, she should be very glad to have us. We should get to the Rōjū—to the New Council compound as quickly as possible, so that she has time to summon us before the evening meal if she needs to."

Mishi didn't like the idea of having to delay her departure from Rōjū City in order to meet with Tsuku-san first; her visions had only become more frequent over the past tenday, and she didn't wish to risk any more time near people she cared about, but she would do as she must. She hoped that Tsuku-san would observe the more formal niceties and allow them one night of rest before summoning them, as that would give her a full night during which to plan and execute her own disappearance, perhaps even after a small bit of sleep. However, if Tsuku-san summoned them immediately, well...she hoped she could make decent progress on a night without sleep.

After a tenday of hard riding she was exhausted, and she was sure Taka and Mitsu were just as tired, although it was possible her recent convalescence had made the toll harder on her than on her companions. Tsuku-san's summons had come only a few days after they had parted ways from her at the pile of cinders that had, until recently, been the Josankō. The three of them had been halfway to the orphanage that had been Mishi and Taka's childhood home by the time they had received Tsuku-san's message. Though they had been on their way to sniff out more about Mitsu and Taka's mystery, they had changed plans immediately upon receiving Tsuku-san's missive and ridden as fast as they could without injuring their mounts. She had to hope that her friends' own exhaustion would delay them in their pursuit of her.

In the meantime, now that they were finally here, they would discover why the leader of the New Council so desperately required their presence.

Tsuku-san's note had been short but unequivocal: *Come at once to Rōjū City. Lives are at stake.*

~~~

Mishi followed Taka's leather-clad form through the hallways of the Zōkame wing of the New Council complex, and Mitsu trailed behind them. The grassy smell of the tatami, combined with the layout of the rooms and halls, reminded her of the school she had grown up in, but the size of the grounds and buildings, combined with the quality and abundance of the artwork that covered the walls and doors, was greater than any she'd ever seen save in her first visit to Rōjū City—before she'd stolen a scroll and set half of the decorative gardens on fire.

She briefly wished for a reality in which she had the time and energy to appreciate what she was sure were intricately painted reliefs on almost every door.

She took a deep breath to keep the thought of this meeting from overwhelming her. She didn't want to bring on any more visions. She had to keep herself together long enough to get away from Taka and Mitsu.

They hadn't asked to bathe, eat, or take any other form of respite before meeting with Tsuku-san, nor had they been offered the opportunity to do so. That didn't bother Mishi in the least in terms of personal comfort, even if it did make her plans to run away from her friends more complicated, but it made her gut tighten to think that things were serious enough that Tsuku-san wouldn't even offer them that much hospitality before speaking with them.

Finally, they turned down a hall that led past two large, ornately painted doors guarded by two Eihei. The Eihei simply nodded at them and opened the doors.

Tsuku-san sat in seiza on a slightly raised platform at the far end of the large receiving room. Whoever she had been speaking to must have just been dismissed, for the kimono clad figure rose and exited even as they entered and approached the dais.

"Welcome, Taka-san, Mitsu-san, and Ryūko-san. I have been waiting for you."

Mishi's shoulder blades twitched at the use of her true name. She had never taken to using it, even after learning it cycles ago, and it bothered her to hear it now. She wondered what purpose Tsuku-san had for its use, as she had never called her that before now.

"We are sorry for the delay, Zōkame-sama," Taka said, folding to her knees before the dais and bowing to Tsuku-san. "We came as quickly as our mounts would allow."

Mishi noted Taka's formality and followed suit by folding herself next to Taka and bowing accordingly. She saw Mitsu do the same beside her.

"And the Council would gladly wait that time a hundredfold for such honored guests as you, Taka-san, but we appreciate your alacrity, as we have great need of your assistance."

Struck by the formality of Tsuku-san's words—after all, the four of them had been travel companions sleeping on the same roadside little more than a tenday before—Mishi took another good look around the room. At least two of the men standing to the side of the receiving room were dressed as scribes. She didn't see anyone else who looked like a council member, but she wasn't sure what they would look like in the New Council as compared to the Rōjū. Tsuku-san's language alone indicated that this was an official meeting and not a personal one, though. Mishi felt her back muscles tighten. Mishi had expected Tsuku-san to ask for their help, but she hadn't expected the request to come as a formal demand of the

New Council. She tried to remind herself that she could still disappear between now and the dawn. The New Council making demands on her wouldn't change that. She hoped.

"It is our honor to wait upon the Council," Taka said, with another bow.

"The Council has three requests," Tsuku-san said. "One for each of you."

Beyond exhaustion, and unwilling to spend any more time and energy on formal wording, Mishi and her companions simply nodded and waited expectantly.

"Taka-san, you are said to be the greatest healer this realm has seen in an age; your services are greatly needed. There is a rebellion to the north of Rōjū City. After we sent forth troops to assist with the change in government and enforcement of the new laws protecting female Kisōshi and yukisō, groups of Kisōshi still loyal to the Rōjū started fighting them in a few towns north of the capitol. Now these men have joined forces and made it necessary for our own troops to form up as well. There is a small battlefront forming and it is desperately shy of qualified healers. Most of our healers have been dispersed to every city and town in order to help spread the new laws and new training regarding josanpu and the treatment of females with kisō. We cannot afford to recall them all, or even most of them. I need someone I can trust, who can help train people as well as lead the healers who are already there, and that person is you, if you are willing. Are you willing?"

Mishi had struggled to keep her mouth from sliding open and her jaw from dropping lower and lower as Tsuku-san had explained the situation. She couldn't believe that men were still fighting after all that she and her friends had done at the battle of Rōjū City. Didn't they understand that the Rōjū were finished? The old council had been disbanded and the new laws set and enforced, why were they fighting it? Did they really want a world where young girls were killed simply because they were born with enough power to become Kisōshi, or were they simply terrified of any kind of change?

Her ire shifted quickly to panic, though, when she realized what Tsuku-san was sure to ask next. If Taka was needed for healing, then surely the fight wasn't going that well. Which meant that Tsuku-san would need more fighters and...Mishi felt her hand begin to shake even as it reached for the katana that was no longer at her waist. She couldn't fight again. She couldn't...

"Ryūko-san, I am honored to have a kitsune-dan Kisōshi as a guest here in Rōjū City, welcome."

Mishi nodded, thrown enough by the use of her rank and true name together to be at least temporarily distracted from her mounting terror. She still wasn't comfortable with the fact that she'd been promoted to kitsune-dan as soon as the New Council had formed and started evaluating Kisōshi. They'd claimed that her part in the battle at Rōjū City had been a very thorough test and demonstration of her abilities, and that they were all agreed she should be ranked far higher than hebi-dan. The debate, apparently, had only been on how high to rank her; some had argued for tora, some for anagumi, or ōkami. Apparently taking her age into account had been the only thing that had kept the ranking as low as kitsune. She had been greatly relieved not to have been promoted further.

"Though I believe you deserve a much longer time to recover, after fighting so hard for Gensokai only a few moons ago, I fear I must ask you to fight once more."

Mishi opened her mouth in order to object then and there, scribes and official requests be damned, but Tsuku-san continued speaking, as though Mishi hadn't made a sound. Mishi swallowed her objection as best she could. She didn't wish to make Tsuku-san lose face, but she was already trembling at the mere thought of having to fight once more. She took deep breaths and clenched and unclenched her fists as she tried to focus on the words that Tsuku-san was saying.

"The Rōjū zantō are not only attacking our forces north of Rōjū City. They are also attacking small towns and villages throughout the far northern region. There is at least one group, possibly more, of sanzoku who are demolishing any place where they find female Kisōshi alive. As you may guess, there aren't many of these places, and where they exist, the female Kisōshi are infants or, more rarely, young children. Still, they have destroyed three such villages already and they leave no survivors. We cannot know in advance where they will strike without knowing where the female Kisōshi are, and now that word of these attacks has spread a bit through the region, people are even less inclined to reveal that they have a Kisōshi for a daughter than they were under the Rōjū. We're worried people will start drowning their own infants this time, simply to spare the entire village. Fortunately, it is not a common problem, and many people still don't even believe that their daughters can have enough kisō to be Kisōshi anyway, but these sanzoku need to be stopped. They've destroyed three villages already. There are bound to be at least a half dozen more that have girls with kisō within their populations. We must find them before the sanzoku do, and we must protect them."

Mishi felt some of the tension leave her shoulders. Perhaps Tsuku-san only intended her to do the task she had set out to accomplish to begin with. Perhaps she would only be asked to seek out newborns with kisō, or the rare girl who had somehow survived the genocide of the Rōjū Council and lived to childhood.

"I know that you wished to seek out new female Kisōshi anyway, and it pleases me that your mission and the New Council's wishes align so well."

Mishi smiled at this and bowed her head slightly. She felt her fists unclench as she realized that she wouldn't be asked to fight after all.

"In addition, your incredible defensive skills will be invaluable to the second part of your assignment."

Mishi tensed again, locking eyes with Tsuku-san. Did the grey-haired woman understand what she was asking?

"This group of sanzoku cannot be permitted to continue to terrorize our people. They must be stopped at all costs. You alone, of course, cannot stop them, but you can lay the trap that will finally allow us to find them and bring them to justice. If you can either track them down, or lure them to you, and notify our forces with sufficient time, we should be able to ambush them and finally put a stop to them."

Mishi saw sorrow in Tsuku-san's eyes as she spoke, and she realized that even if the woman didn't fully understand that Mishi could no longer fight, she at least understood the danger of what she now asked her to do.

Mishi wanted to do this for Tsuku-san, she wanted to find girls like herself, help them, protect them, but she couldn't fight. She was terrified to hold her katana once more, terrified of what she might do with it, of who she might hurt. What if she injured one of the girls? What if she got lost in a vision and attacked townspeople? Who would stop her?

She would have to refuse. She didn't want to make Tsuku-san or the New Council lose face, but she simply couldn't do it. She—

"Ah, Kusuko-san, there you are. Please come in."

Mishi turned to see the person Tsuku-san addressed, and felt rage consume her.

~~~

Mishi opened her eyes and was supremely grateful that she wasn't wearing her sword.

Mitsu held one of her wrists and Taka the other, and she was thankful that the visions hadn't chosen that moment to consume her along with the rage, else she was confident that her friends would now be dead, as would the beautiful, tiny, ornately dressed assassin who now stood across from her in front of Tsuku-san and the scribes on the dais.

"Kusuko-san is on our side now, Ryūko-san."

Mishi took a deep breath and reminded herself that what Tsuku-san said was true. Kusuko had fought with them at the battle in Rōjū City at great personal risk. She was no longer the enemy. Mishi knew that, but some part of her consciousness saw the young woman and thought only of the enemy, only of the hishi that had killed Sachi-san and led to the destruction of the only home she had ever known. That part of her had filled her with a rage so encompassing that she had stood up without realizing it and reached for a sword that was no longer there.

Luckily, Taka and Mitsu had restrained her and kept her from doing worse, and Tsuku-san had interpreted her reaction as a lack of information, or a grudge, and seemed willing to dismiss it at that.

Mishi bowed to acknowledge the reminder and relaxed her arms to let Mitsu and Taka know that she no longer needed to be restrained. She could sense that they were both still close enough to reach her easily and, she was reassured by their proximity. She didn't wish to attack Kusuko, or anyone else. If anything, this was simply one more reason she needed to be gone by morning.

"Now then, I have requested Kusuko-san's presence because I believe she will be critical to this new assignment."

Mishi cringed; Tsuku-san couldn't be serious. She wasn't going to send Kusuko with her, was she? Mishi could barely refrain from killing the woman when she walked into a room, so how could Tsuku-san expect her to work with the assassin?

"Kusuko-san will be accompanying Taka-san on her assignment."

⇁ Taka ⇁

Taka followed behind the Eihei who led her to her guest room with unseeing eyes. She wasn't sure what disturbed her more, Mishi's uncontrolled rage and what lay behind it, or the fact that Kusuko was supposed to accompany her on her mission.

No, that wasn't true. She was far more concerned with Mishi's mental state, but it was a testament to how worried she was for her friend that it overshadowed her alarm at being paired up with the beautiful young assassin.

She would have to think about that later. For now, she needed to focus on Mishi and what was wrong with her. She thought that the two episodes, the one on the road to Rōjū City and the one when Kusuko first appeared, were different in many ways, but neither of them aligned with the Mishi she knew from childhood. Even more, they didn't align with the Mishi she'd come to know over the moons since they had finally been reunited.

She looked up and found herself standing dumbly in front of a sliding door, with the Eihei who had led her there looking at her expectantly. She shook her head and slid the door open, vaguely waving off the Eihei when he asked if she needed anything else.

The room was small and clean, with a fresh pot of tea waiting on a low-lying table in the center, and saddle bags already arranged against the far wall.

She sat in front of the tea and poured herself a cup.

What could she do to help Mishi-san? She had to do something, and soon. Mishi would be horrified enough by what she had done to try something drastic, and Taka didn't want to wait to find out what it would be.

She stood up and left the room, determined to find Mitsu and see if he could help her protect her friend. Her tea sat forgotten on the small wooden table.

⇍ Kusuko ⇍

After placing the warmed sake on the table, Kusuko retreated to a corner of the small, dimly lit room that reeked of spilled sake, old squid, and burning oil. Once there, she kept her head bowed low and awaited further requests.

She hadn't expected Mamushi-san to be meeting with anyone tonight, but now she was even more certain she'd made the right choice when she'd put on her brown serving kimono, left her hair in a simple tie at the base of her neck, and removed all of her makeup before making her way across the city to where she suspected her father to be. When she hadn't found him in his chambers in the Security Compound that abutted the New Council Compound, she had decided to try one of his many meeting places on the outskirts of the city. In these clothes, without any of her usual adornments and her hair loose enough to at least partially cover her face when she angled her head demurely, no one noticed her. She was simply another scrawny serving girl, and no one of rank would pay her any heed at all.

She had learned that lesson well enough when her father had sent her to live with the compound's cleaners for a cycle during her training. Despite many cycles of hearing her beauty acclaimed by most of the people who knew her father, all of whom were used to seeing her presented in the fine kimono he provided for her, on her very first day working with the palace cleaners one of the scribes who had flattered her with compliments only a tenday prior had almost tripped on her as she scrubbed the floor, and then called her an ugly, clumsy beast before continuing on his way.

If she needed any further proof, the man who sat across from her father, who she clearly recognized as the former First Rōjū despite his attempts to disguise himself as a merchant, paid her no attention at all, and indeed spoke as though he and Mamushi-san were the only two people present.

"The New Council is weak. The people deserve a governing body that can protect them better," the First Rōjū said, from across the low table before which he and Mamushi-san both sat in seiza.

Mamushi-san filled the First Rōjū's sake cup. When the First Rōjū made no move to return the favor for Mamushi-san, Kusuko bowed and shifted forward to fill it for him and then silently resumed her place.

"They may be weak," Mamushi-san replied, once he had taken a sip of his own sake. "But many people love them for their policy allowing even the lowliest farmer to come forward and speak at their council meetings."

"The people are foolish, and can be easily swayed. They won't love the New Council if the New Council fails to defend them."

"Ah, and the people are in need of more protection these days aren't they?"

"I hear it can be very dangerous in the mountains, and there are those violent rebels to the north of the city..." The First Rōjū's voice trailed off, and he sipped his sake.

"I believe, however," he continued, "that there is more that can be done."

"Oh?" asked Mamushi-san, never willing to give away more information than he had to.

"The New Council has allies," the First Rōjū continued. "Allies that could help turn the tide in protecting the people from these new threats."

"I see."

"Do you? These allies, abominations though they are, could be just as useful to us as they are to the New Council. Before they are neutralized, they should be...offered a chance to change allegiances."

"Strong allies are unlikely to change sides so easily," Mamushi-san mused, taking another sip of warm sake.

"I believe it is part of your skill set to discover people's motivations and exploit them, is it not?"

Mamushi-san only smiled.

"I will see what can be done," he replied at length, pouring sake for the First Rōju once more.

"Excellent," said the other man, draining his cup and then rising from his place on the tatami floor. Just before he reached the door, he turned and pulled a small, but heavy looking, bag from his waist belt. "I almost forgot. It disgusts me to have to deal in the stuff personally, but I suppose it can't be helped if I must pretend to be a merchant."

He dropped the bag by the door. It jingled weightily, and then he slid the door open and left.

Kusuko kept her head bowed until Mamushi-san addressed her.

"Welcome, Kusuko-san," he said, cueing her to raise her head. "That was well done. I only recognized you after the First Rōju had left."

She kept her face carefully blank, though she secretly rejoiced at the rare praise. She inclined her head slightly to acknowledge the remark.

"And what do you make of our recent guest?" Mamushi-san asked.

Kusuko again was careful not to show her emotions, but she was both surprised and delighted to be asked her opinion on the matter. Her father generally kept no one's council but his own.

"I find it interesting that he considers the New Council's allies worth manipulating."

"Do you not think they are powerful enough to be worth the effort?" Mamushi-san asked.

Kusuko considered carefully before answering.

"I think that they are indeed as powerful as the First Rōju suspects, or even more so. What interests me is that he is willing to admit their power, and their potential usefulness to his own cause, and yet call them abominations in the same breath."

Mamushi-san smiled.

"Many of the Rōju have shown an amazing capacity for hypocrisy, I find."

Kusuko had to make a great effort to prevent the shock from showing on her face. Her father was never this candid with her. Had he grown to trust her more in the moons since the battle at Rōjū City? Or was this another of his tests? Suddenly wary, she was careful of her reply.

"The illusion of power can make men blind to many things." She felt confident that the phrase her father had taught her as a small child would serve her well in this moment.

"Very true, Kusuko-san. Of course, the First Rōjū has been under the illusion of power for a very long time. What do you think will come of his plan?"

Kusuko decided this must be a test.

"Who am I to say? I have only a small portion of the knowledge needed to judge such things."

"Mm... Indeed. It is possible though, that the First Rōjū has even less knowledge of this topic than you do, as you are the person who has been placed closest to the New Council's allies."

"Yet I have no knowledge of the First Rōjū's situation, or that of his closest allies," she replied.

"None?" Mamushi-san asked.

Kusuko left her face blank, and said nothing. Her father had taught her long ago the value of never letting anyone know the full extent of her own information.

Mamushi-san smiled yet again, and if Kusuko hadn't known the man her whole life she might have thought the sake was going to his head. He was never this voluble.

"Do you think the New Council will be as easily toppled as the First Rōjū believes?" She decided to hazard a question of her own, while Mamushi-san seemed to be in a talking mood.

Mamushi-san took another slow sip of his sake, and quirked an eyebrow at her.

"Any government is as easily undone as its most influential members," he replied.

It was another lesson from her childhood, but that didn't make it any less true.

"And do you think Tsuku-san is so easily undone?"

Mamushi-san stared at her for a moment.

"I do not yet know what would undo Tsuku-san, or any of the other high-ranking members of the New Council," he replied. "But I'm fortunate to have an informant among them who will tell me as soon as she discovers it."

Kusuko-san bowed then, and decided it was past time for her to take her leave. She felt certain this was a test of some kind, but she didn't understand the rules. Failing Mamushi-san's tests could be fatal. She decided to go before she said the wrong thing, and alluding to her current assignment was often as close as her father ever came to giving her a direct dismissal.

"I will send you my reports as I can," she said.

"Inari-san will collect them for me," he replied, just as she reached the door.

She managed not to stutter step before she passed the threshold, but only barely. She had been half convinced that her father was finally beginning to trust her, given the amount of information he had just shared with her, but if that was true, why was he sending his other most trusted hishi to check up on her?

≈ Mishi ≈

Mishi sat in front of the tree and watched the fog swirl around the mountain top. She wondered if she was inside of a cloud. Yet the moonlight shone brightly on the rocky outcropping before her, and a glint of silver and gold caught the corner of her eye.

"What troubles you, child?"

The voice that sounded like earth moving and distant thunder made her sigh in relief. It had been too many moons since she'd heard that voice. The giant head, scaled in silver and gold with eyes almost the size of Mishi herself, appeared before her, and, suddenly, she couldn't find the words for all that troubled her. Her voice caught in her throat as tears sprang to her eyes. Eventually she managed to stutter out, "I'm a monster, Tatsu-sama."

"Hmmm... I'm inclined to agree with you, after you've gone so long without even coming to say hello."

"What?"

The statement was so absurd that she almost laughed despite the tears that still choked her.

"Have you been avoiding me?"

"Avoiding you? Tatsu-sensei, I've been traveling! I told you I would be gone for moons."

"Yet here you are."

Mishi thought about that for a moment.

"Isn't this a dream?" she asked.

"Hmph..." Tatsu snorted, and a bit of smoke flared from his nostrils. "Does that make it any less real?"

"Doesn't it?"

"Child, did you have a question for me, or didn't you?"

Mishi considered that for a moment. She wanted to know if this was real. She desperately wished to be visiting Tatsu-sama right now. She had thought that the only way to reach him was to be physically present on the top of his mountain. Surely, he would have told her if that wasn't the case...wouldn't he? She shook her head. Real or imagined, she had a rare opportunity to talk to her mentor. She shouldn't waste it.

"I want to know what's wrong with me."

"Hmm...what makes you think something is wrong with you?"

"I have visions...nightmares in the day time...I'm a danger. I keep hurting people. I injured Taka-san and Mitsu-san on the way to Rōjū City. What if I had done worse? I could never forgive myself."

"Ahhh...interesting choice of words."

"What?"

"You would never forgive yourself if anything happened to Taka-san, ne?"

Mishi shook her head.

"Never."

"And will you ever forgive yourself for protecting her at the battle of Rōjū City?"

"What?"

"Mishi-san, you would do anything to protect the people you love, and indeed you have. You have killed to protect the people you love. Now, will you forgive yourself for doing so?"

Mishi thought about that.

"I don't know how," she said at length.

Tatsu nodded, his usually mischievous eyes solemn.

"The how is often a great challenge," he said. "Yet first you must accept the why."

"And why should I forgive myself? I don't deserve it. I attacked my best friend and a man who has done nothing but try to help me."

"And did you intend to attack them?"

"Of course not! I was consumed with a vision. I couldn't tell dream from reality, and when they touched me...I thought I was being attacked by Eihei."

"So, it was an accident."

"Yes, but Sensei, the people I've killed, I meant to kill. I've done great evil. And my dreams...in my dreams..." She couldn't bear to form the words to tell Tatsu-sama the truth of her dreams. "I'm a monster," she repeated instead.

"A monster, child?"

Mishi locked eyes with Tatsu then, and she let him see everything within her.

Tatsu's eyes grew heavy with sorrow then, and Mishi thought that he must have seen the truth and was now mourning the person she once had been.

"Look at me, child."

She did.

Tatsu opened his jaws, then turned to the mountain top, away from Mishi, and released a giant gout of flame that could have destroyed an entire city if it had been aimed at one. Trees and grass turned to ash, rock turned to molten lava, the mountain top was seared clean in the wake of that flame.

He turned back to her.

"I am capable of great violence," he told her. "I have killed, child. Many times in my long life it has been my duty to do so, to protect that which I hold dear. Am I a monster?"

Mishi shook her head.

"Don't be ridiculous, Tatsu-sama. You would only kill if you had to, and—"

"So quick to forgive me my evils, child, and yet so reluctant to forgive your own."

"But Sensei, that's—"

Mishi's eyes opened and she looked at the ceiling in the guest room she'd been provided in the Zōkame's wing of the New Council compound. A soft breeze blew in through the window that opened onto the small balcony of her room and she wondered if she'd left it open. She didn't remember leaving it open.

She wanted to spend time thinking about her dream with Tatsu-sama. Had it been real? That is to say, it had clearly been a dream, but had Tatsu been there, too? He was a dragon kami, after all. What was to stop him from showing up in people's dreams if he felt like it? Then again, she had never dreamt of him before now, so if it were possible for him to visit her dreams, why had he never done so before? Or was it that she hadn't visited him?

She put those questions aside for the time being, and got up to check her belongings. She needed to be ready to leave as soon as she'd met with Tsuku-san in the morning. She had finally decided that leaving in the night had the potential to attract too much attention from the guards, and she was desperate to avoid having to hurt anyone else. If she left in the middle of the morning, it was likely no one would be the wiser until the evening meal. In addition, she would have time to explain to Tsuku-san why she couldn't accept the assignment that she'd been given.

She approached her laid out saddle bags and took in the shapes of her belongings as they lay in the moonlight. All her things were laid out almost exactly where she had left them....

Now she was left pondering a new question: why had someone been in her room?

18日 2月 新議 1年

18th Day, 2nd Moon, Cycle 1 of the New Council

≈ Mishi ≈

MISHI SAT ACROSS from Tsuku-san and tried not to fiddle with the sleeves of her uwagi. Tsuku-san, as always, was impeccably dressed in a sedately ornate kimono, with her long grey hair pulled into a simple coil at her neck. Mishi was dressed in her travel-worn brown and green uwagi and hakama, and she felt as though the older woman's deep brown eyes were scrutinizing every faded thread of fabric, even though she knew that Tsuku-san was far more likely assessing her physical and mental state.

In an attempt to stop fidgeting, Mishi looked around the small tea room that sat in the middle of the central garden of the New Council compound. From where she sat, she could see the small koi pond just beyond the tea house's small porch, as well as some of the shaped, decorative trees that adorned the garden. Warmed by the small brazier that Tsuku-san was using to prepare the tea, it was a calm and peaceful place. Or it would have been, if Mishi hadn't felt so anxious about her planned departure and the reasons behind it.

Mishi looked back to Tsuku-san just in time to receive the small cup of macha that the older woman had finished preparing, and she nodded in thanks as she received the chawan with both hands.

After they had both taken a small sip of tea and had a moment to savor it, Tsuku-san spoke.

"Why did you ask to see me, Mishi-san?"

Mishi was tempted to ask why she was "Mishi-san" again here in the teahouse, when she had been Ryūko-san in the official receiving room yesterday, but decided it wasn't worth the time. She had more important things to discuss.

"I cannot complete the task you've assigned me," she said quietly. Hearing the words spoken aloud, even coming from her own mouth, turned her stomach, but what else was she to do?

"Oh? And why is that?"

Mishi took a deep breath.

"I cannot fight anymore, Tsuku-sama. I am…broken." She didn't want to admit to being a monster, not to Tsuku-san, not if she didn't have to. "I cannot hold a katana or wakizashi without posing a threat to all the people around me. I cannot be trusted to protect the children you would send me to find, and I refuse to be a threat to them. There are enough people who wish to hurt them as it is."

A long exhale followed that statement. She'd practiced it many times that morning. She hoped she'd remembered everything. She needed Tsuku-san to understand.

Tsuku-san took a few more contemplative sips of tea before speaking again, but Mishi could read nothing in her face.

"Every Kisōshi poses a threat to the people around them when they wear their katana and wakizashi…and even when they don't. What is different about you? No, don't answer yet."

Mishi had indeed been about to object, but she swallowed the reply and let Tsuku-san continue.

"Every Kisōshi is a danger to those around them. All trained warriors are, but especially Kisōshi. That is why Kisōshi are required to complete cycles of training before they are allowed to wander freely in society."

Mishi's eyebrows rose and her grey eyes widened as that statement sank in. She had never thought of it that way. She had always thought that Kisōshi were "allowed" to train for cycles to become better fighters, to learn to use their kisō. She knew it was required, but she had always thought of it as a privilege, not an obligation. For the first time, she thought of it from the perspective of someone who did not have kisō. Would those people want men and women *with* kisō to simply do as they pleased in society, without receiving cycles of strict training and discipline? Probably not. After all, a person without kisō could train all they liked, but they would never have the advantage of an element to aid them in their fight. They would never stand a chance against someone who had that kind of power, not without huge numbers on their side.

Mishi caught Tsuku-san's gaze then, and realized that the elderly woman had watched her moment of comprehension. Now she continued.

"It is because of that training and discipline that people do not fear having Kisōshi live among them, though, to be honest, many still do. You have had the same training, the same discipline, instilled in you as any other Kisōshi, and your kisō still comes to your call. That power not only comes with the need for training, it comes with a great weight. You are only responsible for your own life, Mishi-san, that much is true, and I cannot force you to help me in this. The New Council's rule will not be like the Rōju's rule. We will not lock up and punish any who refuse us, if they have broken no laws. And yet...who shall I send to do this task instead of you, Mishi-san? I have sent a handful of my best Kisōshi to seek out the sanzoku and do you know what I have found?"

Mishi shook her head.

"Corpses. I have found the men I sent lying dead on the roadside, leagues from where they were supposed to be. The sanzoku know who we are, they know what we intend, and they are hiding in the woods like cowards between each of their attacks. Everyone I have yet sent to track them has either returned with nothing, or has not returned at all."

Mishi felt the blood leave her face as she considered what Tsuku-san was saying.

"I know that what I ask of you is incredibly dangerous, and I am aware that you have been feeling...unwell, but there is no one else I can send on this mission who I believe will succeed at it."

"I'm not a tracker," Mishi objected, before her brain could stop her. Tracker or not, she still couldn't go on this assignment. She was just as likely to harm the people she was protecting as the sanzoku were.

"I'm aware of that. I'll be sending Mitsu-san with you on this mission, in case that talent becomes necessary. He's the best tracker we have, in all honesty, but I was reluctant to send him lest the same fate befall him as did all the others. He has two advantages, though."

Mishi quirked one eyebrow in silent question.

"He is a natural tracker, unlike the others, who were merely trained to track…and he will have you to protect him."

⇁ Taka ⇀

Taking a deep breath of the cool spring air that wafted through the window to her guest room, Taka refolded the three kimono that Tsuku-san had gifted her with for the third time since she had begun packing, and cursed the need for any clothing other than her leather leggings and tunic. Her saddle bags lay in the center of the small, tatami floor and were the focus of her entire attention. Mishi-san had seemed preoccupied at the morning meal and Taka had decided she had better pack sooner rather than later, in case she needed to go running after her friend soon. Now she was fully absorbed in preparing her few belongings for immediate travel.

Perhaps that's why she didn't hear the small knock on the shoji before it slid open.

"Taka-san?" asked a quiet voice from the doorway.

"Hmm?"

She turned distractedly toward the door and then sputtered when she realized who was there.

"Kusuko-san! Hello. I…I'm sorry. Can I help you?"

She was surprised at how embarrassed she felt at being caught unable to fold kimono properly by the beautiful young assassin, but suddenly her tongue felt like an exhausted donkey that had to be prodded to do its task.

"I was just coming to see if you needed any assistance preparing for our trip," said the diminutive young woman.

Taka shook her head.

"No, I'm just wrestling with these kimono. I'm no good at folding them properly, I always wind up with creases. Comes from never wearing them, I suppose. Silly things if you ask me."

Her cheeks reddened before she could get her mouth to stop running. Kusuko, of course, was dressed immaculately in a dramatically colored kimono of black and deep scarlet, with enormous sleeves. Kusuko was always dressed in ornate kimono. *Wonderful,* thought Taka, *I've insulted my travel companion before even setting foot on the road.*

"They are tricky, ne?" Kusuko agreed, before Taka could even begin to mutter an apology. "But here, I'll show you a trick I learned."

Before Taka could stop her, the young woman had swept across the room and was laying out one of the three kimono Taka now owned.

"Line up the hems like so," she said, demonstrating as she went. "And then fold here and here, folding the sleeves in last."

Kusuko held up a small, perfect rectangle of kimono that would pack away nicely into Taka's saddle bags. Taka nodded dumbly, although she very much doubted she would be able to replicate the procedure.

It must have showed on her face.

"Why don't you pack your other belongings while I fold these, ne? It's a small thing that I can do for you."

"My other belongings are already packed," she said, before she could stop herself. The woman didn't need to know that she owned next to nothing. Taka took a deep breath. She was far more rattled by Kusuko's presence than was reasonable.

"I'll just go find Mishi to take my leave," she said, looking for any escape, and also reminded of her original hurry.

"Oh, you didn't hear?" Kusuko asked, already folding the next kimono.

"Hear what?"

"No one had seen Mishi since the morning meal, and then one of the guards reported seeing her leave through the western gates not long ago."

20日 2月 新議 1年
20th Day, 2nd Moon, Cycle 1 of the New Council

~ Mishi ~

DESPITE THE MANY conflicting emotions still battling for supremacy within Mishi's mind, the tall pines, clear blue sky, and steep mountain backdrop allowed her to be distracted by the gentle spring sun on her face as she walked along the northern road. The air still held winter's bite, but she could feel the season begin its turn and she looked forward to the coming warmth that would melt what remained of winter's grip. Perhaps she was too focused on those thoughts of promised warmth, or perhaps the man was just too stealthy for her, but she had no conscious notion that Mitsu was there until his hand clamped down hard upon her shoulder.

"What exactly do you think you're doing?" he asked, as she turned to him with her arms in a defensive posture.

She stepped back quickly and wondered which part of her had recognized it was Mitsu before she saw him. Some unconscious part of her must have, or she was certain that he would be dead by now.

"Currently? Restraining myself from doing you real physical harm," she said, looking pointedly at his hand on her shoulder. "But just before that, I was enjoying the beginnings of spring."

Mitsu removed his hand from her shoulder, but kept pace with her as she turned to walk along the road once more.

"I mean, what are you doing on the road already? You left without telling anyone. We were supposed to depart together. Instead it took me a day and a half just to find you."

Mishi took a deep breath and returned her eyes to the road instead of keeping Mitsu's green gaze.

"I was hoping you wouldn't find me. I can see that was wishful thinking." She glared at him and wondered how he had tracked her so easily. She had made good time, been careful to avoid other people on the road, and even allowed herself to be seen leaving through the gates on the wrong side of the city, just to throw off any pursuit. She had thought it would take him much longer to find her, and had hoped he wouldn't find her at all. She was as much a danger to him as she was to Taka. Now she would have to find some other way to leave him behind. "And I had hoped…especially after my talk with Tsuku-san, that perhaps she and Yasuhiko-san would consider letting you stay behind if I left without you."

Mitsu snorted derisively.

"That's ridiculous," he said. "It only made them send me to catch up to you, in case you decided to try something foolish like go up against a band of sanzoku alone."

Here he paused to look pointedly at her, but she didn't react. That hadn't been her plan…at least, not at first.

"Besides," he continued, "you forgot your katana and wakizashi, so they insisted that I bring them for you."

He gestured toward the roll on his back, out of which poked the ends of her katana, and Mishi grimaced. She had left the blades behind on purpose.

"I can't take those," she said, as she felt her hands begin to tremble and her entire body start to shake. "Don't let me near them."

She felt her stomach souring and she worried that the visions might overtake her once more. She took deep, calming breaths, and looked away from the blades, focusing on Mitsu's face once more. Perhaps she should keep talking. Perhaps that would remind her of where she was…and where she wasn't.

"You experienced firsthand what I did on the road to Rōjū City. Imagine how much worse it would have been if I had been wearing my swords."

Mitsu's eyes widened, and he turned so that the blades were no longer visible to her.

"It's all right, Mishi-san," he said. "You don't have to take them. I'm sorry. I….Look." He reached into a pouch that he kept slung across his chest and pulled out a small scroll. "Taka-san told me to give this to you."

He handed her the scroll, but was careful not to touch her, and to keep himself aligned so that she couldn't see the swords in his traveling roll.

"I have others as well, one from Tsuku-san and some from your friends, but read that one first. Taka-san said it was important."

Mishi, unsure what Taka could possibly have to say that would help, but willing to do anything that might distract her from a new onslaught of visions, opened the scroll and began reading.

Dear Mishi-chan,

I know that you never meant to hurt Mitsu-san or me the other day on the road to Rōjū City. I understand that you're not feeling like yourself these days. I wish that I could help you, but I understand that you didn't wish to risk hurting me again. I assure you, I think the risk is worth it, but we find ourselves once more on different paths as the New Council has asked me to lead their healers, and has asked you to fight again. I'm not sure which task seems more impossible.

Since we cannot all travel together, Mitsu-san and I have discussed it and we agree that Yanagi-sensei may be able to help you. Will you agree to travel with Mitsu-san as far as Yanagi-sensei's forest? It's near the northern province that is plagued by sanzoku anyway, and Yanagi-sensei may be able to help you in a way that I cannot. He helped Mitsu-san when he lost his family, and he helped me too after I lost Kiko-san.

I know you don't think you're worthy of my friendship right now, but I love you, and I would be devastated if I lost you too. Please consider at least meeting Yanagi-sensei.

With love,

Taka-san

Tears came to Mishi's eyes as she realized just how well her friend knew her and her thoughts. She sighed, rolled up the scroll, and tucked it inside of her travel roll.

"I suppose I'm stuck with you," she said, turning to Mitsu once more. "But that doesn't mean I won't accidentally kill you between here and Yanagi-sensei's forest. We'd best travel hard and fast. If I'm exhausted each night you might have a better chance of surviving."

Mitsu's face changed completely as laughter lit the corners of his eyes.

"Come along then!" he called, even as he turned to run ahead of her.

~~~

They had finally stopped running long after dark, when Mishi had decided that exhaustion would pull her down into sleep before any more visions would be able to plague her. Mitsu had insisted that they needed a hot meal though, and she had blearily gone about starting a fire while he traipsed off into the craggy forest to snare them something to eat. She had taken her time about it, using a flint and steel as anyone else would, rather than calling to it with her kisō.

Now Mishi listened to the fire crackle as her eyes took in the cracks of starry sky that peeked through the trees and mountains above her, and she breathed in the crisp spring air that held a hint of smoke and cooking rabbits. She was grateful for the exhaustion that kept her limbs heavy and her head clear. Even the smell of smoke and cooking meat, which had brought on the visions more than once while they were traveling to Rōjū City, weren't enough to stir the memories in her now. She simply watched the fire and let her mind wander freely.

Enjoying the companionable silence as fat hissed and dripped from the two hares that Mitsu had caught and prepared for them, Mishi took a moment to appreciate the fact that Mitsu didn't always feel like talking. If he had nothing to say, he said nothing. Mishi approved of that kind of companionship. Eventually, though, she noticed a change in the silence and she looked at Mitsu to see what might be troubling him.

It was difficult to tell. Mishi wasn't an expert at reading people outside of battle, but eventually she decided that he seemed nervous, as though he expected an enemy to arrive at any moment. Then she realized that he probably thought the enemy was already here.

"I can move farther away if you like," she said, trying to keep her tone casual, when she saw Mitsu shudder momentarily as the fire shifted in the wind.

His green eyes snapped to hers and held them for a moment.

"Why would you do that?" he asked, sounding suspicious.

"Because you're afraid of me," she replied. "I can see it now, in the way you sit. And I've noticed it at other times."

She waited, but he said nothing.

"It's all right," she said quietly, though she didn't really feel as though it were all right. Something inside of her didn't like the thought of Mitsu being frightened of her. "I understand."

Mitsu shook his head as though chasing off an insect, and then spoke.

"It's not you. I'm not afraid of *you*."

Mishi didn't believe that.

"You're intimidated by fire," she said.

"Exactly! I'm afraid of fire...even this cooking fire disturbs me. Watching the way it devours that wood, and changes the nature of the hares..."

"But, Mitsu...I *am* Fire. If fire makes you nervous, then I should terrify you."

"I know you won't hurt me, though," he protested. Mishi almost laughed at how comically untrue that statement was, and was about to point out that she had already disproved it quite viscerally, but Mitsu continued before she could speak. "This fire has no conscience, it has no soul, it just is. And fire consumes, that's simply what it does. It has no choice. You have choices, and you choose not to harm, whenever you can. So, yes, I'm afraid of fire and its nature, but I'm not afraid of you."

"Perhaps there is more of fire's nature in me than you imagine." Mishi thought of her dreams, and all that she had done, and shuddered slightly.

"Just because it's the element you are called to doesn't mean you must act like it in all ways. I'm tied to wind, but you don't see me blowing down people's homes or tearing up trees, do you?"

Mishi laughed, because the image that came to mind of Mitsu doing either of those things was humorous to her, but then another thought struck her and she stopped laughing.

"Mitsu-san, you and Taka-san both agree that I'm...unwell enough that I need to seek Yanagi-sensei's help. Couldn't it be that the fire within me is taking over? That it's bending me to be as destructive as the soulless fire that you fear?"

Mitsu was silent for a long time, and Mishi began to wonder if he ever planned to reply.

"I don't know what it is that's causing the visions exactly, or why they take reality from you, but I think the core of you is still there. I think the part of you that wishes to help people rather than harm them is not only there, but still the driving force behind your actions."

"How can you say that?" Mishi asked, panic rising in her chest at the memory of what she had done to Mitsu and Taka. "How can you say that after I attacked you and Taka-san outside of Rōjū City like that? Isn't it clear that I've lost myself?"

"Mishi-san, you may have accidentally hurt us when you were lost in a vision, but think of what you did next. Once you realized what was happening, you were so concerned with protecting us that you tried to run away."

Mishi was silent for a long time.

"I assumed everyone would think I was simply shirking my duties to the New Council."

Mitsu actually laughed at that.

"Oh Mishi-san, I don't know what the rest of Rōjū City thinks, but for Taka-san and I, and probably the Zōkames as well, it was as clear as anything that you were leaving in order to protect us."

Mishi said nothing then, silently accepting the hare that Mitsu passed to her and eating her fill before she could fall asleep where she sat.

Even as sleep claimed her that night, she kept coming back to one question: Why did it please her so to discover that Mitsu-san knew her well enough to understand why she had run?

27日 2月 新議 1年

27th Day, 2nd Moon, Cycle 1 of the New Council

~ Mishi ~

MISHI HAD NEVER run so much in her life, but she was truly glad of the exhaustion she had felt each night as they collapsed into whatever small clearing or copse they used for shelter against the light winds and rain that followed them into the north. Mitsu always had the energy to find them a small animal for the evening meal, whereas she barely had the energy to strike flint to steel and coax a fire to life in whatever small space they managed to keep dry long enough for her efforts to take hold. Mishi often wondered if perhaps Mitsu called on wind and earth to help him run so quickly for so long. She decided she would ask him the next time that she could catch her breath.

Nine days after leaving Rōjū City, more than a day's travel away from the road they had taken north, they arrived in a clearing that was nestled in a small valley, amongst the broad-leafed trees of a dense forest. A stream trickled nearby, and there was a strange woven mat lying against a rock face that joined the steep incline that shaped the valley.

"It's still daylight," Mishi said, as they rested against a thick log that had been flattened on top and seemed like it had been moved to the clearing just for the purpose of making a table or backrest. "Why are we stopping?"

She feared she wasn't exhausted enough to hold off the visions.

"It's a shame that Taka-san isn't here to show it to you," Mitsu said, "but this is the home she has known for the past eight cycles." Mitsu walked up to the woven mat as he spoke, then pulled it aside, revealing a small cave that contained a much-used fire circle near the entrance and a low, flat stump that looked as though it might be used as a table. When Mishi stood and went to look more closely at the cave, she saw a stack of woven mats at the back of the room that likely served as a futon.

"We won't have to sleep in the rain tonight," Mitsu said.

The sky was still clear above them, but it had drizzled on them the night before and Mishi thought that she had seen clouds behind them before the mountains had cut them out of her view as they had come into the valley. The prospect of staying dry through the night was a pleasant one, but she didn't like the idea of sleeping so close to Mitsu and leaving him without an easy escape if she should wake up to one of her dreams.

"You can have the cave," she said. "I'll sleep beneath the stars."

"You'll be sleeping beneath the clouds," Mitsu replied. "I promise to be on my best behavior."

Mishi didn't laugh, though she could see the mischievous twinkle in Mitsu's eye.

"It's not your behavior I'm worried about," Mishi said.

"You won't hurt me, Mishi-san," Mitsu replied, his eyes no longer twinkling.

Mishi didn't dignify that with a response. She wouldn't argue with him, she would simply sleep outside. There was another fire circle in the small clearing in front of the cave, where she could keep warm enough without shelter.

"I'll make a fire," she said. She didn't wait for Mitsu's reply, but exited the cave and started searching for kindling and fallen branches that would be dry enough to catch, even after the light rains of the past few days. She needed to keep busy and, if at all possible, to tire herself out enough to keep her from being a danger to Mitsu. She would search very thoroughly for deadfall in hopes of using up more energy.

She wished they had needed to run farther today. She could already feel the tightness in her chest that often accompanied her visions.

Eventually, she had collected enough wood and kindling that she could no longer put off starting the fire. She was dismayed to see that Mitsu had already returned from his hunting excursion and prepared a small brace of hares for cooking. She had hoped he would still be busy.

Mishi knelt by the fire circle in the clearing, deciding that the weather would likely hold off long enough to let them cook the hares and eat, and began assembling the kindling and smaller pieces of deadfall. Then she took out her flint and steel and struck sparks into the cradle of kindling. It didn't take her long to get the small fire blazing, and then she added more and more wood until the fire was large enough to cook the hares Mitsu had brought down. It would take some time for it to reach a temperature appropriate for cooking, but she had collected enough wood to fuel the fire through the night.

She looked up to find Mitsu staring at her intently.

"Why not use your kisō to start the fire?" he asked. His voice was casual, as though the question were of little consequence, but she could see from the set of his jaw that it wasn't an idle query.

Mishi took a deep breath. How to answer without lying?

"Why use kisō when I have a perfectly effective flint and steel? There are far better uses of kisō than starting a simple campfire."

There, Mishi thought, *a question couldn't be a lie, and the statement was true enough. Perhaps that answer will appease him.*

She tried not to catch Mitsu's gaze, but found her eyes caught by his as she went about setting up the crossed branches that would support the spit for roasting the hares. His gaze told her that he was unconvinced, yet he didn't press her any further.

Eventually they set the hares to cooking and it wasn't long before Mishi was inwardly cursing how little they had run that day. The smoke alone had brought memories too close to the surface, but once the hares were set above the fire, the smell of searing flesh pulled even harder at her mind.

She heard screaming in the distance and told herself that it wasn't real. She looked at Mitsu, just to be certain that he hadn't heard it as well, but he was calmly rotating the hares over the flames.

She began to take deep breaths, and to put herself on the far side of the fire. She didn't want to be too close to Mitsu. Perhaps she should walk into the forest...but no, he might follow her.

"Mishi-san, are you all right?"

She blinked and tried to focus on what was in front of her instead of the distant screams that she was fairly certain were only in her mind.

"Mishi-san?"

Suddenly, Mitsu's face was right in front of hers. She blinked again.

"Yes?"

"What can I do to help?" he asked.

"I don't know," she replied, because it was the truth. She had never yet stopped the visions from coming once they had started.

"Do you want to hold my hand?" Mitsu asked.

Mishi thought about that. She could still hear screams in the distance, and the smell of smoke and cooking rabbit was being replaced with the smell of blood and battle.

"I might attack you," she replied, shaking her head. Her vision was still clear, but the sounds of battle were getting stronger. "You should get away from me."

Now Mitsu was the one shaking his head.

"I won't leave you alone when you're like this," he said. "You could hurt yourself."

Mishi might have laughed at that if she had been capable of feeling any humor at that moment. Instead she simply said, "I'm far more likely to hurt you. You should get away."

Mitsu shook his head once more, and began to reach for her.

Panic took hold. She wasn't lost in a vision yet, but she knew it was only a matter of time. She didn't want to hurt Mitsu at all, but she knew that if he followed her and the vision got worse he would be in real danger. In this moment she could still control her actions.

So, she grabbed his wrist, turned with his body weight, and threw him to the ground. She made sure the impact was hard enough to knock the wind from him, and then she did the only thing she could think of to protect him. She ran.

~~~

Mishi stopped running when the muscles in her legs felt like wet sand instead of charged lightning and the sounds of battle had receded back into memory and were no longer playing in her ears. She collapsed then, heedless of the underbrush still wet from snow-melt that lay beneath her, and simply stared at the tree branches that obscured the sky above her as she took in staggered breaths of damp, spring air.

"You know, when Taka-chan runs through the forest like that she doesn't generally stop to lie on the ground," a voice that sounded like shifting earth and wind blowing through trees rumbled, as willow branches moved into her line of sight. "But I think she should rethink this. It is always good to stop and appreciate the earth from time to time."

A face—was it still a face when it consisted of bark and moss?—came into view then, and Mishi knew that she must be meeting Yanagi-sensei, Taka and Mitsu's longtime mentor. She sat up and slowly took in the bark that shaped itself into a nose and mouth, eyes the color of hardened tree sap, bushy eyebrows of moss and lichen, and the body of what looked like a willow tree. It had as many long, arced and trailing branches as would be found on any normal willow, but also seemed to have legs, or something approximating them.

"You must be Mishi-san," the talking tree continued, and Mishi found that she was struggling to reply. Somehow, even though she was good friends with a dragon who resided on a mountaintop and came forth from a small statue only when the sun went down, the marvel of this walking, talking tree held her speechless. She managed a nod.

A wide smile cracked the gnarled face of the tree.

"It is a true pleasure to finally meet you, Mishi-san. I have heard much about you! How wonderful that Taka-chan finally found you once more. At least, I assume she has found you once more even though she is not here with you. Friends are one of the best parts of life, ne? How do you like my forest?"

Mishi laughed. She couldn't help it. She wasn't sure what she had expected when she thought of meeting this thousands-of-cycles-old kami, but she was fairly certain that an effusive and expressive moving tree hadn't been it.

"The pleasure is mine, Yanagi-sensei," she said, the tree's chatty nature seeming to unblock her tongue. "You aren't what I expected," she added, before she could stop herself.

"And what did you expect, youngling?"

To her relief, the bark and lichen face was still smiling.

"Well…." She wasn't sure how to explain her expectations. "The only other being I know who is as old as you are is a somewhat ornery dragon."

"Ah, yes, Tatsu-san mentioned that he had a new student."

Mishi had been training with Tatsu-sama since the age of ten, so she wasn't sure what it meant that he "had a new student." She supposed that with beings as long-lived as a tree-kami and a dragon, her entire lifespan would be considered recent.

"Do you and Tatsu-sama speak to each other often?" she asked.

"Hmmm…difficult to say."

Mishi wasn't sure if the walking tree was being evasive, or was simply struggling with human time frames.

"But Tatsu-san spoke very highly of you, as has Taka-chan," he continued.

Mishi didn't know what to say to that. She had never thought very highly of herself, and lately…well, lately she considered herself a danger to the world around her. After all, she was here because she had just run away from a friend she was worried she might kill. She certainly didn't consider herself worthy of anyone's praise.

"Hmm…" Yanagi's large eyes studied her, and the humor seemed to have left his face. "What troubles you, youngling?"

Mishi shook her head. She knew better than to try lying to someone like Yanagi, but she didn't know what to say. How could she explain that she was a danger to all of her friends and the world in general? If she told Yanagi-sensei the truth, wouldn't he condemn her? She felt certain she would deserve it, but she wasn't anxious to find out what the tree-kami might do to someone like her. After a long moment of silence, in which Mishi could think of no safe reply, Yanagi spoke once more.

"You are skittish like a sparrow, youngling. Do I frighten you— ah no, but you weren't frightened when you first saw me, and Tatsu-san is your mentor, so it can't be that. Hmm…what then?"

The tree paused briefly, but Mishi made no effort to help him. She simply sat on the forest floor and gazed up at him, her emotions in turmoil.

"You are not afraid of me, and, judging by what Tatsu-san told me about his newest student and her ability to fight, you are unlikely to be afraid of most things that a youngling would be frightened by...and you only began to act like a startled swallow when I asked what troubled you...oho! That's it! You are frightened of yourself! It is your own troubles that scare you, ne?"

The tree's face lit briefly at seeming to have solved a puzzle, but when his gaze met Mishi's again it had lost all of its briefly held triumph.

"And why should one as young as you be so haunted?"

Mishi's throat caught as she tried to find words...and couldn't. She stood up, finally, but no answer came to her save the hot tears that streamed down her face. She wasn't sure why she was crying, but she supposed it didn't matter. Her eyes flowed freely and she didn't bother to wipe at them. She didn't think they planned to stop anytime soon.

"Hmmm...Child...no that's not right. I call many creatures children, but one who has as much darkness around them as you do can no longer be called a child..."

Darkness? Was that what was wrong with her? Had she absorbed too much darkness? Had it made her evil?

"Will you let me take a look at you, Mishi-san? I understand that you fear yourself, but what I cannot understand is why. And if I do not understand why, then I cannot begin to help you. I would like to help you. Would you like that?"

"I'm not sure."

She hadn't meant to speak, but the words were out, and as she said them she knew them to be true. She wasn't sure that she wanted to be helped, or rather, she wasn't sure that what little help could be offered would be worth the risk of someone truly understanding what was wrong with her. She was very afraid of what lay beneath the visions that haunted her dreams, both waking and sleeping.

Yanagi-sensei seemed to think for a long moment, and Mishi realized that a face of bark was very difficult to read.

"If what Taka-san and Tatsu-san have told me can be relied upon, along with what little I can know of you from our brief encounter here...then I think it is safe to assume that what would frighten you most is the idea of hurting the ones you love. After all, you are afraid, but instead of seeking solace from your companion you run alone into the woods. And why would you do that, if not to protect your friend?"

It was true that she feared hurting the people she cared about more than anything, and the fact that she had already hurt them once left her with a guilt she thought she would never be without.

"What if I can help you protect your friends, Mishi-san? Would it not be worth it, whatever it is you fear I will discover, to know that they would be safe?"

Mishi thought about that, and was too busy hoping that what Yanagi-sensei offered was true to worry about how closely he had guessed what she had been thinking. Could he really ensure that she would never hurt the people she loved the most? No matter how bad the darkness got, if she could be sure of that, she thought she might be able to manage.

She nodded, finally, the tears still streaming down her face from too many emotions to name.

"Yes. Help me protect them."

~~~

Having Yanagi-sensei inspect her kisō was similar to, and yet quite different from, having Taka do it. The brush of Taka's kisō was so familiar that having her lifelong friend follow the ebbs and flows of her energy to the deepest well within her did not seem like any kind of an invasion.

Yanagi-sensei's presence didn't feel like an invasion either, because she was allowing it, but it felt quite foreign. She supposed that shouldn't be surprising, considering that he was a who-knew-how-old tree-kami and not her lifelong friend...but she couldn't quite fathom how it was different, simply that it was. Perhaps she could sense the age and power behind his touch, or perhaps she only thought that she could because she knew that he was old and powerful. One thing she was certain of was that the kisō that joined with her own felt of earth and wind and even water…she'd never sensed three elements in one being before, and the sensation startled her.

She felt Yanagi-sensei's kisō touch her own, pausing to await her permission for further contact, and then became distinctly aware of a presence not her own, information, ideas, and identity flooding her senses.

Male yet female, old, as old as the mountains that surrounded them, and ever dying, yet constantly renewing, and always new. At first she was surprised that he had allowed her to know so much about him, but then it occurred to her that it might have just been a simple way to distract her from what might otherwise be an overwhelming experience. She had rarely connected with Tatsu-sama this way, and the few times she had, it had been while she was in desperate need of healing and in no state to notice what his consciousness felt like. Now she wondered. Would it be overwhelming? Would the connection trouble her?

Slowly, the tide of "otherness" that was Yanagi-sensei's initial contact reduced until it felt more like the kind of contact she was used to establishing with Taka. She was surprised, however, to find that his kisō already permeated her own. It normally took Taka longer to reach all the way into her fuchi and begin assessing her.

She took a deep breath to maintain her calm. What had Yanagi-sensei already learned about her in that short period of time? Did he know what was wrong with her? Could he truly help her? Or would he simply discover the terrible truth about her and then let others know that she was not worth helping?

She inhaled deeply through her nose, the cool air bringing with it the scent of pine needles, wet leaves, and still lightly frozen earth. She let it out, trying to focus on her too fast heart to slow its pace.

She felt Yanagi's earth kisō reach for her own fire. What did he hope to discover that way? His kisō prodded hers gently, and she felt the fire within her respond, wishing to play.

No. She couldn't. It wasn't safe. She could hurt someone. She wouldn't allow it. She hadn't allowed it for so long.

Then she felt Yanagi-sensei's kisō unlock something within her.

The world exploded.
Mishi screamed.

~~~

Mishi looked up at the trees around her and wondered why there was no fire above her. Had the whole thing been a dream? Had she collapsed while running away from the camp? Perhaps she'd never met Yanagi-sensei at all. Perhaps the whole thing was a creation of her mind and nothing more.

"Hmm...well, that was impressive, I must say."

The deep voice, which sounded like wind rustling leaves and moving earth, came from somewhere near her feet. She sat up.

A bark and lichen encrusted face, hosting eyes of hardened tree sap, met her gaze.

"How long has it been since you called forth your fire, youngling?"

Mishi thought about that. She hadn't used her kisō since the battle of Rōjū City, when she'd used so much at once that she'd almost died—would have died, if Taka hadn't been there to save her. At first she'd been under strict healer's orders (Taka's and Tatsu's both) not to use her kisō lest she do herself irreparable harm, but when that ban had been lifted she still hadn't resumed using her kisō. The reason was simple—she didn't trust herself not to hurt any of her friends with the powerful fire that coursed through her and called to her from within and without. The pain of losing Sachi-san and Kuma-sensei was a raw wound that she couldn't touch and the thought of losing anyone else was more than she could bear. The thought of losing someone to her own violence was beyond paralyzing. No, there was no safe way to use her kisō, and the longer she held that decision the more justified she felt about it. Her dreams and terrors had only taken a more and more solid hold of her mind as more time passed. She could not be trusted, could never be trusted, to wield her kisō safely again.

"A few moons," she whispered, as all those thoughts cascaded through her mind.

Yanagi-sensei's face looked dire.

"It is a very dangerous game that you play, youngling. You could hurt someone you do not mean to hurt."

"I know!" she cried before he could say any more. "I know, I can't be trusted! That's why I haven't used it at all. Not since the battle of Rōjū City."

"What I mean, youngling, is that you cannot allow your kisō to build up in this fashion. It is very dangerous. You have to release a small amount of it daily, or else you risk an explosion like the one that just happened."

Now Mishi's face blanched and her attention was once more drawn to the trees that surrounded them. She saw no sign of fire anywhere.

"It was real then?" she asked, her voice tiny.

Yanagi nodded.

"Indeed, youngling. Luckily, since I was here, and knew what was coming, I was able to prevent it from damaging even the smallest leaf. All the creatures that call this forest home are safe, worry not on that account."

Mishi felt the tension in her shoulders and back release slightly at the reassurance. She was glad to know she hadn't hurt anything living.

"But you could easily have done so, and indeed, if you don't use your kisō every day, you will do so."

Mishi shook her head. She was just as afraid of using her kisō as she was of picking up her sword. Perhaps more so. There were people who could stop her, even with a sword in her hands, or at least slow her down, but her kisō? It wasn't that she thought she was more powerful than anyone else, it was simply that fire could do so much damage, so quickly, that there was little anyone could do to defend against it. Even Taka, whose water kisō was easily equal to or better than Mishi's fire kisō, would be hard pressed to find a way to stop the damage that she could cause with a single burst of flame.

"Mishi-san, I understand that you think your kisō is likely to hurt someone, but believe me, if you refuse to use your kisō at least once a day, you will wind up with another explosion like this one, just waiting to be unleashed. And it could happen anytime, especially if you lose yourself in visions again....Which, by the way, are caused by the blocked kisō, did you know?"

"What?" Mishi was losing track of the conversation quickly.

"The visions, they're a sign of the sickness that comes from a buildup of kisō. Or, I should say, the intensity of your nightmares and visions is a sign of the buildup of kisō. The nightmares and visions are a thing your mind has created because of all the horrors you have faced. They may never go away entirely, but they shouldn't be as overwhelming if you use your kisō daily. It is remarkably unhealthy to go so long without accessing your kisō. Think of it like a spring-fed well that is sealed shut. Eventually the reservoir of water reaches the seal, and then pressure slowly begins to build. Leave it long enough, and a geyser pours forth when it is finally broken. In the meantime, the pressure may harm the interior of the well; the water, seeking an exit, will try to break its barriers in order to relieve the pressure. In the case of kisō, however, the barrier is your mind, and your kisō will seek the parts that are most easily ruptured. Your nightmares are like small cracks in your mental barriers, and your kisō, seeking an exit you refused to give it, sought to fill those cracks until they burst."

"You make it sound as though my kisō has a mind of its own."

Yanagi shook his giant head and hundreds of willow branches shook with it.

"No, youngling, only that it behaves as water does. It has a nature, just as anything else, and it must do as its nature bids it."

"If I try to release it, won't it just explode again?"

"Not if you release it frequently. At least daily. Surely Tatsu-san explained all of this to you? Did he not instruct you to use your kisō every day?"

Mishi nodded. Of course, Tatsu-sama had told her to practice her kisō every day, but that had been before...before she'd discovered all the terrible things she was capable of. And after her injury, after she'd been carefully instructed not to access her kisō for a tenday or more in order to heal, she assumed that she could simply refuse to access it, despite what she'd first learned, and thus protect her friends. She hadn't known it would make her sick, she had simply thought...

"Tatsu-sama always said that practicing with my kisō daily would help me to channel it and also help me grow my power. That every time I used it, I made the reservoir a tiny bit deeper, and so I thought..."

Yanagi's branches bobbed up and down in what Mishi could only assume was a nod.

"You thought that if you stifled your kisō the reservoir might shrink? That it would eventually dwindle, and stop flowing? That you would deplete your own power and thus free yourself of your responsibility?"

That took Mishi aback. She had secretly thought she might rid herself of her kisō entirely, but she had done it in order to take responsibility for how dangerous she was. Hadn't she?

"Certainly, youngling, your life would be easier if you did not have so much power. And to have so much so young...I do not envy you that, truly. But I'm afraid there is no way to cut yourself off from it, short of your own death, and I imagine, as one who wishes to protect her friends above all else, that you do not wish to put them through the pain that your death would cause them."

Mishi felt the blood drain from her face as Yanagi-sensei addressed the thoughts that had run quietly in the back of her mind for the past few moons. She hadn't seriously considered taking her own life, but after the day when she had hurt Mitsu and Taka, her thoughts had started to wander that way. Yanagi-sensei's reminder put a stop to that.

"So, we are back to the best way to protect your friends, ne?"

She nodded.

"You must release your kisō daily. If you practice with it, as you always did before your injuries, then you should find it reliable once more. If you do not treat it with the same respect you always have, if you cease to nurture it as you should, then, and only then, it may betray you."

Mishi swallowed, and the hairs on the back of her neck rose. Her kisō called to her, even when she didn't use it, but she hated the thought of calling it forward again, and the damage that she might cause. A deep longing rose in her, though, as she realized that a core part of her had been desperate to reach for the fire within her for moons now.

Slowly, she nodded.

Then she took a deep breath, centered herself, and called forth the fire within.

~~~

Mishi watched the firelight dance before her—now the sole focus of the night-blackened forest that surrounded her—and she took a deep lungful of smoke-tinged air as she let the fire leap back and forth from her fingertips to the circle of stones that—mostly—contained it.

Mitsu hadn't been at the campfire when she had returned from her encounter with Yanagi, and she hadn't gone looking for him. After all, she still thought he was safer the farther away from her he stayed. The hares had cooked, and she had set them aside to cool before starting to practice her new promise to Yanagi. She wouldn't risk her friends by not accessing her kisō. She would be diligent about practicing with it once more.

So she played with the fire in her hands, simply rolling it back and forth between them, eventually closing her eyes and imagining the shape of the fire in her mind's eye. She had used this exercise to shape fire as a child, and she decided it was a good one to take up again. It would help her use enough kisō to keep her promise to Yanagi, yet it was something simple and playful that she didn't think was likely to harm anyone.

She pictured the fire as a sly fox, and felt the shape of the heat between her hands conform to the image in her mind—sleek body, large ears, and puffy tail. Then she pictured the fox scampering from her hands back into the fire, and she felt the "fox" act accordingly.

She smiled at the feel of the fire working with her to mold itself to her imagination. Next she imagined a tiny Kisōshi, complete with a katana. Then she imagined the figure going through the steps of a slow kata. She was happy that the forms still came to her easily, even though she hadn't practiced them in moons.

She winced then, reminded of why she hadn't lifted a sword in that time.

Without bidding, images of the battle of Rōjū City flashed before her eyes. Hundreds of Kisōshi locked in battle surrounded her, and her own opponents were going down one by one, taken by her sword, or by the fire that issued forth at her command.

The smell of smoke filled her nostrils, and she could hear the screams of the fallen. She moved to block and strike, block and strike, her blade becoming a shroud of steel.

Her breath came faster and faster, as her enemies kept coming.

"Mishi-san?"

Was that Taka crying out for her? More opponents rushed her, and she fought them back.

"Mishi-san?"

No, a man's voice. Kuma-sensei? Kuma-sensei was injured. Did he need her?

"Mishi-san, can you hear me?"

Not Kuma-sensei. Someone younger. Katagi-san?

"Mishi-san, it's Mitsu. Can you hear me?"

Mitsu. Yes, Mitsu might be nearby. Hadn't he been the one who brought the scroll to Tsuku-san? Where had he gone once the fighting started?

"Mishi-san, can you hear me?"

She could hear him, but she couldn't see him. Why couldn't she see him? The flames around her were growing higher, the smoke thicker—she could barely see her opponents now.

"Mishi-san, can you see me?"

She shook her head. She didn't have the breath to say no, there were too many of the Rōjū's Kisōshi to fight off. She blinked the sweat out of her eyes.

"Mishi-san, we're in Yanagi-sensei's forest, just outside of Taka-san's cave. Can you see me?"

Mishi blinked again. Yanagi-sensei's forest? Taka's cave? Not in battle. Not in Rōjū City. She'd been sitting by the fire, working with her kisō.

She blinked once more.

The firelight glowed behind Mitsu's face. Why was it so close? Green eyes stared into her grey ones. She blinked again. Could she still smell smoke? That was just the camp fire, wasn't it?

Suddenly Mitsu's face was as close to hers as possible, his lips pressed against hers. She blinked rapidly, completely bewildered, but once more sure of where she was, physically at least. She was standing in front of the fire outside of Taka's cave, and for some reason Mitsu was kissing her. She ignored the small flip that her stomach performed and pushed herself away from him, jumping backward onto the log that she had been sitting on earlier.

"I'm sorry," Mitsu said, his eyes sparkling slightly in the firelight. "I shouldn't have done that without your permission, but I thought that slapping you was probably a good way to get killed."

Mishi nodded. She wasn't sure if she was accepting the apology, or agreeing that slapping her might have resulted in Mitsu's death, perhaps both.

"Do you wish to talk about it?" Mitsu asked.

Did he mean the kiss or the vision? Not sure which he meant, or which terrified her more, she shook her head.

Mitsu nodded, then turned and walked into the cave.

28日 2月 新議 1年

28th Day, 2nd Moon, Cycle 1 of the New Council

⇒ Mishi ⇐

THE NEXT MORNING, as they sat in the clearing beyond the cave waiting for their morning rice to boil, with birds chirping in the soft spring sunlight, Mitsu pulled a stack of rolled parchments out of his pack.

"I meant to give these to you days ago, but we were running so hard each day that I kept forgetting each night when we made camp," he said, as he handed them to her. "Now that Yanagi-sensei has insisted that we rest for a day, I've finally remembered. One is from Tsuku-san. I believe the others are notes from your friends in the south, which arrived the day I left Rōjū City."

Mishi sighed. She had remembered that Mitsu had said that he had other messages for her on that first day, but she hadn't asked for them on purpose. She told herself it was because she was too tired to read after they had run so hard each day on the way here, but in truth, she wasn't feeling particularly eager even now.

She was curious to know how Ami was doing with rebuilding Kuma-sensei's Kisōshi school and filling it with new students, and she supposed she didn't mind reading whatever Tsuku-san had to say to her either, but she was rather dreading reading the scroll from Katagi—especially after the looks he'd given her ever since she'd told him that she didn't wish to have him accompany her on this journey.

"Well?" asked Mitsu, after Mishi had rerolled the third scroll and placed it into her pack.

She just looked at him. She wasn't about to volunteer any of the topics Katagi had brought up in his letter. Mitsu didn't need to know that Katagi felt abandoned by her, or that he was still professing his love for her even though she had insisted on leaving him behind.

"What did Tsuku-san say about our assignment?" he prodded.

Mishi thought for a moment before answering, and swallowed before she spoke. The message about their assignment hadn't been all that heartening.

"She said we're to keep in touch with Riyōshi and send word as soon as we have a good idea of where the sanzoku are establishing themselves between raids. She reminded me again that the men who tried to track them previously have all wound up dead. She suggested we use extreme caution, but repeated that it is urgent we stop the sanzoku as quickly as possible. I wonder if she knows that those ideas don't exactly work well together."

"I'm sure she's just worried about you."

Mishi was silent for a long time as she stared into the steam that rose from the boiling rice.

"Mishi-san, it's all right to be frightened by this assignment. It's quite dangerous. There's a good chance the sanzoku will kill us if they catch us, and we're basically laying ourselves out as bait for them. Being nervous is perfectly natural."

Mishi raised her grey eyes to meet Mitsu's green ones. She didn't smile, but the corner of her mouth quirked to one side.

"I'm not frightened of the sanzoku, or of what might happen to us if they catch us. Though you're right that it would be perfectly reasonable to feel that way."

"Oh?" Mitsu's eyebrows rose in clear surprise at this statement.

Mishi shook her head.

"I'm just worried that I'll kill you by accident before the sanzoku even get to us."

Mitsu's eyebrows jumped to his hairline, but Mishi didn't laugh, even at his reaction. It was true. She was worried she would injure him, or worse. She had hoped that the visions would leave her after working with Yanagi, but if last night was any indication, that wasn't happening. Yanagi had said that the visions might improve with time, but how long would it take for her to harm Mitsu-san?

She particularly didn't like it that he still carried her swords. It would be too easy for her to take them from him.

She was distracted from her concerns, though, when a high-pitched keening rent the air. She watched Mitsu look skyward and saw him check the ties on the leather bracer he wore on his forearm. Then, a large red-tailed hawk backwinged into the clearing and landed forcefully on Mitsu's outstretched arm.

"Riyōshi! It's good to see you," Mitsu said, as the bird eyed him cautiously.

Mishi wondered if the bird would nip Mitsu's ear the way it always did Taka's, but was disappointed to see it keep its beak to itself.

Mitsu went quiet for a while, and Mishi assumed that he was communicating with the hawk. She wondered idly what it must be like to be able to exchange images and emotions with a mind as different as a hawk's, but her thoughts abruptly shifted when Mitsu turned to her, his face suddenly quite grave.

"What is it?" she asked.

"Riyōshi has spotted what might be a sanzoku scouting party moving toward a town a few days travel from here."

Mishi extinguished the fire beneath the rice, and grabbed her already packed travel roll.

"Lead the way," she said to the hawk.

⇌ Kusuko ⇌

Kusuko watched the dark shape in the trees for a long time and then thrashed a bit in her bed roll, as though she were sleeping fitfully and could wake at any moment. Then she stilled, and listened to the quiet night sounds, the sounds of Taka breathing nearby, and the soft animal and insect noises that filled the night. She waited until the moon slid behind a cloud, taking away the soft glow that had covered the forest, and then she slipped from her bedroll to the ground behind a log that lay in between her and the small fire they had made.

She continued that pattern, waiting until the moon hid behind the clouds and then moving to another rock, tree, log, etc., until she came up behind the dark shape in the trees. Then she pulled her dagger from her obi, reached carefully around to press it to his throat, and whispered, "Follow me."

~~~

The moon had barely crossed a tree's span of sky when she stopped, turned around, and looked Inari-san in the eyes.

"How kind of you to check on me," she said, her voice an emotionless monotone.

"That was clever," said Inari, with a wide smile on his face. "I was sure you were still in your bed roll."

She nodded.

"I used the thrashing to push my bed roll into a more or less Kusuko shaped blob."

She wouldn't have bothered to explain, but she was fairly certain that Inari knew exactly what she had done, even if he hadn't known she was doing it at the time. And perhaps he even knew that. Inari was tricky, like the fox he was named for.

"Ah yes, I remember that trick," the older hishi said. "Always a favorite with the youngest trainees."

Kusuko nodded again, though she wasn't sure if his assertion was true. She had never trained with the other hishi, outside of combat training. Her father had taught her everything else himself.

"Why did my father send you after me?" Sometimes the best way to get information was to be blunt, and Inari could lead a person through a verbal maze if that person wasn't careful. Kusuko didn't have time for word games, or romps down memory lane.

Inari smiled.

"What makes you think he did? Perhaps I'm simply curious to see how you perform on this mission."

Kusuko rolled her eyes, because she knew it would amuse Inari.

"Yes, of course. I'm sure that following me through the northlands is precisely what you would choose to do with your free time."

Inari laughed.

"Very well, I was sent...but what makes you assume your father cares to know anything other than that you are well? He worries about you, you know."

This time Kusuko only rolled her eyes mentally, allowing nothing to show on her face. She knew full well that Mamushi-san considered her nothing more than another operative. He had taken an interest in her training only to ensure that she was the best hishi she could be. He certainly didn't "worry" about her the way any normal parent would.

"Ah yes, I'm certain he's greatly concerned for my wellbeing. Of course, he would send one of his best and most trusted hishi to ensure that I am well. That is a perfectly reasonable use of resources."

Her tone was completely flat, and she imagined that even Inari might have trouble deciding if she were being serious or sarcastic.

"Mm....Well, I'm here, anyway. Do you have anything to report?"

She supposed it was silly to think that Inari would tell her the real reason that he was following her. She suspected that Mamushi-san didn't trust her to complete her mission for some reason, perhaps because her latest hifu had allied itself with the New Council? Perhaps he hadn't believed her when she'd insisted that it was only her hifu that had changed allegiance, and not her true self.

She certainly wasn't about to ask Inari if he knew anything about *that*.

"The Rōjū zantō are causing trouble to the north of Rōjū City, as are the sanzoku farther north, who are most likely also Rōjū zantō. They are keeping people from believing that the New Council is stable enough to rule, and they are causing people to be afraid of harboring females with enough kisō to be Kisōshi. I've been assigned to follow Taka-san, to heal on the front lines and help her as best I can while collecting information."

She deliberately didn't share more than she thought Inari likely already knew. It wasn't that she didn't trust Inari—though of course she didn't, since all hishi were trained to spy on each other—it was simply that information was valuable, and one never knew when one would need an additional edge.

"And Taka-san's companions? The ones you worked with before the Rōjū were overthrown?"

"They've been sent on a different mission."

If Inari expected her to elaborate, he was disappointed. She wasn't sure when or if she planned to tell him about Mishi's mission, but for now she decided it was best to stick to the assignment she'd been given herself.

Inari smiled then, much to Kusuko's surprise.

"Nothing else?" he asked, far too brightly.

She shook her head.

"Ah, to be young again," Inari said, apropos of nothing. "I wish you the best of luck on the front lines. I've heard it's getting nasty over there. The Rōjū zantō are fighting with the kind of dedication one expects of zealots or crusaders. It's strange to witness in person, and I imagine it would be frightening to have to fight against it. Keep an eye on that healer of yours."

Kusuko nodded once, and turned to leave.

"Oh, and don't be surprised if you get some new orders from me in the near future," Inari said, no longer smiling. "You know how Mamushi-san can be."

What was Inari hinting at? He'd called Taka "hers," which made her wonder if he knew something that she didn't, and then he'd warned her of her father changing her orders. Would it be the puppy all over again?

She shuddered once, despite having felt appropriately dressed for the weather only moments before. Then she took a deep breath and returned to her bed roll.

It might be for the best if she put some distance between herself and Taka. Just in case…

30日 2月 新議 1年

30th Day, 2nd Moon, Cycle 1 of the New Council

⇒ Taka ⇐

TAKA TOOK A deep breath and instantly regretted it. The stench of rotting flesh mingled with the smell of hundreds of unwashed bodies, horses, and cooking fires.

While her stomach and nose battled the pervasive odor of the camp, her eyes took in the tents that filled the open pasture in front of her and extended well past her field of vision. The largest tent was right in front of her, a tent the size of the town hall she'd grown up with. She assumed it was the healing tent, judging by both the smell and the sounds emanating from it. Groans, sighs, and the occasional scream drifted on the same wind that brought her the smell of rotting flesh.

She did not take another deep breath, but she did take a moment to prepare herself for what was to come. Tsuku-san may have called her the greatest healer in Gensokai, but Taka had never been in charge of other healers before; indeed, she'd never even had to heal more than one person at a time. At least, not more than one *human* at a time. She had, once, when there had been a very bad storm in Yanagi-sensei's forest, had to heal multiple animals in the same day, and she had been forced to organize them by the severity of their injuries as well as how time sensitive the healing would be. Thankfully, she'd had both Yanagi-sensei and Riyōshi to help her organize, assess, and communicate with the animals that needed help.

She didn't know who would help her here. Indeed, even Kusuko, who had left Rōjū City at the same time as Taka, had gone her own way after traveling with her for only a few days, stating that she had a matter she needed to attend to and that they would reunite at the camp to the north.

There had been enough people traveling the road from Rōjū City that Taka hadn't worried about traveling alone, especially since that was the way she had traveled for cycles until she'd been forced to travel with Mitsu last fall. She had actually enjoyed the chance to appreciate the change of scenery, hunt and cook for just herself each night, and sleep under the stars without anyone else to worry about. She felt slightly guilty about it, but it was a relief not to have to worry about Mishi and her state of mind at every moment. She still fretted about her, but she trusted Mitsu, and she knew that Mishi would do everything she could to protect them both.

She had enjoyed having the time to think about whatever came to mind, and embrace her own solitude once more. However, she had thought too often about this very moment, and she still hadn't sorted out how it should go. She was supposed to walk in here and offer not only her services as a healer, but advice and instruction to other healers.

The only other fully trained healers she knew were male, and none of them had been willing to accept a female yukisō. Of course, that was before the Rōjū Council had been disbanded and female Kisōshi had been accepted as fact rather than fiction. They had also been at the Josankō, and she had a feeling that any of the healers who had been willing to become instructors there had not been the type of men she would ever wish to work with. Perhaps the men she was about to meet would be different.

Well, standing out here fretting about it wouldn't tell her one way or another. She centered her kisō, reminded herself that she had been trained by Yanagi-sensei and that she had orders from the leader of the New Council, and then pulled aside the flap of the healing tent.

~~~

"I'm looking for Iruka-san," she said to the first person she came across, a young man wearing a dark brown kimono covered in various stains of questionable substances.

The young man's eyebrows rose, and Taka wondered if she should have changed into one of the kimono that Tsuku-san had insisted she bring with her before making her appearance. But where would she have changed? She didn't know where her quarters were yet, and besides, she felt most comfortable in her leather leggings and tunic, even if people looked at her strangely because of them.

"In the back," the young man said, even as he returned to whatever it was he'd been doing.

Taka took in the expanse of the healing tent. There were hastily assembled palettes all over the floor, with a hundred men or more spread out on them. There seemed to be walkways established between certain rows of men, but beyond that she couldn't instantly detect any sort of order to how the men were arranged. Perhaps it would be explained to her after she'd introduced herself.

She saw a few men, dressed in the same dark brown kimono that the man who'd given her directions had been wearing, walking amongst the injured and ill men, and they seemed to minister to them. She reached out with her kisō to the nearest one, to see if he was a yukisō or simply a volunteer who aided with the sick.

She sensed enough kisō that he could have been a healer, but it wasn't very strong. She wasn't overly surprised. The men who had worked at the Josankō hadn't been overly powerful either. Perhaps Iruka-san would prove more capable. Powerful, she chided herself. She knew quite well that one didn't have to be excessively powerful to be a capable healer. The female instructors at the Josankō had been excellent examples of that. They had been weak enough in their kisō to avoid being drowned at birth, and yet most of them were quite adept at treating women throughout pregnancy, and caring for young babies through all kinds of illness. She would keep an open mind. Just because she had more kisō than any of the men here didn't mean she was necessarily a better healer.

"Can I help you?" asked a deep voice, pulling her from her musings. The man was a full head taller than she was, although barely any wider. His tone made the words sound like a threat, rather than an offer of assistance. As did the way he loomed over her, as though trying to get her to take a step backward.

"I'm looking for Iruka-san," she said, holding her ground.

"You've found him," he said.

When he offered nothing further, Taka held out the scroll that Tsuku-san had sent along with her.

"I've been sent by Tsuku-sama and the New Council," she said.

Iruka-san looked at her and quirked an eyebrow.

"Never seen a female messenger before," he said, as he took the scroll. "A bit young, aren't you? To be out traveling alone?"

Taka swallowed the first reply that came to mind and simply jutted her chin toward the scroll.

"I suggest you read that," she said.

The man scowled as though she'd insulted him, but must have decided that her manners were something he could correct later.

Taka's anxiety increased slightly. She had a feeling that this man wasn't going to like what he read in the scroll she'd just handed him. She watched his eyes widen as he progressed through the scroll, saw the way that his gaze flicked to her and his scowl deepened. She saw his neck redden, and she prepared for the shouting that she was sure would come.

Then it didn't.

"Follow me," the man hissed.

Taka was so surprised not to be the recipient of the ire that had so clearly built up in the man's gaze that she failed to move for a moment. Then she hurried to catch up with his long stride as he walked straight out of the tent.

He walked quickly through the first few rows of tents and then stopped in front of one. It was identical to all the others they'd passed, but Iruka-san gestured to the entrance flap.

"These will be your quarters. We were told to expect additional healers."

The man grimaced, but didn't say anything else for a moment.

"I'll send someone along to fetch you after you've had some time to unpack your things and make yourself comfortable."

Taka nodded, grateful for the chance to clean up some after a full tenday on horseback through steep, narrow, winding mountain paths. She smiled politely, said thank you, and entered the tent.

~~~

After the first candle burn, in which she managed to get acquainted with her tent, unpack her meager belongings, find a basin for washing, put it to use, and dress herself in the plainest of the kimonos that Tsuku-san had sent with her, Taka began to wonder where the person that was meant to fetch her was.

After the second candle burn, she wondered if they expected her to have found a hot spring somewhere and taken a full bath, or if they simply assumed that she took an inordinately long time to primp. Perhaps they thought she needed a nap.

About halfway through the third candle burn, Taka realized that Iruka-san had never intended to send anyone for her at all. This mystified her briefly. Did he think her incapable of finding the healing tent without help? Or was he simply testing her to see if she had the confidence to return to the tent without a guide?

She sighed, rose from the small sleeping palette where she had sat down to begin writing a letter to Mishi, brushed herself off, and got ready for a confrontation.

~~~

Taka opened the flap of the healing tent, only to find the same young man who had given her directions earlier blocking the entrance.

"Healers only," he said.

"I am a healer. Please move," Taka replied.

The man didn't budge.

Taka wished that she were wearing her leathers instead of this damnable kimono. In her leathers, she carried a hunting knife on her belt and could easily look threatening by reaching for it. In a kimono, she had to hide her hunting knife away in her obi, and it was difficult to draw attention to it without actually pulling it out and brandishing it. That was far less impressive an action for her to take, as she didn't truly know how to fight with it. She only used it for preparing animals for meals after she'd snared them. So she settled for glaring at the young man instead, and wishing that she were as tall and imposing a figure as Mishi.

"If you don't move, I'll render you unconscious and you'll be of no use to anyone," she said, when the man still didn't move.

He stared at her as though she hadn't spoken.

"I did warn you," she said, as her hand darted quickly to the young man's neck and she sent her kisō running into his, pulling his consciousness away. He crumpled to the floor, and as soon as he was down she made her way directly toward Iruka-san, who was standing over an injured man to the right-hand side of the tent.

"Your assistants leave much to be desired," she said, when she reached him. "That one guarding the door has fallen asleep on the job. Have you been having trouble with insurgents? I assume you must, if you have to place a door guard."

She said it all in the most cheerful and matter-of-fact tone she could muster. She was willing to confront the man, but she was curious what he would choose to do if she simply defied him with a smile on her face instead.

"How did you get in here?" he asked, ignoring her earlier comments.

"Well, your door guard is asleep, as I mentioned, but why on earth would I have trouble getting in here? Surely he is only trying to keep out the riffraff?"

Iruka-san glared at her without pretense.

"You are the riffraff," he hissed.

Now Taka decided a change of tone was warranted.

"I am a fully qualified healer that your leader has put in charge of this healing tent. I don't know what you have against me aside from my gender, but as it appears that that's enough to get your balls in a twist, I'm glad that you won't be in charge anymore. No one so easily unhinged should be responsible for the well-being of so many."

She may have made a point of saying the last part a fair bit louder than was strictly necessary, but she was trying to make a point.

"Get out," he said, not quite yelling. "Get out of my hospital."

Taka took a deep breath, despite the putrid smell, and said, "I'm afraid that if you wish to attempt to make me leave, you will wind up unconscious like your door guard."

Iruka-san's hand rose to point at the exit, and his other hand reached for the collar of Taka's kimono.

"GET—" he began to shout.

Then he fell over limp.

"I did warn you," Taka muttered, letting go of the hand that had grabbed her collar.

Kami curse it, she thought. *I really was hoping someone would explain where I could find everything.*

1日 3月 新議 1年

1st Day, 3rd Moon, Cycle 1 of the New Council

≈ Taka ≈

TAKA STIFLED A yawn as she pulled her hands back from yet another soldier, watching the tight lines of pain recede from his face as sleep took him. She had been working constantly for a few candleburns in quick succession now, and the healers she had worked with had either been untroubled by her age and gender, or they had simply been too busy to pay attention to who was giving orders and triaging patients.

Or perhaps they had simply watched her heal enough men to decide that she must know what she was doing. Whatever the case, no one had given her much trouble after she'd rendered Iruka-san unconscious, and she had been able to help a number of soldiers in that time as well.

Most of the injuries weren't that grievous, and she would have wondered why they were waiting in the tent to be treated if she hadn't realized that leaving the tent without treatment would likely mean that they would have to fight again with an injury. Any men who weren't in the healing tent were returned to battle at once. Only a few men had injuries that required them to be completely immobilized or bed ridden, but many had injuries that would make fighting dangerous if they weren't treated.

Taka stretched her arms above her head, and looked around the tent once more. She'd found another healer who had been willing to tell her how the pallets were organized, and what system they were using for triage, not long after she had incapacitated Iruka-san. Now she inspected some of the areas that were lower down on the priority list.

Traitor's Hope

Iruka-san himself had been attending to the high priority healings, so she had taken those over as soon as the man was unconscious. She had just healed the last high priority patient, though, so now she was looking farther down the line.

There was a man moaning on a pallet that was farther away from her in the section meant for patients who would likely last a few days before they needed immediate care, and something in her gut made her move closer to the man.

When she got to him, she saw that his face was covered in a thin sheen of sweat and that his breath was ragged and stuttering. She gently placed a hand on his forehead and reached out with her own kisō.

Infection. It didn't take long for her to sense that his body was fighting off something strong, and that it was beginning to lose the battle. Taka took a deep breath and prepared to push her kisō further.

A hand clamped on her wrist and pulled her away from the man on the palette.

"I thought I told you to get out," said a deep voice, as she looked up to see Iruka-san looming over her once more.

"And I told you," she said, keeping her voice as level as she could, "that if you didn't let me go I would be forced to render you unconscious. Do you need another nap, Iruka-san?"

The man glared at her, but dropped her arm.

"I won't have all my efforts of the past few tendays ruined by some idiot girl."

Taka held her chin high as she replied, "That's true. You won't."

Iruka-san looked at her as though she'd suggested they both go have sex with dolphins, but she held her ground.

"This man doesn't have time for me to stand here arguing with you. He needs immediate attention."

Iruka-san snorted derisively.

"This man is fine. His wounds aren't deep, he can wait. That's why he's in this section of the tent."

Taka shook her head.

"Whoever assessed him when he first arrived must not have assessed him with kisō. His superficial wounds have led to an infection, and if he doesn't get help soon, he'll die."

"Ridiculous! His coloring is perfectly normal, there isn't any pus at the wound site, he—"

"Stop using your eyes and use your kisō! His blood is tainted. It's possible the blade that cut him was tainted too, but it doesn't matter now. Now all that matters is stopping it before it's too late."

Iruka-san glared at her and put a hand on the man on the floor. His face was set in a grimace, and his temples had begun to sweat.

Taka didn't want to let Iruka-san take the time to assess the man again, but she'd have to forcibly remove the other healer at this point if she wanted to treat the ill man, so she simply waited and hoped he was quick about it.

Iruka-san's face paled, and then his mouth set in a firm line.

"It's already too late. The infection has spread, he only has a few more minutes."

Now Taka *did* push Iruka-san out of the way.

"Get out of my way. Let me work."

Iruka-san stepped back and watched her with the same set face.

"He's beyond what even I can treat, child. You're wasting your time and energy. You'll probably just wind up hurting yourself."

But Taka had already tuned out the older man and his nay-saying, placing a hand on the infected man's chest. She sent her kisō immediately to work. She was soon so deeply focused on sending her kisō to route out the taint in the man's blood that she barely felt the hand that grabbed her shoulder and pulled on her, or heard the commotion that followed when that hand suddenly let go before it could part her from contact with her patient.

She had to work quickly. The infection, as Iruka-san had said, was everywhere, and moments were vital to staying ahead of it. Taka spread her kisō wide, seeking out the water of life that called to her just as any water did, and finding the parts that didn't belong, the parts that attacked what did belong, the things that made a man so ill that he could die without ever shedding more than a drop or two of blood, and sometimes not even that.

After a long time, though Taka had no idea how long, she blinked. Her eyes finally opened once more, no longer looking inwards, and saw the world before her. The man on the palette was asleep, breathing slowly and evenly.

Taka took her own deep breath, and smiled.

The faces that greeted her when she raised her head were not smiling, but Taka barely noticed their expressions, since she was too busy taking in what their bodies were doing.

Iruka-san lay on the floor facedown, still conscious, but unmoving, and Kusuko sat on top of him with a small dagger held casually to his neck.

The other healers in the tent were all completely still, some remaining next to their patients, others circled around Taka and the tableau on the floor. Taka wondered briefly if Kusuko had ruined her chances of collecting information with this display, but before she had time to worry about it, she realized she needed to fix things before they got out of hand.

"He's healed," she said. "Now, before anyone else moves, I'd like to point out that pulling me away from a patient is never a good idea. Not only could it kill the patient, as it certainly would have in this situation, but as you can see, I am not without my defenses."

And so what if my "defenses" are a tiny woman in full kimono, she thought to herself. *They are obviously effective regardless.* Taka decided that if Kusuko had brought this much attention to herself then she might as well take full advantage of it, and try to make it so that her services as "defense" were never needed again, at least not against these men.

"Now," Taka continued. She stood up and almost instantly went down again. Kusuko was immediately by her side, holding her by the arm. "I need rest," she announced, perhaps unnecessarily. "I will be returning to my quarters for the night, but if there is an emergency I expect to be sent for. If not, I will return in the morning and expect no more trouble."

She said that last with as much command as she could muster, and hoped that, between her tone of voice and the threat of Kusuko's dagger, her words would be heeded.

Then she let Kusuko help her through the tent flaps and out of sight of the healing tent entirely before finally collapsing. She was surprised to feel herself lifted into a set of arms, and to look up and see Kusuko's face smiling down at her as she was carried across the camp.

2日 3月 新議 1年
2nd Day, 3rd Moon, Cycle 1 of the New Council

~ Kusuko ~

KUSUKO WATCHED TAKA'S chest rise and fall in the flicker of the low candlelight, her slow, somnolent breaths barely discernible against the constant background noise of a military camp, and wondered what it must be like to save lives rather than take them for a living.

She had pulled Taka out of the kimono she'd been wearing, as it had been covered by more than its fair share of blood and other fluids. She hadn't thought that Taka would appreciate soiling her bed roll that way on her first night in her quarters.

Now Taka was tucked away in her bedroll, sleeping the sleep of a woman who had just saved a life and impressed the devil out of more than twenty other healers. She wondered if Taka knew that none of the men in that room were capable of doing what she had done.

Kusuko knew, not only because of Iruka-san's reaction and his attempts to "pull her away from that man before she hurts herself," but also because she could see it in the faces of all of the healers who had watched Taka cure that man. The surprise, astonishment, and even envy on some of them had been clear within a moment or two.

She hadn't meant to show her true abilities anywhere near so soon in the assignment. After all, people would be far more willing to speak in front of her if they thought that she was a quiet, demure maidservant. Yet she rather relished the idea that those men, who had secretly hoped that Taka would fail in her attempt to heal the infected man, would attempt to stop Taka again, and this time get a true stomping.

She had thoroughly enjoyed taking the pompous Iruka-san down a few notches in front of all of his healers. It was always particularly entertaining to take down a man almost twice her height, especially with an audience. So, the men would be reluctant to say anything to her or in front of her, at least for a tenday or so, but eventually they would forget. They always did. She was so small, and she dressed like a doll, and they were so unused to women being able to fight...they would forget. But, for a little while at least, they would be leery of trying to force Taka out of the healing tent, and perhaps that would be long enough for Taka to make her own impression on them. If she hadn't already.

When Kusuko considered what the other healers had been saying when they'd been trying to get Taka away from the sick man—"He's beyond saving," "She'll just hurt herself," "Using that much kisō will kill her,"— and then when she considered the looks on their faces when Taka had finished, still conscious and with the man clearly resting peacefully...she thought perhaps Taka had already impressed them.

Not that she'd been given a choice, but the healing arts had never appealed to Kusuko. Of course, perhaps that was because she was a fire kisō and wouldn't be able to use her power for healing anyway. Even still, she preferred learning how to defend herself, and how to incapacitate her enemies, to learning how to heal the wounded or sick.

It wasn't the killing that satisfied her, it was knowing that she could outsmart her enemies, learn their weaknesses and exploit them. It was the power of knowing that she could protect herself.

Then she thought of Taka rendering those men unconscious with the touch of her hand, and remembered her doing something similar in the battle at Rōjū City. Perhaps the woman wasn't completely without defenses then, but she still wouldn't like to be as unprotected as the young healer was.

She shuddered.

That was all right, she would be here to protect Taka, to make sure that none of the men got the wrong idea about her, or tried to hurt her out of jealousy or spite.

Then she wondered why she felt so protective of the young woman. She was just another assignment, she told herself.

Inari's subtle warning rang in her mind again. *You know how Mamushi-san can be.*

A shiver ran down her spine. Yes. She did.

~~~

Kusuko threw the ball to the puppy and squealed with delight when the puppy caught it. Her small, rounded face was alight as the small red and white dog trotted over to her with a triumphant grin on its face.

"Do you like puppies?" her father asked.

"Yes, Otō-san, I love puppies!" she shouted gleefully.

"Excellent," her father said. "Now, please hate puppies."

Kusuko looked quizzically at her father for a moment.

"But, Otō-san, I love puppies."

"No, child, you hate them."

Kusuko had already learned in her five cycles that her father could turn angry very quickly, and she did not wish to anger him. She had already disagreed once, and she knew better than to do it again.

"Yes father, I hate puppies."

"Now, please convince me that you hate puppies," he said, in a calm voice that made her wary.

Kusuko thought about that for a moment.

"Go away, puppy!" she shouted. "Go away, I hate you!"

The small red and white fluffball looked at her with one ear raised and the other half folded, its small head tilted to one side, but it didn't move.

"Go AWAY, puppy!" she shouted again, now afraid of what would happen if the puppy persisted in staying with her. The puppy just looked at her, then began to whine.

"You don't sound like you hate the puppy, Kusuko-chan," her father said. His voice was still calm and even, which made Kusuko scared. If this was a lesson, then she couldn't predict what would happen. Mamushi-san never reacted the same way twice between one lesson and the next.

"I HATE YOU, PUPPY!" she screamed, trying to will the puppy to run from the courtyard. The puppy looked at her and whined again, probably desperately wondering why she was afraid.

"Kick him," her father suggested.

Kusuko blanched. She had been willing to scream at the puppy and chase it away, but kicking it would hurt it and she didn't think the puppy deserved to be hurt.

"Go on," her father prodded. "Kick him."

She knew she shouldn't refuse, that it would make her father furious, but she couldn't bring herself to hurt the small creature. It was so tiny, and it trusted her so much. They had just been playing and it had been so happy with her, why did she have to hurt it?

"I can't," she whispered, terrified of what the punishment would be for failing her father this time.

"Yes, you can," he encouraged. "You have to."

She tried to picture herself kicking the small, trusting furball, but she couldn't make herself do it.

"He trusts me, Otō-san," she replied.

"And you must kick him, or else I will kick him, and you don't want that, do you?"

Kusuko thought about that for a moment. Did she want her father to kick the puppy? It would mean that she wouldn't have to kick the puppy, which was good, but her father was much bigger than she was, and much stronger too. Wouldn't it hurt the puppy more if he kicked it?

She stepped forward to kick the puppy. She even pulled her leg back. But the puppy just sat there, whining, wondering what was causing tears to stream down his playmate's face, and she couldn't do it.

"I can't Otō-san, I'm sorry."

She closed her eyes and waited for the beating that would befall her. Perhaps it would be the same as the time she had failed to lie successfully to the maids who worked in the nursery. She waited, but no beating came. Instead she heard a loud crack and a muffled yelp, then her father's footsteps leaving the room.

When she opened her eyes, the blank stare of the puppy met her gaze, and she sat in the small courtyard crying until the sun came down.

~~~

Kusuko startled awake and wiped a hand across her eyes, but found them dry. She didn't think it was coincidence that she'd had that dream tonight. Her memory knew well what Mamushi-san could be like. She would have to be very careful going forward. She knew that she had good reasons for this hifu to befriend Taka, even good reasons to take it further than that. It could be very advantageous to her current assignment to get as close to Taka as the young healer would allow, but she would have to be careful indeed if she didn't want Mamushi-san to misinterpret that closeness, or consider it a threat.

She sighed, as she turned to check on Taka's sleeping form a few armspans away from her. She would have to make sure that her core-self felt none of the affection for Taka that her hifu might feel, and then she would have to be very careful to prove that to her father.

3日 3月 新議 1年

3rd Day, 3rd Moon, Cycle 1 of the New Council

~ Mishi ~

MISHI CAUGHT THE smell of smoke and rotten meat on the wind and she turned to look at Mitsu. He nodded, but said nothing, and they both quickened their pace as they descended through the densely forested valley toward the creek and the small village that lay next to the nearest road.

They had left the road for a few days after Mitsu had picked up the trail of what might have been a sanzoku scout, thanks to Riyōshi's warning, but either the man had realized they were following him, or they had simply lost him. Now they headed down through the valley toward a small village that they had heard was one of the few places to report the birth of a female Kisōshi since the overthrow of the Rōjū Council.

Despite the change in the laws that governed Gensokai, and the efforts the New Council had made to spread word of those changes and support the new laws, there were almost no reported births of females with enough kisō to become Kisōshi. It was difficult to know if this was because the births were that rare, or because none of the parents felt confident yet that their children would actually be spared.

With these latest attacks from sanzoku on towns supposedly harboring female Kisōshi, Mishi could hardly blame the parents. It didn't seem that there was any guarantee that their children would be protected, and what good did it do to proclaim them to the New Council? Children couldn't attend schools for Kisōshi until the age of five. Why risk anything before then?

Traitor's Hope

Yet, the village they were nearing had done precisely that, or the parents of the child had, and now Mishi's stomach was turning as the smell of smoke and rotten meat grew stronger, the closer they got.

It wasn't long before both Mishi and Mitsu were running, by unspoken agreement, though Mishi wasn't sure what good they thought it would do to get there more quickly. Still, the feeling of apprehension was only getting stronger, and Mishi supposed it couldn't hurt to find out for certain what had happened sooner rather than later.

When they got to the village, Mishi thought she could have gone a lifetime without seeing what had happened.

It was a slaughter.

The village itself seemed empty. The first few houses they passed looked as though they had been abandoned suddenly, but there was no sign of what had happened to anyone. They only found that when they reached the village square. It wasn't a particularly large square, but it appeared that it could hold the entire population of the town.

At least, that was Mishi's best guess, as she took in the mound of bodies that filled the square. Men, women, children. No one had been spared. All the bodies were heaped into the center of the square with no regard given to who they had been, or that they had been people at all.

On the wall of the village hall standing next to the square was a message, scrawled in dried blood.

"The Yūwaku shall never rise again!"

And below that, "No female monsters shall be allowed to live."

Mishi was too busy preventing her gorge from rising to pay much attention to the words of the message, but Mitsu asked, "The Yūwaku?"

Mishi nodded, even as she pulled the sleeve of her uwagi up over her nose and mouth.

"The all-female regime that ruled Gensokai for over a century," she replied.

"But that was over a thousand cycles ago," Mitsu muttered, as he covered his own face. "Why would they care about that?"

Mishi shook her head. She wasn't entirely sure how the Rōjū thought and made their arguments, but she had a guess.

"The supposed 'threat' of women with power rising up and taking over is what made the Rōjū Council accept the laws that killed newborn babes in the cradle for centuries. It makes sense that they would continue to use that mindset, even with their hired mercenaries."

Mitsu was quiet for a moment, as they both took in the devastation at the center of the village square. It seemed as though no resident had been spared.

"You think these men were paid?"

Mishi thought for a long moment, then nodded.

"It would make sense. I mean, it's possible the remaining Rōjū have found a large band of men who are allied with them and believe the same things as deeply as they do, but it's more likely that they have hired men who don't care who they are asked to kill, and perhaps a few of them have been convinced that female Kisōshi need to be prevented from existing, regardless of the cost."

Even as she said the words, Mishi felt the skin on her spine crawl like an army of beetles. She hoped that they could leave this place soon.

"Mitsu-san, can you sense if there is anyone in that pile who might be living?"

Mitsu's face paled.

"Do you really think they would have left someone there?"

Mishi shrugged. She glanced at the pile of dead and felt bile rise in her throat.

"Given what they've already done…I wouldn't put it past them."

Mitsu nodded, his face still locked in a pale grimace.

He closed his eyes, and Mishi wondered if that helped him to focus his kisō or if it simply prevented him from having to look at the pile of corpses that took up the main part of the square. Perhaps both.

After a long pause, Mitsu started to speak.

"Nothing. They didn't leave any—"

His voice cut off abruptly.

"What?" Mishi asked, suddenly on alert. She felt her hand go to her hip automatically, clenching and unclenching in the place where her katana should have rested. Instead, she saw the scabbard and hilt poking out of the roll on Mitsu's back. She had insisted that he continue to carry both of her blades, simply to make it that much harder for her to use them against him.

"I think someone's alive," he said.

~~~

Mishi would never have thought to look in the mud puddle that sat on the edge of the town square, and she supposed that the sanzoku hadn't thought to either. After all, who on earth would cover themselves in mud, almost drowning in it, in order to hide? Mishi's gaze flicked to the town square once more, and she thought more people might have, if they'd known what they needed to hide from.

Yet this mud puddle was where the life that Mitsu had detected was coming from. They had almost missed it, because he was checking the pile of bodies in the square and not the surrounding area.

They approached cautiously, fully aware that they could be falling into a malicious trap, but thinking it unlikely. After all, who would come upon the town in its current state and think to check the large mud puddle where a collection of murky water and thick muck gathered between quick changes in slope from the square to the road. It seemed an unlikely place to leave an ambush, but perhaps a spy, or some other trickery, awaited them.

Mishi reached the pile first, her hands opening and closing, her flames calling to her like a faint itch, asking to be brought forth. She inhaled deeply and let out her breath slowly. She could just make out the outline of two bodies in the mud.

They were children.

"Mitsu-san," she whispered, "are you sure they're alive?"

Mitsu was beside her then, and she could see him nod in her peripheral vision. The two small bodies were as still as statues, and it took a moment before she could see the soft rise and fall of their chests. They were completely covered in a thick layer of mud, with most of their bodies submerged, the tops so thoroughly coated that they only left a vague outline of a human shape. It would take a close inspection indeed to ever have spotted them. And if Mitsu hadn't detected their life force anyway, they never would have looked.

"You're safe now," she said, hoping that it was true. "We mean you no harm."

"Can you move?" Mitsu asked the small, motionless human shapes.

Suddenly, two small hands shot forth and wiped away a thick layer of mud from one small face. A pair of dark brown eyes blinked open and inspected both of them very carefully.

"You cannot take my sister away," said a high voice.

Mishi nodded, knowing very well what it was to fear being separated from the person you were closest to in all the world.

"I promise we won't try to take your sister away," she said, putting kisō behind the statement to see if the child would sense it.

The boy's eyes widened slightly, but he said nothing, only looked at her more closely. Mishi sent out her own kisō then, even as she felt his reaching for her, and was surprised to find enough kisō to make a fairly formidable Kisōshi.

"Do you know how to sense lies, little one?" she asked.

The child nodded.

"Then I'll say it again, with none of my own kisō, and you can decide for yourself if I mean it."

Another nod.

"We mean you no harm, and we promise not to try to take your sister away from you."

There was a brief pause, in which no movement came from either of the two forms in the mud, but then the child who had already cleared its face sat up, and the child next to it began its own slow rise.

The two muddy figures stood, and Mishi wondered how to say what she had to say next.

"I'm sorry children, but you appear to be the only survivors."

"They killed the whole village?" the first child asked.

Mishi only nodded.

She was startled when the second child spoke in a voice even higher than the first.

"Good," it said. "They deserved it."

~~~

Mishi watched the now familiar silhouette of the red-tailed hawk circling in the clear blue sky above their camp, and wondered how long the bird had been keeping an eye on them. Riyōshi had come down to check in with Mitsu most evenings while they had been making their way through the wilderness between Yanagi's forst and these northern villages. She hadn't seen him for a few days, though, and she wondered if the hawk had news, or had simply gone off hunting. Either way, the bird had been circling for some time, but didn't seem inclined to land.

The air held the smell of thawing earth, and, while tinged with the tang of mud from their two small companions, it was free of the smoke and rot that had made breathing in the village so difficult. She didn't think it was the smell that was keeping the bird away, but he generally didn't spend this much time circling before he landed.

Her gaze drifted to the still mud-covered children.

"How did you know to hide?" Mishi asked. The children had been virtually silent since leaving the village. They had walked hand in hand, saying nothing, between Mishi and Mitsu as they had made their way to this camp about a league away from the village. Now they had settled into a small copse of trees and Mishi had set a cooking fire (an act that had caused both children's eyes to widen substantially, as she had used fire she called forth from her hands) so she thought it was time to find out more about the two resilient little ones.

The boy—Mishi was fairly certain that the children were a boy and a girl, though with all the mud caked onto them it was difficult to tell—shrugged his shoulders.

"The people in the town have been trying to separate us for moons now. When we heard there were Kisōshi coming, we thought they must be coming to try again. We couldn't get away before someone found us, but once the fighting started we knew we had to hide. They would have seen us if we'd run from the square."

Mishi didn't need to see the terrified expression on the boy's face, which she could barely make out through all the mud. She knew what had happened to anyone who had been caught running away from the square.

"So you hid in the mud?" she asked, hoping the boy would continue.

He nodded.

"I like mud." The way he said the words made it sound as though that were the only explanation anyone could need. She supposed it probably was.

"How long did you stay there?" Mitsu asked, as he returned to the copse of trees they'd made their camp in. Mishi assumed he must be finished with scouting the area to make sure that no sanzoku were nearby.

The boy looked unsure.

"The sanzoku came before it was light out," he replied.

Mishi nodded, repressing a shiver. It would be sunset soon, so the two children had spent almost the entire day lying still in that mud. She sent a bit more kisō to the fire, increasing its heat. It was a cool day as it was, and the children would be freezing as soon as the sun went down, if they weren't already. She wished they had some clean clothes for them, but Mishi and Mitsu were both traveling with just the clothes on their backs. Tomorrow, when there was plenty of daylight to dry them off, and they could be sure they were far away from the sanzoku who had destroyed the village, they would find a stream and let the children wash.

Mitsu began preparing three large rabbits that he must have caught while he was scouting the nearby woods, and Mishi took a moment to marvel at how quickly he could find supper every day. She was in no danger of starving in the woods, but it would certainly have taken her longer to secure the camp's perimeter and also find a meal than it had taken Mitsu.

She returned her attention to the two small people before her.

"Why were the villagers going to separate you?" she asked.

The boy looked shy, and didn't respond. For the first time since they had left the village square, the girl spoke up instead.

"He's a Kisōshi, and the villagers insisted on sending him away to train."

Mishi nodded.

"They do that with all Kisōshi," she said quietly. "Even girls now are being asked to train."

The little girl frowned.

"There are no female Kisōshi," she said. "Everyone knows that."

Mishi raised an eyebrow at that. For one, the two children had just seen her light their camp fire from her hands, a fairly obvious sign that she was a Kisōshi herself. For another, the little girl had clearly been lying when she made the statement—Mishi's kisō told her that, along with her gut. What shocked her most was that the girl had used kisō to reinforce the lie.

It seemed that she was looking at not one miniature Kisōshi, but two.

4日 3月 新議 1年

4th Day, 3rd Moon, Cycle 1 of the New Council

～Mishi～

MISHI STARED AT the slowly lightening sky and tried to let the horror of the previous day leave her consciousness. Her nightmares had been even worse than usual, but she had expected as much, and made Mitsu sleep between her and the children. She had tried to insist on sleeping outside of the camp, so that if she were caught in any of her dreamscapes she wouldn't be able to harm anyone, but Mitsu had insisted that she stay close to him, as he had for all of their journey so far. His arguments were the same as they had been for the past tenday; he was far more likely to wake up and defend himself if she were close by and he could sense her movement and react accordingly. He would be able to stop her from reaching the children, or at least distract her long enough for the children to escape. He had quietly added that she was warm, and the nights were still cold, as he did every time Mishi brought up the argument anew, and she had asked him if he was willing to die for warmth. He simply smiled, and said that a person had to die for something, and that was the end of the debate.

In truth, Mishi had let it lie because she thought that his first argument was a strong one. When they had been traveling alone, sleeping beside her was Mitsu's best chance of waking before he could be attacked, so that he might somehow escape her, and now that the children were with them it was still their best chance of survival. She ignored the tiny voice inside her that said she found Mitsu's presence through the night comforting.

Last night, they had discussed taking turns to keep watch, but Riyōshi had arrived then, having delayed until both children were asleep, and—after reporting that he had flown all day and seen no sign of the sanzoku who had attacked the village—had insisted that he would roost nearby and warn them of any intruders. Knowing that the bird was very quick to wake, and had keener senses than either of them unless they were using kisō to aid them, they had agreed.

Mishi's dreams had changed, and now included piles of corpses and the screams of innocent children. She hadn't slept well, and a final nightmare had woken her just before dawn. But she hadn't woken with dream visions still ruling her sight and mind, and she was thankful for that.

Instead, she had woken to the sound of two small voices whispering in the darkness.

"Do you think that they know?" the boy asked.

"No. Why would they?" replied the girl.

"I think that lady is a Kisōshi."

Silence had greeted that statement, and Mishi had heard nothing more from the children as she lay awake watching the sun recapture the sky from darkness.

After the little girl had lied to her yesterday, she and Mitsu hadn't asked them any more questions, aside from their names. The boy had replied that they didn't have any, and the four of them had eaten in near silence, with the children drifting into an exhausted sleep when they had barely finished their portion of the food.

She understood all too well why the little girl would have lied about the existence of female Kisōshi. Why she would have done anything to hide the truth of what she was. And it was now clear why the two children would have done all that they could to keep from being separated. The two of them together could pretend that the strong level of kisō they presented was only the boy's, as long as no one looked too closely. But if the boy was taken and sent to train as a Kisōshi, the girl would be left alone with her own kisō exposed to anyone who might look for it, and no way to deny that it was hers. Apparently, she hadn't yet mastered the art of damping her power, as Mishi had been forced to do in childhood. Yes, she understood the siblings' motivations to stay together all too well. What she didn't understand was why the little girl hadn't shown the slightest remorse that the whole village had been killed, why she had said that they all deserved it.

It was clear that the two children didn't trust them at all, and with good reason, Mishi thought. After all, aside from arriving and saying they meant them no harm, what had they done to prove that they were worthy of trust? Especially considering all that the children had just been through. She tried to imagine lying still in a pool of mud while hearing a group of people you had known by name being slaughtered. Even if the girl truly thought the villagers deserved their fate, hearing them die horribly couldn't have been anything less than terrifying.

She would have to build some trust with them today, if she could. She would like to know which elements they were tied to, and offer the girl training, if she wanted it. Either way, these children would need her and Mitsu to protect them until they could be safely escorted to the Zōkame estate, or to the school that Ami was rebuilding in the south.

That thought in mind, Mishi rose from her bed roll and began doing her old morning routine of unarmed kata.

As she had hoped, both children, who were now awake and had enough light to see by, were keenly interested in watching her. Once she had their attention, without breaking her concentration, she called a small globe of fire to her hand and began moving with it through the forms of her unarmed kata.

Both children gasped when they first saw the globe, and their attention only grew more intense as she began to roll the ball around her arms and upper body with the fluid movements that came from cycles and cycles of practice. After she had finished her fifth form, she stopped and turned to the children.

"Would either of you like to try?" she asked.

The children both looked eager for a moment, before their faces fell in unison. At least, that was the impression Mishi got through the mud; it was difficult to tell for certain.

"I'm not a fire kisō," the boy said, hanging his head.

Mishi looked at the girl, but she just averted her eyes and said nothing.

"You don't have to be a fire kisō," she said. "What element can you call?"

The boy glanced sideways at his sister before replying, "Earth." Then he muttered, "And a bit of water."

Mishi sensed the lie, wondering how often he had repeated those words, and if anyone had believed him. Of the very few people who could call more than one element, no one was ever able to call both water and earth, or both wind and fire. No one knew why exactly, but Tatsu had always told her it was a question of balance and the way the elements interacted. If a person was able to call more than one element, it would be a healing element like water or earth, and a combative element like fire or wind, but water and fire cancelled each other out, as did earth and fire, so the only options for working with more than one element were earth and wind, or water and wind. Earth and wind allowed people to be kisōseki, strong trackers like Mitsu, and water and wind…well, very few people had that combination, but Mishi had heard that they were called raiko, or stormcallers, and the legends of their powers were terrifying. If Tatsu hadn't assured her of their existence, she would have simply thought them a myth created to frighten travelers around a campfire.

She supposed that if his sister were a water kisō then pretending that he could call water as well as earth would make sense to a child who didn't know that no such combination of kisō existed.

"I see," she said, looking between the two children. "Well, you can call forth a ball of earth or water for this exercise, though it's typically done with wind or fire."

In fact, it was only ever done with wind or fire as far as Mishi knew. She was well aware that earth and water Kisōshi became yukisō like Taka, and wind and fire Kisōshi became senkisō like herself, but she didn't know if that was the way it had to be, or the way that society said it should be. For centuries, the people of Gensokai had insisted that female Kisōshi could not exist, but that had never been true; it had only been an illusion used to force society to conform and eliminate a supposed threat. What else had been forced upon them in all those centuries?

She didn't know if earth and water Kisōshi would make good senkisō, but judging by what she'd seen Taka do over the cycles they had spent growing up together, she thought it likely that the girl, at least, would be able to do a simple form with a water globe. Earth would likely be more difficult, but if the boy was resourceful, he might be capable of it anyway.

And so, without meaning to, she began an impromptu lesson on kisō, and unarmed combat forms. Mishi made a point of addressing both children, even though the girl kept looking away and feigning disinterest.

The sun was halfway to its zenith by the time that the boy managed to create a ball of earth that he could take at least partway through a form.

"Excellent!" Mishi said, her eyes alight with enthusiasm. She turned to the girl.

"Now you try," she said.

The girl's eyes widened, and she shook her head frantically.

"I can't," she whispered.

"I think it would be easier with water than with earth," Mishi said, smiling. "I've already shown you that I can do it with fire." When she still saw fear in the little girl's eyes, she got down on her knees so that she was eye level with her and continued. "Do you really think I would turn on another female Kisōshi? I have been training to fight men like the ones who attacked your village since I was your age. My sisters and I all trained together to stop them. I thought we had succeeded when we helped take the Rōjū Council out of power." She frowned then, as the truth of her next words sank in. "I hadn't considered that there would be men evil enough to keep harming innocents even once they knew the truth of their own actions. I had thought that once they realized that the Rōjū were treating infant girls as the enemy, no Kisōshi would stand with them, and they would be left powerless. I suppose I should have known better. It seems that others knew what would be coming."

She stopped speaking then, thinking of the Zōkames and how they must have had some idea of how much more work would remain to be done after the rebellion. She thought of how old Tsukusan had looked in their last meeting, how heavily the weight of all

Traitor's Hope

the New Council's decisions seemed to weigh on her. She shook her head as if the action would make the burden of that knowledge go away.

"That's why Mitsu-san and I are here now," she continued. "We are looking for female Kisōshi, either newborns and their parents, or girls like you and me, who managed to survive somehow when the Rōjū were still actively killing us off. We're trying to find them and tell them that they can be trained now, if they want, in healing, or as senkisō, Kisōshi of rank, to defend the people and protect them from the kind of men who are attacking villages like yours."

"It wasn't our village," the girl said, and Mishi was so startled by her reply that she said nothing for a moment.

"What do you mean?" she asked, when the girl offered no further explanation.

"It was never *our* village," the girl explained. "We were born somewhere else, and brought to another village when were three cycles old. There was a nursemaid who brought us, but she went away. We left that village moons ago, and then we came here. The people of the village never liked us. They just wanted to take my brother away from me. And then…." She paused and took a deep breath before she continued in a whisper. "And then they were going to give her to those men."

Mishi blinked, confused.

"Give who to the men?" she asked.

"The baby. The baby who was like me. The sanzoku came for her, and at first her parents hid with her, but then the villagers…they found them and brought them to the square. They gave her to the sanzoku. They were going to let them kill the baby, without even trying to fight."

Mishi's mouth closed into a tight line. It was a child's interpretation of what had happened, of course. There were probably…reasons. The sanzoku had in all likelihood threatened the whole town, a threat they clearly could make good on. Still, something inside her fractured slightly at the thought of people offering up a baby to those monsters, simply to protect their own skins. She supposed they had paid for it, and dearly, despite whatever "deal" the sanzoku had offered them. She felt her stomach tighten, and wasn't sure which horror was worse, the fate the villagers had been willing to hand an infant over to, or the fate the villagers had all received.

At least now she thought she understood why the girl had said that the villagers deserved what had happened to them. She wasn't sure that she agreed, but she wasn't sure that she could argue the point, either.

She sighed then, all at once weary of the world and the kind of people that brought these things to pass.

"If you ever wish to learn how to fight those kinds of people," she said, locking eyes with the tiny brown-eyed girl before her, "you let me know, and I will be sure that you do."

The little girl nodded once.

Mishi stood then, and took a brief look at Mitsu, who had somehow prepared the morning meal without any of them noticing what he was about.

"What can we call you, children?" she asked. "I know that orphans often don't have the names that their parents gave them, but we always used to name ourselves. What do you call each other?"

The boy looked at his sister, waiting until she gave him a brief nod before speaking.

"I'm Tsuchi," he said quietly.

"And I'm Mizu," the little girl added.

"Mizu-chan, Tsuchi-kun, it's a pleasure to meet you. My name is Mishiranu, but you may call me Mishi, and this is Mitsu-san."

Mitsu smiled and added, "Mitsuanagumi is my full name, but you can call me Mitsu. And Mishi-san's real name is Ryūko-san, but she tries not to tell people that."

Mishi ignored the jibe and instead bowed to both children.

"It is a pleasure to meet two fellow Kisōshi."

≈ Mizu ≈

Mizu scanned the woods around her, looking up and downstream along the creek. Having confirmed that there was no one nearby, she turned to her twin.

"We need to go," she said.

"Why, Mizu-chan? They seem nice."

"The villagers seemed nice. That doesn't mean we trust them."

"But that lady is a Kisōshi, just like you."

"She might be a Kisōshi, but she said she was trained, and she has a real name. She can't be just like me, or like you. We can't trust them. Even if they're nice, they'll try to separate us. All grownups do. They won't let us stay together because they'll try to make us go to different schools. Even if they don't want to kill me for being a Kisōshi, they'll want to train me, and they'll want to train you, and do you think they'll let us train together?"

Tsuchi shook his head. He knew as well as she did that the grownups *always* tried to separate them.

"So we have to go," Mizu said again.

After a moment's hesitation, Tsuchi nodded.

"Is that why you asked to go pee?" he asked.

Mizu nodded.

"They won't come looking for us for a little while yet. We'll stick to the creek. I'll ask the water to hide our steps, and you can keep the earth from telling on us."

Without further discussion, they took off up the stream, heading farther into the woods and mountains, planning to leave the roads behind them.

~~~

They'd gotten nearly a league away from the camp they'd made with Mishi and Mitsu when Mizu heard a shrill whistle from the tree tops that made her stop in her tracks.

"That was no bird," she said to Tsuchi.

The boy said nothing, but she could sense him pushing his kisō outwards, trying to figure out what waited in the trees that towered above them.

She felt a small but sharp pain in the back of her neck and briefly wondered why Tsuchi had pinched her, then she heard him cry out and her world went dark.

Mishi

Mishi wiped another splash of creek water from her face and shivered, as she felt the icy water soak its way into her hakama. Her view consisted of Mitsu's back, and she was close enough that she kept getting water in her face, but the alternative was to let him get far enough ahead that she might lose him. The man could move damnably fast, even over a rough creek bed filled by a swift moving current, and they were trying to move as quickly as possible. Her only chance of keeping up with him was staying so close that she could place her feet wherever he placed his, thus avoiding obstacles that remained invisible to her.

It had taken them far too long to realize that the children were missing. When they had finally gone to check on them, Mishi's first thought was that they had been abducted by sanzoku, but Mitsu had quickly established that they had left on their own, since he found no signs of anyone else in the area. Mishi supposed that made sense anyway, as the sanzoku surely would have tried to take Mishi and Mitsu as well, rather than only the children. They had no reason to suspect that the young girl was a Kisōshi, after all, whereas Mishi was well known as one, and an enemy of the Rōjū at that. Besides, they would likely have heard the commotion if there had been any sort of altercation nearby.

No, it made sense that the children had simply run away, though she was sad to think that she hadn't really gained their trust that morning. The problem was that they'd run farther into the mountains, and now she and Mitsu would have to do all that they could to try to reach them before they stumbled on a group of sanzoku, who would have no qualms about killing two small children simply to keep their location a secret.

They were almost running, Mitsu in the lead, using his connection with the earth and wind to discover which direction the children had gone. Mishi was surprised that they'd kept to the creek bed, as the water was cold and there were times when it was quite deep, but she supposed that with a water kisō to aid their travels they would have been able to make decent time, and it was certainly an excellent tactic to avoid being followed.

Unless it was Mitsu who followed you.

Mishi was yet again impressed by his abilities. She had asked him once how his tracking skill worked, but he had only said, "The earth and wind speak to me, as I imagine fire speaks to you."

She didn't think of fire as speaking to her, really. She thought it called to her and that she called back. Was that any different? Perhaps not, but she didn't think that fire actually told her anything. Not information, anyway. Not the location of game, or the way a quarry had gone. Though she supposed she never asked it those kinds of questions.

She was so focused on Mitsu's movements, and so lost in her own contemplations, that she almost missed the sound of the arrow that split the bark on the tree behind her, as an archer missed the shot he'd taken at her head.

Without thinking, she tackled Mitsu to the ground—half in the creek and half on the bank—and came up in a single motion, her katana gripped tightly in her right hand, taken from the pack on Mitsu's back without conscious thought. At the same time, her left hand called forth the fire that always lingered near its surface, and she sent it soaring toward where she calculated the archer to be, not waiting for the scream that confirmed her aim before turning to seek out her next target.

She was vaguely aware of Mitsu rolling to his feet and running into the trees to her right, the creek behind them both, as she ran to the left and brought her sword up, just in time to parry the blow of the katana held by the nearest sanzoku, a man who had apparently been waiting behind a tree for her approach.

She didn't wait for his next blow, or even try to engage him blade to blade, she simply called forth fire to the leaves at his feet and sent it shooting upward, searing his skin and causing him to drop his sword, as she ran him through the chest and moved on to the next ambusher.

She heard a cry from her right and hoped that it was Mitsu's opponent and not Mitsu himself who had issued the sound, but she had no time to check, as she saw a man ahead of her standing over two small prone forms that lay still on the ground. The man was facing her, rather than the children, and he stood between her and them. She hoped that they were still alive, since he seemed to be guarding them, and she was relieved to see that he wasn't preparing to injure them. His sword was out and pointed toward her, so she launched a fan of flames in his direction, making sure it was aimed high enough that it didn't risk scorching the children. The man ducked, then rolled toward her, closing half the distance between them, and Mishi obliged him by charging in his direction.

Instinct and many cycles of practice with an archer for a sparring partner made her roll hard to the left, partway through the charge. She regained her feet in a fluid movement, rolled again to the right, then charged the rest of the way on a diagonal. The arrow shafts vibrating in the ground behind her were the only evidence that she wasn't crazy. The archer remained out of sight.

But the angle and depth of the arrows gave her some insight into where the archer might be, so she threw more flames into the nearby trees, hoping that she and Mitsu would have time to quench any fires she might be igniting in the forest during this fight. It was something she would have to worry about later. Now she had drawn level with the man who guarded Mizu and Tsuchi and he claimed her full attention. She had to hope that she had either eliminated the archer, or that he would be too concerned about hitting his ally to take any more shots at her now.

This swordsman was more prepared than the last had been, or perhaps was simply a better fighter, but he dropped away from her as soon as he saw her raise her hand in the motion she used to call forth fire. She felt flames lick at her own feet as the man tried to use the same tactic on her that she'd just used against his ally.

The difference, of course, was that fire wouldn't harm her. Tatsu said that was true of all the most powerful Kisōshi, that the element they were tied to was also one that they were immune to. She didn't understand why it wasn't true for all Kisōshi…shouldn't the element that aids you refuse to hurt you? It was true for Taka and water, and it was true for her and fire. As a child, she had simply thought it was the way of things, but after she began training with Kuma-sensei, she had learned that many Kisōshi were still susceptible to their own element.

She let the fire her opponent had thrown at her grow in the leaves beneath her, and she smiled as she caused the flames to grow, then willed them toward the man who had called them into existence.

His eyes widened so much that she saw as much white as she did iris, and his eyebrows reached for his hairline. She pushed the flames at him in a final single burst, then charged right behind them, unafraid of the heat that flowed around her even as she came in with a high strike that her opponent barely managed to block.

In three more moves he lay at her feet with a gut wound that was likely to keep him down permanently. Gut wounds were vicious, and Taka wasn't here to heal the man, so she ran him through the heart.

As she pulled her sword out of the corpse, Mitsu came running through the trees and stopped beside her.

"I only sensed five, plus the children. I think we're safe."

She nodded, suddenly self-conscious about how she had killed the man at her feet even after he was already down. She knew it was the humane thing to do, but she still thought it felt wrong to take a man's life so callously.

Then she shook herself. She was a monster, and it was only appropriate that Mitsu understand just how much of a monster she was. She didn't need to be self-conscious about it, she just needed to protect Mitsu and the children. It was that simple.

She moved toward the stream to wash the blood from her katana while Mitsu checked on the children.

Mitsu might understand the kind of monster that Mishi was, but she didn't think a five-cycle-old girl and boy would. She focused on rinsing the blood from her blade and did her best not to make eye contact with any of her companions.

"I want to learn how to do that," Mizu's voice chimed from behind her.

Mishi turned, wondering what the girl was talking about.

"Can you teach me to fight like that?"

7日 3月 新議 1年
7th Day, 3rd Moon, Cycle 1 of the New Council

⇒ Taka ⇐

TAKA TOOK A deep breath and found that the air smelled mildly of blood and sweat, but it wasn't overwhelming and didn't make her want to gag. She smiled, taking in the inside of the healing tent and its occupants, and couldn't help but feel rather proud. There were very few patients left, and the handful of men who needed longer periods of rest to recover were mostly helping to treat those who were still unable to get up from their palettes.

It wasn't that the healers who had been working before she arrived at the camp didn't know what they were doing, not really. They had a good general knowledge of healing, and they did the things that they understood quite well. It was that none of them had apparently ever studied the human body as thoroughly as Taka had. Strange to think that she had been taught most of what she knew from a talking tree and then had mostly practiced on animals, but between her understanding of kisō and her understanding of the human body, she was able to heal almost all of the wounds that came to them, and prevent infection as well. If a man was still breathing when they brought him to her, it was likely she would be able to save him. And she also found that she had a much deeper reservoir of kisō than any of the other healers here. She could heal more people, more rapidly, than any of the men who had thought of her as a "little girl" on the first day that she had arrived at camp.

None of them seemed to think of her as a little girl now. The first few days had been tumultuous, certainly, but with the help of Kusuko—and she owed the young woman much—she had managed to get all of the healers in the camp to take her seriously. The same was true for most of the soldiers. It hadn't taken long for stories of her healing prowess to turn into the stuff of legends amongst the soldiers. Soon she was greeted warmly whenever she walked across camp, recognized as the reason that many of the men and their comrades were still walking on two legs.

Of course, once or twice she'd been greeted a little too warmly. The first time she'd rendered the man unconscious before he did anything more than make lewd suggestions. The second time, the man had one arm around her chest before she'd known what was happening, and then he'd suddenly been on the floor with a dagger pressed to his throat and Kusuko sitting on his chest. Taka still wasn't sure if the young woman had been following her, or simply happened to be there at the right moment. She wasn't sure she minded either way. She had nothing to hide, and she certainly appreciated having the additional protection from any of the men who got the wrong idea, even if she was livid that some men seemed to think her objections to a liaison were something they could overrule.

She shook her head and returned to her survey of the tent. It wasn't that it was cleaner, or better organized, although she had improved the system of triage by insisting that a healer who could use kisō to assess patients be in charge of the entry and organization. It was a combination of how few patients were left, and the hopefulness of those who remained. There was quite a bit to be said for a patient's outlook on their own recovery, in terms of their chances of healing properly after Taka had done what she could. The mood in the healing tent seemed to have changed substantially since she had arrived, in that regard.

And that was why she was here, even though it wasn't her shift. She scanned the tent once more, and this time she spotted Iruka-san toward the back, talking with one of the other healers.

Taka took another deep breath before she started toward the tall man. It wasn't that he was still fighting her assignment to be in charge. After the first three days, and only the one intervention by Kusuko, he had accepted that she was the healer in charge. It was just that…well, there was acceptance, and there was acceptance. He seemed willing to relinquish control because all of the other healers had finally recognized her as the more experienced healer, but he did not seem to appreciate his own demotion. Every time she gave him an order, it seemed to create an internal struggle for the man.

As she walked, she slowly let out the breath she'd taken, and reached for a calm that she did not feel.

"Iruka-san," she said. "Pardon the interruption. Do you have a moment?"

The man turned to her with his habitual glare in place. She'd begun to think that it wasn't just for her—he seemed to have a similarly sour expression when most people engaged him in conversation.

He bowed slightly, gesturing to a corner of the tent that was currently unoccupied. She bowed and led the way.

"What can I do for you, Taka-san?" he asked.

His tone was perfectly polite, but there was something about his posture, gaze, and facial expression that made the question sound like a curse. It was an impressive talent, Taka thought, to sound that polite and clearly not mean it at all.

"Starting tomorrow, I would like to begin admitting patients from the town," she said, keeping careful watch of his facial expression. "There are people who aren't soldiers who are either getting mixed up in the fighting, or else are simply suffering from everyday maladies, but cut off from access to healers because of the military forces to either side. They need treatment, and we've got enough room and time to be able to treat some of them."

She could see the corners of Iruka-san's mouth turn even farther down as she spoke, an effect that was almost comical, as the man hadn't been smiling when she started speaking anyway.

"Absolutely not! We are needed to treat soldiers, not children with stuffy noses, or women moaning about their moontimes. It has been—"

"I'm sorry, Iruka-san. You seem to be confused. I wasn't asking."

The man's mouth snapped shut at the interruption, and his glare deepened as she spoke.

"Please make the arrangements so that anyone from the town who needs treatment knows where to come, and who to ask for."

"It's fine if *you* wish to waste your time taking care of the riffraff from this town, but you cannot expect the rest of—"

Traitor's Hope

Taka was saved from having to cut the man off again by someone else doing it for her. The healer who had been stationed at the door for admittance was standing in front of both of them, looking decidedly nervous.

"I'm sorry, Taka-san, Iruka-san, but I think this is urgent."

"What is it?" asked Taka, before Iruka could regain his composure.

"It's the latest soldiers seeking admittance," the man said.

"Well, what's wrong with them?"

"They...they say they surrender, but...well...they're from the Rōjū zantō."

⇒ *Kusuko* ⇐

Kusuko stood outside the healing tent and watched the injured soldiers limp their way across the camp. She wondered how many there were in total. She wasn't surprised that the Rōjū were providing too few healers, or perhaps just poor ones, but she'd never heard of a mass of men decamping just to receive medical treatment from their opponents. She thought it particularly strange that men who were fighting to keep women with kisō from making it into adulthood were now begging for medical treatment from precisely the kind of person that they would have drowned in the cradle. She wondered if any of the men had thought of that. Perhaps they didn't believe the part of the stories that said that the healer they sought was a woman.

It was that irony that made her question her father's sanity sometimes. Mamushi-san made use of women with Kisōshi for his hishi. She wasn't the only one. How did he reconcile the women he considered useful members of his network of spies and assassins with the abominations the Rōjū insisted all female Kisōshi must be? Of course, the Rōjū had known about his use of female Kisōshi and said nothing for cycles and cycles, so perhaps no one in power questioned that kind of hypocrisy. She wondered how many members of the now defunct Rōjū Council had female relations with enough kisō to be yukisō or senkisō who were still alive now solely because of their affiliation. Did they all live with the hypocrisy, or did some of them actually believe what they claimed to be the truth?

She needed to avoid asking questions like that if she wished to survive her next meeting with Mamushi-san. He would never accept that kind of questioning from his subordinates, and she knew better than to think that being his daughter would offer her any protection from his wrath. *It must be this hifu,* she thought. *This hifu has become a bit of a rebel, and far too interested in Taka and her friends.*

Yes, her hifu questioned the Rōjū and her father's decisions, not Kusuko. The true Kusuko knew that her father was simply being practical. He would take money and information from the sources that offered it, in exchange for certain services. He would follow the path that served him best in his endless quest for information and influence. She should do the same. No matter what stirrings she felt when she looked at Taka across a room. No matter how her mind tried to ally her with her hifu's feelings on the matter.

She sighed, and the wind rustled the trees behind her, carrying a slight chill with it. It was warmer now than it had been a few tendays prior, but winter was slow to release its grip on the land here in the north. She listened to the birds singing in the trees behind her for a moment, then moved to follow the last of the men who had been shuffling through the camp into the healing tent, slipping between men and shadows, generally going unnoticed even though she was still dressed in full kimono.

She told herself that she was here to work, simply following her assignment. After all, Taka might need her to stop someone from doing something stupid. She told herself that it was not that she would simply get a chance to watch the incredible woman work.

⇌ Taka ⇌

Taka tried to ignore the flutter she felt in her stomach as she noticed Kusuko weaving her way through the influx of enemy soldiers who had marched their way into the tent only a moment after they had been announced by the triage healer. She was suddenly quite

Traitor's Hope

busy, and she didn't have time to be distracted by beautiful assassins, or anything else.

Where she had only moments ago been appreciating how uncrowded the healing tent had been, there were now men filing into every corner of the space. Taka wondered, if these men were all from their opponent's side, how many men were still left to fight?

"Does this usually happen?" she asked Iruka-san, more to distract him from the objections he seemed to be silently sputtering than because she actually thought it might be normal.

"No," the man said, his head still swiveling to take in all of the new patients. "The enemy does not generally surrender a large chunk of their fighting force in order to receive better medical treatment."

She nodded.

"Do you think it's a trap?" she asked.

She was amused as she watched the man's face pale, and his eyes widen. It appeared he hadn't considered the option until she had mentioned it.

"It could be," he admitted, looking quite a bit less composed than he had only moments before.

"Don't worry," she said, casually. "I saw Kusuko come in a moment ago. If they start attacking, she'll be here to defend us."

She wasn't sure if the man would find that statement more antagonistic than reassuring, given his personal history with the former assassin, but she was pleased to see that he relaxed some with that piece of information tucked away. *How quickly he warms up to her now that he considers her to be on his side,* she thought.

"Do you need me?"

Taka barely managed to avoid jumping at the sudden appearance of the young woman they had just been discussing. Her heart fluttered this time, but she thought it was just as likely to be surprise as attraction.

"Actually," she said, managing to keep her composure because she was supposed to be in charge, and that made it easier to remain serious, "we could use another set of hands to help with treating the minor wounds after we've triaged the more urgent needs. How are you with bandages?"

Kusuko smiled.

"I have always been excellent at tying people up," she said.

Taka's first thought was that of course an assassin would be good at restraining people, but then Kusuko winked at her, the flutters returned to her stomach, and she thought that maybe Kusuko wasn't talking about her work.

Taka swallowed and nodded, handing Kusuko a roll of bandages.

"Follow Oga-san, please, and start cleaning and bandaging anyone he says is low priority."

Kusuko nodded and walked away. Taka was both disappointed and relieved to see her go. Was that normal? To want someone to stay because they make you feel alive, but want them to leave because you can't function normally in their presence? She shook her head, certain that she was going crazy, and needing to focus on things other than petite assassins who could stop daggers with their smiles.

"Focus, Taka-san…focus…"

She glanced furtively around, to be sure that no one was listening to her, but luckily Iruka-san had wandered off to speak to another healer, and everyone else was just as busy.

She inhaled and counted to ten, exhaled to the same count, and then got down to the business of saving the lives of the enemy.

⇌ Mishi ⇌

Mishi scanned the skies above them, clear blue and lit with a gently warming sun, and was once more disappointed at the lack of any nearing black dots that might be Riyōshi. They were closer to the sanzoku than they had ever been before, that they were sure of. Yet she and Mitsu couldn't agree on what to do next. The obvious answer was that they had to get the children to safety, but if they left now without knowing where the sanzoku had established their base of operations (if they indeed had one), then they left without doing anything to stop them from demolishing another village. If, however, they continued to stay near the village where they had found Mizu and Tsuchi, they risked being found by the sanzoku and killed.

Mitsu argued that he should scout out the sanzoku alone and that Mishi should escort the children to the Zōkame estate. But Mishi knew that was a suicide mission, even as good as Mitsu was at tracking, and she refused to let him go alone. She had tried to insist that *she* should go on her own to find the sanzoku while Mitsu escorted the children to safety, but Mitsu retorted that if it was suicide for him to go alone, the same was true for her. What he lacked in ability to fight multiple opponents, she lacked in tracking and stealth. Mishi had to confess that his argument was sound, and stifle the thought that she might not mind a suicide mission. They hadn't gotten anywhere close to a decision, when Riyōshi had joined them and offered his services as a scout. The sanzoku had evaded, or captured and killed, all scouts so far, but how many of those had been in the air?

Mishi and Mitsu agreed, finally, that if Riyōshi was willing, they would wait while he checked the surrounding area and reported back. They would wait only as long as it took him to find them again, and if they thought the sanzoku were approaching, they would simply flee and Riyōshi would have to find them later.

That had been three days ago.

Each day that passed without the arrival of the temperamental red-tailed hawk increased Mishi's creeping sense of dread. If he hadn't arrived by midday today, she would tell Mitsu that they should leave anyway. Something about this was all wrong.

"Do you think they somehow caught him?" Mitsu asked, from right beside her.

She managed not to jump. She was beginning to get used to how easily he could sneak up on her; something no other human (especially one with kisō) was able to do.

"I don't know. How does one catch a hawk?"

"I suppose it's possible, but it would be difficult with even an average hawk, and Riyōshi is not an average hawk."

She turned, noticing that Mitsu had his pack on his back. Apparently he'd had the same feeling about things that she had. He handed her pack to her, complete with katana and wakizashi.

"I'm tired of being tackled every time you need your sword," Mitsu said.

Mishi opened her mouth to object, but snapped it shut when she heard a rustle of fabric in the trees behind her.

Without thinking, she tackled Mitsu to the ground and cried out to the children, "Run!"

Mizu and Tsuchi, who had been practicing with balls of earth and water while Mitsu was preparing the morning meal, dashed into the trees together at once, just as an arrow whistled through the air where Mishi and Mitsu had been standing, thudding into a nearby tree.

Mishi was up and charging at the archer, her katana already drawn from her pack, before she could see if the children had made cover, or if Mitsu would be able to follow them.

She spotted a small glint of steel in a tree ahead of her, and she threw a wave of flame at it as she ran. She heard the archer cry out in pain, and saw him fall from the tree.

And then she saw more steel flashing from the tree tops, and glinting between the trees. At least thirty men. Mishi weighed her odds. She could fight quite a few men on her own, perhaps with Mitsu's help...

She rolled sideways, and came up running. Arrows thudded into the ground beside her, and wind and fire tore into the trees and leaves that surrounded her. She dropped again, rolled, and turned back toward camp. She could see no sign of Mitsu, Mizu, or Tsuchi. Had they been captured, or had they already made their escape? She dropped and rolled once more, turned away from everything, zigging and zagging between the trees as she ran, and kept running. At the very least she could distract some of these men. If she was lucky, perhaps she could pick off a few that followed her.

She had to hope that Mitsu and the children were together, and had made their escape.

8日 3月 新議 1年

8th Day, 3rd Moon, Cycle 1 of the New Council

⇌ Kusuko ⇋

"YOU HAVEN'T LEARNED much that we don't already know," Inari-san said, from the other side of the low table laden with sake and small plates filled with everything from pickled vegetables to slices of raw fish.

Kusuko nodded, but didn't reply for a moment, only taking a small sip of warm sake and thinking. The small, warm room was hardly private—no room in an izakaya truly was—but it contained only the two of them, the food on the table, the smells of warm sake and cooking fires, and the sounds of quiet conversations floating through from the other rooms nearby.

But it wasn't the lack of privacy that kept Kusuko from wishing to tell Inari-san more of what she had learned.

Kusuko had dutifully reported all of Taka's actions since arriving at the camp. She didn't feel that any of that information would be of great importance to the Rōjū, or to her father. Taka's healing prowess was already well spoken of within the New Council, and the spies her father had in place there were already quite familiar with it. Perhaps having further confirmation of just how powerful she was would prove useful to someone, but she understood Inari's point. They had other spies who could easily have (and perhaps already had) confirmed Taka's healing prowess. She hadn't yet proved herself useful on this assignment, and she well knew what sort of response failing to be useful inspired in Mamushi-san.

"I believe I can get more information from Taka-san," she replied at length. "I've already helped her considerably with a few threats around the camp. She may be more open now to…some of my other charms."

Inari chuckled.

"Surely your other charms are quite potent, after so much time in the world of winds. Practical of you, but I thought you preferred to avoid romance whenever possible."

Kusuko smiled a smile that said nothing.

"I don't mind as much when the target is female," she replied. It was a truth she didn't mind giving Inari, as she was fairly certain that her father was already aware of it, so perhaps Inari was too.

She stood up to leave, though, as she didn't wish to give Inari any more truth than that for today.

Inari's face turned somber then.

"Guard your healer well, Kusuko-san. There may be…trouble ahead."

Kusuko merely nodded and turned toward the door.

"And guard your heart, Kusuko-san," he added, just as she was leaving. "Our hearts can be traitors to our plans."

Having no reply to that, Kusuko simply walked away.

Had she already told Inari too much?

⇌ Mishi ⇌

Mishi felt the rough bark cut into the skin of her palms, and she tried to relax her grip on the branch beneath her. It had taken her a full day of running and fighting to get away from the sanzoku who had been chasing her. Ultimately, she had been forced to stop and fight the five men who had still been tailing her as the sun went down. She had been beyond exhaustion, and knew that her only chance at rest would be to dispatch them. It hadn't been pretty, as the small gash on her left arm attested, but it had been mercifully short. She supposed that the men had assumed that she would be too tired to fight all five of them after such a long pursuit, and that was why they had closed ranks on her when she finally turned to face them. She hadn't been altogether sure that they were wrong, but she'd fought hard, reminding herself of the pile of bodies in that village every time that her energy had almost failed her. In the end, desperation and rage had borne her through.

That night she had slept deeply, although she was still plagued by dreams. She had dreamt of the usual violence that haunted her, and then—suddenly, in the way that only dreams can turn—she had been talking to Tatsu again on his mountainside. When he had asked her why she had come, she had told him that she hadn't, that she was asleep. He had told her that if she was there at all, in dreams or waking, she was there for a reason. So, she had told him about all the killing. About how it didn't seem to matter if she wore her swords or not, she still killed without hesitation. Despite the visions that had haunted her in daylight, and still haunted her at night, her instant reaction, when faced with battle, was to destroy the enemy.

She had killed more men a few days ago, she explained, and then again today. She told Tatsu that she was sure that there was something wrong with her.

Tatsu had stared at her for a long moment, his giant reptilian eyes regarding her with silent consideration, and then, in his calm voice of distant thunder and rolling earth, he had reminded her that the men she had killed had executed an entire village: men, women, and children; the elderly and the young. They had shown no mercy, and they'd had no provocation. They killed as a means to an end; they did it with little thought and, seemingly, no regret.

The men she had killed deserved no mercy, he explained, and they certainly didn't deserve the remorse that their deaths were causing in her.

She had woken up then, and after contemplating Tatsu's words for a time, wondering if they were truly his or simply an extension of her own conscience, she had risen in the predawn light. Not knowing what else to do, she had started back toward the last camp she had shared with her companions. Her hope was that either Mitsu or the children would return to it, seeking out the rest of their party, just as she was. Her fear was that it would be full of sanzoku waiting for precisely that.

So, instead of waiting in the open where anyone could see her, she waited here, high above the camp, with an excellent view of every point of entry. She didn't have Mitsu's tracking prowess, and since they hadn't established any other meeting place, her only chance of finding her companions was to see if any of them returned to camp. She supposed that there was a chance that Mitsu might lead the children to the Zōkame estate or Yanagi's forest, but that would only happen if he was with them, and not also trying to find her. Besides, it would take a tenday to get to the Zōkame estate from here, and only a few days less to Yanagi's forest, so if Mitsu and the children didn't show up by midday tomorrow, she could head that way anyway. For now, she would wait.

She did not have to wait long, as it turned out.

She had arrived around midday, and it was before sunset when she sensed someone else's kisō approaching. Mitsu must have known she was there, and must have been trying to make sure that she knew it was him coming and not some sanzoku returning to finish what they had started. Certainly, he could have snuck up on her as usual, if he'd tried, or she assumed he could have, although perhaps her perch in the tree would have prevented him. Either way, she thought it was wise of him not to try, as she was just as likely to stab first and ask questions later, at this point.

She pushed her own kisō out to him so that he would know she had sensed him, but she didn't move from her hiding spot. There was always a chance that he had been captured and was being used to lure her into a trap.

Mitsu walked into the small clearing where they had made camp two nights before, and sat down on the fallen log beside their fire circle. He held up two rabbits by their legs, waving them in her direction.

"I've caught us the evening meal, but I could use some help with the fire," he said.

Mishi might have laughed, if she hadn't noticed the absence of the two children.

"The children?" she asked, not yet moving from her perch.

"I followed them far enough to determine that they've been taken."

"Taken, or killed?"

"There was no blood on the ground, but beyond that I can't be sure. It seems reasonable to think that they might keep them alive in order to lure us into a trap later, now that they know we exist."

"And Riyōshi?"

"He found me last night," Mitsu said, already beginning to prepare the rabbits. "The sanzoku had spotted him, so he led them on a merry chase through the mountains. They must have multiple teams of scouts, though, since the men that were chasing him were still following him as of yesterday, and he was not close to this camp."

Mitsu sighed, and finally looked right at her, his green eyes piercing the distance between them as though she were sitting right next to him instead of high in a tree ten tatami lengths away.

"I thought they had killed you," he said, his mouth a hard line. "I came back here thinking I would track you to wherever they had finally cut you down."

Mishi climbed down from her perch in the tree as he spoke, dropping to the ground once her legs dangled near head height.

She lit the fire as she approached Mitsu, locking her grey eyes with his.

"You have that little faith in my fighting ability?" she asked.

He didn't smile, but his eyes seemed to brighten, and he stepped closer to her as she drew near. She felt a small flip in the center of her stomach, despite all the worry, all the guilt, and everything else these past few days and moons had wrought.

Would she throw Mitsu if he tried to kiss her again? She hadn't the last time, but she had been distracted then. Was she actually expecting him to try? Surely the last time had only been to pull her from her visions. He wouldn't want to do it again...and why did she care, anyway?

"May I kiss you?" he asked.

She felt her head dip in a nod, even though she hadn't decided on an answer. Apparently, her body had made its own decision.

His lips met hers, and she didn't throw him, or punch him, or stab him. She didn't feel like running away, either. She leaned into him, and let his arms wrap around her. Gradually, she held him in return. After a long while, during which Mishi decided that kissing might actually be a thing that she enjoyed, he pulled away, but she still felt the warmth of him despite the distance.

"What now?" he asked.

Mishi thought for a moment.

"Now we figure out how to rescue Mizu-chan and Tsuchi-kun."

10日 3月 新議 1年

10th Day, 3rd Moon, Cycle 1 of the New Council

⇒ Kusuko ⇐

KUSUKO HAD BEEN surprised to find herself a capable healer's assistant, a role she'd never expected to play in life, despite the number of roles she had needed to portray as a spy and assassin. Yet she found that the work involved was strangely satisfying. She'd certainly done many jobs as bloody, and filthy, as this before. Her various assignments had led her to do everything from cleaning the palace latrines to mucking out horse stalls. She was familiar with most of the unpleasant substances she was asked to deal with when she assisted Taka in her work, and she found that the end result, helping people to heal, was surprisingly gratifying to someone who had spent most of her life doing precisely the opposite.

Perhaps that explained why she looked at Taka with an admiration that grew daily. The young healer spent all of her time dedicated to bringing life back to the dying, the sick, and the injured, receiving nothing in return, as far as Kusuko could tell. It was that point that had prompted the questions that Kusuko had started asking her daily. She told herself that the interviews were simply an attempt to gain information that would make her more useful to Mamushi-san.

"When you haven't been ordered to heal soldiers by the New Council, what do you do for your living?" she asked one day, as she helped Taka fold newly cut bandages.

"I live in a small cave in the mountains. I hunt when I need food, and I heal the animals of the forest when they need it. I have everything I need there, so I suppose I don't have much of a living, at least not in the way that most people would talk about it."

"So, why are you here, then? If you don't need the housing and food, what sway does the New Council hold over you?"

Taka had quirked an eyebrow at that, and had looked at Kusuko sidelong, even as she continued to fold bandages.

"They don't have any hold on me, I suppose. Tsuku-san is a friend of sorts, but I wouldn't say that she has a hold on me, no. And the New Council holds no more sway over me than any governing body, but...well, I suppose you could say that I have a vested interest in seeing them succeed."

"Because of Mishi-san?" Kusuko asked.

Taka shook her head.

"No, she has her own reasons for helping them, and I have mine."

Kusuko could tell that Taka didn't trust her enough to say more on that subject, so she tried another tack.

"I'm still not sure how Mitsu-san fits into all of this," she said, hoping that Taka would jump at the change of subject.

Taka did seem to warm to this alternate topic. She smiled, even as she said, "Where indeed?"

She paused, folding yet another bandage in silence, before continuing.

"He's a bit of mystery, Mitsu-san. He was quite different when I first met him, even though that was only a few moons ago. He was...angry. But I suppose that's not what you asked. He was sent to help me find Kuma-sensei, which wound up leading me to Mishi-san. I believe you're familiar with that story?"

Kusuko only nodded, not wanting to interrupt, and also preferring not to remind Taka of *why* she was familiar with that story.

"Well, he did that, and in doing so...it turned out we had more in common than we thought."

Kusuko waited, but Taka said no more. Was Taka in love with the man? She hadn't seen any signs to suggest that she would be, indeed, she had reason to think that Taka's romantic interests ran similarly to her own. What did that mean then, that they had more in common than they had thought? She pondered it for a moment, and almost laughed aloud when her mind gave her the answer.

"He's your brother?" she asked, before she could stop herself.

Both of Taka's eyebrows rose to her hairline, and her hands stilled mid fold.

"Mishi-san said once that you were much smarter than you made yourself appear," Taka said, and Kusuko was pleased to see her cheeks redden after the words escaped her mouth. "That is, she meant it as a compliment, or at least…she was explaining that you did a very good job of playing the empty-headed courtesan when you wished."

Kusuko smiled.

"I pride myself on my ability to make others underestimate me," she admitted.

Taka nodded, smiling softly.

"I only said it because no one else has guessed, not even Mishi-san."

Kusuko wasn't overly surprised. Mishi had so much else to concern her.

"You look a bit alike, when I think about it. Not so much that I would have guessed without additional clues, but I can see it now that I have reason to make the comparison."

Taka's eyebrows rose once more. She still hadn't resumed folding bandages.

"I hadn't even thought that we looked all that similar. In fact, we're still not sure that we're related, it's just a theory. I don't know who my parents were."

Kusuko regarded her for a moment, then said, "If I were a gambling woman, I would put money on you being brother and sister."

Taka laughed at that. Kusuko had just opened her mouth to explain her comment, when a series of shouts at the front of the tent cut through their conversation. They both turned to see what was happening.

"Taka-san," called Inari, from the front of the tent. "They're attacking the camp. We need to leave."

≈ Taka ≈

Taka was not going to let these men die just to save her own skin.

Two other healers had followed Iruka-san when he insisted on leaving the camp to its fate. The other seven had stayed with her. She was still amazed that they hadn't all abandoned her the moment Iruka had said he was leaving, but Kusuko had stood beside her and asked how she could help, and then most of the men had simply stayed as well.

The battle was close enough that they could hear the shouts and cries, and Taka was reminded of the way she had felt during the battle at Rōjū City. There was a certain single-mindedness behind what one had to do in these situations—the details of what was necessary became exceedingly clear, and the rest just faded into the background.

In Taka's case, what she needed to do was assess and treat the stream of injured men that now flowed into the healing tent. There weren't enough healers to keep up with the number of men who were limping their way into the tent, and Taka didn't want to think about how many other injured men must still be lying in place out in the camp. Unlike most days, there were no free hands to help the injured who couldn't manage on their own to make their way to her. Today, all hands that were able held weapons, and had no time for the fallen.

She didn't have time to wonder why the Rōjū zantō had chosen to invade the camp, she didn't have time to consider what that might mean for this campaign, and she certainly didn't have time to think about what would happen to her if the men who had attacked them succeeded in overcoming the New Council's troops.

She only had time to focus on one soldier at a time. Seek out internal blood loss, assess for high priority injuries, heal anything that was life threatening until it was stable, then move on to the next patient.

She would not allow herself to become overwhelmed with how many men were still waiting, or how much closer the battle sounded now than it had when they had first started. She simply kept going, one assessment at a time.

~~~

When she finally raised her head from the last patient who had seemed likely to die without immediate attention, she could no longer hear fighting in the distance. In fact, she couldn't hear much of anything, save the soft night sounds outside and the small grumbles and twitches of sleeping men.

She turned and was almost surprised to see Kusuko beside her, proffering a damp cloth. The former assassin was still here…after all this time? She had been so focused on what she was doing that she hadn't paid much attention to who was handing her the supplies she requested. Yet now that she had a moment to appreciate it, the fact that it was Kusuko was…interesting. She hadn't expected the woman to stick around at all after the fighting had started, let alone stay by her side and hand her bandages, healing salves, and water.

"Why are you still here?" she asked, before she could stop herself. Her cheeks colored as she realized how rude that must sound, but she'd said it now, so she just waited for a reply.

"It is difficult to defend someone who is not in the same room with you."

Taka smiled. "And it's your job to protect me?" she asked.

Kusuko raised an eyebrow at that, winking as she said, "Just in case you can't render everyone unconscious before they reach you."

Taka didn't particularly like the idea of needing protection, but she couldn't argue with the fact that she wasn't a warrior. She was good at many things, but she had never wanted to learn to fight. However, her life lately had made her question that choice. She was surrounded by violence, it seemed—perhaps it was time for her to learn how to protect herself better.

"You could always put yourself out of a job," she mused.

"Oh?" Kusuko asked, looking startled.

"You could teach me to defend myself," Taka replied.

Kusuko smiled then, and something about the gesture made Taka's insides turn in a warm, pleasant way.

"And if I don't wish to be out of a job?" she asked, with a playful tilt to her head.

"Surely you must be tired of keeping an eye on me. This must be the most boring assignment you've ever been given."

Kusuko actually laughed aloud at that comment. She looked around the room as though assessing whether or not anyone else could hear them. They appeared to be the only ones awake at this hour, but appearances could be deceiving, as Taka imagined Kusuko knew all too well.

"You underestimate how boring our training assignments can be," Kusuko said, as her gaze returned to Taka. "And you underestimate how much I enjoy your company."

Taka could feel the blood rushing to her neck and cheeks, but she tried to ignore the reaction, deciding to change the subject instead.

"Earlier, before the attack, you were asking about Mitsu-san. Why?"

Kusuko shrugged, and Taka wondered, not for the first time, if the woman was excellent at dissembling, or if Taka could trust what she read in her face. She had seen Kusuko keep a carefully blank face in front of Tsuku-san...could she also look genuine when she wasn't? Mishi had said that she had believed for days that Kusuko-san was an air-headed courtesan, but then she had proven herself to be an incredibly insightful spy and assassin. Taka tried to remind herself that the beautiful face she saw before her belonged to a hishi, but she had a difficult time believing it. Not because she doubted the woman's fighting abilities, far from it, but because she saw something in her that seemed too...sincere. Perhaps she was just fooling herself.

"I wanted to know more about you, and...Mitsu-san and Mishi-san seem as though they mean quite a lot to you."

Taka nodded, then yawned. They had been working throughout the day, and half the night was probably gone as well.

"Shall we return to the tent?" she asked.

Kusuko assented, and they walked out of the tent together.

"So, how did you discover that you and Mitsu were siblings?" she asked as they walked.

Taka considered whether or not she should share this story with Kusuko, but she couldn't think of a reason not to. What importance could her familial ties possibly have to a spy?

"When we were traveling together this past winter, Mitsu-san and I were staying outside of the village where he lived with his parents before they died in the fire that took their house and, he believed at the time, his sister as well. I didn't know any of that, but we made camp for the night and I had a dream in which I was trapped in a burning house, searching for a small hawk figurine. In the morning, Mitsu-san went to visit the small shrine he had made for his family. I saw the same hawk totem on it that I had seen in my dream, which led me to tell Mitsu-san about it. Apparently, I'd gotten a number of details right about...things I shouldn't have known unless I had been there."

"And the figurine?" Kusuko prompted.

"Mitsu-san informed me that it had been the totem his parents had given, first to him, and then to his baby sister, to help them sleep. His baby sister called it "Taka," and it was one of the only words she could say at the time his parents were killed."

"She?"

"Well, I, apparently, although it's not as though I remember any of it."

"So you don't know how you survived?"

Taka shook her head. She didn't remember much of anything until after she'd arrived at the orphanage.

"I only know that everyone at the orphanage called me Taka. I once asked Haha-san why, and she said that I'd had a scrap of parchment with that word on it in my hand when they'd found me on the doorstep. I always thought she was just making up a story for me, but now..."

By now they had reached Taka's tent, which was where Kusuko had been staying most nights as well, since the first time that Taka had found herself with an unwanted nighttime visitor.

Taka pulled back the flap to enter, but Kusuko put a hand on her arm.

"Does Mitsu-san know why his parents, your parents, were killed? You made the fire sound as though it wasn't an accident."

Taka shook her head.

"He's never said. I can only assume it was because of me. If it had become known that our parents had somehow kept a daughter with enough kisō to be a yukisō...I would guess that someone reported them to the Rōjū, or at least to the local magistrate."

Taka saw Kusuko's face change slightly in what little moonlight was available, and she wondered if it was sadness or some other emotion that crossed her face.

"The Rōjū must never be allowed to regain power," she muttered.

Taka only nodded, pulling the tent flap back once more.

When she turned to enter the tent, her world went black

≈ Kusuko ≈

Kusuko saw the sack go over Taka's head, and had her hand on her shuriken before Taka could be pulled inside the tent.

She rolled low, directly behind Taka's disappearing form, and quickly threw three of the small multi-pointed blades into the three men she could just see on the other side of the opening.

Luckily, they were only treated with a sleeping draught, not poison, as she had no idea who these men were or why they had been sent to take Taka. If she killed some of Mamushi's men by accident…well, he would blame them for being sloppy, but he wouldn't be happy with her, either.

Of course, the effect of the sleeping draught wasn't instantaneous, so she rolled once more to get through the door, quickly sweeping the legs out from under the man who restrained Taka's arms. He went down, but he pulled Taka with him. Kusuko decided that he wasn't a priority; Taka could likely render him unconscious herself, now that her arms were free, and the sleeping draught would take effect soon.

In fact, just as Kusuko was regaining her feet and turning toward the next opponent, he dropped on his own, and she heard the man behind her collapse as well.

"Well, that was interesting," she said, standing up and brushing the dirt from her kimono. "Are you all right?"

She reached a hand down to help Taka up as she asked the question. Taka had already removed the sack from her head on her own.

Taka merely nodded. She looked paler than usual, and she shook ever so slightly, but she wasn't panicking.

"More reason for you to teach me to defend myself," she said eventually.

Kusuko found that thought amusing, but was intrigued by it too. Taka was athletic enough in her own way, excellent runner that she was, so she could probably be taught a few things about fighting that would help her in a situation like this. And teaching her could have…potential. If she wanted to get close to the young woman, sparring was an excellent way to do it. She ignored the small shiver of excitement that ran up her spine at the prospect, and instead focused on the present. She reached for the flap to the tent and checked outside, then continued to hold it open.

"We shouldn't stay here tonight. Whoever sent those men could send more. Come with me, I'll show you to the inn I was staying at before."

The room she'd rented the first few nights after their arrival might not be available anymore, but something would be, and Kusuko didn't like the idea of sleeping anywhere predictable after this.

Taka nodded, gathered a few belongings, and turned to follow her, but Kusuko gestured for her to exit first.

Kusuko waited until Taka was outside of the tent, and then in a breath that was barely a whisper she said, "I'll talk to you later Inari-san."

The shadow that hid within the shadows behind the tent flap that she held open only nodded, a motion that even Kusuko wouldn't have seen if she hadn't been looking for it.

Then she stepped outside of the tent and led Taka away.

⇌ Taka ⇌

Taka lay with her eyes open, staring at the ceiling of the room in the small ryokan that Kusuko had led her to, and listened to the soft sounds of Kusuko's breath and the silence of the inn. She breathed in air that smelled of tatami and cooking fires, and she wondered what was keeping Kusuko awake.

The young assassin's breathing was soft and regular, but she was not asleep yet. Taka could tell that her heart was not following the steady, constant pattern that it would if she were asleep.

Was the young woman also lying there wondering if more men would seek them out tonight? Did Kusuko have any idea what those three men had planned to do with her?

Taka was still rattled by the attack that had come when they'd reached her tent. It was somehow different from the other attacks that she'd endured since she arrived. Was that because there had been more than one attacker? She certainly wouldn't have been able to escape the three men who had been waiting for her if Kusuko hadn't been there. The other two men who had attacked her over the past tenday…she probably could have rendered them unconscious before they hurt her, which somehow had made the attacks less threatening. That wasn't true of tonight's attackers. If Kusuko hadn't been there, she would be in their power right now. She shuddered. She didn't know what they had planned for her, but she was very glad that she wouldn't be finding out.

She noticed that she was shaking and took a few deep breaths to the count of ten to try to stabilize her breathing. When that didn't work, she closed her eyes and thought of her woodland home. Visualizing the small creek that ran near her cave and the animals that she often encountered there helped her to regain a feeling of calm.

Once her breathing was even, she tried to maintain that breath pattern, slow, calm, measured breaths, until she fell asleep. It didn't quite work, though. Her brain was alight with concerns, and no matter how carefully she breathed, her mind would not allow her to rest. Even with her eyes closed. Even when she curled up on one side in the position that was most comfortable to her for sleeping.

She was surprised then, when she heard Kusuko get up from her palette. For a moment, Taka thought that the young woman was coming over to join her, and she wasn't sure if she was disappointed or pleased when it turned out not to be true.

She was certainly confused when she heard the shoji door slide open and closed, and then she began to feel confusion give way to dread when she realized that Kusuko had "snuck" away thinking that Taka was asleep.

She tried to tell herself that she didn't care if the assassin was trustworthy or not, that it didn't matter if the former hishi was actually loyal to the New Council, or still somehow loyal to the Rōjū. She knew that was a lie, though, as she began to suspect the latter. She did care, and the thought made her quite sad.

So she did nothing when she heard the young assassin return in the hours just before dawn, and she never asked where the young woman had been.

⇒ Kusuko ⇐

At least she didn't have to go far to find Inari-san this time. The warmly lit room, filled with the familiar scents of sake and cooking food, was just across the road from the ryokan where she and Taka were staying for the night.

Kusuko poured the warm sake, careful not to drip onto the sleeves of the server's kimono she had "borrowed" from the back room of her own inn, and settled herself across from Inari-san.

"Is there anything else I can get for you, okyaku-sama?" she said, addressing Inari-san as befit her role of izakaya server.

"I would like some information," he replied.

"I'm afraid I have nothing of interest to report," she said, keeping her tone as neutral as possible.

"After all the time you've been spending in close company with Taka-san, you have nothing to report? I find that difficult to believe."

Kusuko bowed, allowing the point.

"I have managed to learn a number of personal details about Taka-san, but nothing that I think would be of interest to any of our employers."

"And is that your decision to make?"

Rather than answer that inconvenient question, Kusuko countered with a question of her own.

"Why were you planning to abduct the woman I've been assigned to protect?"

Inari-san looked at her with an assessing gaze. For a long moment Kusuko wondered if he was going to refuse to tell her, and if so, on what grounds, but he eventually replied.

"The Rōjū have decided that she would be of greatest use if she came to be on their side of the current conflict, and had hoped to…persuade her to heal their soldiers."

"An interesting choice….Did they really think that she would agree?"

Inari-san shrugged.

"They perhaps planned to neutralize her, if she did not wish to aid their cause."

"I see."

Kusuko thought about that for a moment. She tried to ignore the hot spike of anger that pierced her at the thought of Taka being "neutralized" for the sake of the Rōjū's aspirations, an emotion she found altogether surprising and disconcerting. Although, she understood their reasoning; Taka had materially altered the outcome of this conflict so far, so much so that the enemy had begun surrendering in order to be treated by her rather than their own healers. What remained of the Rōjū and their allies must be facing a war of attrition at this point, and that was likely not a situation they embraced. Perhaps they thought that there would be a way to manipulate Taka into working for their side. Perhaps they had something they thought Taka would consider valuable enough to make her comply. She considered that.

She took a moment to weigh what she knew of the players. There was Mamushi-san: ever practical, but merciless when it came to his own people and their loyalties. Then, the remaining Rōjū: increasingly desperate as their chances of reestablishing themselves as the dominant force in Gensokai dwindled with each day that the New Council did not fall. And Taka: stubborn, loyal, and with a deep hatred of the Rōjū that could likely only be overcome if she needed to save the lives of people she cared about deeply.

Finally, she considered, briefly, her own wants and her own emotions. She wasn't sure exactly what she felt toward Taka, but she was certain of one thing: she did not want the young healer to die. But the Rōjū were desperate enough that they would certainly kill her if they knew that she would refuse to serve them. Was there anything she could actually do to keep Taka out of the hands of the Rōjū? She could try, but that would risk Mamushi-san's ire and the outcome was by no means guaranteed. No, the best way to keep Taka alive would be to make sure that she would comply with the Rōjū, should they manage to capture her. She calculated all of this in a few cold seconds of thought, and then spoke.

"Are you aware that Taka-san has a brother?" she asked.

Inari's eyebrows rose, and Kusuko began to tell the tale that Taka had shared with her earlier that night. Inari's face was carefully blank through the whole telling, except when she reached the part about the fire, and Taka disappearing and then showing up at the same orphanage that Mishi would be taken to a cycle later. It was barely a twitch of the brow, and if Inari had been responding to the story as a normal person would she might have thought nothing of it. But Inari had schooled his features, as he often did during her reports, and that twitch was as jarring as if he had jumped up and down screaming.

Inari knew something about the story that Kusuko was telling, which meant he knew something about Mitsu and Taka that he wasn't telling her.

11日 3月 新議 1年

11th Day, 3rd Moon, Cycle 1 of the New Council

⇒ Taka ⇐

TAKA WAS SURPRISED that she'd fallen asleep again after hearing Kusuko return in the middle of the night. She had assumed that the time she'd spent lying awake waiting for Kusuko to come back and do something sinister, be it return with Rōjū zantō or simply try to poison her, would have led to her being unable to sleep for the remainder of the night. Yet she had awoken with the dawn feeling as though she had slept for at least part of the night.

Her mind resumed its worrying, though, as soon as she was awake, and she could do little to distract it from wondering whether or not Kusuko could ever be trusted. Then Taka had wondered if it was reasonable to even *want* to trust Kusuko. Mishi had warned her that the woman was deceitful, and she *knew* that Kusuko was a trained spy and assassin, so was it crazy to wish for her to be trustworthy? Was she being naive to think that a person like that could ever develop real loyalty beyond her current employer?

She sighed, then looked around the slowly brightening room to see if Kusuko had heard her, but the young woman appeared to be asleep and, this time, her heart rate and breathing confirmed it.

Taka's eyes wandered around the small, simple room, only six tatami mats large, and unadorned save a single small painting on the sliding door that led to the hallway.

Was it possible that Kusuko had gone somewhere benign in the night? Could she have left to go bathe, and simply taken a luxuriously long time doing so?

Taka shook her head. She was being ridiculous. When a "former" hishi pretends to sleep, then sneaks out of a room in the middle of the night, she doesn't do it to have a bath. She does it because she is serving more than one master and doesn't wish for the one to know of the other.

That was ultimately the conclusion that Taka had come to the night before. If Kusuko was sneaking off in the middle of the night, it was because she wasn't working for Zōkame-san and the New Council alone.

A knock on the shoji startled Taka from her musings. She pulled off the blankets that she'd slept in through the night, and was just reaching for the door when Kusuko was suddenly beside her. She saw the woman holding a dagger discreetly by her side, even though her arm was in a natural and relaxed pose. Taka wondered vaguely if she always answered the door like that, or if she expected trouble.

Either way, she decided it was best to stay behind the petite assassin while she slid the door open, just in case.

"What do *you* want?" Kusuko asked.

As she hadn't attempted to stab whoever she was speaking to, Taka decided that it was at least safe enough to take a look at the person at the door. She shifted so that she had a clear view of the doorway, and almost gasped in shock.

The man standing on the other side of the door was someone she had met before—he was the Kisōshi of the golden hakama, the one who had almost caught her a cycle ago when she had been searching for documents about Kiko's origins. He was the man who had fought her, but hadn't tried to stop her, a man who had perplexed her entirely.

"I have news," he said, looking between Taka and Kusuko, and seeming to recognize Taka in some way. "Mitsu-san and Mishi-san haven't reported in for days, and there has been a new village destroyed in the area they were sent to investigate."

13日 3月 新議 1年

13th Day, 3rd Moon, Cycle 1 of the New Council

~ Mishi ~

THE SMELL OF damp and rotting earth filled the tent, and Mishi wondered what the children had hoped to accomplish by covering themselves from head to toe in mud once more. She supposed they had been trying to use mud to hide from the sanzoku again when they had been caught. She sighed inwardly, and took another look around the small, sparse tent. There were no decorations, no arms.

Mishi struggled against the bonds on her wrists, hissing at the rub of the coarse rope against her skin.

"Stop that!" shouted the man at the door, who came over and slapped her across the face.

She whimpered and shied back from the strike, as though very much afraid of having it repeated. She wished she had Kusuko's knack for dissembling, so she could also bring tears to her eyes, but that was beyond her power.

Mizu and Tsuchi did not seem to have any problems bringing tears to their eyes, but she thought that was probably because the guards had talked about not needing to keep them around anymore now that they had successfully lured in the "dangerous female Kisōshi." The guards had actually laughed when they said "dangerous," and cuffed Mishi one more time, to make her cower.

Mishi had found it very interesting that they had been trying to lure her in, though. She had just assumed that they wouldn't kill her immediately if she surrendered, and had hoped that would give her enough time to find Mizu and Tsuchi. Instead, they had taken her directly to Mizu and Tsuchi, and she had learned that they had been trying to capture her. Had that been true a few days before, when they had initially attacked? She didn't think so. The arrows she had dodged had been meant to be fatal. So what had changed?

Something to contemplate later, she suspected. Right now, she had to focus on other concerns. Like the armed guard at the door, the forty other armed sanzoku who inhabited the camp, and whatever had happened to Mitsu after she'd surrendered herself to a sentry. Of course, knowing that the sanzoku might not plan to kill her after all might be useful knowledge for the immediate future, but she couldn't count on it without knowing more. Perhaps they had planned to lure her in to find out what she knew, and then kill her. She couldn't trust that they wouldn't take her down as soon as she escaped with the children. So she had to stick to the original plan. As long as Mitsu was able to manage his part.

Just then the tent flap rustled, and a guard dragged a bedraggled man into the tent and threw him, trussed like a pig on a feast day, to the floor.

"Found this one sniffing around the commander's tent. Was told to keep him alive for questioning."

Mishi glared at Mitsu as he rolled onto his back and his face became visible. The sanzoku who had thrown him on the floor spat on the ground, then walked out. The guard who had been slapping Mishi around since she arrived hit Mitsu across the back of the head as well.

"I suppose this is as good a place as any to spend your final days. And if you're lucky, the commander will get around to questioning you sooner than that."

He laughed at his own statement, as if this were the highest form of humor, and Mishi just barely stopped herself from rolling her eyes. She was supposed to seem meek…

The children, mud covered and terrified, were huddling in the corner and seemed truly upset by the words that the guard uttered. No doubt they expected to have to watch Mitsu's execution. Indeed, if Mishi didn't get them out of here, they probably weren't wrong. That seemed precisely the kind of thing these men were capable of, though Mishi couldn't fathom why. Was it simply that once you started accepting violent orders from someone else, regardless of who the victims were, you stopped caring? Or were these men truly depraved? Did they enjoy hurting people?

Yet another thing she would have to contemplate later.

The guard moved back toward the tent flap. Mishi readied herself.

It was difficult, certainly, to get her legs under herself with her arms tied behind her back, but Mishi managed it while the guard was looking around the flap to check in with the guard on the other side. When he returned, she dove—straight at Mitsu's prone form, knocking the wind out of him.

The guard was instantly on her, pulling her up from Mitsu and away, holding her arms and then her shoulders.

"Now, stop that," the guard said, as though scolding a child. "You won't get a chance to silence him before the commander speaks with him, that's for certain."

He held her up by her shoulders as he spoke, and seemed surprised to find that they were eye to eye. He glared at her, refusing to look away, as though the height of her gaze was some form of challenge.

"You're a tall one," he said. "Now, don't make me teach you a lesson. The commander said we weren't to kill you, but that doesn't mean I can't give you a good beat—"

The man was cut off by his own wakizashi slitting his throat. Mishi's gut turned at having killed a man before he was aware of the threat. It felt cowardly. But he'd been looking right at her the entire time. It wasn't her fault that he hadn't noticed that she'd burned through the bonds tying her wrists behind her back, or that he hadn't been fast enough to see her arm come forward to grab his wakizashi from his belt and raise it to his throat. It wasn't as though she'd attacked him from behind.

She grabbed the man as he fell, gently guiding his body to the floor as the life drained from him. She studiously avoided looking at either of the children. She hadn't heard either of them scream, thankfully.

She moved to untie Mitsu.

"You look ill," Mitsu commented, as she helped him stand.

"I've never killed a man who wasn't trying to kill me first before."

Mitsu nodded, paling slightly himself.

"Just remember what these men did to those villagers, and that they would kill any of us without question if they were told to do so."

Mishi nodded. She understood that what Mitsu said was true, but that didn't quell the queasiness in her gut.

Once Mitsu had stripped the guard of his uwagi and hakama and donned them himself, Mishi positioned herself just inside the tent flap, readied herself, and then nodded to Mitsu.

Mitsu then called to the guard outside.

"A little help," he called, loudly enough that the guard outside would hear him, but not so loud as to draw anyone else's attention.

The outside guard stuck just his head into the tent, and Mishi struck the underside of his chin as quickly and forcefully as she could. He began to collapse toward Mitsu, who grabbed the man's shoulders and dragged him inside before laying him down.

Mitsu glanced at Mishi.

"He could wake up at any time and raise the alarm," he said softly, perhaps to avoid the children hearing him.

Mishi shook her head.

"I know, but he should be out long enough for our needs and…I couldn't do it again. I can't kill men that way. It feels…wrong to me."

When they had first made this plan, she had thought that killing the guards would be the same as killing any of the other men she had fought. She was already a monster, after all, how difficult could it be? Not difficult at all, as it turned out, but completely different from anything she'd done before, and not an experience she wished to repeat. She knew the man wasn't innocent, but somehow killing someone unprepared for battle…it didn't sit right with her. It made her feel too much like a hishi. She would take her chances that this man would wake up. Hopefully, they would be far enough away by then for it not to matter. Besides, she had hit him quite hard in the one spot that Kuma-sensei had assured her would always render a person unconscious for a good length of time.

Mitsu looked worried, but nodded.

"*You* could kill him now, if you like," she said, with a sharper tone than she'd intended. If he was so worried about making sure that they had infinite time to get away, he could bloody his own hands.

Mitsu locked eyes with her then, and where she expected to see anger, or disgust, she saw sadness.

"You're right. I'm sorry. They're just as likely to discover the bodies after we leave as this man is to wake up. Either way, we'd best hurry."

Mitsu helped her disrobe the sanzoku guard, and she reluctantly exchanged her own uwagi and hakama for his. Where hers were the green and brown of Kuma-sensei's line, all the sanzoku wore the crimson and black of the Rōjū.

Not for the first time, she was jealous of Mitsu's leather leggings and tunic. He had been able to keep his clothing on beneath the guard's. She would have to abandon her clothes here, and hope the man she'd taken them from bathed regularly. She supposed she still got the better end of the deal though, as the uwagi she had taken from the door guard wasn't soaked in blood. They were lucky that the uwagi were crimson anyway, so the blood would likely go unnoticed unless closely scrutinized.

When she'd first raised the idea that they dress as guards from inside the camp, Mitsu had raised an eyebrow.

"And how are you going to disguise yourself as a man?" he had asked.

Mishi had actually laughed at that.

"Most men think I'm a man already," she said. "Especially when I'm wearing uwagi and hakama, complete with wakizashi and katana. It doesn't matter that the rules have changed; no one expects a female Kisōshi. Since I'm tall and slender, I blend in particularly well, but I imagine if you put Kusuko in my clothes everyone would assume she was a man as well."

It had been Mitsu's turn to laugh then, but he acknowledged that it was probably true and that had ended the discussion.

It was only after they were both clad and armed with the guards' kit that she finally looked at the children. They both looked pale beneath the mud that coated them, and their eyes were wide, but they were no longer crying.

Mishi cleared her throat, still ashamed of the man that she'd killed, before speaking to them.

"We're going to lead you out of here," she explained, "so we'll leave you tied and need you to act like prisoners. Do you understand?"

They nodded mutely.

Not wishing to waste any more time, Mishi grabbed Mizu, while Mitsu grabbed Tsuchi, and they left the tent with the children dragging along. She wasn't sure if they were excellent actors or if they were terrified right now anyway, but the children were as rigid and wide-eyed as any true prisoner being transferred.

Every now and again, the children would fidget and Mishi or Mitsu would shake them and tell them to step lively.

They made it to within sight of the edge of camp, and Mishi was just beginning to think they might make it to safety before someone stopped them. Her stomach tightened and her hopes dropped when she heard someone shout.

"Where are you taking those children?" a man called out behind them, without preamble.

Mishi cursed silently, and tried to think of a suitable lie. They had planned to say that they were taking the children to the commander, but they were too far toward the outside of camp for that to be plausible. She wasn't sure exactly where the commander's tent was, but she was fairly certain they must be walking away from it at this point.

"We were on our way to the commander's tent when this scamp insisted that he had to piss," Mitsu turned around and improvised, before she could say anything.

It was a decent attempt, she thought, but as she turned to see if the man had bought it, she saw him reaching for his katana.

"Run!" she said, as she shoved Mizu-chan to Mitsu, drew her own katana, and charged the man who had stopped them.

~ Taka ~

Taka ran as quickly as she dared, focused on keeping sight of the dark spot in the sky above her without tripping over the roots, branches, and brush that littered the forest floor. Her lungs took in deep, even breaths of pine-scented air, and her legs pushed her farther and farther along the small game trail that followed more or less along the same path that the red-tailed hawk above her pursued. Trees flashed by in her peripheral vision, and she hoped that she was fast enough. She had to be fast enough.

~ Kusuko ~

Kusuko moved as quickly as her body was capable of over the uneven forest floor, and was grateful that she had decided to change into the flowing charcoal leggings and tunic of her hishi garb rather than remain in her kimono. It wasn't that she couldn't move swiftly in her kimono, she'd taken great pains to be sure that she could, it was just that keeping up this pace for so long would have been nearly impossible in the more constricting outfit, and she was unable to keep pace with Taka anyway. As it was, she had to follow the hawk ahead of her and hope that she arrived in time to prevent Taka from getting killed.

She had been surprised enough when Inari-san had arrived and informed them that Mishi and Mitsu were in trouble, but she had been almost shocked enough to react visibly when Inari had informed them that he would join them in heading to the last known location of Taka's friends. Even now, the older hishi kept pace just behind her—she had been gratified to note that he couldn't match Taka's pace either.

She didn't know what Inari had planned. In all likelihood, he hoped to get Taka in the same place as Mishi and Mitsu, which would make it easier to apprehend all three of them and present them to the Rōjū, or at least the Rōjū zantō that had been stirring up trouble in this area, but she thought that whatever he had planned had been turned upside down when the red-tailed hawk that Taka and Mitsu could both communicate with had arrived at their camp this morning and informed Taka...

Well, she wasn't sure what the hawk had communicated to the young healer, she only knew that Taka's face had grown more and more concerned as the hawk delivered its message. At the end she had turned to Kusuko and Inari, said, "I know where they are. Follow me!" and then taken off running.

It was starting to seem that knowing where they were was a very general claim, as Taka appeared to be following the flight of the red-tailed hawk rather than leading them to a concrete destination that she could have found on her own. Consequently, they had to ford the occasional stream, jump over small gullies, and move around the odd set of small cliffs. She supposed that the hawk didn't recognize any of these things as obstacles, and it had made for a tiring day. She didn't know how Taka still had the energy to run at all, let alone at the seemingly inhuman pace she was keeping. Kusuko had lost sight of Taka's form long ago, and were it not for the sight of the circling hawk high above she would have had no idea where to find her.

She would have sighed, if she'd had the breath for it, but she had nothing more than the air she needed to keep running.

⇌ Mishi ⇌

Mishi glanced longingly over her shoulder at the tantalizingly close edge of the sanzoku camp, even as her katana met the blade of the man who had stopped them. Her hopes surged for a moment as she saw Mitsu and the children draw near the perimeter.

Then her attention was consumed with the battle before her.

She had already drawn a second opponent, and she didn't know how many more would come to investigate the sounds of steel on steel before she was able to make any progress toward the edge of the camp.

She had known, when she started her charge, that she might be overwhelmed before she could rejoin her companions. She had to hope that she could at least give them enough time to make their escape. She doubted that the sanzoku would still be willing to let her live after this escape attempt, but perhaps whatever orders they had would take precedence.

In the end it probably didn't really matter, since she doubted she would get through this battle alive. She wasn't going to stop until they cut her down, anyway. That was the only way she could buy enough time for Mitsu and the children.

In the time it had taken to contemplate all of that, she had already slain the man who had first stopped them. His death weighed on her, just like those of all the other soldiers she'd killed, but she didn't feel soiled the way she had when she'd killed the guard inside the tent.

How strange my mind is! she thought. To be so concerned with how and when a life is taken, instead of being simply horrified that it had to be taken at all.

She shook her head and refocused on the task at hand, as another three men surged forward to join the fray. She smirked as she noticed that, even as they added men to the fight, they were pushing her farther toward the edges of the camp. She wondered briefly if Mitsu and the children had made it past the perimeter yet, but she didn't chance looking.

Her world was narrowed to every block and parry, every stroke of the enemies' swords. She had to keep her opponents shifting constantly. If she led the dance correctly, they couldn't attack her at the same time without the risk of killing their fellow sanzoku. She couldn't let them flank her, or they would cut her down before she could recover. All the while she worked to pull them with her to the edge of the camp, it would be her only chance at escape.

As a fourth and fifth sanzoku joined the fight, she decided that it was time to start using her kisō. She had been putting it off, hoping to avoid the attention that smoke would draw from the rest of the camp.

Unfortunately, now she had little choice, if she still hoped to make her own escape. She threw a fan of fire behind the melee that she was part of, just to discourage anyone else from joining them, and then she started throwing flames at nearby tents to create enough smoke to blind her opponents. Then she started flicking flame at the ground right in front of her while exchanging blows with the men who attacked her, trying to deter some of her attackers long enough to put the others down.

It almost worked. She had just cut down the sanzoku closest to her, giving herself enough space to raise a wall of fire in front of her remaining three opponents, and turn toward the edge of the camp, when another three men came running toward her from the perimeter, cutting off her only route of escape. She flung a wall of flame in front of them and took off running between two tents, but she was no longer running toward the perimeter. Now it was only a matter of time before she was trapped.

⇒ Taka ⇐

Taka almost tripped over the two children lying in the mud next to a small pond, but thankfully she sensed their kisō before she could step on them. As she realized what they were, she was torn between staying to see if they were injured and in need of help, or running onward to the camp that she could now just make out in the distance.

"Taka-san?" a familiar voice asked, followed by a familiar scruffy, green eyed face.

"Mitsu-san!" she cried softly, as she ran forward to throw her arms around his neck. "You're all right?"

Mitsu nodded, though his face looked troubled. Was he not pleased to see her?

"What's wrong?" she asked, even while her gut tightened with fear as she noticed what was missing. "Where is Mishi-san?"

Mitsu's eyes darkened, but his answer wasn't as dire as she'd feared.

"In the camp, distracting the sanzoku so that we could make our escape."

She took a deep breath, thinking about what that would mean.

"We should wait for the others, then," she said after a moment.

"Others?" Mitsu asked.

"Kusuko-san and...an older man. I'm not sure who he is. I think he might be a hishi."

They both turned to look at the sky when they heard the piercing cry of a red-tailed hawk, and Riyōshi swooped to land on Taka's outstretched arm.

⇒ Kusuko ⇐

Kusuko had lost sight of the hawk, but it didn't matter at this point. She could see the vague shape of a military camp in the distance, even through the trees, and she followed the trail of bent and broken branches that Taka had left behind. The young healer must have been getting tired by this point, since she had gotten careless about leaving a trail that could be followed. Or maybe she had done it on purpose, in order to let Kusuko and Inari know where to follow. Either way, Kusuko no longer needed the distant dot of the bird in the sky to tell her which way to go.

"I wonder what trouble they'll have found by the time we reach them," Inari said, from just behind her.

She was truly impressed with the man's ability to run. She wasn't sure how old Inari-san was, but she suspected he was around the same age as her father. That was far from old, at least as she judged it, but he wasn't a young man either. The fact that he was still with her, and had breath to speak, was truly impressive, especially since she had been under the impression that the man preferred assignments that included copious food and sake, and little or no running. Clearly, the man had hidden depths.

"No doubt they're doing their best to be killed by the sanzoku," she replied drily. It wasn't that she thought Taka and her friends were reckless, it was just that she knew their objectives ran contrary to those of the sanzoku, who appeared to need little reason to kill anyone they found in opposition to their schemes.

She ran on, with Inari close behind.

She wondered, then, how things would turn out with Inari present. She would have to be careful in how she presented herself to the man who was Mamushi-san's favored spy—second only to her-

Traitor's Hope

self—though perhaps not that anymore. After all, Mamushi-san had sent Inari to keep an eye on her, so perhaps he trusted the man more than he trusted her. Would Inari insist on pushing Taka-san and the others into the arms of the sanzoku? Would he be willing to help extricate them from their current predicament, only to trap them again later on?

She considered whether it would be in her best interest to turn around, slip a poisoned dagger into the man's ribs, and leave him here in the forest. But it would be too easy for someone to connect his last known whereabouts to her and report it back to Mamushi-san. She didn't think he would like the idea that she had killed his favorite spy, even if she made up some story about him turning against her…. No, it wasn't worth it. Besides, she thought that Inari-san might be useful to her yet. The man seemed…flexible. Perhaps he would be open to helping her prevent Taka-san's death if it were presented in the right light.

By the time they reached Taka-san, she was with Mitsu, the red-tailed hawk, and two tiny, mud covered children.

They made an almost comic tableau, but Kusuko didn't take the time to appreciate it.

"Where is Mishi-san?" she asked.

Taka and Mitsu looked grim.

"Still within the camp," Mitsu said.

"Is she alive?" Kusuko asked.

Mitsu nodded.

"She was when I left, and…" he gestured toward the camp, which was visible at a distance through the trees.

Kusuko took a good look and saw that new plumes of smoke were sprouting up here and there around the closest edge of the camp. Either Mishi-san was still alive, or else someone was randomly setting fire to tents as the day wore on.

"How long has she been fighting?" she asked.

Mitsu frowned.

"Too long," he said.

Kusuko nodded in understanding.

"Who is that?" asked Mitsu, jutting his chin in Inari-san's direction.

"This is Inari-san," she said. "An associate of mine."

"Your servant," Inari said, bowing a polite distance.

Mitsu merely inclined his head, making his distrust quite apparent. Kusuko couldn't blame him, really, but she didn't need him worrying about that right now.

"What is our plan?" she asked.

"We don't have one," Taka replied, matter-of-factly.

"We need a distraction," said Mitsu, "something that will give her a chance to escape."

Kusuko thought about that for a moment.

"Mishi-san is a fire kisō, yes?"

Mitsu and Taka both agreed.

"Then I believe I have an idea."

⇒ Mishi ⇐

Mishi's katana felt like more like a blacksmith's hammer than the fine steel weapon it was, and her legs felt like boiled seaweed. Each block and strike took more out of her, and she didn't think she had long before the three men who had her pinned between two tents would overwhelm her. She had been lighting fires all over the camp as she was chased, hoping to cause enough damage to distract a large portion of the fighting force that was trying to capture her. It had worked for a time, but there was almost no wind, and the fires were easily controlled and weren't spreading.

She parried a blow from one attacker, but barely had the strength to fend off the next man's slash, so she wound up taking part of the hit to her right arm. She felt blood drip down her sleeve as she barely managed to deflect the next attack.

She had let herself be cornered, in the end, because that at least limited the number of attackers who could come at her at one time. There was barely space for the three men who came at her now, and they had to alternate stepping forward to strike her, so she had exchanged having no place left to run for being able to fight her enemies one at a time.

But she knew she could not hold. She had been fighting for too long. She wasn't sure how long it had been since Mitsu had escaped with the children, but she had already been fighting far longer than she'd ever fought before, except during Kuma-sensei's most grueling training days.

She reached for her fire, and felt that she was pulling at the ends of her kisō. If she wasn't careful, she would pull beyond what she had, and the drain would kill her.

Ah well, if she was going to die anyway…

Mishi gathered herself for one last spectacular display of fire. She wasn't sure if it would kill her, or simply leave her unconscious, since she couldn't be exactly sure how drained she had to be to get one result rather than the other, but the men who attacked her weren't likely to leave her alive either way, she thought, so best to go out with as large a display as possible. If it took a few of these men with her, so much the better.

It was strange, here at the end of everything, given the number of times she had considered herself unworthy of life over the past few moons, how angry she felt to have the chance at life taken from her. It wasn't that she feared death; she simply wished to live. Now, in the final moment before death would take her, she violently, deeply, wanted to live. She thought of the laughter she had shared with Taka, Ami, Sachi, Kuma-sensei, Tenshi. The times that Katagi had kissed her, the times that Mitsu had. The wonder she felt staring at the night sky, and listening to Tatsu explain the stars. The exhilaration of battle, of pitting her skills against those of another. She didn't embrace the killing, but she did relish the challenge. She was going to lose all of it, and the thought both angered and saddened her. She pushed the thought aside, embraced the anger, and allowed it to help fuel the kisō she was about to draw on.

One deep breath in—even while she somehow mustered energy she no longer felt she had to parry another strike—she gathered her remaining kisō and…

A giant ball of fire, the size of which Mishi had never seen before, consumed several nearby tents. Mishi almost looked down at her hands in shock, as all three of her enemies turned to stare at the spectacle. She hadn't released any fire, let alone enough to take out that many tents at once. But she didn't let the surprise distract her from a much-needed opportunity. With a surge of energy she had never expected to feel again, she ran through the closest man to her, pushed the one beside him into the third as hard as she could, and then slipped past the stumbling trio as they tried to regain their footing.

She didn't stop to wonder how the fire was spreading so rapidly from tent to tent, or how it had managed to encompass so many tents at once, she simply ran as fast she could for the edge of camp, blissfully unheeded by the men who were running pell-mell to try to squelch the fire that threatened to encompass their entire camp, with all of its stores, weapons, and horses.

She would have laughed, but she didn't have the energy. Running was all she could do.

⇌ Taka ⇌

Taka stood at the edge of the camp, watching the fireball that Kusuko and Inari had let loose on the sanzoku and hoping that it would be enough to help Mishi escape. She marveled at what the two Kisōshi were able to accomplish together. The fire that they sent roaring through the camp was larger and more vicious than any flame she'd seen Mishi control. Kusuko's fire, fanned by Inari's wind, ate through the tents as though they were kindling. It had helped, Taka supposed, that they had started with the tent that held all the food stores, as well as the sake. The rice wine seemed to be adding fuel to the inferno, and the men in the camp couldn't haul water fast enough to make even the smallest dent in the blaze.

She was so focused on the fire, and all it consumed, that she barely noticed the figure running into the woods just south of her. When she finally registered the movement, her legs took off without her mind even registering the command. Mishi was over a hundred tatami lengths away, but Taka felt as though she covered the distance in no time at all. One moment, she was seeing Mishi run from the camp, and the next, she stood before her lifelong friend.

Mishi smiled when she saw her.

"Taka-chan," she said, her mouth a grin that showed all of her teeth.

Then she collapsed.

Taka cried out and leapt forward to catch her friend, but just barely managed to keep Mishi's head from hitting a root as her body slammed into the forest floor. Fear gripped Taka's stomach like a vise, but moments after she sent her kisō pushing into her friend's body to assess the damage, she started to breathe easier.

She jumped, almost dropping Mishi's head from her lap, when a deep, breathless voice directly behind her asked, "Is she all right?"

Taka swallowed the shout she wanted to direct at Mitsu for startling her so, but the concern in his voice gentled her reply.

"She's fine. She's exhausted, and she's lost a bit of blood, but it's nothing a bit of rest and a bandage won't cure."

"Thank all the kami," said Mitsu. And then he truly shocked Taka by wrapping her in a very firm hug. "Thank you for coming after us, and bringing those two hishi with you."

Taka laughed then, though she wasn't sure if it was from Mitsu's statement or simply from the release of tension now that she knew Mishi was safe.

"It would have been more difficult to leave them behind," she said.

Mitsu released her and looked around the forest.

"We can't stay here. Once they get that fire under control, they'll remember us. And they may have scouts out looking for us already."

Taka agreed, so she helped Mitsu hoist Mishi onto his shoulders. Taka was the better runner, but she was too short to carry Mishi's tall form for very long without allowing her legs to drag. Mitsu was at least as tall as Mishi, so he was able to carry her by wrapping her legs about his waist, as Taka secured her arms in front of him using the belt that carried her small hunting knife and pouch.

By the time they had her secured, Kusuko and Inari had found them, bringing along Mizu and Tsuchi, still covered head to toe in thick mud. Taka had already forgotten about the two small humans that she had briefly seen when she had first come upon Mitsu in the forest, but she remembered them now as they appeared with the two hishi, and wondered, for the first time, where they had come from.

She supposed they would have time to discuss everything that had happened over the past tendays once they had safely made camp for the night.

"Can the children run?" she asked.

Mitsu looked at the two five-cycle-olds and smiled.

"They run fairly well. They'll certainly be able to keep up with me, hauling Mishi."

Taka smiled briefly, then took off running. She could find a decent camp for the night as well as Mitsu, and she supposed he needed to save his energy for running with a person-sized load on his back.

14日 3月 新議 1年

14th Day, 3rd Moon, Cycle 1 of the New Council

~ Mishi ~

MISHI ABSENTLY FIDDLED with the bandage on her arm, as she listened to birds singing in the nearby pines and adjusted the cooking fire for the morning meal. As usual, Mitsu had managed to catch a few rabbits the night before, and today there were leftovers, as well as some fish that Inari had produced from somewhere, presumably the same nearby creek where the children had gone to wash off the mud that still covered them from their various hiding spots over the past few days.

Kusuko and Inari had strayed into the woods, ostensibly to check for signs of sanzoku, but Mishi privately thought they might be exchanging information. She was reluctant to think ill of either of them after they'd saved her life the day before. Indeed, Inari had even offered her a spare hakama and uwagi this morning, enabling her to shed the soiled set she'd taken from the sanzoku guard. Inari had been nothing but helpful since she had met him. And yet, Mishi couldn't help but wonder where both his and Kusuko's loyalties truly lay.

Mishi stared intently at the fire in front of her, ignoring the chill morning air and the slightly overcast sky, still amazed that she was alive to see it. It was strange, she thought, to truly believe you were about to die, only to find yourself alive on the other side of things. It felt as though something had shifted inside of her. A piece of her that had been stuck somewhere now floated free. A rough patch that had been smoothed no longer pricked her skin, or a small bit of puzzle that had been misaligned now lay flat in line with the rest of her.

It was too new for her to put words to it, so she sat and stared into the flames of the fire and simply *felt* it. She used her kisō to shift the fire in its pit, creating patterns in the flames beneath the slow roasting rabbits.

"Where are you, Mishi-chan?" Taka asked, as she sat beside her friend on a low rock.

"I'm not sure," Mishi replied. She knew better than to lie to Taka about how she was feeling, and she wouldn't have wanted to, anyway. "Did you do anything to me yesterday?"

Taka shook her head gently.

"I used a bit of kisō to help that wound close, since you seemed exhausted enough as it was without having to heal anything on your own, but aside from exhaustion and a bit of blood loss there wasn't much for me to treat."

Mishi nodded, staring into the fire.

"Nothing wrong with my kisō?" she asked tentatively.

Taka shook her head once more.

"Your kisō seems fine to me now. Mitsu-san said that Yanagi-sensei was able to help you...he didn't really explain how."

Mishi thought about that. She supposed she shouldn't be surprised that there was nothing different about her that Taka could detect. Yet she felt decidedly different.

"Does something seem wrong?" Taka asked.

Mishi shook her head.

"Not wrong. Just...different. I don't know how to describe it yet."

She thought for a moment, but couldn't come up with anything that made sense, so she said, "Let's talk of something else. When I figure out how to explain it, I'll try."

Taka smiled, then.

"Perfect, because I came over to ask you about those two little ones you and Mitsu managed to pick up."

Mishi smiled a bit at that. She had regained consciousness shortly before they had made camp for the night, although she hadn't bothered to tell Mitsu to put her down, even after she was awake. She had known better than to think she could move well on her own at that point, and while it had stung her pride to be carried, she had let it go in order to keep from slowing the whole group down. In truth, none of them had been moving overly quickly, save Taka. They'd all had a long hard day of travel, and when camp had finally been found and made no one had even had the energy to eat much of the evening meal that Mitsu caught and prepared for them. Hence, the rabbits that were still there to eat this morning. The seven of them had said almost nothing to each other, simply forcing themselves to swallow a small amount of meat, before each had curled up in his or her own space and slept. They hadn't even discussed setting a watch, and Mishi wondered if Riyōshi had kept an eye on them during the night, or if the hawk had been as exhausted as the rest of them.

So, there had been no chance for them to share their stories, and there were likely many questions all around. She frowned when she thought of the story behind how Mizu and Tsuchi had joined their ranks, but she took a deep breath and explained it all to Taka anyway.

Taka was in turns horrified and impressed as she covered the state of the children's village, the fate of the villagers, and then how the children had hidden—not just from the sanzoku on that day, but from every adult they had ever encountered their whole lives.

"Are they twins?" Taka asked.

"I believe so. They haven't said as much, but they appear to be the same age. At least, as much as I can tell through that much mud. I haven't gotten a very good look at them yet, to be honest, since they've gone from mud puddle to mud puddle over the past few days and this is the first time we've rested near water long enough for them to wash up properly."

Even as she said the words, she could hear the two children approaching from the woods. She and Taka both turned to see them, and indeed Mishi found it refreshing to be able to make out their individual features. Mizu-chan's face was slightly more rounded than her brother's, and her nose curved up at the end, while his was straighter and his cheekbones were more prominent. They both looked like children finally, rather than statues, and indeed, so similar that she thought they must be twins. They were too close in height and weight to have much difference in age at all.

She turned to Taka to see what she made of them, and almost drew her sword when she saw the look on her friend's face.

"Taka-chan? Are you all right? You look like you've seen a spirit."

"I think I have."

⇌ Taka ⇌

Taka felt trapped in her own mind as the memories crashed over her: Kiko-san questioning the instructors and getting sent to the cages, Kiko-san saying her name in the hall as they awaited their punishment, Kiko-san laughing quietly on the palette next to hers as they impersonated the instructors that terrified them most.

Kiko-san.

Kiko had been ten cycles old when Taka had first met her at the Josankō, and only thirteen when she had died in childbirth, but Taka had spent hours memorizing that face. If she had ever worried that she would forget Kiko-san with time, here was the living proof that she would not.

Even still, it took a moment for Taka's mind to catch up with what her eyes so clearly saw.

She was looking at Kiko's children. Yet how could that be?

She had never been certain that Kiko's children had survived birth, and she certainly thought that the instructors would have considered them an inconvenience to be gotten rid of rather than humans to be taken care of. If nothing else, she couldn't imagine how the instructors at the Josankō, the very people responsible for training Josanpu in how to detect and eliminate female Kisōshi at birth, had not done precisely that with Mizu-chan.

Yet here she was, clearly female, clearly a Kisōshi, and clearly alive.

Taka could feel the tears building in her eyes and her throat tightening, but she wasn't sure what the driving emotion behind the reaction was. Sadness, in memory of Kiko? Joy, at finding Kiko's children alive? Shock, at having both the joy and sadness thrown at her so suddenly? She couldn't begin to isolate one, and wasn't sure it

Traitor's Hope

mattered. She simply let the tears come, and let the sob fill her throat.

"Taka-san, are you all right? What is it?" asked Mitsu-san, who had just emerged from the woods, with yet another rabbit.

In her peripheral vision she could see that his eyes were locked on her, and she wondered if he had seen Mizu and Tsuchi yet without the mud covering their faces. She couldn't remove her gaze from the children, though. Even Tsuchi, now that she took a good look at him, resembled his mother.

Finally, Mitsu followed her gaze, and then she heard the soft thump of a rabbit hitting the earth. She turned to see his eyes as wide and white as hers felt.

"It can't be," he said. "You said they were dead."

"I thought they were."

A long moment passed in which no one said anything, and then Mizu, her hair still wet and her clothing damp, asked, "Why are you staring at us?"

Taka finally realized that, as familiar as the children's faces might seem to her or Mitsu, they would have absolutely no idea who she was, or what connection she might have to them.

She cleared her throat, but it took a few attempts before she could speak.

"I'm sorry, children. You must think me incredibly rude. I...well, I believe I knew your mother."

Now it was Mizu and Tsuchi's turn to stand there wide-eyed and staring.

"We don't even know our mother, how could you?"

"I can't be positive," she said, after some thought. "But you both resemble her, and, Mizu-chan, you look like her in miniature. Mitsu-san knew her too, and he agrees with me."

Mitsu nodded emphatically before speaking.

"I suppose I didn't notice before because of all the mud," he said, when the children looked to him for confirmation. "But you do look just like Kiko-san."

"Kiko-san?" asked Tsuchi. "Where is she?"

Taka felt the tears well up once more, but she found she was still able to speak.

"She died." She couldn't bring herself to add any more, but Mizu seemed to have figured it out.

"She died when we were born, didn't she?" the young girl said.

Perhaps she had made up the story long ago, trying to fill in the blanks of her existence, and was simply eager to have it confirmed. Hadn't Taka done the same a thousand times in her own childhood?

"Yes, but...well, it's more complicated than that."

Rather than looking worried or guilty, as she had feared they might, both children seemed to be relieved. They shared a brief smile and nod, then turned back to Taka.

"And our father?"

Taka's own face darkened with the memory of what had been done to Kiko, and she chose her next words very carefully.

"I never knew who your father was," she said. It was the truth, or part of it, at least. How did you tell a child that her father was one of at least five men who had forced themselves on a twelve-cycle-old girl as a "punishment"? You didn't, as far as Taka was concerned. Perhaps someday she would explain in full what had been done to Kiko-san, but not today. "I know absolutely nothing about him, not even his name."

The children shared another look, and this time seemed a bit disappointed, but neither of them seemed overly upset.

"How did you know our mother?" asked Mizu.

Were there any safe answers she could give?

"That's a very long story," she replied, after some thought. "But I guess you could say that we went to school together."

School wasn't the word she generally chose to describe the Josankō and all the evils it held, but she didn't know what else to call it without explaining more than she felt comfortable with to the children.

In a flash of rustling trees and general commotion, Inari appeared in the middle of their small gathering.

"I hate to cut short this touching—albeit one-sided—reunion, but the sanzoku could be closing in on us even now. We must decide where we are going, and then break camp as quickly as possible."

Taka frowned.

"What do you mean, decide where we're going? Aren't we taking the children to the Zōkame estate? Surely it's not safe to keep them out on the road like this."

Inari said nothing in reply, but looked pointedly at Mishi and Mitsu, who exchanged a glance.

It was Mishi who spoke next.

"We had actually been torn between taking the children to safety and staying to keep an eye on the sanzoku, hopefully executing our original mission."

Mitsu nodded, before adding, "It may be our best, perhaps our only, hope of stopping them before they strike again."

Taka considered this, realizing what must be making them look so uncomfortable.

"You want me to take the children to the Zōkame estate without you," she said.

They both nodded. She thought about that, and what it might mean. Despite the attack by the Rōjū zantō before she had left, the New Council's soldiers had still had the upper hand in that exchange. The commander of the camp had assured her, before she left with Inari and Kusuko, that the situation would be well enough in hand without her. He had also assured her that the healers would be permitted to continue to treat townspeople in her absence. She hoped it was true, because it seemed that now it would be a question of tendays, rather than days, before she could return there. She fervently hoped the fighting would end before she had a chance to go back.

Yet, the problem wasn't her responsibilities as the New Council's chief healer. The problem was that she wanted to stay with Mishi and Mitsu, to ensure that they were all right. She couldn't help them fight, but she could do her best to make sure that they didn't die. She almost said as much, but she knew what the response would be. They would be all the more likely to get hurt if they had to worry about keeping her safe as well. She knew better than to make that argument, and she also knew perfectly well that Mishi and Mitsu would be unwilling to leave the children in anyone's care but hers.

"Fine," she agreed. "But I'll need some help."

She looked expectantly at Kusuko, and ignored the small flip that her stomach performed when the young assassin smiled, agreeing to join her without hesitation.

"Now," said Inari, before any more questions could be raised. "We really must be going."

Inari received no argument on that point.

As they packed their meager belongings and prepared to break camp, Mishi maneuvered herself close to Taka's side before asking, in a whisper "Do you trust Kusuko-san to help you?"

Taka cringed a bit at the question, not because she thought it was unfair, but because she didn't have a simple answer.

After a pause, she said, "She has had ample opportunity to hurt me, or worse, over the past few tendays. If her goal was to do me harm, wouldn't she have done so by now?"

Mishi caught Taka's eyes with her grey ones.

"Is that enough for you to trust her with Kiko-san's children?"

Taka thought about that for the span of several heartbeats.

"You and Mitsu-san are needed elsewhere, and I certainly don't trust Inari-san…. It seems foolish to travel alone with the children. I suppose it will have to be enough, for now."

Mishi looked a bit helpless for a moment, then finally nodded her assent.

"Be careful, neh?"

Taka smiled.

"I'm the careful one, remember?"

15日 3月 新議 1年

15th Day, 3rd Moon, Cycle 1 of the New Council

⇌ Kusuko ⇋

KUSUKO DIDN'T LET the soft sun, light breeze, and clear skies lull her into a sense of safety, though she could understand the temptation, as winter slowly released its grip on northern Gensokai. Instead, she kept her senses open to whatever might lie just off the road, or ahead of them around a bend. The mountain forest that surrounded them, full of pine trees and dappled sunlight, was beautiful, but it would provide easy cover for anyone who wished to surprise them.

If she was meant to be the protection for their small group, then she was determined not to fail at what might be the easiest assignment she'd ever taken. Safe passage to the north for a woman and two children was perhaps not the given it would have been a cycle ago, before the remnants of the Rōjū's allies had started their attacks, but it was still easier than almost anything she'd ever been assigned to do. Protecting Taka alone in the New Council military camp had been substantially harder than she expected this assignment to be, and even that she had considered light work.

She had spoken to Inari briefly, before he had left to do kami-knew-what—he certainly hadn't told her what he was up to, but he hadn't given her any additional instructions, despite his vague remarks earlier about guarding her heart. When she had asked him directly about his intentions toward handing Taka over to Mamushi-san, he had responded with standard Inari-style vagaries.

She was not reassured.

Yet, she suspected that if Inari planned to hand Taka over to Mamushi-san, he might have insisted upon it while they were on the road, with only her for a companion. It certainly would have been easy enough for them to overwhelm her on the journey from the military camp to the sanzoku stronghold, but he had never once suggested it.

Was it a test of loyalties somehow, to see if *she* suggested it?

She would put nothing beyond her father and Inari-san, but she wondered if she was reading too much into it.

The sound of one of the children laughing distracted her from her contemplations, bringing her mind back to the present.

She watched Taka and the children walking along the trail ahead of her, and wondered how they felt about Taka's revelations about their mother. She pondered what it would be like to meet someone who had known her own mother. Of course, Mamushi-san had known her, but he never spoke of her, and Kusuko was uncertain whether he'd ever held any affection for her, or if she had simply been a woman he had impregnated. She knew that her mother had died in childbirth, and that Mamushi-san had not allowed the josanpu to drown her on her first day of life, and that was all.

Had the children spent the past five cycles of their lives wondering about their origins, or had they been too busy surviving to give it much thought? Surely there was always time to wonder.

It surprised her to hear either of the children laugh, and made her wonder what Taka must be telling them in order to make them forget their troubles, even briefly.

As she paid closer attention, she realized that Taka was sharing a story about the children's mother.

"She ran so fast, even I couldn't catch up with her," Taka was saying.

Both children laughed.

"All for a scroll?" Mizu asked.

"Yes," Taka said with a nod. "We were very curious. We both wished to learn more about healing than the Josankō was willing to teach us. We snuck into that library often at night, so we could choose the scrolls that actually interested us rather than just the ones on animal husbandry—interesting though those were, in their own right."

"And they didn't catch you?" Mizu asked, still wide-eyed and smiling.

Taka's face clouded suddenly, her smile hiding like the sun behind a cloud.

"Not that time," she said.

"Did they ever catch you?" Mizu persisted.

Taka nodded, the light gone from her eyes, and Kusuko felt her own gut tighten to see such a change overcome the young healer.

"What happened?" Mizu asked.

Kusuko could see the pain cross Taka's face, her eyes tightening, her cheeks paling, her mouth a hard line.

"Mizu-chan," she said, not knowing what Taka was going through, but feeling a desperate need to make it stop. "Did you know that Taka-san can run faster than anyone I have ever seen?"

She said it with a determined brightness and interest that made Mizu-chan look between her and Taka with curiosity. Kusuko could tell the little girl was not distracted, but she seemed willing to change topics.

"Oh?" she asked. "Have you seen many fast runners?"

"Oh yes," Kusuko replied, her shoulders and neck loosening as the topic was accepted. "I was in Rōjū City once when they held a competition to find the fastest runners in all of Gensokai."

Taka's face still held traces of the pain that had gripped her earlier, but she smiled as Kusuko began her tales of watching such a competition.

Kusuko tried to ignore the warmth that spread through her when Taka mouthed "thank you" to her, as the children peppered her with questions. She told herself it was just this hifu that was thrilled with Taka's gratitude, not her true self.

She told herself that many times, as the day wore on, and she continued watching Taka interact so easily and playfully with the children.

She told herself the same thing when a deep sense of longing filled her that night as they made camp by the roadside. She was not capable of romantic love. Love was nothing but a liability, especially in her profession. Love was dangerous. Attachment led to pain. She had been taught that lesson over and over again by Mamushi-san.

She was an expert at feigning attraction, even feigning emotion; she watched those around her closely and was well aware of what love, lust, and longing all looked like, and what they did to a person.

But she had never felt those things herself. She had never wanted to. She still didn't want to. It could lead to nothing good. Her father had taught her that love was a liability, and made one thing perfectly clear: anything that she loved would be taken from her.

She fell asleep that night with the crack of a puppy's neck ringing in her ears, and tossed and turned with nightmares until dawn.

17日 3月 新議 1年

17th Day, 3rd Moon, Cycle 1 of the New Council

⇒ Mishi ⇐

MISHI WATCHED MITSU prepare their breakfast again, wondering if she would tire of rabbit soon.

"Are there other animals that you like to eat?" she asked.

Mitsu shrugged.

"Rabbits breed quickly, and often. It seems a kindness to help rid the world of a few of them, and squirrel doesn't taste very good."

Mishi smiled at that.

"Is that all you can catch then, squirrel and rabbit?"

"They're the easiest things to snare," Mitsu explained. "But I can hunt just about anything with the right tools."

"Oh? What would you use to hunt a fox?" she asked.

"Why would I hunt a fox?" Mitsu looked indignant. "They barely have any meat on them, they're clever and useful creatures, and they keep vermin populations low. There's no point in hunting a fox."

"You wouldn't want to hunt one just to say that you had?"

Mitsu looked as perplexed as if she'd just suggested that they dance in the treetops naked.

"Why would I?"

Mishi thought about that for a long moment. She'd never hunted much. When she needed to survive in the wild, she knew of a handful of herbs and berries that were safe to eat, and she thought she might be able to set up a snare for a rabbit now that she'd watched Mitsu and Taka do it enough times. But she was trained to kill people, not animals, and she didn't know if it would be possible to take down a deer with a katana. She didn't think she would enjoy killing an animal that had never done anything to harm her if it wouldn't provide much food, though she'd had no qualms about killing the chickens they'd eaten at Kuma-sensei's school, and she didn't think snaring rabbits would bother her. But she could understand why Mitsu wouldn't want to kill a fox. She wondered why some men seemed to take pride in killing animals that they considered dangerous.

"Do you think it would be interesting to hunt an animal that could hurt a human?"

"A fox can hurt a human just fine," Mitsu replied.

"What about a wolf, or a bear? One of the large cats?"

Mitsu shook his head.

"All of those animals help keep deer and other animal populations lower, which in turn protects the trees and the rivers. I wouldn't want to reduce their numbers. They struggle to survive well enough as it is."

"Why do some men hunt them, then?" Mishi didn't think that Mitsu would have a new answer that she did not possess, but she wondered what he thought of the matter. She liked the idea of knowing how he thought. He had an interesting mind, similar to hers in some ways, but decidedly different in others.

"I think they fear things. Perhaps the animals they hunt, or perhaps what others will think of them if they don't hunt them. Either way, I think their actions are driven by fear."

Mishi considered that, and decided it rang true. Men did seem to be motivated by fear all too often. After all, wasn't that the reason why the Rōjū Council had been formed to begin with? Fear that something like the Yūwaku would form again, followed by fear that women with power would rise up against the establishment that had suppressed them over centuries. Mishi wondered if fear had ultimately driven the leader of the Yūwaku, all those centuries ago. Had she, too, been led by fear to commit the atrocities that she was now famous for?

"What are you afraid of, Mitsu-san?" she asked, after a long pause.

Mitsu stared at the fire silently for a long time.

"I'm afraid that the person I love won't love me in return," he said quietly, barely loud enough for Mishi to hear.

Mishi swallowed, wondering what he meant by that. She didn't know what she was supposed to think about that kind of statement. Did he mean her? Did he mean someone else? He could just as easily be referring to his sister, couldn't he? Or was he just speaking in generalities, and didn't mean one person at all? And what did he mean when he said love? What kind of love? Romance? Family? Friendship?

She was bewildered for a long moment, but eventually she decided that she liked his reply. It was honest, and she thought it was a good answer, no matter who he was talking about. If it was her, she worried that he was right. She wasn't sure if she was capable of love, and she certainly didn't think she deserved it. If it was Taka he was referring to, she thought he was probably safe. Taka had grown very fond of Mitsu in the short period of time they'd known each other, and Mishi thought that her friend was well on her way to considering the man an older brother regardless of what they discovered about their own history. But the thought of Mitsu loving her troubled her, and she didn't know what to say in reply, in case that was what he meant.

"What do you fear?" he asked.

Mishi considered that for a long time, even though the answer came to her immediately. She wondered if anything else scared her more than what first came to mind. Certainly, the remaining sanzoku were frightening, their large band of trained Kisōshi bent on destroying the lives of those who had never harmed them. And whatever was behind that band of sanzoku frightened her even more. While the sanzoku were just men, and might simply be following orders, something was leading them. Something was causing them to attack innocents, and ransack villages, and she thought it unlikely that they all uniformly agreed on how to go about it without any kind of leadership. Their attacks were too well organized, too well staged for maximum effect on the people who would stumble across the wreckage. Someone was organizing all of that, and that meant that someone believed very strongly in a cause that wished to wipe her, and everyone like her, from existence. That frightened her too, but it was a vague fear, and one that she couldn't control, so it made little difference to her on a day to day basis. When she focused on it, it frightened her, but it was a distant fear.

No, the answer that came to mind instantly was truly the thing she feared most. She almost hated to say it aloud, but she had already resigned herself to the fact that she wasn't worthy of Mitsu's love, so she went ahead and said it anyway.

"I'm afraid of killing the people closest to me," she said, in a voice just above a whisper. She knew that she could have phrased it differently. She could have said hurting, or harming, but she worried that then he would take her statement as a figurative fear. That he would think she feared pushing people away, or causing them emotional pain. She didn't fear those things, not really, but she thought she would always have nightmares about killing the people she loved.

"You would never hurt someone you loved," Mitsu said, with a confidence Mishi did not share at all.

"You can't know that," Mishi protested. "You don't understand what I'm like. You don't know me. Not really."

Mitsu shook his head.

"I may not have known you as long as Taka-san, who, for the record, doesn't think you'd ever hurt the people you love either, but I've seen so much of you in the past few moons. I know you wouldn't hurt anyone who hadn't done anything to hurt you."

"You don't know that." Mishi felt like she was just repeating herself over and over again. "You've never seen me in a rage. You've never seen what I can do when I'm truly angry. And besides, what did the men I've killed ever do to deserve death? They were only ever following orders."

"Only following orders? Mishi-san, they were trying to kill you! Orders or not, if you hadn't killed them, they would have killed you. You didn't start this war. You didn't ask them to attack you."

"Didn't I? I infiltrated their city, stole their scroll. I knew I would have to fight to defend myself. Why didn't I use the sleeping draught that Tenshi-san concocted on all the men I battled in Rōjū City during my escape? Why didn't I keep my sword treated with it at all times? I could have just nicked the skin, and they would have collapsed without a fight."

"Could she have made enough for all those men? Would it have still been on your blade by the time you escaped? And did you even have your own blade with you, at that point? I thought you said that you were pretending to be a young Kisōshi's maid. Did you have your katana with you?"

Mishi sat in silence and fumed for a moment. It wasn't as though Mitsu was wrong about those points. In fact, she hadn't had her own sword with her. It had been vital that she not be caught with anything resembling a weapon for the earlier part of their plan to work, but that didn't make Mishi feel any better about the men that she'd killed. Nor did it make her forget the night that Sachi had died. It was that, above all, that haunted her.

"You don't understand, Mitsu-san. I didn't kill only men who tried to kill me. The night that Sachi was poisoned, I..." she paused, unsure if she could actually tell Mitsu what she had done. Mitsu just looked at her expectantly, and she found she could only continue if she stared into the fire. "I hunted them down, Mitsu-san. After they'd poisoned Sachi-san, once I knew she was dying, I...I tracked them down and killed them. I had the sleeping draught on my blade. I didn't have to do permanent damage to them. A scratch alone would have brought them down, but...I couldn't bear it. I couldn't bear the thought of losing her, and I couldn't bear the thought of losing anyone else to those kami-forsaken hishi. They would have just come back to fight us again, and I couldn't stand the thought feeling that pain again. But it didn't matter, did it? They still took Kuma-sensei from me. I'll never see him again, no matter how many hishi I kill. And I'll never see Sachi-san again, never hear her laugh. And now I can't even bear to be around Ami-san or Katagi-san." Mishi was crying now, tears pouring silently down her face while she spoke, her voice unbroken. "I can't bear to be around either of them, Mitsu-san, because they were both there that night, and they were both there when Kuma-sensei died, and they both knew him, and they knew about his life, and seeing them just reminds me of all the things I'll never share with Kuma-sensei or Sachi-san again. Do you have any idea what that's like? To push away all your friends because you can't overcome the loss of someone you loved? To turn away the first person who loved you because you know you don't deserve him and, more importantly, because you can never give him what he needs, since you can barely stand to be in the same room with him?"

Mishi paused, startled, as she had never meant to bring up Katagi-san and his feelings for her, or hers for him, but she realized it didn't matter, since Mitsu was never going to love her anyway, not after all of this, not after he knew the truth. So she just kept talking, for the first time since Kuma-sensei had died, she just said everything that she felt and let the tears and words pour out, like blood from a wound.

"The nightmares that I have every night? The ones that I wake up screaming from? Do you know what those are? Taka-san is convinced that I wake up reliving the battle at Rōjū City, or maybe the night that Sachi-san died. She's half right. I relive those moments, those terrible moments, but ultimately, by the end of the dream, I'm forced to watch Sachi-san die, over and over again, or some nights it's Kuma-sensei, even though I never saw him die to begin with…. But the part that never changes, the part that stays the same every night, is that in the dream…I'm the one holding the sword."

Mishi took a deep breath, shuddering as she let it out.

"So don't tell me that I would never hurt the people I love, Mitsu-san," she said defiantly, through the sobs that now wracked her body. "I have killed them. Two of the people I loved most in the world…and I kill them, over and over again, every night."

She finally stopped, then. That was the worst of it. The part she was sure that no one could understand or forgive, the part that she was sure marked her as a monster, deep within. After all, you could pretend to be good all you wanted, but if your mind made you evil in your sleep, you had to know the truth, didn't you?

Mitsu was silent for a long time, and Mishi prepared herself. She expected the rejection to hurt. After all, try as she might, she had still come to care for Mitsu quite a bit more than she had planned to. So she tried to take some deep breaths to steel herself against what was coming. She assumed it would be bad, though she didn't know if it would take the form of anger, or merely disappointment. She took another shuddering breath, and waited.

When Mitsu finally spoke, his voice was quiet, but he sounded as though he, too, had been crying. That thought made her cringe, but she found herself unable to turn and look at him. She didn't want to see the rejection in his eyes any sooner than she had to. Instead, she listened to his voice and hoped that, whatever he had to say, he would say it quickly. She didn't want to draw this out.

"Yanagi-sensei used to ask me about my dreams," Mitsu said, and Mishi wondered for a moment if he'd even listened to her before he made his reply, but she kept her silence. She deserved whatever it was he chose to tell her. "I would wake up screaming in the night, long into my childhood," he continued. "And Yanagi-sensei would ask me every morning what I'd dreamt of, but for the longest time I refused to tell him."

Mitsu paused for a long moment, taking one of the sticks that sat beside the fire and using it to adjust some of the logs. It was a completely banal movement, but one that Mishi found oddly comforting in its normalcy.

"But every night I would wake screaming, and every morning Yanagi-sensei would ask me what I had dreamt. Eventually, after a few moons of this, I finally told him the truth, or at least part of it. I told him that every night I watched my parents burn in the fire, heard my sister's screams from within the house, and sat in silence, hiding inside the log where my mother had hidden me."

Mishi cringed at the thought of a small boy reliving such a terrible memory, night after night. She wanted to reach out and take Mitsu's hand, but she didn't want to risk him rejecting her touch, so she simply sat beside him and watched the fire in front of her.

"But that was only part of the truth. The dream, as I told it to Yanagi-sensei, would have been an accurate account of what had happened. I sat hidden in my log, and listened to my family burn in a fire that was claimed to be an accident, although some believed it had been set by hishi. But the dream was much worse than that. In the dream, all those details were the same as my memory, all but one. In the dream, I was the one who had set the fire."

Mishi gasped briefly, and now understood why Mitsu was telling her this story.

"It took me a long time, cycles and cycles, to finally tell Yanagi the truth of those dreams. And in those intervening cycles, the dreams stayed the same. I would dream them over and over again, and every time, I was the one who had started the fire. It got so bad that for a period of time I wondered if I really had been the one who had set it. After all, no one else had been around to confirm or deny my story. I could have set it. What if I had set it and had simply forgotten about it? What if I had set it and had somehow remembered it differently when I was awake, because I couldn't take the horror of being the reason my family was dead? I had almost believed that, for a cycle or more, when Yanagi finally pried enough to get me to admit what was happening in the dreams. And then, he told me something about dreams that helped me to accept that it wasn't me who had killed my family, no matter how responsible I might have felt, for whatever reasons. He said that dreams, good dreams, can represent our greatest hopes, and nightmares, especially the terrors that haunt us after something horrible has happened to us, represent our greatest fears. You already answered my question honestly. I know that. Your greatest fear is that you'll hurt the people you love. What better way to present that fear, than with you killing the people so dear to you that you've already lost? My mind did it to me after my parents were killed, when I thought that Taka was dead, and I used to blame myself for their deaths all the time. Even when I knew I hadn't killed them, I thought I was somehow guilty for not having died with them, or for not being able to prevent their deaths."

"But you were a five-cycle-old boy, you couldn't have—"

"That's right, I was a five-cycle-old boy, and there was nothing I could have done to stop my parents from dying in that fire, or to have prevented it from being set. I couldn't even have resisted my mother, when she took me to that log and hid me there. All I could have done was gotten out when I'd been told not to, and possibly died with my parents."

"They wouldn't have wanted that, they would never have wanted that."

"Of course not. No one wants their children to die with them, not anyone sane, at any rate. But that doesn't mean my mind always understood that, or that my sleeping mind would let me escape the thought that I had somehow done the wrong thing."

Mitsu took a deep breath, and Mishi wondered what he would say next.

"For a very long time, I thought I was a monster. I thought I was an evil child, who had managed to kill his own parents. I didn't think I was worthy of anyone's love or friendship, and it was only with the help of Yanagi-sensei and Kiko-san that I started to understand that I was worthy of love, and hadn't done anything wrong."

He turned to look at her, and Mishi couldn't help but turn to meet his eyes this time.

"Mishi-san," he said, reaching forward and grabbing her hand. "I can't imagine what you've gone through. I've never had to fight the way that you have, or had to kill just to stay alive for as long as you have. I can't understand all that you're going through, but I know what it's like to believe that you're a monster, and to think that you're responsible for hurting the people you cared about most in the world. I can't fix any of this for you, and I don't think you need me to, but...I care about you, and I believe that you deserve that, and while you may think you're a monster still, I know that you aren't. And if you'll let me believe in you while you try to believe in yourself, I'd be happy to do it. I would be honored to be a part of your life. I would be honored if you would let me love you, even if you can't love me just yet...even if you never can."

Mishi couldn't break her eyes away from Mitsu's green ones, and she didn't know how to react to all that he'd just shared with her. Words failed her. She still couldn't believe that she wasn't a monster, despite all that Mitsu had just told her. Mitsu's story had moved her, truly, but he had been a boy who had just seen his family killed before his eyes, while she was a fully trained Kisōshi. She'd been taught to kill, and she'd used that knowledge to harm others, sometimes in self defense, but once in a rage spurred on by revenge. She knew that she wasn't as innocent as Mitsu had been.

But he'd heard her story. He knew the whole truth now, and he insisted that he still wanted to love her. She didn't know how she felt about that. She was sure she ought to try to convince him that it was a terrible idea. He should know it himself, but she would remind him of it if she had to. Still…he knew the truth, and he wasn't turning away from her. In fact, if anything, those emerald pools that he called eyes were beckoning her closer, and the memory of the other night surged forward. She felt a rush of blood through her body as she remembered the kisses they'd shared.

She knew she shouldn't let Mitsu love her, but a part of her was smart enough to understand that she had little choice in the matter. If he loved her, he loved her, she couldn't control the way he felt. But did she love him? She didn't know. She'd wondered the same thing about Katagi, once. He'd offered his love to her, and she'd wanted to accept it, but she'd never been sure how she felt about him. She'd often worried that she'd wanted his affection simply because no one had ever shown her that kind of attention before. She'd never considered him as an object of her affection until after he'd told her that he cared about her. Then, whatever feelings she might have had for him had been buried under the grief she felt for the loss of Kuma-sensei and Sachi-san, the fear that she might hurt Katagi or Ami, and a mix of memories that she would just as soon have forgotten.

Mitsu, on the other hand…she'd been attracted to Mitsu from the moment she'd met him. Something in the way he moved had drawn her to him, in a way that she'd never felt drawn to Katagi. And the time they'd spent together since then had only made her feel more connected to him.

She'd always felt as though Katagi didn't really know her, and had only fallen in love with an idea of her, rather than the person she truly was. She was still convinced that she didn't deserve Mitsu's affection, but she couldn't deny that he understood who she was. He had just made that much perfectly clear.

Did she love him? She didn't know. She wasn't sure she wanted to love anyone again, after losing two of the people she cared about most. It was devastating enough to think that something might happen to Taka, or Ami, or Katagi, or even Tenshi. She didn't think she wanted to add to the list of people whose loss could hurt her so badly.

But she enjoyed his company, and his kisses thrilled her. She wondered if that could be enough for him. She didn't think that was how love worked, but what did she know?

"I...." She wanted to say all of the things that she'd just considered in that long silence. She wanted to be honest with Mitsu about how she felt, and what she feared. But when it came time to put it all into words, she found she didn't know how to say any of it. "I can't," she muttered, her face flushing with embarrassment at how poorly she had translated her feelings into words. She looked away, unable to face her own cowardice.

Mitsu said nothing for a long moment, but he eventually let go of her hand and stood up.

"I understand," he said, as he moved to deal with the rabbits.

Mishi thought he probably did, despite the fact that she'd completely failed to explain anything, and she wondered what she'd done to deserve his understanding.

~~~

Mishi's eyes widened, and her jaw dropped, as she took in the sight below her. She and Mitsu sat high in a tree, staring down at a crimson and black serpent that slithered its way through the valley below, silencing the usual forest sounds and replacing them with the footsteps and barked orders of over a hundred sanzoku, with half that many horses, marching along the trail to the southwest. The sky was clear and sunny, but that did nothing to stop the chill that coursed along her spine as she thought of what a force like that could do to a small village, or even a much larger town.

They descended from their vantage point only after asking Riyōshi to follow the sanzoku horde and report back to them. They would attempt to follow in parallel, but couldn't risk being seen. They wouldn't be able to overcome the number of archers and armed soldiers that the sanzoku would send after them in the open forest.

As they ran from there, Mishi wondered where the additional sanzoku had come from. She hadn't thought the camp they'd nearly destroyed a few days prior had held nearly that many men. Were there more bands of sanzoku still hiding in these mountains? Was that why they were so difficult to pin down? Had they split into multiple bands, only coming together in order to wreak havoc on their next target? The thought made her ill. Now she doubted that the New Council would be able to send a force large enough to enact the ambush they had originally planned, but they still had to try.

She was brought suddenly out of her musings, back to the present—where she was following on Mitsu's heels while they flew through the woods as fast as their feet would move them—when she nearly ran headlong into Mitsu's back as he came to a very abrupt stop.

Perhaps he had been as distracted as she by the overwhelming sight of so many sanzoku, or perhaps he had been so focused on using his kisō to be sure that none of the sanzoku followed them, that he hadn't been focusing on what lay ahead.

Which was a band of twelve sanzoku, headed straight for them.

Mishi tackled Mitsu, noting the archer who already had an arrow nocked and ready, and wondering idly how many arrows she'd kept out of Mitsu's hide since they had met. She was rolling away from him even before they'd hit the ground, and she came up running, charging the closest sanzoku with a fierce battle cry intended to draw the enemy's attention to her.

It worked, perhaps too well, as she found herself dodging another arrow and more than one thrown wakizashi—surprising, as the short swords weren't balanced for throwing, but she supposed the sanzoku were rather desperate to disable her. She dodged them all, her body falling into the rhythm of the fight as easily as it always did, and she was finally glad that she had begun traveling with her katana at her side once more. She had decided it wasn't sensible to add the extra step of retrieving from Mitsu's pack every time they were attacked, especially now that she had no need to protect Mizu and Tsuchi.

She had her katana out and slashing through the closest archer before he could switch from his bow to some close-range weapon that might have served him in defending against her. She moved to the next man, and the next, dodging arrows as she went, suddenly grateful that these men were mounted and that she and Mitsu were not, as she found plenty of cover from her next target between the trees and the fallen men's horses. Between her attacks and Mitsu's, the group of twelve mounted men seemed disordered and confused, and she wondered if they were truly meant to be scouts or if they had been sent out for some other purpose. There seemed to be no organization to their attacks, and they had seemed genuinely surprised to encounter two opponents in the woods, though they'd let fly their arrows readily enough once they'd spotted them.

Soon Mitsu was by her side, and they had taken down six of the twelve men. She was shocked to find the remaining six splitting up. Three abandoned their fellows and made off in the direction of the hundred men that she and Mitsu had spotted earlier. She expected the other three to engage her and Mitsu, but they turned in the direction they had been traveling and kept riding that way. Mishi and Mitsu exchanged a brief glance, and then turned to follow them as best they could.

It wasn't long, however, before they saw where the men were headed. Then they promptly turned and ran, hoping that no scouts followed them.

Over the ridge that they had been following when they had first encountered the small group of sanzoku lay a valley filled with yet another band of a hundred or more.

~~~

Exhaustion swept over Mishi as she and Mitsu collapsed into a tiny clearing long after sunset. They hadn't stopped running since they'd come across the second mass of sanzoku.

Luckily, Riyōshi was content to keep track of the movements of at least one of the bands, both if he could, and report back to them. He had clear warnings to avoid detection, lest a scout try to follow him back to their location. Of course, no scout would be able to keep up with his unencumbered air speed, but at this point they didn't even want to point anyone in the right direction.

Mishi could barely move her legs and arms after so much running and the fight with the twelve sanzoku besides.

"I'll get us some rabbits," Mitsu said, after lying still to catch his breath for a moment. "We'll need to eat."

Mishi's jaw sank to her chest, or would have, if she had been able to spare the movement from the intense breathing she was still engaged in.

"You have the energy to hunt now?"

"Catching rabbits takes little enough energy, and if we don't eat, we'll be good for nothing at all tomorrow. Rest up. Start us a fire, if you've the kisō to spare."

She lay still for another handful of heartbeats after Mitsu had disappeared into the gathering dark, and then she stood to gather some wood for the fire.

Of course, she could use her kisō to power a fire without wood, but it would take a stupid amount of energy to maintain it. If she had fuel for the fire, she could simply light it and then control its temperature with a minimal use of her kisō. It seemed only reasonable to manage her kisō as sparingly as possible, considering what they might be up against in the coming days, so she set about collecting deadfall from the woods that surrounded them. She looked for the drier bits of wood and pine needles, even though it technically didn't matter; she could call fire to even the wettest wood.

By the time Mitsu returned, she had a cozy cooking fire burning and had even set up a spit, which rested between two sets of crossed branches, tied with a thin creeping vine she'd found on a nearby tree, so that they could suspend the rabbits over the fire with ease. Considering how stiff her limbs were and how taxing she found even small movements, she considered this a great accomplishment.

Mitsu made no comment on her accomplishments, but simply produced a brace of already skinned and cleaned rabbits, which he then proceeded to skewer with her spit and set above the fire.

Once their dinner was cooking, he produced a full water skin. Mishi was once more impressed by his comfort in the wilderness.

"You seem more at home here, days away from the nearest village or road, than anywhere else," she noted aloud. She wasn't sure why she bothered to say it, but the notion intrigued her. Mitsu seemed as comfortable in the widerness as she would have been in her own room at Kuma-sensei's school, before it had burned to the ground.

Mitsu smiled.

"The wilderness is my home, much as it is Taka's now, but I've been living in the wilds since the age of five, and Taka only began to live in the wilderness at the age of twelve. And of course, I'm older than she is, so I had a head start anyway."

Mishi contemplated that.

"How old are you anyway?" she asked, her curiosity piqued.

"Twenty-one cycles," Mitsu replied, as he took a moment to turn the rabbits on the skewer.

That made him five cycles older than she was. For just a moment, the thought made her feel young, as though Mitsu had experienced more of life than she had. And perhaps he had, but the feeling didn't last long, as she remembered all of the things she had experienced, especially during the past few moons. She shook her head, trying to dislodge the memories that came pouring back into her mind's eye. She didn't want to remember any of those things, not the past few tendays, not the moons before that. She just wanted all of the death to go away.

She tried to take deep calming breaths, but the air was tinged with the smell of cooking rabbits, the smell of fire and flesh only helping to call forth memories of screams and shouts, the sounds of the dying and those still fighting for life.

She felt Mitsu's presence beside her suddenly, though she hadn't heard him leave the opposite side of the fire. She felt his hand rest gently on her shoulder. She was reassured that she recognized that it was him, and aware that she was in front of a fire and not in the battle that played out before her eyes.

"Mishi-san, what can I do?" he asked.

She tried to take another deep breath, and this time she was able to recall that it was rabbits cooking, and not human flesh burning, close by.

"Keep talking to me," she whispered.

"Very well. What shall I say?" Mitsu asked.

"Tell me about the woods around us. Tell me what your kisō enables you to sense that I can't sense."

"Well, I'm not entirely sure what you can sense, but I can describe what I sense well enough, I suppose."

She felt his hand begin to leave her shoulder, and she felt her muscles tense in response. It wasn't a conscious movement, just the reaction of her body.

"Would you like me to keep my hand there?" Mitsu asked quietly.

Mishi nodded. Mitsu returned his hand to where it had rested on her shoulder and Mishi felt her muscles relax. *How odd*, she thought. *I once almost killed Mitsu when he put his hands on me in this state, and now my body insists that he maintain the touch.* She almost wanted to laugh at how paradoxically her body and mind sometimes behaved, but the images that still flowed before her eyes drove any humor from her mind.

"I can sense the animals," Mitsu began, and Mishi felt herself relax further, as some part of her that wasn't experiencing images and smells from a hellish memory did its best to pay attention to Mitsu and his voice. "I can generally tell where they are, and where they've been. I'm not sure why I can sense life so well, aside from the idea that some amount of earth is in every living thing. That's certainly what Taka believes. In addition, the earth itself tells me things. There are the things I can track with my eyes, shapes and trails left behind in the ground after someone has passed by, but there are also things that the soil tells me when I call to it. And, of course, the wind brings me scents and sounds. Does fire ever tell you anything?"

Mishi was fascinated by what she heard, and she was so busy trying to discern what Mitsu meant by fire "telling her things" that she barely noticed that the nightmarish memories that she had been experiencing moments ago were fading.

"I don't know what you mean, exactly. What are you asking? I call to the fire, and sometimes it calls to me, but I don't know that it ever tells me anything."

Mitsu's voice continued right next to her, his hand still firmly planted on her shoulder.

"When the earth tells me things, it…it's not like a voice conveying information. It's not even like the animals that send along their emotions or ideas, which I can then discern a message from. It's more like…it's like what someone's skin can tell you if you touch them."

Mishi considered that for a moment, and thought that perhaps she understood what he meant.

"You mean the way an opponent's body might tell you what they plan to do next by the way that it moves?"

"Something like that. Or...or the way that a lover's skin might tell you that they're enjoying your touch."

That suggestion made the blood race to Mishi's face, and she wondered if Mitsu had said that just to get a reaction from her. But even as her embarrassment faded, as she convinced herself that Mitsu was simply talking in general terms, trying to explain this phenomenon to her, her thoughts strayed back to the way that her skin had felt the last time that Mitsu had kissed her.

She remembered, unbidden, the way that her skin had reacted to his. The way that having his lips pressed to hers had sent an electric jolt through her body. The way that his hands on her back had felt, as his arms embraced her.

She cleared her throat and tried to focus on the present, but she thought she had a much better idea of what Mitsu was talking about when he talked about a lover's skin reacting to something.

"I think I understand you," she said, trying to swallow the feeling of embarrassment that tried to rise up inside her. She had nothing to be embarrassed about. Mitsu had brought up the subject of lovers as an example, and it was perfectly natural for her mind to conjure images of that to help her understand what he was speaking of.

"Mishi-san?" Mitsu's voice was much quieter than it had been earlier, and she couldn't help but notice that his hand had strayed from her shoulder to her exposed collarbone. She felt fire race along her skin where his fingertips touched her, and she worried briefly that she had actually allowed fire to course over her. That worry was erased when Mitsu's hand remained where it was, then began to trace the line of her shoulder.

Her breath caught, momentarily, when she realized that she was no longer seeing images from her past. Her eyes opened, and she was surprised to find that Mitsu's eyes were the first things that she saw. She hadn't realized that she'd tilted her head to meet his gaze. His green eyes flared with an emotion that her mind refused to identify, and she considered closing her eyes against the sight of it.

"Mishi-san?" he asked again, but this time his hand stayed in place, and she wondered if she'd been imagining his hand wandering earlier. She wasn't sure what he was asking her.

"Yes?" she asked, wondering if perhaps all he wanted was a demonstration that she could still hear him, a sign that she wasn't lost in the visions again. She refocused her eyes on his face, and then raised them to meet his gaze once more, just to prove that she was still present.

Mitsu held her eyes with his for a moment, and tilted his head to one side as though asking a question that she didn't understand. When she didn't make any sort of reply, a small bit of the light seemed to leave his eyes.

"Are you all right?" he asked at length.

Mishi nodded, though she didn't say anything. She was well enough. Confused, still slightly embarrassed about the misunderstanding about lovers and skin, but well enough.

Mitsu removed his hand from her shoulder, shifting his seat so that he wasn't pressed quite so close to her. Mishi hadn't noticed just how close he was, until his absence left traces of cold all along her side, and she instantly wished she had answered differently. Whatever answer would bring him back to her was the one she wished she had given.

She shivered slightly, the cool air feeling frigid after having had Mitsu's warmth pressed against her.

He seemed to notice the shiver, and shifted closer to her once more.

"Are you cold?"

Mishi gave the barest of nods, not willing to answer aloud, because she wasn't truly cold. She knew that he would be able to sense the lie if she uttered the words. But she had felt a chill and she wanted him close to her again. Even if she didn't know what to do with him so close, she longed for him to return.

She felt herself relax as he resumed his earlier proximity. He wasn't pressed against her quite as closely as he had been before—she could tell because there were parts of her skin that still felt chilled, compared to a few moments earlier—and she decided to make up the difference herself, scooting closer to him.

"Tell me more about what you sense in the wild," she said. She wasn't sure if she wanted him to speak because she enjoyed the sound of his voice, or because she was interested in what he told her. She thought it was likely a combination of the two. She certainly enjoyed his voice, but she found herself intrigued by the way he described his kisō.

"So…the earth tells me things, or rather, I can sense its reactions to the things that have traveled before me. The signs that most people can detect are just one layer of the things that I can sense. I can also sense what the plants and animals have experienced, as well as what the earth itself has experienced, through its reactions."

"You read the earth?" Mishi mused, as she stared into the fire and let Mitsu's voice wash over her.

"I suppose you could say that."

She could hear the smile in his voice. She leaned against his shoulder, watched the fire cook the rabbits that would serve as their dinner, listened to the creatures that shifted and called out in the forest around them, and began to understand how someone could feel completely at home in the wild.

~~~

After dinner, Mishi banked the fire so that it would continue to burn at a reasonable rate throughout the night while generating enough heat to keep them both warm. It was spring, but the nights were still quite cool this high in the mountains, and sleep would be difficult if they let themselves get too cold.

Mishi was trying to figure out where the best place to lie for the night would be, relative to the fire and the warmth it would create, when Mitsu indicated an area he had just cleared of rocks and layered with pine needles.

"The pine needles will help to keep us warm."

Mishi hesitated when she realized that Mitsu intended for them to sleep near each other once more.

"I shouldn't sleep beside you," she said, fear clawing her chest as she remembered the visions that had gripped her while the rabbits had cooked. "What if I wake up from a nightmare and don't recognize you? What if I don't wake up from the nightmare at all?"

"Then I'll let you know it's me, and you'll stop."

Mishi shook her head.

"You know that's not how it works. I'm lucky I haven't hurt you already on this journey. Kami curse it, I'm lucky I haven't had any more visions, with all the things we've seen over the past few days."

"It will be fine. You've never hurt me before."

Mishi only raised an eyebrow at that.

"Well, you've never hurt me once you realized it was me," Mitsu corrected hastily.

"You don't understand," Mishi insisted. "I could kill you."

Mitsu shook his head, but Mishi didn't allow him time to speak.

"Mitsu-san, you've seen it. When I'm trapped in those visions I don't recognize anyone. Everyone becomes the enemy. I can't be trusted."

"We'll leave your blades on the far side of the camp."

"I don't need my blades to kill you, Mitsu-san." Mishi hated to say it, but she knew it was the truth, and so did Mitsu.

"Mishi-san, if you can't be trusted, then I'm not safe no matter what side of the camp or fire I'm sleeping on. Right beside you or a dozen meters away will make little difference. We've discussed this before."

"But if you're farther away, you'll have more time."

"Only if I wake before you do, and realize you're having a nightmare. How many times must we have this same argument? Mishi-san, if you're right here, at least I can easily sense you, sense how you're sleeping. If you start thrashing in your dreams, I'll know to give you space. I'll have more time to react than if you were to wake in the night on the other side of the camp and come toward me."

Mishi was about to argue, when Mitsu spoke up again.

"Besides, if you're cold in the night you won't sleep as well, and you'll be far more likely to have nightmares to begin with. If you stay between me and the fire, you'll be warm and you'll sleep calmly."

Mishi opened her mouth to object, but Mitsu cut her off one more time.

"And if you leave me to sleep alone, I might freeze to death. I don't have fire at my beck and call, and can't just decide to be warm the way that you can. If you sleep beside me, you can be certain that you won't awake to a Mitsu-cicle in the morning."

That made her laugh. She remained unconvinced that Mitsu would be safe with her beside him, but she was tired of arguing and she was half convinced that Mitsu was right, as he had been when the children were with them. Besides, she would stay awake all night if she had to, in order to keep Mitsu safe.

She lay down, curling up in front of the fire. She instantly recognized that the pine needles made a great deal of difference in how warm she was. She resolved to ask either Mitsu or Taka for lessons on surviving alone in the wilderness.

Despite her best intentions to the contrary, it wasn't long before the gentle warmth of the crackling fire, and the warmth of Mitsu at her back, allowed exhaustion to claim her.

She didn't wake reliving a terror that was causing her to attack Mitsu. She did wake up screaming.

Mitsu's arms wrapped gently around her, not hard enough to make her feel restrained, just enough to remind her that she wasn't alone.

She took great, gasping breaths, trying to remove the images of Kuma-sensei's death from her mind. In reality, it was something she'd never actually seen. She had been busy fighting the First Rōjū when it had happened, and she'd only ever heard it described after the fact. But in her dreams, not only did she see the event up close and personal, with Kuma-sensei's eyes pleading for life even as the blade bit into his shoulder and cleaved him to the lung…in her dreams, she was the one who held the blade.

"Mishi-san?" Mitsu's voice asked, from behind her. The skin on her neck danced to the feel of his warm breath against the tiny hairs that stood up there.

"Yes?" she asked, as she worked to get her breathing under control.

"Is there anything I can do?" Mitsu asked, his voice quiet and calm.

Mishi took a deep breath, considering the question. She wasn't lost in a vision. She didn't need the kind of reminder that would pull her back to reality. She was free of the images that had woken her, but the essence of them remained. The sick feeling that she had done something horrible, something that could never be undone. That she had killed something beautiful, and lost a bit of her soul with it. That feeling stayed with her, and she didn't have the slightest idea how to get rid of it.

"Don't let go," she whispered.

If she'd learned anything from her experience earlier in the evening, it was that she would regret the loss of warmth she felt right at this moment. In fact, she took a moment to register just how close Mitsu was to her. Just like earlier, when they'd been sitting by the fire, he'd pushed himself much nearer to her than she'd realized while she had been lost in whatever was tormenting her.

This time, she took stock of how she could feel his arms wrapped gently around her shoulders, the muscles of his forearms pressed against her own, the muscles of his chest pressed against those in her shoulders.

His stomach pressed tightly against her lower back...when she registered his legs and how they tucked against her own, she noticed something else, and her memory was suddenly thrown back to conversations with Sachi that now seemed like they'd happened a lifetime ago. Detailed conversations about men, which she had never had with anyone else before or since.

She wasn't sure what it meant that she could feel that particular part of Mitsu's anatomy, but she had some guesses, based on those long-ago conversations.

She took another moment to luxuriate in the feel of Mitsu's body against hers, and she was glad that she'd asked him to continue holding her. Something about it was chasing off the feeling that had overwhelmed her as she woke from the dream, and she wondered if she would be able to sleep again that night. So far, she'd never been able to find sleep again, after a dream like the one she'd just had.

Then she felt Mitsu's breath against the back of her neck, and thoughts of sleep left her.

"Mishi-san?" Mitsu asked again, and she wondered why the timbre of his voice made the bottom of her stomach drop away.

"Yes?" she whispered, afraid that speaking any louder would chase away whatever was happening between them right now.

"May I kiss you?" Mitsu asked.

Mishi's skin felt a rush of heat at the mere suggestion, and she nodded softly, only to realize that Mitsu was behind her and probably couldn't see.

"Yes," she whispered.

She had been about to shift her weight to roll toward him, as she expected him to kiss her mouth, but before she could move she felt his lips graze her throat. She felt her heart increase its pace as the light sensation continued—from her neck, down to her collarbone, and then out across her shoulder, carefully shoving the cloth of her uwagi out of the way as it went.

Mishi had worried, for the tiniest moment, when Mitsu had first asked to kiss her, that she would waste the moment comparing the kiss to her first kiss with Katagi. Instead, she found all memory of that first kiss erased by the sensation of the warm lips that traced from her collarbone to her shoulder, and back again. When he reached the place where neck met collarbone, he traced back up her neck, to the soft spot behind her ear. When he came forward to trace her jawline to her mouth, he finally shifted them both, so that he was suspending himself above her. She lay with her back to the earth and her face toward the sky, his green eyes holding hers for a long moment, just before his lips found hers and kept them. Quietly at first, without demanding, just testing to see if they were welcome. Mishi, so caught up in the sensations she'd been drowning in for the past few moments, turned into the kiss and returned the gesture with enthusiasm.

It had been so long since she had been able to feel anything without the pain of her past overwhelming her. For a long moment, as their lips met, she forgot who she was, and where and why, and she put all of her being into returning that kiss.

Mitsu simply met her there for a moment, but then something about her reaction turned his gentle quest into something hungrier, and soon his lips were demanding more, his tongue begging for an entrance, which she eagerly granted.

Mishi soon found that, as close as they were already, she wanted more. Her arms quested upward, without her direction, wrapping themselves behind Mitsu's back, around his neck, to pull him closer. Soon, she found herself rising from the ground to close the distance between them, and Mitsu's arms seemed to be supporting her efforts, doing their best to keep her raised up and pressed against him.

One of them moaned, but she was never sure which of them it was, and she didn't care. All she knew was that she felt a fire coursing through her body, and for once the sensation came without doubts, or fears, or any other feelings at all. She felt good, truly good, for the first time in more moons than she could count, and she never wanted it to end.

Eventually, though, she felt the space between them grow again, and though she lamented it, she understood that exhaustion was bound to claim them both after a time. She finally pulled back enough to look at Mitsu's face. His eyes sparkled in the moonlight that danced around them, and his lips curved up at the sides in a smile that warmed her more than the fire that still smoldered beside them.

"Why did you want to kiss me?" she found herself asking, before her brain could stop her.

Mitsu's eyebrows rose, touching above his nose as he spoke.

"I thought it was fairly obvious."

Now Mishi raised an eyebrow of incredulity.

"I've wanted to do that since very shortly after the first time that we met," he said.

"You mean that time in the woods, when I thought you were a stray hishi come to capture me?"

Mitsu nodded.

"I almost killed you. It made you want to kiss me?"

Mitsu nodded again, this time more vigorously.

"You're insane," she said.

Mitsu merely shrugged.

"I find you very intriguing," he said, as if that was the only reason a person could have for kissing someone.

"And beautiful," he added, making Mishi entirely suspicious of him.

She must have narrowed her eyes at him, for he looked at her with honest shock.

"You can't tell me you don't know that you're beautiful!?"

Mishi continued to glare at him.

"I don't dislike the way I look," she said. "But I know that most men find someone like Kusuko attractive, and I am well aware that I don't look a thing like her."

"All to the good, in my mind. Kusuko looks lovely enough, but she's small, and…well, she looks too much like a doll for my liking."

Mishi chuckled at that.

"And what do I look like?" she asked, before she could stop herself.

"A warrior," Mitsu said simply.

Mishi didn't reply to that, but she decided to lie down in the crook of Mitsu's arms once more, and let sleep take her. This time, she didn't dream of anything but moonlight on skin, and the warmth of a glowing fire.

18日 3月 新議 1年

18th Day, 3rd Moon, Cycle 1 of the New Council

⇒ Mishi ⇐

MISHI WOKE TO the sound of breathing, and it was a long moment before she remembered where she was, and with whom. The sky was just getting light, the sun still hidden beneath the horizon, and the sounds of small animals and birds filled the space around her. She took some time to enjoy the warmth of Mitsu's body pressed against hers, and the memory of last night brought blood to her face—and other places. She wasn't ashamed of what they'd done. Long ago, after overhearing a conversation between Mishi, Ami, and Sachi, Tenshi had explained that it was perfectly normal for two people to please each other in such a way, especially if they cared for each other. Nevertheless, Mishi was glad that they hadn't done anything that would require her to take the herbs that prevented pregnancy. She didn't have any with her, and she was unsure where to find them, or how to treat them to make them potent. She was fairly certain that Taka would know all about them, and she would ask her friend if they became necessary, but for the time being, she was glad she didn't need to have that discussion. Would it be strange to admit to Taka that she cared for her brother? She didn't think Taka would mind, but then, she'd never had a brother. Taka was fairly new to having a brother, so perhaps she wouldn't mind either.

She shook herself. Did she really think that Mitsu would continue to care for her now that he knew the truth? Could he really love someone who was so…damaged? He'd been understanding yesterday, when she'd told him the truth, and he'd still seemed to care for

Traitor's Hope

her last night, but surely the morning light would make it clear to him that she wasn't an acceptable target for his affections.

She would do her best to remind them both of that.

That much decided, Mishi rose from the pine bed, careful not to disturb Mitsu, and started a small fire with some of the remaining deadfall she'd collected the day before. They would be getting an early start, surely, after all they'd learned yesterday, but they could at least cook the extra rabbits that Mitsu had caught.

Once the fire was crackling peacefully, with another two rabbits skewered above it, she stood beneath the tall pines that surrounded their camp, silhouetted against the lightening sky, and began to warm herself by running through the kata she had learned for unarmed combat. She would let Mitsu sleep while she practiced. If she was going to return to violence, and the last few tendays proved that it was inevitable, then she should do all she could to control herself, and practice was the key to control.

She was so deep into the forms of her kata that she almost didn't hear the branch snap in the forest behind her.

For a moment, she pretended that she hadn't heard it. She caught sight of Mitsu out of the corner of her eye. He had risen from the pine needles and begun to tend the rabbits not long ago. Now, with nothing more than a brief glance in her direction, he continued tending them, as though he hadn't heard anything either.

She started a new kata, one whose pattern would take her closer to the forest, turning as the kata required, which lined her up with her target.

Her peripheral vision showed her Mitsu finding a reason to move to the far side of the fire, as though he were deeply involved in tending the rabbits. As soon as he was in position, she sprang.

The man hiding in the shadows was taken by surprise, as evidenced by the whites of his eyes flashing as he turned to run into the forest, but he was quick enough to react before Mishi reached him. She wasn't sure she would have been able to catch him if Mitsu hadn't been covering his escape.

Between Mitsu's speed, and the angle at which he moved to intercept, it wasn't far—barely a handful of sprinted paces—before they had caught up with, and successfully tackled, the spy.

Mishi was disturbed to note that the man was dressed in hishi garb, but as he hadn't yet thrown any poisoned blades at her, and had instead attempted to run away, she decided he didn't deserve death before she'd had a chance to speak with him.

So, as she and Mitsu wrestled his arms behind him, before he had the chance to draw a weapon, Mishi hit him hard at the base of his skull, watching him crumple to the ground beneath her.

It was only after she had tied his hands, when Mitsu rolled him over and pulled off his mask, that they recognized Inari-san.

~~~

Mishi stared at the unconscious form of Inari-san, trussed up by the fire, and wondered what on earth he was doing following them, when they'd been traveling with him voluntarily only a few days before. Of course, it was possible that he was still working for whatever remained of the Rōjū, or that he'd defected to the sanzoku, but neither of those seemed like reasonable explanations for his presence.

"What do you think he was doing?" she asked Mitsu, who stood beside her with an equally dumbfounded expression on his face.

"You mean, aside from spying on us?" he asked.

"Obviously. He was watching us for a long time, more than just what he would need to ascertain our position and report back. Why should he care what we were doing?"

"Shouldn't you just ask him that?"

"People are more likely to tell the truth if they think you already know it."

"But you can sense if he's lying."

"As can you."

"So he has little reason to think lying will work."

"But silence can be very effective."

Mitsu was quiet for a moment, and Mishi wondered if he were considering the various ways to force another human to speak. Mishi didn't think she could stomach any of them, not to mention Kuma-sensei had always insisted that torture didn't usually work.

"Perhaps an exchange of information, then?" Mitsu suggested at last.

"What could he possibly wish to know that we would be glad to tell him?"

"We could always lie."

"He's a Kisōshi as well. He can tell if we're lying, and as a hishi he's likely trained specially for it."

Mitsu stared hard at the man on the ground.

"He was surprisingly easy to catch," he mused.

"And he made no attempt to bite down on the small capsule of poison most of them keep in their mouths."

Mitsu's eyebrows rose at that. Apparently, that was a piece of information he'd been without, until just now.

"How do you—"

"The other hishi, aside from Kusuko, chose that escape when we caught them at Kuma-sensei's school. Kusuko might have as well, but we'd learned our lesson and taken hers from her mouth while she was unconscious."

"So, if he was easily caught, and hasn't tried to kill himself with a capsule of poison…"

"He's either not a real hishi, or he planned to be caught."

"Interesting notions, both."

"Indeed. Shall we sweep his mouth before we wake him, just in case?"

Mitsu nodded, proceeding as asked. They found no capsule of poison. They didn't have any of the restorative balm that Tenshi had used to wake the hishi they'd interrogated moons ago, so they resorted to a skin of cold water to the face.

Inari sputtered to consciousness.

"Good morning, Inari-san," Mitsu said, bowing slightly with the water skin still in his hand.

"Would you be so kind as to tell us why you were watching us?" Mishi was striving to keep her voice polite. She thought the incongruity might throw the man, making him more likely to make a mistake.

"Kind of you not to kill me," was his sole reply.

"Well, we like to keep our options open," Mitsu replied. "I wouldn't make any promises about changing our minds, though."

Inari nodded, as though that was only reasonable, but didn't say any more.

"What is your purpose here?" Mishi asked, deciding to get straight to the point.

"What is any man's purpose?" he replied. "Can any of us truly know, until we're dead?"

Mitsu was clearly working to repress a chuckle, and Mishi was convinced that they made a terrible pair of interrogators.

"You wear the garb of a hishi," Mishi continued. "Why is that?"

"Quite comfortable, really. Light, breathable, fairly quiet when one is running in the woods."

"Would you be a hishi then?" Mitsu asked, still struggling not to smile. She wondered if this line of questioning was even worthwhile, since they already knew that he was an associate of Kusuko's, and they knew for certain that Kusuko was, or at least had been, a hishi.

"It's possible," he replied, with a small smile. "I would be most things, if given the opportunity."

Mishi was angry with herself for liking Inari's replies, and angry with Inari for evading all of their questions. He wasn't lying about anything so far, merely dodging questions deftly with word games, and she was learning nothing aside from the fact that the man had a good vocabulary and a solid sense of humor. She wished that he hadn't been here spying on them. She thought she might enjoy his company under other circumstances.

"Sir, I'd very much like to continue this chat sometime—you are as entertaining as a fool and as wise as an old fox. But I'm afraid we need to be going, and we can't take you with us. Unless you can prove that you're no threat to us, somehow, we'll be forced to kill you and leave your body for the crows. Is there anything you'd like to share with us, to help us make the decision?"

Mishi knew she wasn't lying—she'd kill the man if he proved to be a threat to any of the people that she loved. But what she didn't tell him was that it wouldn't take much to prove to her that he was no threat. She was in no way eager to take his life, especially after he'd helped to save hers once already.

The man's face paled somewhat, and she wondered if he'd taken the threat to heart, or was merely that talented an actor. To say that she didn't trust anything about the hishi would have been a gross understatement.

"I was sent to monitor your actions and report back on what I saw. I report to the leader of the hishi, not to the band of sanzoku who attacked you earlier. After all, if I wanted to hand you over to them, I wouldn't have bothered to help save you from their camp a few days ago, would I? I've no interest in giving away your position to them, and by the time I return to my master, you'll be long gone from this clearing, and I'll have no idea where you are."

"Why would the leader of the hishi be interested in us?" Mishi asked, though she thought she might have a guess.

"You keep interesting company," the man said, before leaning back against the tree on which they'd propped him, and closing his eyes for a moment.

Mishi wondered if he meant Taka or Kusuko, perhaps both. Which would be of more interest to the leader of the hishi: a healer so effective she could turn the tide of a war, or one of his former—possibly former, she reminded herself—hishi?

"Come now, tell us something useful so we don't have to kill you," Mishi said.

"Define useful," Inari-san said.

"Something we don't already know," Mitsu replied.

"You have your mother's eyes." Inari smiled as he spoke, though his eyes looked more sad than amused.

Mitsu glared at the man.

"Very funny."

"Not a joke, Yoshida Mitsuanagumi-san."

Now Inari's face was entirely serious.

Mishi glanced at Mitsu, seeing that his face had gone from a forced glare to sincere astonishment.

"How did you learn my name?" he asked.

Inari's smile faded, and his eyes grew sad.

"I met your mother once, very briefly. Your father, too."

Mitsu opened his mouth to reply, but no words came out. Mishi wanted to ask how Inari had known who Mitsu was, if he'd never met him and had only met his parents briefly long ago, but she thought it was Mitsu's place to ask, rather than hers.

Finally, Mitsu found his voice.

"Why would you tell me this?"

Inari smiled once more.

"It's a pleasure to see that you and your sister have found each other."

Mishi now began to wonder how much of her personal history Taka had shared with Kusuko. Had the young "former" spy already passed that information on to this man? If so, why was he bringing it up now?

"He's been traveling with Taka-san and Kusuko-san," she reminded Mitsu, whose face was darkening from astonishment to something more sinister. "He could easily have gotten information from them, or listened in to private conversations."

Mitsu nodded, but his expression didn't clear.

"Good. You shouldn't trust me. My master is one who would take advantage of the information. But I hope you'll believe me when I say that I'm very glad to see that you've found each other. Everyone should have some kind of family."

Mishi wondered what other mysteries this man would reveal, if they kept him around long enough. Perhaps that was his only goal, to make them think he was worth keeping.

"What else can you tell me?" Mitsu asked, when he finally regained his voice. "About my parents…"

"Only that they were good people. And that they didn't deserve to die." Inari sighed, before continuing, "But then, most people don't, when it comes down to it, and yet everyone gets there eventually."

Mishi watched Mitsu's face closely as he listened to the hishi, and considered stepping forward to restrain him as he moved to grab Inari-san's grey tunic.

"Did you kill them?" he asked, when he was nose to nose with the older man.

Inari shook his head, sadly.

"I did not. But I didn't stop it either, so I may as well have."

Mitsu's fists clenched in the folds of the man's clothes, and Mishi reached out to stay his arms. She had never seen Mitsu enraged before—although he'd been something close to it when they'd found Mizu and Tsuchi's village laid to waste—but now she could see the anger burning behind his eyes, causing his hands to shake with restrained violence. Finally, after a long moment, he dropped Inari to the ground.

Mitsu walked away from the small clearing, and Mishi let him go.

"Strange way to make yourself seem valuable," Mishi said, crouching in front of Inari, who said nothing but only watched Mitsu walk away.

"Did you really know his mother?" she asked.

Inari-san met her eyes.

"I wouldn't say I knew her, but I did meet her once, briefly."

"And you're sure that he and Taka are siblings?" she asked, because neither Taka nor Mitsu had been certain of it, despite their suspicions.

Inari nodded.

"Of that, I am now certain."

"I would imagine that however you came to know that is information that Mitsu and Taka would find worthwhile," Mishi admitted. "Now, if you can just convince me that you don't mean us any harm, I'll untie you."

Before Inari had a chance to speak again, Mitsu came running back to their camp, with Riyōshi still clinging to the leather brace on his forearm.

"One of the bands of sanzoku appears to be heading for a walled town less than a day's travel from here," he announced. "Now is our best chance to stop them."

⇜ Kusuko ⇝

In the dim light of the izakaya's kitchen, Kusuko looked at the tiny rolled parchment that she'd carefully collected from the empty sake cup. She inhaled the warm air, filled with the scent of cooked rice, warm sake, and steaming vegetables, and ran the information through her mind again and again.

The practical thing to do was to let it all play out without her interference. The sanzoku were in place, the Rōjū had their plan in motion, and she certainly shouldn't interfere. Mamushi-san would be furious with her if she interfered. And what did she care anyway? Taka was safe. The children that Taka seemed to care so much about were also safe. Surely that was enough. Mishi and Mitsu meant nothing to her, even if this hifu respected them as both adversaries and allies. And Inari-san...well, she knew how resourceful he was, and she didn't think Mamushi-san intended for him to die, so perhaps she would see him again.

No, it was not in her best interest to do anything with the information she'd been given, save to make note of it in her mind and keep heading northwest, toward the Zōkame estate.

She slipped into the narrow alley behind the izakaya, dark, empty. She changed out of the serving kimono she'd "borrowed," leaving it on the back step, where the next person to empty a slop bucket would be likely to see it.

She followed shadows between the shadows, returning to the inn where she, Taka, and the children had found a room for the night.

She made no sound, as she returned to the palette beside Taka's sleeping form. Made no noise, as she lay there for a moment, watching the moonlight shine on the young healer's face, and the quiet rise and fall of her chest.

She should sleep, and in the morning they would continue their trek to the Zōkame estate.

She reached a hand to Taka's shoulder.

"Taka-san," she whispered urgently. "Taka-san. We need to leave."

19日 3月 新議 1年
19th Day, 3rd Moon, Cycle 1 of the New Council

⇒ Mishi ⇐

AS MISHI'S FEET pounded through leaves and underbrush, weaving her through the sun-dappled forest, she watched the wall in the distance loom larger, and she pondered Inari-san's strange behavior that morning.

He had spied on them. That was something she could understand. He was a hishi; his purpose was either to gather information, or to kill.

What she didn't understand was why, after Mitsu had announced that the sanzoku seemed to be heading for the walled town that now loomed ahead of her, he had seemed to blanch, albeit so briefly that Mishi thought she'd imagined it, and then begged them to let him go.

He had seemed almost frantic, and they hadn't known what else to do with him anyway. It wasn't that they trusted him, but they simply didn't see how he could be any more of a threat to them than the one hundred sanzoku that they were about to try to prevent from demolishing yet another town.

Besides, they had needed to move quickly, in order to reach the town with enough time left to warn them and help them prepare their defenses. Not that they'd told any of those particulars to Inari-san. In fact, they waited until he was well away from them before they discussed their own plan, and especially before they sent Riyōshi off with their request for reinforcements.

Then they had made their way toward the walled town, with the help of Riyōshi's description and Mitsu's tracking abilities.

They hoped to have ample time to warn the townspeople before the sanzoku arrived. After all, they were traveling light and there were only two of them, whereas the horde of sanzoku they had run into the previous day were encumbered by their numbers, their heavily laden horses, and their supplies.

As they drew closer to the town and its impressive walls, Mishi's attention was drawn away from the puzzle of Inari's behavior, focusing instead on the size of the walled town. From what she could see, the wall looked like it was at least three times the height of a man, perhaps four, and patrolled by a number of guards.

The sight gave Mishi hope, for she didn't know how long the town would last, walls or no, if they had no soldiers to defend it. She could only hope that the soldiers were well trained, that perhaps a few of them had some amount of kisō, or that, at the very least, they had a few capable archers among their ranks. She didn't know how long it would take the New Council reinforcements to arrive, and she didn't think it likely that she could single-handedly fend off over a hundred sanzoku for a matter of days.

She and Mitsu finally reached the gates, which were wide open and unguarded, and she felt a shiver run down her spine when they passed through them. For a reason she couldn't name, it felt like being swallowed whole.

~~~

As soon as they ran through the gates, Mishi was shouting for the nearest guard, telling him to call the townspeople inside, sound whatever alarm they had, and close the gates.

When the man only stood and looked at her, she added, "Over a hundred sanzoku are headed this way. Do you want your gates open wide when they get here?"

That seemed to spur the man to action, and he proceeded to alert his fellow guards. Shouts rang out along the wall, and runners began cutting away from the gate and across the town.

"Who's in charge here?" she asked the man she had initially warned, once he returned from sounding the alarm.

Traitor's Hope

"Our resident Kisōshi is away, so Namura-san is in charge," the man answered.

"And where might I find him?"

"Now that the alarm has been raised, he should be heading to the western gate," the man said.

Mishi thanked the man, and turned to Mitsu. They had entered through the eastern gate.

"Ready for more running?" she asked.

Mitsu smiled.

"Always," he said.

She was glad that he didn't tire easily, given what might be coming, but she said no more as they both took off down the main road that headed west.

Aside from the wall that surrounded it, Shikazenji appeared to be a normal town. While it wasn't overly large, it was quite a bit bigger than the village from which they had rescued Mizu and Tsuchi. They ran down a road that appeared to be large enough for two carts to pass each other, glimpsing at least two guest houses, three izakayas, and all the merchants and rice vendors that one would expect to see in a small city. Mishi was surprised at how long the main road was, and wondered how many people lived here to support so much commerce. Even so, they reached the other side of the town in good time.

There was quite a bit of activity around the western gate, but it wasn't yet closed.

"I'm looking for Namura-san," Mishi said to the first guard that she and Mitsu came across.

"On the wall," replied the guard, with an upward gesture, before continuing on his way.

All the guards seemed occupied now, and Mishi wondered how many there were in the town, and how well trained they might be. She also wondered if the resident Kisōshi would be the only one who might be available to help defend the town, or if any of the guards might be Kisōshi as well.

She was relieved, as she climbed the narrow stairs that led to the top of the wall, to find that Namura-san was indeed a Kisōshi. A man in his middle cycles, he was stout—a full head shorter than

Mishi, but wider by a fair margin—and commanding. Mishi had to push her way through a number of guards who were awaiting his directions in order to reach him.

"Namura-san," she said, surreptitiously checking the markings on his hakama that indicated his rank. She was slightly disappointed to find that he was fukurō rank. She outranked him, which meant that, by default, she was in charge. That might be useful, but it made her uncomfortable, since the man was at least twice her age. "We are the ones who warned your guards of the coming sanzoku. I'm here to offer any assistance I can in protecting your town."

Namura-san nodded briefly, even as he gave orders to the men who waited nearby, and then he seemed to finally see her for the first time.

"What are you?" he asked with a sneer.

Mishi's eyebrows rose together.

"I beg your pardon?"

"You're dressed as a Kisōshi, but you're a girl. That's an offense punishable by death, you know."

Mishi narrowed her eyes at the man.

"Not anymore," she said. "Any woman who is a fully trained Kisōshi may dress as one. Or did you not receive the latest decrees from the New Council in this backwater village?"

Perhaps she didn't mind that she outranked this man, after all.

"Just because the New Council says that a woman trained as a Kisōshi may dress as one, doesn't mean any woman can dress so whenever she likes. A katana and wakizashi are dangerous, you know; they're not toys."

Mishi wondered if the man's kisō was so weak that he truly couldn't sense hers, or if he was simply being obtuse in order to fluster her. She briefly considered demonstrating just how dangerous her katana could be, but reminded herself that, as tempting as it was to lash out at this man, he hadn't done anything to truly deserve it.

"And who are you?" asked Namura-san, turning to Mitsu, who had been standing by with his eyes narrowed.

"No one of importance," Mitsu replied coolly.

"Are you her protector, then? The man who keeps her out of trouble, while she runs around pretending to be a Kisōshi?"

Mitsu only snorted at this, and turned to look out over the wall

"As much as I enjoy you wasting our time this way," Mishi said, "There are more than a hundred armed sanzoku on their way here, and we've come to help. How many trained Kisōshi do you have in your ranks?"

"The presiding Kisōshi and I are the only ones available to this town. Our presiding Kisōshi is not here, which leaves me, and perhaps this man you've brought with you, if he has as much kisō as he appears to."

"Then the three of us are the only Kisōshi here?"

The man snorted.

"I count two Kisōshi here."

"I'm afraid we don't have time for your persistent ignorance," Mishi said.

"And I don't have time for this charade," the man countered, his voice hardening with anger. "Now get off this wall, before I—"

Mishi didn't wait for the man to finish.

"Mitsu-san, is there anyone in, or near, that guard shack?" She indicated a small, empty wooden building that sat just beyond the western gate. She was fairly certain that it was empty, but she wished to be quite sure.

Mitsu shook his head.

"No one is near it."

She turned to look at Namura, and, without dropping his gaze, she called forth the element that sang in her blood. Flames immediately engulfed the little shack.

"Do you need further proof?" she asked.

She watched Namura turn to Mitsu, as though preparing to accuse him of setting the guard shack alight on her behalf.

"Earth and air are my elements," Mitsu said, before the blustering man could accuse him. "And you're wasting precious moments that we could be using to plan for the enemy."

Mitsu glared at the man, and Mishi could sense Namura's kisō reaching out to Mitsu's, his eyes widening as he confirmed, finally, that Mitsu was not capable of calling the fire that Mishi had.

The man only inclined his head the slightest angle. He was clearly not happy with this discovery, but she saw that he realized he had little choice but to accept that she was Kisōshi, and that she outranked him.

"What do you propose for our defense?" he asked, his teeth almost grinding as he choked out the words.

"I think I have a plan that will keep them busy. We only have to—"

Mishi was cut off mid sentence, as a shout from the guards along the wall drew their attention.

A guard was pointing to the road that led west from the town, and they looked out to see the horde of one hundred sanzoku that they had been warned of approaching in the distance. Yet even as they were turning back to exchange worried looks at the sight, a runner topped the wall and almost fell before Namura's feet.

"Namura-san, the enemy is close," he panted.

Namura glared at the man for a moment.

"I can see that," he said. "I didn't need you to come running to tell me something I can see with my own eyes from atop the gate."

"You can see the eastern gate from here?" the man asked, his eyes wide.

"What?" Namura asked, his own face beginning to imitate that of the runner's.

"The enemy is within sight of the eastern gate."

Namura turned to look at the enemy that approached the western gate, and then shook his head.

"How many?" he asked.

"A hundred or more," the runner replied.

"We're surrounded, then," Namura said, to no one in particular.

~~~

They had no choice, in the end, but to listen to the demands of a small group from the main fighting force that approached the western gate.

The demand that was issued—to hand over all female Kisōshi within the town's walls, or else be destroyed by the force of sanzoku that now surrounded them—did not surprise Mishi. The reaction of the townspeople did.

The request had barely been made before Mishi's jaw dropped at the sight of two babes in arms, only a few moons old, being pulled away from their mothers, who were frantic and doing their best to resist.

Even before the horror of it registered in her mind, she saw Mitsu sprinting down the stairs, running from the top of the wall to where the men were wresting the babies from their mothers' arms. Then her body kicked into motion, and she followed on his heels.

"What are you doing?" Mitsu demanded, as soon as he reached the men who were separating the mothers from their daughters.

The men turned to look at him as though he were crazy. Three of them sneered at him, but none of them replied. Mitsu had no authority here.

But the men's expressions changed when Mishi appeared at his side, dressed as the Kisōshi she was, including the katana and wakizashi that she had been reluctant to wear for so long. She hoped they would assume, as Namura had initially, that she was a man, and pay more attention to her presence as a Kisōshi than as a woman.

"You've been asked a question," she said calmly.

It seemed that they did assume she was a man, as most of them averted their eyes and began muttering.

"A clear answer, please," Mishi said, still without raising her voice. She stood tall, hoping her height would further the impression that she was male, and she tried to call forth the calm confidence that Kuma-sensei had always used whenever he needed to get his students to do something they didn't wish to do.

"You there," she nodded toward the man holding the smaller of the two babies. "Give us an answer."

The man cleared his throat, looking at the ground before him.

"We've seen what they do to the towns that hold girls like these," he said. Though he spoke barely above a whisper, it was still clearly audible to everyone in their immediate circle. "It's not worth it," he continued quietly. "Saving them isn't worth it, if it means everyone else in this town has to die. We knew, when we saw them coming, what they were going to do. We thought that maybe, if we threw the girls out the gate when they got here, they wouldn't want to kill the rest of us."

Mishi's mouth formed a hard line, and out of the corner of her eye she saw Mitsu's face go rigid with his own ire. Without even hearing the demands of the sanzoku, these men had simply started rounding the girls up, as soon as they'd known the sanzoku were approaching.

Mishi reached to Mitsu with her own kisō, sending him an idea.

When Mishi next spoke, her words were magnified for the whole crowd to hear, and quite a crowd had gathered before the gate by now.

"I understand that none of you wish to die to save these children," Mishi began, turning to look each of the people arrayed around her in the eye, one by one. "Or, even if you might give your own life to save them, you may not feel that allowing your whole town to be slaughtered on their behalf is a reasonable expenditure of human life." She paused, letting everyone think about that for a moment. "You might be right. Perhaps that is too great a price to pay to save the lives of two small humans."

A number of people in the crowd were nodding. Mishi felt her stomach twist, thinking of what would happen to these babies if they were handed over to the sanzoku.

"What would you say, though, if I told you that I can guarantee our victory against these monsters? If I told you that they will never be able to do here what they have done in all the other villages that you've heard about? Would you fight? Would you protect the children you are so quick to hand over to those who would kill them?"

A number of the people around her showed patent disbelief at this idea, but some of them seemed intrigued, as though they genuinely wished for some way to protect the children. The babies' parents in particular seemed to like the idea.

She could feel the mindset of the crowd around her begin to change, and she felt a brief flicker of hope. Then she remembered just what she was promising, and how unlikely it was to be true.

Mishi felt the viselike clamp of a hand on her arm at the same time that she heard the incredulous hiss in her ear.

"What in the name of all the Kami do you think you're doing?"

She turned to face Namura-san, making a point of standing as tall as she could. She needed to remind everyone that she outranked him, and hope they still believed she was a man, or else this would all come unraveled quickly.

"We should be throwing you to them as well," Namura hissed. Mishi wondered why he was grabbing her arm and hissing at her in a voice too quiet for others to hear, when he could easily announce her gender to the world and have his guards try to seize her. Then she took a good look at his face and eyes, and realized that he was terrified. She wondered if he was more afraid of her, or the men that surrounded them. Could he sense that she was a monster? Well, a monster she might be, but she wasn't about to let these babies be slaughtered.

"And what would that accomplish, do you think?" she asked, in a voice that carried, turning away from Namura-san, as she forcibly removed his hand from her arm. "Do you think that the men outside your gates will truly leave you in peace if you hand over the girls that they seek? Do you think that's what they did with the towns they destroyed? Do you think those people were any more reluctant to hand over their daughters than you were?"

She was speaking to the whole town, not just Namura-san. It was important that they understand that giving in would gain them nothing. Mishi wasn't so naive as to think that they should sacrifice their entire town for two babies, even if that's what she would do, given the choice. She didn't want to see that kind of slaughter again, and she knew it was a real possibility, if they fought. But she knew it would be a certainty if they opened the gates to hand over these children, who had done nothing wrong save be born with a combination of gender and power that the men on the other side of the walls disapproved of.

"We have seen what these men do to the towns and villages they come across. They are not honorable men. They will not simply take these two babies, then be on their way. They didn't come here in these numbers just to steal away two tiny souls, leaving the rest of you in peace."

Mitsu was once more aiding her, magnifying her voice, and she turned to make sure that everyone heard her.

"They came here today for a slaughter. They serve the Rōjū. It aids their purpose to leave destruction and terror in their wake, because that is the only way that the men they serve have any chance of regaining power. They hope to make people too frightened to support the New Council, so frightened that they will accept the Rōjū once more, even if it means abandoning their daughters to be killed. The truth of the Rōjū Council is now known, and men trying to cling to the power that they once held are using these soldiers, and your fear, to regain what was lost to them. The soldiers outside these walls have come here to raze your town, whether you open your gates to them or not. But I promise you this: if you open those gates and allow them to take your daughters, they will overwhelm us instantly, and there will be no hope of defense."

She took in the faces of all those around her, and saw the fear of that truth echoed in all of their eyes.

"You would kill innocent people, just to protect these abominations?" Namura-san asked, this time loud enough for everyone to hear.

Ahh…now Mishi thought they were getting somewhere. Abominations, were they?

"Anyone who attempts to hand these children over to those monsters is far from innocent," she said simply.

"Even though they're only acting in the interests of the town? Trying to save the greater number of lives? Do you think so highly of your own kind that you would sacrifice all of these townspeople, just to save them?"

"I've already told you—I'm not asking anyone to sacrifice themselves, only to defend their own."

As she spoke, she saw the Kisōshi flinch closer to his katana, and she wondered what would finally make him draw against her.

"You must be delusional, if you think your skills are sufficient to fight off the army that's waiting outside of these gates."

"Hardly."

Mishi almost jumped at the new voice that cut across the crowd to join them.

"Far from delusional, Namura-san. If you'd ever seen her fight, you'd only wonder what extra trick she was hiding up her sleeve, not whether or not she'd lost her mind."

Surprise, quickly followed by deference, registered on Namura's face. And Mishi couldn't help allowing her own eyebrows to rise when she turned to see none other than Inari-san, making his way through a crowd that parted quickly before him. He was no longer dressed as a hishi, but rather resplendent in a pair of golden hakama and a white uwagi, both the swords of a Kisōshi riding openly in his obi, the rank of kuma plainly embroidered in the hem of his hakama.

"Ryūko-san, it is good to see you again," he said, his eyes alight with mischief as he addressed Mishi by her birth name. "I see you've met Namura-san. You'll have to forgive him for mistrusting you. He was not present at Rōjū City to see you wage battle against more trained eihei than could be easily counted in the time it took you to defeated them."

"Inari-sama," Namura said, quickly dropping to his knees. "I didn't know you had returned. I await your orders."

"My orders are simple enough," Inari said, turning and inclining his head to Mishi. "Do whatever this young woman tells you to do to try to save our town."

~~~

Mishi was nearing exhaustion. There had been no time to question Inari's presence in this town, or the fact that it seemed to be his Kisōshi holding. No time to wonder at what that meant, or why it should matter. There had been no time for anything but taking up her place on the top of the wall, with Mitsu at her side, and doing all that she could to help protect this town, which had finally decided to fight for its own survival rather than hand itself over to the sanzoku who had come to destroy it.

She was oddly grateful for her encounter with the camp full of sanzoku a few days before, as she realized that it had made her push her fuchi and body to the brink. She thought it likely that she would need every drop of power in her to get through this battle, but as she pulled at her kisō, she thought the well might be just a little bit deeper, thanks to that previous fight. She only hoped that it would be enough.

Standing side by side with Mitsu, on the wall above the eastern gate, she prepared herself to throw another fire storm at the men approaching the wall.

She had taken the example of Kusuko and Inari to heart, and decided that using that tactic was the best chance they would have of defending this walled town. They were outnumbered by no small margin, and there was only so much that a small group of two dozen soldiers could do to defend the wall from over two hundred sanzoku. The four Kisōshi they counted among them were hardly a match for those kinds of numbers, especially when the sanzoku boasted at least three times that many Kisōshi of their own.

Mishi knew that their only hope lay in keeping the sanzoku away from the wall, and keeping them guessing. She had been grateful to discover that Namura was also a fire kisō, and thus was able to work with Inari in a similar way as she would work with Mitsu. Of course, the results were less impressive, but they were still enough to keep the sanzoku back from the western gate.

What Mishi and Mitsu had achieved, however, had surprised even Mishi. She knew that her kisō was strong, and she knew that Mitsu's was as well, but she hadn't anticipated the magnitude of what that strength could render when they wove their elements together.

The firestorm that Mishi and Mitsu were releasing on the sanzoku was terrifying, and Mishi found herself slightly frightened of what they could do together. More than the wall of flame that Kusuko and Inari had used against the sanzoku in the woodland camp, this was a typhoon of fire; great whorls of flame that could have encompassed half the town, if Mishi and Mitsu had been bent on destruction, rather than defense.

As it was, the sanzoku were barely able to approach the town before Mishi and Mitsu sent another storm of devastation and flame against them. It was death to any of the men who were caught in the storm, but the sanzoku had quickly learned to flee as soon as they saw Mishi and Mitsu's presence above the wall. They had promptly taken to crouching behind the crenellations on the wall, only standing up to rain fire down on the sanzoku below.

But the sanzoku knew that time was their ally. Mishi and Mitsu might have a great deal of power, but they had limited energy. If the sanzoku harried the walls long enough, the fire storms would eventually cease.

Inari and Namura had already sent a runner from the western gate to let Mishi know that they were tiring, and wouldn't be able to continue much longer. Mishi thought that she and Mitsu would tire not long after them. Besides, how much would their continued efforts matter, if the western gate was lost to the sanzoku?

She took a deep breath, peering through the embrasure to see what the enemy was doing. Another band of two dozen sanzoku was approaching the gate once more. It was probably just another feint to get them to use up their kisō, but the men carried hatchets, and six of them hefted a metal-tipped battering ram between them. She had no doubt that, if she and Mitsu failed to fend them off with fire once more, they would make an attempt on the gate. They couldn't allow that. Once the men got close enough, any attempt to set them ablaze would just as likely set the wooden parts of the gate aflame as well. Their defense would be worth nothing if they burned the town down with their efforts.

She locked eyes with Mitsu, who looked as exhausted as she felt, and his head bent in acknowledgement of their next attack. Moving as one, they stood and turned toward the men moving in the direction of the gate.

Mishi called forth her fire, and Mitsu brought forth wind to spread it farther and faster than she would ever have been able to alone. The inferno that hurtled toward the men approaching the gate was formidable, and Mishi was careful to control the flames so that they didn't reach for any target they shouldn't consume. It wasn't long before her exhaustion began to tug at her, and she turned to Mitsu, ready to pull them both down behind the wall.

Yet for some reason, as she reached for him, Mitsu's eyes widened. He began to fall away from her, off the side of the steps that let them stand above the wall's zenith, toward the deck below.

She didn't register the arrow sticking through his shoulder, or the blood that trickled from his mouth, as he fell from her; not really. All she could see were the whites of his eyes, and the limp hand that she had tried to grab, as he slipped from her and collapsed on the deck below.

Her heart stopped. The world stopped. And then she screamed, even as she leapt the steps to land on the deck beside him.

~~~

There was too much blood. That was all she could think. There was too much blood, and why, why, why did the kami-cursed archer have to shoot Mitsu? Why couldn't he have shot her? Wasn't she the bigger threat anyway? Couldn't they tell that she was the monster, and that Mitsu was…good? Whole? A person who didn't deserve to die?

She thought she might be crying. Her face was wet, but she ignored that. She was too busy pressing the cloth from her hakama against the wound around the arrow shaft, trying to remember everything Taka had ever told her about arrow wounds. She knew that, in general, bleeding was something one wanted to stop, and that pressure helped, but she couldn't remember if she was supposed to take the arrow out, or leave it in. She knew Taka had told her once, and she thought Kuma-sensei had too, but she'd never had to heal an arrow wound before, and now she couldn't remember. So, she did the only thing she knew to do—she pressed against the blood that seeped from the arrow through Mitsu's shoulder, trying to ignore how far away his mind felt, and how weak his kisō seemed.

She wished, desperately, that Taka were here. She had never wished for anything so hard in all of her life.

Perhaps that was why, when Taka suddenly arrived beside her, she wasn't completely surprised.

~ Taka ~

"He's not breathing, Taka-chan! Why isn't he breathing?"

Taka had just barely reached the eastern gate when she found Mishi, crouched beside Mitsu's prone form, his legs sprawled awkwardly beneath him, lying far too still.

Taka looked closely at the arrow sticking out of Mitsu's shoulder, and thought she could guess why his breathing might have stopped, but she didn't take time to speculate or to speak. She maneuvered herself to Mitsu's side, gently pushing Mishi farther away from the wound so that she could have full access to it, but not so far that it would prevent Mishi from touching him. If Mishi was lending him her kisō, as Taka suspected, it wasn't something she wanted to interrupt. It might be the only thing giving him the strength to function right now.

Taka closed her eyes, pressing her hand to Mitsu's exposed neck and sending her kisō spreading easily through his body. She was relieved to find his heart still beating, but unsurprised to find his lungs unmoving. Between the arrow embedded in his right lung, and the impact of his fall to the wooden decking that circled the wall halfway up, she didn't think his lungs would be moving without help anytime soon. She would have to work quickly.

She felt Mishi's kisō brush against her own, and she took a moment to direct it, without words, to the beating of Mitsu's heart. Mishi couldn't manipulate Mitsu's blood the way that Taka could, but she could give the heart the energy it needed to continue, even with a stalled blood flow, and that would help Taka immensely as she worked to heal his lungs and get them back to working on their own.

She took a deep breath and focused her kisō on the area around the arrow shaft. Then she looked up, opening her eyes.

"You," she said to the nearest warrior, who stood waiting for his turn at the archery slot. "I need you to come break this arrow and pull it from his shoulder—can you do it?"

She couldn't focus on all the repair work she would need to do while also breaking and removing the arrow cleanly herself.

The archer, who had greying hair and a small scar coming from the corner of his mouth, said nothing, but he nodded and stepped forward. She supposed that, if he were old enough and had seen real battle, he might not be unused to removing arrows from his fellows.

Taka kept most of her focus on the internal war being waged within Mitsu's chest, doing her best to keep more blood from finding its way into the lungs themselves, even as the archer went to work breaking the arrow and pulling it from Mitsu. Luckily, Mitsu was unconscious already, and he did little to struggle against the painful procedure.

Taka worked as quickly as she could, after that, and only took a brief moment to mentally thank Kusuko and all the kami for bringing her here in time to save Mitsu. There was much to be done. She did her best to bring the tissues of his lung together, so that they would seal well enough to take in air once more, as well as sealing the blood vessels that had been severed by the path of the arrow. She tried to clean up the blood that had already leaked its way into Mitsu's lungs, but there was only so much she could do at one time, and getting the flesh to heal enough so that his lungs could move on their own had to be her top priority.

Eventually, she felt Mishi's kisō flagging, and knew that her friend had already pushed herself beyond what was reasonable.

"Mishi-san, you've done very well. Stay with me here, and hold his hand, but that's enough kisō from you. He won't thank me if I let you kill yourself, and I can do the rest."

Taka didn't open her eyes, or stop her treatment, as she said this, and she hoped that Mishi wouldn't object. She barely had the energy to continue her work, let alone argue with a stubborn Kisōshi. She, Kusuko, and the children had been traveling non-stop for the past day and a half, and she had little energy to spare.

Taka didn't think it was a good sign for Mishi's health that she did as she was asked immediately, but she waved the thought away and continued to focus on Mitsu.

She now had to keep his heart running while she finished the repairs on his blood vessels. She would need to get his lungs moving again soon, though. The blood that she was circulating through his body via his heart didn't have enough oxygen in it, and would soon fail to do its job.

So she left off cleaning up blood vessels, and instead asked Mishi to use Mitsu's own uwagi to bind the hole that remained close to the skin. She had healed most of the internal damage, but she would have to rest before she could bind up the outer wound. For now, she would have to rely on the pressure of the securely tied garment. Mishi responded quickly, setting about the process while Taka continued to work with the internal torn flesh and the heart.

When Mishi was done, Taka decided it was time.

"Mishi, I need you to pinch Mitsu's nose closed and breathe into his lungs for him."

"What?"

Taka was still focused on keeping Mitsu's heart beating, so she didn't open her eyes to inspect her friend's expression, though she imagined it was confused.

"Tilt his head until his mouth opens, then place your mouth over his so that it covers it completely, and then breathe the air from your lungs into his."

She didn't think Mishi would be squeamish about the procedure, but she realized it might be a difficult thing to understand from a simple verbal explanation. If Taka could have done it herself while still keeping the rest of Mitsu's vital organs going, she would have, but she was too exhausted from all her efforts to heal him so far, and she didn't want to risk letting his heart stop its rhythm.

Mishi didn't ask any further questions, as the second explanation apparently sufficed, and after a moment she heard her friend take a great breath of air and then exhale it forcefully.

"Now sit back!" Taka added, hoping she'd spoken in time.

Taka hadn't performed this breath on many patients, but the few that she had performed it on had vomited blood or water shortly after their lungs had restarted.

She could sense the air that had been forced into Mitsu's lungs, and only broke contact when he turned and coughed up blood onto the deck. She opened her eyes and saw that Mishi had, in fact, turned him, and that Mitsu's eyes were still closed.

"He's breathing," Taka whispered.

Mishi said nothing, but she nodded, her hand still on Mitsu's shoulder.

Taka closed her eyes again, this time in exhaustion, and let the tears slide quietly down her cheeks. After a moment, she felt Mishi's hand grab hers, and she let out a deep breath that she hadn't known she'd been holding.

⇒ Mishi ⇐

Mishi took a deep breath and looked around her. When Mitsu had begun breathing again, it felt as though the world had suddenly opened up to include something other than the tiny circle of Mitsu, Mishi, and Taka.

He was still unconscious, but he was breathing on his own, and Taka was right here. Mishi took a long look at her friend.

"How?" she asked, unsure of how to finish the question, but knowing that Taka would understand her.

"Kusuko-san," Taka replied. "She woke me in the middle of the night, and told me that you and Mitsu were in grave danger."

Mishi didn't answer for a moment, wondering, silently, how in the world Kusuko had known about the danger in time for them to get here, but before she could voice her concerns, Taka continued on her own.

"We only stopped moving long enough to alert the New Council troops that we encountered on their way to the Zōkame estate, and tell them that they were needed to apprehend a horde of sanzoku."

At that piece of news, Mishi's jaw dropped, all questions about Kusuko's sources forgotten.

"You brought New Council soldiers with you?" she asked.

Taka nodded.

"They're riding in behind the sanzoku to take them by surprise. Kusuko and I came ahead."

"How many men? And how did you get through the sanzoku and past the gates?"

"Seventy-five men, but they're all trained Kisōshi. Kusuko and I found a set of tunnels that led us under the wall. She seemed to know where they were, but she didn't mention how. I decided to ask her...later."

Mishi thought about that reply, deciding that Taka had her own reasons for trusting or not trusting Kusuko-san. It wasn't her place to question that trust, at the moment. Instead, she decided to focus on more urgent issues.

"Seventy-five trained Kisōshi might help us turn the tide of this battle, but if Mitsu and I aren't defending the wall, it may not be enough."

Taka's face paled a bit.

"It's that bad?" she asked.

Mishi nodded.

"Didn't you see, as you came in?"

Taka shook her head.

"We went north through the woods, and then found the tunnels that Kusuko knew of. We never got close enough to the sanzoku to see them. We didn't want to risk the children, or ourselves, if they should decide to attack us."

"The children?" she asked.

"We had to bring them. We had no safe place to leave them. I had just taken them to Inari-san when I felt you calling for me."

Just as Mishi began to wonder if the children were safe with Inari-san, a high-pitched keening stole her attention, and a flash of wings and wind landed on Taka's arm.

Mishi knew better than to ask what Riyōshi was saying until Taka volunteered it, so even though she was desperate to know what information the hawk had brought them, she waited.

When Taka turned to look at her, there was a smile ghosting her lips and eyes.

"There are a hundred New Council soldiers headed to the western gate."

20日 3月 新議 1年

20th Day, 3rd Moon, Cycle 1 of the New Council

~ Kusuko ~

KUSUKO RESISTED THE urge to shift her weight, as she knelt on the tatami floor in Inari's receiving room. She was sure she was being watched, but even if she were not, her training would not allow her to demonstrate that kind of discomfort, no matter how long she was kept waiting, kneeling on a floor in full kimono. Instead, she focused on the peaceful paintings that decorated the wall ahead of her, and the pleasant scent of grass mats on a warm day. She pointedly ignored the sensation of bloodless legs that hadn't been allowed to move since she'd been led to this room, over a candleburn ago.

It was convenient, she thought, that Inari was the Kisōshi in charge of this town, at least in terms of her needing to report to him. It was perfectly reasonable that she be asked to meet with him after helping to save Shikazenji from destruction. Besides, Taka and her friends all knew that she was associated with Inari somehow, so fooling them was no longer part of her concern.

What did concern her was that she had never known that Inari maintained the persona of a Kisōshi with a holding. She had known him her entire life, and she had never once heard him speak of this place, or these people.

She thought she shouldn't be surprised, really, considering Inari's occupation, and the intentionally limited ways in which they'd interacted, but it seemed like the kind of information she should have learned, especially given the number of times that she had spied on the man.

Finally, Inari entered the room, dressed in his usual golden hakama and white uwagi, katana and wakizashi at his side. He folded himself to the floor before her, bowing a polite amount before looking her in the eyes.

"I'm surprised to see you here," he said.

His face was the usual blank puzzle that he presented when receiving a report, and Kusuko once more fought the urge to shift her weight, though this time from nerves rather than the discomfort in her knees. She wasn't sure how much Inari knew about the orders she had received from Mamushi-san, or how he would feel about her choices. There was a chance, she thought, since the results of her choices had saved this town, that Inari would agree with her decisions and withhold the truth from her father. She didn't think it was likely, since Inari had worked with Mamushi-san for so many cycles. The likelihood that he held the same "practical" views as her father, that he wouldn't take into account his own emotional ties to the town, and would only be concerned with the fact that she hadn't followed her orders, was still quite high. Most importantly, she needed to come up with an explanation that didn't let on how much her decision had been based on her desire to protect Taka. If it got back to Mamushi-san that she had tried to protect Taka's friends…she might as well paint targets on them all, and invite a team of hishi to their sleeping quarters.

"I'm surprised to find *you* here, Inari-san. I would never have guessed you led such a peaceful existence outside of your work."

Inari laughed, which caught Kusuko off guard. She had expected more of his careful blankness.

"Would you call it peaceful, then, to be besieged by hundreds of sanzoku?"

Kusuko allowed a smirk to play across her mouth.

"Is that a regular occurrence here?" she asked. "Do you always have sanzoku surrounding your town?"

The smile didn't fade from Inari's mouth, but some of the mirth left his eyes.

"The reason I built a wall around this town is indeed because we face an inordinate number of mountain bandits, and the like. As you've no doubt ascertained, my work requires that I often leave my town without its primary defense—me. I decided that the simplest solution was to build a wall that could be defended even without a Kisōshi presence. Though I'm afraid I never expected anything like the mass of enemies that came upon us yesterday."

"Indeed," Kusuko replied. "Yesterday's numbers were entirely *unpredictable*."

She let the emphasis of that word sit for a moment, hoping that Inari would take her meaning. After all, the last time that she had seen him, he'd been deep in the mountains, along with the rest of them. Had he known in advance that his own town would be attacked, or was it merely coincidence that he'd returned home before the sanzoku had arrived?

"And yet, you and Taka-san arrived with reinforcements just in time to save us all," he said, turning her trap around on her.

She didn't sigh, but she wanted to.

"I had my orders," she said, wanting to see if Inari actually knew what they had been.

"And did those orders instruct you to arrive here with New Council soldiers in tow?"

"My orders are none of your business," she snapped. It was a risky move, but the truth was she didn't officially report to Inari-san. She had started doing it only to save him the trouble of spying on her, and to leave herself the chance to misinform him, if necessary. She reported directly to Mamushi-san and no one else.

Inari-san bowed his head slightly, though it was difficult to tell if the movement was one of agreement, or deferral. She supposed it didn't really matter. A silence stretched between them for a long time.

"Have I ever told you about the two times I directly disobeyed the orders Mamushi-san gave to me?"

Kusuko didn't allow her face to register the surprise she felt, but it took all of her lifetime of training to prevent it. She shook her head.

"I'm certain you haven't," she said, trying to sound disinterested.

Inari-san took a deep breath, and then began to speak.

"It was long ago. I was your age...perhaps slightly older. You know that I've never minded contradicting Mamushi-san, and as long as I only do so in private, he has allowed it. But there were

Traitor's Hope

some orders that neither of us had the power to contradict. Things that neither of us could stop, whether we would have or not. I don't know how often Mamushi-san wished to go against these orders. You know him well enough to know he doesn't discuss his choices, or his views. Yet there are things that I've been asked to do that I have flatly refused, in private, and when this happens Mamushi-san simply assigns another hishi to do it. So my refusal has no effect on whether or not the thing is done, only whether I am the one who has to do it. But that is now. There was a time when I didn't know the world well enough to know that there were things even a hishi should not have to do. Times when the idea of something proved to be very, very different from the reality.

"I was once given an assignment that took me to a tiny village, not at all far from here. I, and a handful of my fellow hishi, were instructed to burn down a small cabin, and kill anyone who tried to escape the flames."

Inari paused in his story, to gauge her response, but Kusuko simply intensified her stare in a silent bid for Inari to continue.

"I wasn't the one to start the fire, nor was I the one who hunted down the two adults who were in the cabin when they tried to escape, but I was the one charged with eliminating the two children who were supposedly residing within. The first, a child of about five cycles of age, had been removed and deposited in a log outside of the home. I knew what I was charged with, but could not bring myself to do it. Duty or not, it seemed a monstrous task. I left him there, and did not inform my associates as to his whereabouts. The other child, a tiny girl of around two cycles of age, was pulled from her mother's arms by one of my fellows and I took her from him, promising to dispose of her. And I did, after a fashion…I took her to an orphanage, almost a tenday away, and left her there, hopeful that no one would ever think to look for her."

Kusuko didn't let the dawning realization show on her face, but her mind raced as she tried to align all that she knew of Mitsu and Taka's childhood with the man sitting before her. A man she'd thought she'd known her entire life.

"And the second time?"

"Not long after that, a few moons at most, I was sent on another assignment that was centered on killing an infant...but this time I volunteered."

Kusuko only raised an eyebrow, but that was as good as screaming "why?!?" as far as she was concerned.

"Not one of all my fellow hishi had thought it strange, or wrong, that we'd been asked to murder children on that assignment a few moons before. Of course, perhaps they just hadn't thought much about it, since I had been the one asked to accomplish the task. But I couldn't abide the idea of yet another small innocent life being taken for no good reason. I decided that I would volunteer for the very next assignment that required it, and try my hand at hiding a child again."

Kusuko was awed into silence at this point, but luckily Inari chose to continue anyway.

"Yet again, I was not alone on this assignment, and my fellows were responsible for killing the adults. Yet again, I did nothing to stop it. But I had once more been assigned to taking the life of a child, this one a girl of only one cycle, possibly less, still a babe in arms. She was hidden well by her parents, and it took me some time to find her. That turned out to be lucky, as it meant that most of my companions had finished their assignments, and made their own escapes. The whole incident was meant to look as though the small family had been set upon by bandits, and our orders had been to leave the scene as soon as we'd taken care of our part. I was left to sift through the wreckage of the carriage that had been overturned and set alight, and I just barely found the infant before she was engulfed in flame. I took her to the same orphanage where I'd taken the first girl, only because I'd been able to drop her there in the middle of the night before, and no one had seen me arriving or leaving."

Kusuko didn't recognize any part of this second story, except that the age of the second girl would have been right for Mishi, based on the story Taka had told her. The idea that Inari-san had saved the lives of those two girls astounded her. It defied everything that she'd known about the hishi and the laws that bound and governed them. Added to that was the thought that Inari had directly helped two people whose lives had become inextricably linked to her own. She was dumbfounded.

"How many others did you save?" she asked at length, curious how Inari could have gone about rescuing girls without further defying Mamushi-san's orders. He'd said that he'd only done so twice.

"None," Inari said placidly, though the regret in his voice was audible to one who knew him as well as Kusuko did. "I do not know if Mamushi-san realized what I was doing, or if it was mere coincidence, but I was never again assigned to a mission that required the death of a child, after I rescued the second girl. I assume that Mamushi-san knew, and did not wish to punish me, but could not allow me to continue and risk being discovered. Regardless, that was the end of my attempts to play the hero."

"What made you do it?" Kusuko asked, after pausing to think about what it all meant for a moment. She couldn't understand how a trained hishi could choose to forget his conditioning so easily. They were not meant to judge their orders, only to carry them out. It was up to the hishi leader to decide if an order was appropriate or not. No individual hishi was allowed to make that judgment, else the whole group would fail in their mission, which was unacceptable. She'd been raised with that mentality, and she knew better than to question it, or at least, she'd thought she had known better.

Yet how different had her own actions been over the past few days? She hadn't contradicted her orders, precisely. She'd been informed that the attack meant to trap Mishi and Mitsu was coming, and to be sure to protect Taka. Yet instead of quietly moving on to the Zōkame estate, she had woken Taka and told her what was coming. And why? Because of her own personal feelings? Wasn't that worse than disregarding an order because she thought it was wrong? Or was it the same thing? She was making a judgment call. She had decided that Mitsu and Mishi didn't deserve to die. What gave her the right to make that choice?

"The person I was then wouldn't have been able to live with himself if he'd killed those children," Inari said simply. "It's not a choice that I regret, especially now that I've met the results. Indeed, I think

I would have regretted the alternative far more, had that been my choice."

Kusuko's eyes snapped to Inari's face, as that comment pulled her from her own musings. So, Inari knew who he'd saved all those cycles ago. Interesting.

"What choices will you regret, Hifu-chan?" Inari asked, as he rose to his feet, heading to the sliding door on the wall behind him. "Don't let your father's obligations betray your soul."

⇀ Mishi ⇁

Mishi's eyes were locked on Mitsu's face, pale in the soft dawn light that permeated the room of the small ryokan where they had been placed the night before, the air filled with the herby scent of the healing salve that Taka had applied to Mitsu's wound.

Inari had offered for them to stay in his private residence, but Taka had insisted that it would be best if her patient didn't have to be moved very far, and the ryokan was a short distance from where Mitsu had fallen. Mishi refused to leave Mitsu's side.

She had spent the night sleepless, legs folded beside the small futon on which he slept, her own exhaustion forgotten as her mind repeated the same horrid scene, over and over again.

Mitsu falling away from her, an arrow in his shoulder. Mitsu hitting the deck below her, blood trickling from his mouth. Mitsu not breathing, his kisō distant, as though he were standing half a league away from her rather than lying right in front of her.

Eventually those scenes had muddled and merged with other horrors—Sachi crying as poison flowed through her body and her end drew near, Kuma-sensei being run through by a sword, a parade of unnamed soldiers that she had put an end to. It hadn't been a restful night, by any stretch of the imagination.

And then, sometime around dawn, she had begun to contemplate what would have happened if Mitsu hadn't started breathing again, what would happen if he didn't wake up again, despite all of Taka's healing efforts.

Even imagining it brought on a hollow feeling that she knew all too well. She cursed herself then, for having allowed Mitsu into her heart. She realized that without wanting to, and in fact having tried to avoid it, she had allowed Mitsu a place in her soul that could hurt her just as easily as the loss of Sachi-san and Kuma-sensei had. She laughed then, silently, mirthlessly, thinking about how little control she seemed to have over these parts of herself. She could no more stop caring for people than she could stop the dreams in which she relived all of their deaths.

She didn't want it, though. She didn't want this hollow feeling that came from even the *thought* of losing Mitsu. The same hollow feeling that persisted, moons later, in the wake of the deaths of Sachi-san and Kuma-sensei. She didn't want any of it.

And besides, how could Mitsu possibly want her? Knowing all that was wrong with her, how could he wish for her company? He couldn't care for her the way he said he did, at least not now that he knew what she truly was.

She looked up then, to see his eyes open and a smile beginning on his lips.

"Mishi-san," he said, in a voice that sounded rough, incapable of more than a harsh whisper.

Without meaning to, she found that she'd placed her hand over his.

"I'm here," she whispered.

"Did we win?"

She smiled then, and squeezed the hand that lay at his side, unmoving.

"Yes, Mitsu-san, we won."

"And did Taka arrive and save my life?"

Mishi nodded.

"She did."

"I'm the luckiest big brother in all the world," he said, still smiling.

"Indeed, and Taka will likely remind you of it for the rest of your days."

"Oh? Do you think so?"

"She still reminds me of the time she put out a fire I started in our orphanage, before I'd learned to control it properly."

"Well, I suppose I can't complain, really, even if she does," he said.

"Nor should you," Mishi replied, smiling. "Besides, you're on strict orders to rest until that wound has fully healed, and complaining is probably not on the list of approved restful activities."

"Hmm…you're likely right."

He closed his eyes for a moment, and when he opened them again he was no longer smiling.

"Mishi-san, when I first awoke you looked sad. May I ask what's troubling you?"

Mishi smiled at how politely he phrased the question. Of course, she didn't really want to explain what she'd been thinking about when he'd woken, but she thought she owed him her honesty, if nothing else.

"I was thinking about how many things we think and feel aren't truly under our control," she began, glancing up from where her gaze had been locked on his hand under hers, and finding his gaze locked on her face.

The corners of his mouth quirked slightly.

"Ah yes, an issue I'm quite familiar with," he said, turning his gaze to the ceiling and then closing his eyes, as though the effort of keeping them open was too much for him.

"Well," Mishi continued hesitantly, "I…I'm afraid, I think." And as she said it, she realized that it was true. "I'm afraid of the pain of losing the people I care about, and whether I meant to or not, I've added you to the list of people I care about. It already scares me to think of how much it would hurt to lose you. I'm terrified of what might happen if I start to care for you any more than I already do."

And that was it, she realized. She had planned to explain that she was also a monster and that she didn't deserve the love that Mitsu offered her, but as she explained her fear she realized that her own shortcomings were just an excuse. Mitsu knew his own mind, and he could no more control how he felt about her than she could control how she felt about him. To say she didn't deserve it meant nothing in the equation, even if she truly felt that way. What really bothered her was the fear, almost overwhelming, that she could lose whatever might grow between them, along with losing Mitsu himself.

She was so sick of the ache of loss.

"That's an honest answer," Mitsu said, after a long moment. "And I like it better than the idea that you think you're a monster who doesn't deserve to be loved. Not that my liking it makes it more valid, but...well, I know how you feel. The pain isn't as recent for me, but...it took me until I met Taka-san to ever let myself care for another person again, and even then.... You know, you weren't the only one to have a deep heart-to-heart with Yanagi-sensei while we were in his forest."

"Oh?" Mishi was briefly embarrassed that she had been so absorbed in her own troubles that she hadn't noticed that Mitsu was also in distress. "What did you discuss with him?"

"Well, a number of things, but one of them was how much it terrified me to have a sister, and...a friend who I found more than a little attractive."

"Terrified you?" Mishi asked.

"Losing my family once was hard enough. Having the potential for it to happen again...frightens me."

He took a deep breath before continuing.

"But Yanagi-sensei informed me that I was being foolish, and that if I had found people who cared about me despite all my many flaws, then I should be overjoyed, rather than frightened."

Mishi laughed. She could imagine Yanagi-sensei delivering the lecture.

"And did he enumerate your many flaws?" she asked.

Mitsu gave a slight nod, and the corners of his mouth turned up.

"Oh yes. I believe pigheaded and foolish were in there, at least once. I'm not sure. He went on for a bit."

He paused for a time, and Mishi wondered if he'd fallen asleep. She started to take her hand away from his, but found that his grip tightened. When she looked up again, he was looking straight at her.

"I expected to be rejected for all of those things, and more. You accept those things about me, or maybe you just haven't realized them yet...but instead you would reject me because you share the same fear that I do. The whole notion is sad enough to be almost comical."

But he wasn't smiling, and he wasn't dropping her gaze, either. Mishi thought she'd never been scrutinized so closely, and she shivered under his gaze, both warmed and chilled at the same time.

Finally, he looked away, to the ceiling once more, and closed his eyes.

"Will you really live your whole life alone, simply to prevent the pain of losing someone?" he asked.

"Are you asking me, or yourself?" she asked, before she could think better of it.

She saw the corners of his mouth turn up again, even though he kept his eyes closed and his face toward the ceiling.

"I've already answered that question for myself. Yanagi-sensei asked it of me, over and over again, as I wallowed in…whatever it was I was wallowing in. And I answered it the moment I decided to travel with you. If I'm not willing to risk that kind of pain again, I may as well die now. It would be less tiresome, and more peaceful. I don't wish to die, though. So, I chose to have a sister, and a friend, and…perhaps more than that, if you ever wish it."

Mishi didn't know what to say to that, so she said nothing at all. Eventually Mitsu drifted into sleep once more.

~~~

Mishi looked out from the top of the northern gate, at the trampled road and vegetation extending away from Shikazenji, and took a deep breath. She was relieved to find the air free of the scent of burning flesh, singed cloth, and spilled blood. The gate stood open beneath her, and the road was empty as far as the eye could see.

She could almost believe that yesterday hadn't happened. Almost.

How quickly things had moved, once the New Council's reinforcements had arrived. Mishi had been relieved beyond words that their leader was high ranking enough to take care of the sanzoku's surrender, custody, and transport, instead of her.

Now they simply had to hope that the force they had apprehended actually represented the bulk of the sanzoku who had been destroying villages throughout this region. She thought it likely that they did. She found it difficult to imagine too many more camps of sanzoku littered throughout the mountains, burning villages to the ground. The number that they had dealt with yesterday was more than sufficient for the damage that had been done to this region.

"When does Zōkame-san expect us to report?" Mitsu asked, from beside her.

She'd sensed him approaching, but hadn't bothered to turn, even when he'd reached the top of the small steps that allowed them to see clearly above the wall.

"Aren't you supposed to be resting?" she asked, her eyes still locked on the road leading away from the town.

"Strong words, coming from someone Taka-san lectured this morning about not overtaxing herself."

Mishi let a small smile reach her lips. It was true. Taka had reminded her sternly, that very morning, that she was to do as little as possible beyond eating and sleeping, so that she would be fully rested for the journey to unite Mizu and Tsuchi with the Zokames. Mishi had pushed her kisō almost to the breaking point too many times over the past few tendays.

"I've only come to look at the view," she said. "And I'm not the one who almost died yesterday."

Mitsu let out a harsh laugh.

"No. It's been five whole days since the last time you almost died."

She turned to look at him then, something in the way his voice had faltered drawing her eyes to his face.

She could read the emotions there easily enough, after their last conversation, and it finally sank in that Mitsu truly did fear the same things that she did. He feared caring for her, because he feared losing her, and he had experienced the threat of it as viscerally as she had yesterday. She took some comfort in knowing that his fears were her fears.

"Would you ask me not to risk myself?" she asked, wondering, even as she asked it, what she hoped his answer would be.

"Never," Mitsu replied, without hesitation. "I have no right to ask it of you, and never would."

In hearing his reply, Mishi knew that it was the right one. She wouldn't ask Mitsu not to risk himself, either. She only hoped that he would recognize that the people who cared about him would be devastated if any harm came to him, and count that in the way he weighed whatever risks he faced.

When she said as much aloud, Mitsu nodded.

"That sounds reasonable to me."

She wondered then if this was what it was like, to care about someone and decide to become a part of their life, to allow them to become a part of yours. Was one always establishing what rights one had to the other person? Did one ever really have rights to the other person at all?

"I don't know how to do any of this," she said, before her brain could stop her mouth.

"Do what?" Mitsu asked.

"Be whatever it is we're becoming," she said, her eyes focused on the woods that spread out from the town. "I don't want marriage, and I can't see myself ever having children, and...I don't know how long any of this will last. What if you stop caring for me someday? What if I stop caring for you?"

"Are those reasons not to care for me now?" Mitsu asked, his voice quiet behind her.

"No, they're just concerns. I want to be honest with you. I don't want you to expect anything from me that I can't give."

"Would it make you feel better to know that I have the same concerns? I don't know how to do any of this either. I've never pictured myself with children, nor have I pictured myself living in a house in a village. I like the woods, and I like to wander. Would you be willing to wander with me?"

Mishi laughed, then.

"And what have I been doing, the past few moons?"

"Good point."

Mitsu's smile was wide.

"I do want to resume the mission that I first set out to accomplish after the battle of Rōjū City, though. I want to seek out female Kisōshi and help them find the training they need. Would you consent to traveling roads, instead of forest trails, and occasionally sleeping under a roof, instead of the stars?"

"And what have *I* been doing the past few moons?"

For a moment Mishi's smile echoed his, and then it faded.

Traitor's Hope

"We're getting ahead of ourselves," she said. "We still don't know what the New Council will ask of us next, and before that we need to see Mizu-chan and Tsuchi-kun safely to the Zōkames."

"True," Mitsu said, but his smile hadn't faded. "But we can do all of that together, should you wish it."

Mishi met his eyes, which were tinged with a hope that would have hurt her heart, if she had felt inclined to give a different answer than the one she had ready.

"It seems to me that I've no more excuses for turning you away," she said, letting a glimmer of mischief show in her eyes. "And Taka probably wouldn't forgive me if I told her we had to leave you behind."

"You'll take pity on me, then?" he asked.

"Never," she replied, smiling.

He didn't say anything in response, but slowly leaned forward, his eyes never leaving hers, asking silently for a permission that Mishi granted by closing her own eyes, and leaning toward him. Mitsu's lips slowly closed on hers, and she felt a delicious warmth spread through her. She pressed more closely against him, his arms enfolding her, even as she reached her hands up his back, pulling him closer.

A low whistle from behind made them pull apart abruptly. Mishi turned, her cheeks flushing red against her will. They'd been doing nothing wrong, but somehow the knowledge that someone had been watching them made her face warm unpleasantly. She glowered at the source of the sound, surprised to find that it came from Inari-san.

"Pardon the interruption, Ryūko-san," he said, while climbing the stairs from the street, as though he hadn't just wolf-whistled them and was only disturbing a friendly chat. "I've been asked to ascertain how much longer you intend to stay with us in Shikazenji."

He smiled politely, as he reached the top of the staircase and stood expectantly beneath them.

"And who is sending the highest ranked Kisōshi in Shikazenji off on such menial errands?" Mishi asked, trying to banish the hostility she felt toward the man for interrupting her conversation with Mitsu.

Inari-san smiled genially, and Mishi wondered if it was only his training as a hishi that enabled him to dissemble so well, or if he came to it naturally.

"My wife, I'm afraid. She has asked me to invite you to join us for the evening meal tonight, if you will be staying with us for a while longer yet."

Mishi did her best to rein in her surprise at discovering that Inari-san was married. She had assumed, perhaps because she had first met him in the role of a spy and assassin, that he would be unattached. Yet, she found that the idea of a wife went well with the persona that Inari-san seemed to have cultivated here in the town, where he was a respected Kisōshi. She shook her head, as if the action might reconcile the two distinctly different impressions she had of the man.

"We were planning on staying one more night, at the least, while we recover from our injuries," Mishi said. "We would like to be as hale as possible for our travels."

Inari nodded, smiling again, to all appearances the generous host.

"Well, then, my wife and I would welcome you at our home this evening if it is convenient, along with Taka-san, Kusuko-san, and the two children, should they be available to join you."

Mishi only nodded, not sure what to make of the invitation, but luckily Mitsu had his wits about him enough to make a coherent response.

"We're honored by the invitation, and look forward to joining you and your wife over a meal. I'm sure that Kusuko-san, Taka-san, and the children will be delighted to join us as well."

Inari-san seemed pleased with that answer, and he bowed respectfully before taking his leave.

"You're not used to formal invitations, are you?" Mitsu asked, when she turned to him once more.

Mishi sighed, chuckling lightly.

"I was trained with the notion that I would be a servant my whole life, as far as anyone else knew. I didn't need to answer formal invitations, only pass them from one person to another. And…I admit that if Kuma-sensei and Tenshi-san tried to teach me any of the more formal rules of society, I may have been running through sword drills in my head instead of paying proper attention."

Mitsu nodded.

"I had to convey messages by ear and mouth only, so I had to memorize all kinds of formal wording."

"Useful," Mishi admitted, staring him up and down. "I suppose I should keep you around."

Mitsu's eyes lit with…something…at that thought, and Mishi tried to fight the heat that rose within her in response.

"I suppose we should go and tell the others about our evening meal plans," Mishi suggested, as she turned to walk down the steps that would take her to the street below. Out of the corner of her eye, she saw Mitsu's hand shoot out beside her. He didn't touch her, only held it there, waiting.

She looked up into his eyes, seeing a simple request.

"For balance?" she asked.

He nodded, and she took his hand in hers.

1日 4月 新議 1年
1st Day, 4th Moon, Cycle 1 of the New Council

～Mishi～

MISHI TOOK A deep breath scented with tatami and the distant smell of cooking rice, and worked to repress the memories that had been trying to flood her ever since her return to Rōjū City. Then she folded herself down before the slightly raised dais at the end of the receiving room, taking a brief moment to appreciate the mountain scenery that decorated the screens on the far wall, and touched her forehead to the floor.

"That's too much deference for someone of kitsune rank to show to a tora-dan," Zōkame-san's voice rumbled. Mishi sat up, looked him in the eyes, and rolled hers.

"If I'm not behaving as a proper kitsune-dan, it might be because someone promoted me beyond my experience."

Zōkame laughed, then.

"There now, that's better."

Mishi smiled, wondering what had made her respond in such a way to Zōkame Yasuhiko. By all rights, she should be much more respectful to him, but there was something in him that reminded her of Kuma-sensei, and Kuma-sensei had always appreciated it when she failed to defer to him on trivial matters.

She was glad to see that Yasuhiko did as well, though the whole exchange created a pang of longing in her, as it brought fond memories of Kuma-sensei to the forefront.

Yasuhiko's eyes lost some of their mischievous glimmer as he watched her, and she wondered how obvious her grief must be, for him to react so.

"I miss him as well," was all Zōkame-san said on the matter, but it was enough to know that the old Kisōshi had followed her line of thinking, and her unrestrained emotions, clearly enough.

"I'm sorry, Zōkame-san, for bringing our thoughts to such a sad topic."

"Hmph, there is no need to apologize, Ryūko-san. Let alone so formally."

"You insist I'm being too formal, yet call me by my formal name?" she asked, feeling annoyed at being corrected again for being too formal, when, if anything, it was her impertinence that needed correction.

"It is not your formal name. It is just your name. Your parents named you Ryūko, and I will not abandon their wishes simply because you were raised to the age of eight without knowing your true name. Kuma-sensei taught you your name cycles ago, and you should not be ashamed of it."

Mishi bowed her head slightly, in deference and agreement, unable to argue with Zōkame-san when the points he made were true. It was only that she didn't feel like Ryūko was really her, she had always thought of herself as Mishi. She thought she might adjust to the name in time, but she hadn't yet, eight cycles after learning it. Of course, it didn't help that almost no one she knew addressed her as Ryūko, and never had.

"I'm not ashamed of it," she said, at length. "I'm just not used to it."

"And you will never become so, if you do not begin to use it."

Mishi only nodded. It was a valid point.

"I'm glad to see you here so soon. We feared that our messengers would have missed you on your travels, and that you would go all the way to our estate before finding yourselves asked to turn around and join us here in the city."

"Luckily, since we were delayed a number of days in order to allow Mitsu to recover, they found us in Shikazenji before we had departed."

Mishi was unconvinced that it had truly been lucky, since she would have preferred to delay their arrival in Rōjū City even longer. It was a place that—for her, anyway—was crowded with ghosts.

"Now then, Ryūko-san, your report please," Yasuhiko-san asked, with a slight bow.

Mishi sat up straighter, locking eyes with Yasuhiko-san.

"Have you had anyone else's report yet?" she asked.

"The Kisōshi commanding the reinforcements that apprehended the sanzoku have reported to Tsuku-san, along with Kusuko-san, and some of my own spies. But don't let that stop you from giving a full account of the events since you left us here. Tsuku-san is meeting with Taka-san as we speak, and I wish to know all the details of your journey, and everything leading up to the attack, not to mention the details of your defense of the town."

Mishi nodded, and began her account of the past moon's worth of activity. She had a feeling that Zōkame was familiar with everything that she told him, until she reached the part about the babies who had been taken from their mother's arms in Shikazenji.

"How many children were being taken to the gates?" he asked, when she mentioned the baby girls for the first time.

"Two," she replied.

"But you only brought one girl here with you."

"The two babies were too young to be taken from their mothers, Zōkame-san. The one I brought with us is one of the twins that Mitsu and I rescued from the first razed village we found." She hadn't yet mentioned that they believed the twins to be Kiko-san's children. She thought it wasn't her place to mention it, and was sure that Taka would cover that part in her report. "The two babies in Shikazenji stayed with their mothers, who promised to accompany them south to Ami-san's school after the rainy season, once they were old enough to walk."

"I see. They did not wish to accompany you now?"

"No. The mothers wished to prepare for the journey better. I offered to return and escort them, should they wish, but they insisted that they would not need it. I think I may return this way for them at the end of the rainy season, just in case. They seemed interested in the training, even if they were a bit shocked to learn that their daughters would be trained to fight as full Kisōshi."

Yasuhiko-san nodded, and thought for a moment.

"And the two children you brought here?"

Traitor's Hope

"Twins. One girl and one boy. Both Kisōshi, both yukisō. Taka will be taking them to train as healers at the school where she has been asked to teach..." Mishi hesitated. She wasn't sure what Yasuhiko would think of what she wanted to say next.

"What aren't you saying, Ryūko-san?"

"Well, I'm reluctant to mention it, Yasuhiko-sama, as it isn't my place, but..."

"I value your input, Ryūko-san, as does Tsuku-san. Please, speak freely."

"It's only that...the young girl, Mizu-chan. She's a water kisō, but...she wishes to learn to fight. On a whim I began teaching her some of the forms, and she's quite good...so, I began to wonder...why is it that only fire and wind kisō are trained as senkisō, while earth and water are trained as yukisō? Is there really an insurmountable difference, or is it only tradition? The forms are a bit harder with water and earth, but not impossible. If a child wishes to train as a senkisō instead of a yukisō, is it fair to force them to do the opposite?"

Yasuhiko-san seemed to think about this for a long while, and he remained silent for so long that Mishi worried that she had somehow offended him, or broken some taboo she was unaware of. When he finally spoke, his face told her nothing.

"Those are excellent questions, Ryūko-san, truly, though I'm afraid I don't have answers to them right now. I think *you* may be the key to answering many of those questions yourself. It sounds as though you have an apt pupil on your hands, so perhaps you should see how far your instruction takes her, and let us know the results. If all goes well with her, perhaps we can conclude that nothing but tradition separates yukisō from senkisō, and that there should be more choice in the paths open to any of us."

Mishi was so surprised by this answer that she couldn't speak for a moment. When she finally found her voice again, she stumbled over her words.

"I...hadn't planned to teach anyone to fight, Yasuhiko-sama. I had intended to take up Tenshi-san's task of finding young girls, or babies, in need of training and directing them to where they need to be."

"I see," Yasuhiko-san said. "Very well. I suppose we can ask someone else to take up the role of instructor for the child. Let me know if you change your mind. In the meantime, please bring the children to join us for the evening meal tonight; I would be interested to meet them, based on all that you've told me about them so far."

Mishi nodded. She thought the children would be happy to join them for the evening meal. Though they had been quite reticent at first, it seemed that with each female Kisōshi they met, the more they were willing to spend time with adults and speak in public.

"Continue, please," Zōkame-san said.

Mishi went on with a detailed description of how the battle had unfolded once she had convinced the townspeople to fight rather than hand over the young girls to the sanzoku. She took a deep breath, then described how the arrow had nearly killed Mitsu. She noticed that Zōkame-san paled visibly upon hearing the incident described in detail. She assumed that his other reports must have lacked the detail that hers possessed on this particular topic.

Eventually she described their tenday long journey here, to the city. After that, Mishi was unsure of what else Yasuhiko might wish to hear from her, though he continued to look at her expectantly.

"You say that you plan to take up Tenshi-san's mission after this, but I wonder if that will be enough."

"Enough?"

"Will that fulfill you, now?"

Mishi simply stared at Yasuhiko-san. She had wanted nothing more than that only a moon ago. She wanted to be left in peace, to find young girls with senkisō and send them to Ami and Katagi so that they could be trained. She hadn't wanted to ever have to draw her blade in violence again, or to use her kisō to hurt another.

She still didn't relish the idea of fighting, but it no longer terrified her the way that it had a moon ago, when she hadn't even trusted herself to be near a blade. And now that she'd been forced to fight again in self defense, it was difficult to think of a life completely devoid of her sword. Perhaps Mitsu would be willing to spar with her, on occasion. Would that be enough for her?

Traitor's Hope

"I don't know," she said, after a long silence. "I hadn't thought that far ahead."

"You don't have to choose right this moment," Yasuhiko said. "I simply wondered if you had considered your options."

For the past six moons or more, she'd been constantly on the move, and it had come to feel like her natural state of being. She wondered if she would ever feel comfortable in a single place again. She shook her head, trying to free herself from the thought, and looked to Yasuhiko once more.

"Is there anything else you'd like to discuss?" she asked, preparing to stand and take her leave.

"Yes, actually," Yasuhiko said, leaning forward, his face grim. "Tell me what you think of Kusuko-san."

Mishi's eyebrows rose in surprise, and her mind stumbled over the question. How was she supposed to answer that?

"She helped to save my life, more than once," she said carefully.

Yasuhiko nodded.

"And?"

"And...she seems fond of Taka-san," she added, unsure where this conversation was meant to lead. She wasn't sure why she was reluctant to tell Yasuhiko about her suspicions regarding Kusuko's loyalties. She knew that Kusuko had already made her report. Surely the young assassin hadn't turned herself in as a traitor, had she? But even if she had, what did he expect her to say? Mishi was reluctant to make accusations against Kusuko-san, though she wasn't sure why. Perhaps because she knew how close Taka had grown to the young woman, and she wanted to spare her the pain? That didn't make any sense. If Kusuko really was a traitor, then surely it would be better for Taka to know it now, rather than find out later, when she was even more involved with her, wasn't it? But, in truth, she had nothing concrete to report on the matter.

"I...question whether she is truly a *former* hishi. Indeed, I wonder if anyone can make such a claim," Mishi finally managed to choke out.

"Oh?" Yasuhiko said, his intonation suggesting that she should continue.

"She worked with Inari-san to save my life at the sanzoku camp, and she led Taka back to us along with a full complement of New Council soldiers…. Yet, I can't help but wonder…"

"Yes?"

"How did she know she was needed in either of those places, if she weren't still getting information from the enemy?"

Mishi said no more on the subject. Kusuko was obviously still a hishi, with a hishi master, but she wasn't sure that meant that the young woman couldn't be trusted. At least, not when it mattered most.

"I see," was all that Yasuhiko said.

⇒ Kusuko ⇐

Kusuko stared into the small koi pond, watching the golden and red fish swirl mindlessly in circles around each other. It was strange to be back in Rōjū City, somehow, though the place had always been her home. She hadn't gone to her own rooms yet, nor had she visited the hishi compound, or attempted to report to Mamushi-san. Instead, she waited in the small garden closest to the rooms that the Zōkame family occupied whenever they were in the city.

As she breathed in the fresh, earthy air that permeated the garden, she wondered when Tsuku-san and Yasuhiko-san, or the New Council—though they were almost one and the same—would decide to imprison her, or exile her.

If this government were run by anyone else, she would fear execution, instead, but she knew Tsuku-san and Yasuhiko-san too well to think that they would have her killed for her crimes. They were far too forgiving.

Was that the very reason that she found herself making the series of small decisions that were leading her away from Mamushi-san and his allies, and toward the New Council and its allies instead?

Or, was the reason a young healer, whose deep brown eyes drew her own in, just as easily as the dancing red and gold fish of this koi pond?

Traitor's Hope

The truth was, she didn't know, and she hated not knowing her own mind. She had never been this unclear before. She supposed this was the very weakness that Mamushi-san had always warned her of.

She knew it would be smart to leave Taka, and all the New Council allies, and return to her father. She knew that it would be the safest thing for her, and probably for Taka as well. She risked all of them, if she disobeyed Mamushi-san.

That decided her, then. She wouldn't risk everyone else. She would leave tonight. She would—

"They'll try to separate us again!"

Kusuko heard the voice of the girl child, Mizu-chan, coming from the other side of the tea house nestled into the trees behind her. She sounded upset. Concerned and curious, Kusuko silently moved closer to the small, open-windowed building.

"Mizu-chan, Taka-san said that we could stay together. That they wouldn't separate us. That we could both learn healing together."

Kusuko thought that voice sounded like Tsuchi-kun's.

"But I don't want to learn healing. I want to learn to fight, like Mishi-san."

"Well, they won't teach you to fight like Mishi-san if we run away again."

"They won't teach me to fight like Mishi-san anyway. They will send you off to learn with boys, and me to learn with girls, and they won't let us stay together."

"But they said they would."

"Adults lie, Tsuchi-kun. They lie to us all the time. Why would these adults be any different?"

"But they helped us!" Tsuchi sounded a bit desperate, and Kusuko wondered if he was always on the losing side of arguments with his twin sister. "And the last time that we tried to run away, those men captured us and were going to kill us."

"They were only after us because they wanted to capture Mishi-san."

"I thought they wanted to get rid of all female Kisōshi."

229

"Well anyway, all those men were captured outside of that walled town because of the men that Taka-san and Kusuko-san brought with them. It's safe now."

"I don't know, Mizu-chan. I don't like the idea of running away again."

"You want them to separate us, don't you? You don't care what they do with me, do you?"

"No! Mizu-chan, you know that's not true. I don't want them to separate us. Not ever. I want us both to be safe."

"Then we need to leave. Tonight, after everyone is asleep."

"I don't know—"

"If you don't come, I'm leaving without you."

Kusuko heard the stamp of little feet, then a pause, followed by more little feet running after the first set.

She sat on the step to the tea house, and thought for a moment. The information she now held could be valuable. Mamushi-san might find it useful to know that someone Taka cared for would be vulnerable very soon, especially if the Rōjū still hoped to bring her onto their side. Were they desperate, now that so many of their schemes had failed them? Or had they, perhaps, finally given up?

Even contemplating the idea of handing the two children over to the Rōjū made Kusuko feel strangely uncomfortable, as though she had swallowed something unpleasant. Then, she thought of telling Taka the children's plans, so that she might prevent any foolish risks the children might bring upon them all. She waited to see if this stirred any feelings of ill ease, and when it didn't, that decided her.

⇌ Taka ⇌

In the quiet of the room that was set aside for her in the Zōkame family wing of the New Council complex, Taka fumbled the tie she was working on and cursed the second under kimono. Then she decided to go ahead and curse the entire outfit, all three layers, all the ties, the padding, the obi, all of it. She hated how long they took to put on, how much they stifled her movement, and how clumsy she felt when she was wearing them. She couldn't imagine how people did this every day. She wished that she could wear her leathers to this dinner, but Tsuku-san had provided her with kimono specifically for the purpose of dressing appropriately for these types of occasions, and she had been dismayed to find that Tsuku-san had had the foresight to provide her with more here in Rōjū City. Taka wouldn't normally dress just to please someone else, but the older woman, once she had learned that the twins were likely Kiko-san's children, and thus her own great grandchildren, had been so enthusiastic about the dinner being a celebration that Taka didn't have the heart to dress down for the occasion.

She cursed again, when she heard a faint knock on the sliding door to her room.

"Come back later, I'm trapped by ridiculous clothing," she muttered, struggling to retie the belt that was meant to hold the excess fabric of the second kimono in place.

She was furious, then mortified, when she heard the screen door slide open and turned to find Kusuko standing in her doorway, looking perfect in her own red and black kimono, as though it were a second skin rather than a trap made of silk.

"Can I be of any help?" she asked, quietly.

Taka wanted to scream at her to leave, but she took a deep breath and realized that was just her own embarrassment rising to the front. She truly needed help, or she was likely to miss dinner entirely. She swallowed, reminding herself that Kusuko was probably very good with kimono, and it was in no way inappropriate for her to offer to help.

"Yes, please," she said, when she'd gotten herself under control. "I'm not used to these clothes."

Kusuko slid the door closed behind her, and moved quickly to Taka's side. She moved with confidence and efficiency, and Taka couldn't even keep track of all the little adjustments that Kusuko made to various layers of the outfit. Before Taka could even ask what the young assassin was doing, she had moved on to the next piece, and in a blur of motion Taka found herself fully dressed, her obi tied in a grand and decorative bow behind her.

She shivered slightly when Kusuko placed a small wooden comb into her hair, and her hand lingered by Taka's neck.

"You look lovely," Kusuko said, her eyes cast at the floor.

Taka was so taken aback by the expression on Kusuko's face that it took her a moment to laugh.

"You must be joking," she said. "I feel like a child in her mother's clothes."

Kusuko met her gaze, then, her eyes flashing with frustration.

"And can you not look lovely, even when you feel uncomfortable?"

"I suppose I could, but I very much doubt that I do."

"Can you not simply believe that I think you look lovely?"

"I have no reason to."

"I just said you did."

"Those are just words."

And then Taka, who hadn't even been sure why she was arguing, except that the notion that she looked lovely in her current circumstances seemed preposterous to her, was shocked into silence when Kusuko stepped forward, closing the distance between them, and pressed her lips to Taka's.

Taka considered pushing the young assassin away from her, but every part of her body objected to that idea. Instead, she found her arms yearning to reach for Kusuko's waist and pull her closer. She stopped them, but only barely.

Only once Taka's whole body was alight with a fire she had not felt before, did Kusuko finally step back and break the contact.

"There," she said, defiance in her gaze. "Now you have more than words."

Taka inhaled slowly, the scent of Kusuko's honeyed soap blending with the grassy smell of tatami that filled the room, and then she exhaled to the same long count.

"How did you know about the danger to Mitsu and Mishi in Shikazenji?" she asked.

The words surprised her, even coming from her own lips. She hadn't meant to ask them. Not right this moment. But Kusuko's kiss had taken her by surprise, and she'd liked it rather more than she felt comfortable with. She didn't trust this woman's affection, though she desperately wanted to, and that was the danger. Anything Kusuko said or did could be part of a trap. She couldn't be sure that Kusuko's words were real. Even when she used kisō to detect lies, she couldn't be sure when words were only dancing around the truth. This woman who beguiled her so easily was a master of deceit, and nothing made Taka more wary than the idea that Kusuko, beautiful, perfectly presented Kusuko, found her attractive.

Kusuko's face was the cold mask that she took on when she was disguising her emotions, which meant that Taka had surprised her. She supposed she should feel accomplished for having surprised a spy, but she only felt a sense of sadness, as the warmth that had been in the young woman's gaze drained away.

"A spy informed me," she replied.

Taka had sent out her kisō to meet Kusuko's, and she knew that the words Kusuko said were true, although that didn't necessarily mean that they represented the whole truth.

"Whose spy informed you?"

"A hishi spy," Kusuko replied, the distance between them growing as she spoke, even though neither of them had moved.

"Why did you come here?"

"To report to Zōkame-sama, as I was bid. You were there when I was given my assignment."

"No, I mean, why did you come to this room, just now?"

"I had something to tell you."

"More information, from another spy?" she asked.

"In a way," Kusuko said, a smile beginning to play on her lips.

Suddenly Taka couldn't take it anymore, the attraction that pulled her to this woman she couldn't trust. She didn't have the energy to try to sort through all the things that Kusuko might say, to play the word games that might be needed to find the truth. She was done with this not knowing, not trusting.

"You should go," she said, before Kusuko could speak again.

"But this information—"

"Go!" Taka said. "I don't want to hear any more of it. Whatever you have to say, you can say to someone else."

Kusuko looked as though someone had slapped her, and instantly Taka wanted to call her back and unsay it all. She was tired from their journey, she was frustrated with having to wear a kimono, and she was flustered by Kusuko's compliments, and her kiss.

Before Taka could form the words her mind supplied, Kusuko was gone, the sliding door closed behind her.

≈ Kusuko ≈

She wasn't surprised by Taka's response, really. She had half expected it. Certainly, it was an understandable and predictable reaction to feeling attracted to a person you could not trust, and she knew better than anyone how little Taka should trust her. What surprised her was how much the reaction had hurt her, as expected as it was, and how much it pained her to find herself running through the former Rōjū complex, heading not for her own rooms, but for those of her father. Knowing what she would tell him, and fearing what it would mean for all of Taka's friends and allies.

At least one thing was certain. With all ties cut to Taka-san, she would no longer be endangering the young healer. At least she could be sure that Mamushi-san would not lash out at the young woman, just to destroy Kusuko's caring for her.

She ignored the moisture that gathered at the corners of her eyes, and the swollen feeling in her throat, focusing on her destination instead. She thought about all of the things that she would tell Mamushi-san, and tried not to think of the few things that she would never tell to anyone at all.

2日 4月 新議 1年
2nd Day, 4th Moon, Cycle 1 of the New Council

～Taka～

TAKA WOKE SLIGHTLY before dawn, rubbing troubled dreams from her eyes, and wondering what she could do to apologize to Kusuko-san. The young assassin hadn't joined them for the evening meal last night, and Taka had gone to bed feeling more than a little bit guilty. In truth, she might have been the only one who had noted the young woman's absence. Tsuku and Yasuhiko were both so entranced with getting to know their great-grandchildren that they had barely paid heed to anything else during the meal, and Mishi and Mitsu had seemed rather preoccupied with…each other. Taka was pleased at that development, as she thought it would be a good thing for both of them, and increased the likelihood that Mitsu would remain a part of her life, but her own worries about Kusuko, and the damage she might have done to what little trust they'd built between them, made it hard for her to appreciate whatever new thing was budding between Mishi and Mitsu.

She stretched, then slid open the screen beside her futon, which opened onto a small veranda overlooking a private garden. The predawn light cast an eerie glow over the small green space that was still coated in morning mist, and she shivered once before rising to dress herself.

Kami curse it, she was not going to bother with a kimono today. She couldn't imagine anyone being offended with her failure to dress for the morning meal, and besides, she could always change if she had to.

Comfortably dressed in her leathers, she headed out to find Kusuko-san.

~~~

Kusuko was not in her rooms in the Zōkame wing, and there was no sign that she had stayed there the night before. Taka thought that the young spy must have chosen to return to her own rooms in the hishi complex, instead. Taka's guilt deepened, as she considered how much she must have offended Kusuko, in order to drive her from this part of the city.

Having gotten used to the twins' early waking habits, over the many days they had traveled together, Taka thought that they were the only other people in this wing who were likely to be up, so she decided to go see if she could interest them in another writing lesson. When the twins had asked what they would be taught at the school for healing that Taka would take them to, they had both seemed very excited when she'd mentioned reading and writing. They had seemed so eager that, as she and Kusuko had first started leading them to the Zōkame estate, Taka had instructed them daily whenever they stopped to eat and rest, and they both had made great strides. She felt a new surge of guilt, remembering how Kusuko had helped them both with their practice characters when they had stopped to make camp in the evenings, while Taka was busy snaring and preparing their supper.

~~~

When she received no response from within the twins' room, after knocking gently on the sliding door, she started to turn away, assuming that the children were still sleeping after so much food and merriment the night before, but, as she turned to go, she noticed a small piece of parchment sticking out beneath the door. Curious, she bent down and pulled it out.

Her jaw slackened as she read the carefully scrawled note, written in the basic characters of a child.

Thank you for your help, and all of the food. See you again.

At the bottom were the characters for earth and water.

She had no time to take pride in the children's ability to write their own names—she was too busy pushing open the door, seeing their tidy futons lying on the floor, unslept in, and feeling the rising panic as she realized what the note and empty room must mean.

It was only when she heard a wail farther down the hallway, from the area where Tsuku-san and Yasuhiko-san slept, that she began to wonder if Kusuko's empty room might be in some way related to the missing children.

~~~

When Taka arrived at the rooms that Tsuku and Yasuhiko made use of whenever they stayed in Rōjū City, she found the sliding door already open, and Tsuku and Yasuhiko standing in the doorway fully dressed. Tsuku-san held an unrolled scroll of parchment, and looked pale and angry.

"Are Mizu and Tsuchi in their rooms?" she asked, as soon as Taka arrived.

Taka shook her head.

"I was just there. The room is empty, and they left a note."

She passed the note, scrawled in Tsuchi's hand, to Tsuku-san.

"Why force the children to write this note, and then send me this?" Tsuku-san asked, passing the scroll to Taka-san.

Honorable Tsuku-san, we have your grandchildren. In exchange for your own life, and the life of your husband, we will return theirs to you. At sundown, bring Yasuhiko-san and meet us atop the northern cliffs outside the city. Bring no one else. If you will not exchange yourselves for the children, then they are of little use to us, and the girl in particular will be made an example of.

Regards,

The First Rōjū

Just as Taka finished reading the scroll, Mitsu and Mishi joined her in the Zōkames' doorway.

"Could they have made them write it as a distraction, in case we found them before they got far enough away?" Taka wondered aloud.

"But we would have started searching for them immediately if we thought they had run away, so how would that give them any extra time?" Tsuku-san replied.

Taka had handed both the note and the scroll to Mishi, as soon as she had arrived, and she had, in turn, passed them both to Mitsu.

"The children might have decided to run away on their own," Mishi said. "They ran away from us after we found them the first time. They're not very trusting of adults."

"But why would they? After all this time traveling with us, surely they trust us by now," replied Taka.

"It doesn't matter why," Tsuku-san said, her face a strange mixture of sorrow and ire. "The Rōjū have them, and we have to get them back."

"But how?" asked Mitsu.

"We'll do as they ask," Tsuku-san replied. "I'll exchange my life for theirs."

~~~

Taka walked back to her room, her legs heavy with defeat. No amount of arguing had been able to convince Tsuku-san not to hand herself over to what was left of the Rōjū Council.

It wasn't that Tsuku-san didn't understand the risk to Gensokai. She understood better than anyone what a precarious position the New Council was in, and how easily it would topple if she were removed. That was clearly what the remaining Rōjū were counting on. It was the purpose of this entire exchange.

No one was suggesting that Tsuku-san should let the children die, but no one had any better suggestions, either.

The morning had been spent trying to come up with some way to keep Tsuku-san away from the Rōjū, while still keeping the children alive. The plan they had come up with did not leave Taka feeling confident. It amounted to handing Tsuku-san over and hoping for the best.

Traitor's Hope

She was looking forward to a few moments alone, to try to come up with a better solution to their troubles. Everyone had agreed to meet again after the noon meal.

She slid open the door to her room and walked inside. It was only when she slid the door closed behind her that she noticed the shape lurking in the corner.

She turned, her hand flying to her hunting knife, and prepared to render whoever was waiting for her unconscious.

"I mean you no harm," a familiar voice said, from the shadows.

When Taka still didn't drop her hand from her hunting knife, Inari-san stepped forward, holding up both of his hands.

"I've come to offer you hope," he said.

~~~

Taka still didn't like the plan, but that was likely because too much of it relied on chance. Or perhaps it was because of who she would be forced to trust, in order for the plan to work.

She took a brief moment to wish that the twins had never been kidnapped, and she wished even more that it didn't look as though Kusuko had orchestrated their abduction. She also wished that Kusuko's involvement didn't matter to her so much.

"All will be well, Taka-san," Tsuku-san whispered, patting her arm gently as they walked along the isolated forest path that wound up from the road leaving the city to the tops of the northern cliffs.

Taka tried to smile in response, but she only managed something that probably looked like a grimace.

"I don't like the chances we're taking," she said.

Tsuku nodded, and Taka wondered if any of them thought that their plan would work.

"What are our choices?" Tsuku asked. "We cannot leave the twins to these miscreants. Even if they weren't Kiko's children, it wouldn't be right."

"But your capture could be the end of the New Council…" Taka said, with hesitation.

"Hmph..." Tsuku groused. "If, after all these moons of practice, that group of fully trained Kisōshi can't organize themselves without me, then they don't deserve to be in charge of anything."

Taka smiled, because she knew that was the reaction Tsuku-san was looking for, but she didn't feel like the gesture was genuine at all. She knew, all too well, from Tsuku's own admission, that the New Council was entirely fragile. Without Tsuku-san and Yashuhiko-san to guide it, organize it, and convey their vast network of information to the New Council, it wasn't strong enough to hold against the chaos being sown by the remainder of the Rōjū.

That part of what the Rōjū were trying to achieve with this scheme was clear. With Tsuku and Yasuhiko removed from the equation, the New Council was primed to fall. And if that happened, leadership would be open to anyone capable of showing the people some semblance of order. The way things were right now, people might even embrace a return to the old ways. After moons of upheaval in almost every town and village, people might be tired and distraught enough to accept a return to the old power structure.

No, the position of the New Council was fragile, at best, and it couldn't suffer many more blows. That was why the apprehension of the sanzoku had been so pivotal. Not only had it stopped a real threat to the people of Gensokai, but it had shown the power of the New Council. It had been a demonstration of their ability to fight for their people, to protect them, and to respond to a crisis. It had taken an embarrassingly long time to manage, but now that the sanzoku were captured, the New Council had a firmer leg to stand on when it came to defending itself against accusations that they didn't know how to govern a people.

But if Tsuku and Yasuhiko were publicly removed, at this point, the New Council might not weather the storm of inquiry and indecision that would follow.

So, while Taka agreed that it was unacceptable to allow Mizu and Tsuchi to remain in the hands of the Rōjū, or the hishi that worked for them, she wasn't sure the risk to Tsuku and Yasuhiko was acceptable.

Despite the fact that almost everyone shared her concerns, she'd been outvoted when they'd made their plan.

Traitor's Hope

And now...

They approached the abandoned barn that perched near the cliff tops carefully, Tsuku and Yasuhiko leading proudly, with her trailing just behind them.

When they reached the barn, they saw that only three of the four sides were closed in. The north end was open to the elements, and they approached that entrance cautiously.

No one stood guard outside, something that made Taka more nervous than reassured, but inside they found, among the open flooring and the small drifts of leaves that cluttered the abandoned space, three men dressed in full Kisōshi garb.

"We bade you come alone," the man in the center said. He wore grey hakama, with a matching uwagi that made Taka wonder if he was only intending to remind people of hishi, or if the color signaled a clear association with that band of spies and assassins.

"Mamushi-san," Tsuku-san replied, coldly. "You can hardly expect us to come and trade ourselves for the lives of the children without anyone to hand the children over to. Are we simply to trust that you'll place them somewhere safe, once we've given ourselves to your custody? Besides, we've brought Taka-san. She's a trained healer—hardly any use, should we wish to fight you."

Taka didn't even bristle at the remark. It was the simple truth. She wasn't *completely* useless in battle, but she was nearly so. She hardly considered that a shame, as she was the only person here who could put people back together again once the violence was over with, which was something she considered to be of much higher value.

She was more concerned with the fact that the man was called Mamushi-san. That was the name that both Yasuhiko and Kusuko had ascribed to the leader of the hishi. It certainly explained the dark grey of the man's uwagi and hakama. She was rather surprised that the man had bothered to show up in person to this little exchange. It only reinforced her worry for Tsuku and Yasuhiko. The Rōjū must consider them quite important, indeed, if they were willing to put the leader of the hishi forward for their capture.

"Chiki-San, Mori-san, I'm surprised to see you here in person. You honor us," Yasuhiko said, nodding to the two other men. Taka didn't recognize the names, but as she took a closer look at the two other men, she realized that they were both members of the former Rōjū voting council. She quietly took a deep breath, unwilling to draw attention to herself, but suddenly very concerned for their wellbeing. She didn't know how many of the Rōjū remained free, but she knew it was only two or three. If these were all the remaining Rōjū, along with the leader of the hishi, then this meeting was of even greater importance to their enemy than she had suspected. And, if that was true, then there was good reason to suspect some kind of treachery.

"We welcome your presence, Yasuhiko-san. We have much to discuss."

"Oh?" Tsuku-san asked, her eyebrows raised in pleasant inquiry. "I thought we had merely come to turn ourselves over in exchange for the children."

"Certainly, certainly," the former Rōjū replied. "But surely you must be wondering what we hope to gain by taking you into our custody."

"I know what you hope to gain by taking us into custody, Chiki-san," Tsuku replied. "You hope to destabilize the New Council, and eventually overthrow them to regain the power you once held. I wish you luck. Now, let us see the children."

Both of the former Rōjū looked disgruntled at being denied the chance to explain their plan, but neither of them denied that what Tsuku-san had said was true.

"Very well. If you are in such a hurry to become our captives..." Chiki-san nodded to Mamushi-san, and Mamushi gave a sharp whistle that was quickly followed by the sounds of shuffling outside the barn.

After a few moments, Taka released a breath she hadn't known she was holding, as she saw Mizu-chan and Tsuchi-kun carried into the barn on the shoulders of two grey-clad hishi. They were both unconscious, but a quick stretch of Taka's kisō confirmed that they were both breathing, and seemed uninjured. She could only imagine the fight the two would put up if they regained consciousness, and she wondered if they'd been drugged from the start, or if they'd simply been allowed to escape from the Council Complex and then captured as soon as they were out of sight of the New Council guards."

Taka stepped toward the two children, but stopped mid-stride at the sound issued by Chiki-san.

"Ah ah ah..." he tsked. "Not until we have the Zōkame family in our custody."

Taka stayed where she was and waited. Her palms were starting to sweat, and she longed for this to be finished. She tried to widen her senses, to take in more of what was going on around them, but she found her gaze sliding to Tsuku and Yasuhiko, as they cautiously approached Mamushi-san.

Mamushi whistled once more, and Taka could hear the sounds of feet approaching the barn again. Two more hishi entered, each carrying a length of rope. They followed Mamushi-san's silent signals, approaching Tsuku and Yasuhiko with caution.

The two elderly Kisōshi did nothing to resist their captors. They stood placidly, allowing themselves to be tied.

Taka looked to the two former Rōjū and raised an eyebrow in query.

"Hand her the children," Chiki-san said, brusquely. He seemed somehow displeased with how smoothly everything was going, and Taka hoped fervently that their plan wasn't unraveling at this very moment.

Not wishing to give anything away, she calmly moved forward and began assessing the two young yukisō before her, checking more carefully for damage than she had been able to during her previous long-distance inspection. She still found the children uninjured, and she pressed her hand to their necks to set about waking them from their forced slumber. She wasn't as effective as a restorative balm, but her kisō could sense and remove the soporific plants used to induce slumber with a bit of time and a direct connection to her patient.

"How will you carry them?" asked one of the Rōjū, surprising Taka almost enough to make her forget her task. Did the man actually care, at all? Surely, he was only asking because he wanted her to leave before they attempted to move Tsuku-san and Yashuhiko-san from the abandoned barn.

Before she could answer, they heard more shuffling from outside the barn, along with a few grunts of pain. The hishi that were holding Tsuku and Yasuhiko shifted their grips, pulling forth daggers. Taka hoped that they hadn't misjudged the Rōjū's desire to leave Tsuku and Yasuhiko alive.

"I found these two trying to sneak past your perimeter guards." Kusuko's voice came from the doorway, as she tossed Mitsu across the opening to the barn and dragged Mishi behind her.

Taka grimaced as she watched Mitsu slide across the wooden floor. He looked like a rag doll, and so did Mishi. She took a moment to appreciate just how strong Kusuko must be, despite her tiny figure, to have moved Mitsu and Mishi, who were both much larger than she was, any distance at all.

"A few well placed sedative darts made them much more pliable."

She dragged Mishi across the entrance, as she spoke, and dropped her unceremoniously next to Mitsu. Then she threw Mishi's katana and wakizashi down a few armspans away from the two prone forms. Taka winced again.

"So," Chiki-san said, turning to Tsuku and Yasuhiko once more, his eyes alight with malice. "You intended to have yourselves rescued by your warriors, did you? How delightfully double crossing of you. I would never have expected it from the honorable Yasuhiko-san, and his most respected wife."

Kusuko brushed her hands off on her kimono, and approached Mamushi-san and the two former Rōjū.

"What would you like me to do with them?" she asked, as she approached. "I wasn't certain you wanted them dead, so I decided to bring them here, first."

Taka shivered at the casual way that Kusuko mentioned the prospective deaths of Mitsu and Mishi. She had thought that, perhaps, having traveled and fought with the two of them over the past few moons would have created some amount of concern in the assassin, but she reminded herself that this was precisely what she knew Kusuko to be, a master of subterfuge who wore other personalities the way that some women wore combs in their hair—a different one for every occasion, and none of them her true self.

She waited to hear what the men would say, and in the meantime continued the work of rousing the children. Chiki-san had asked how she would carry them, but the answer was that she couldn't carry both of them easily enough to make good time getting away from this place, so the children would need to be conscious enough to move themselves—unless she had help.

She glanced at Kusuko, while the young assassin looked expectantly at her masters, with Mitsu and Mishi lying still and silent at her feet.

No, she couldn't count on any help, at all.

⇒ Kusuko ⇐

Kusuko waited for her father to tell her what he wished her to do with Mishi and Mitsu. She wondered vaguely what Mamushi-san would choose. She thought that the Rōjū would probably wish to eliminate such strong enemies, a preference that they'd made clear before, but she wondered if her father wished the same. Would he simply express that wish because the Rōjū expected it, or would he surprise them all by acting from some other motivation entirely? She could never really be sure how he would react.

She found it very difficult not to look at Taka, but she knew it was essential that she not do it. If she looked at Taka now, she was sure that her father would read her feelings clearly on her face, and she knew what would happen then. Nothing she cared for was ever allowed to remain. So she kept her gaze focused determinedly on the three men standing before her, and didn't even spare a glance for Tsuku and Yasuhiko, or the grey-clad hishi that held them.

"Kill them," her father said, without consulting anyone else. "They aren't worth the trouble they might cause."

The Rōjū didn't object, so Kusuko turned on her heel, in order to approach Mitsu and Mishi. She tried to avoid Taka's gaze, but the young healer's eyes were so wide, and her gaze so insistent, that Kusuko couldn't help but meet her glance, if only for a second. The panic written across Taka's face made Kusuko's heart stumble, but she did everything she could to keep her face a mask of disinterest.

She couldn't let anyone see her concern, she couldn't. If her father—

"On second thought," she heard her father say, and her stomach turned to ice inside her, even before she could turn to look at him once more. "Let them remain to take the children to safety."

Kusuko turned at the small gasp that came from Taka's mouth. She could see the relief spread across her face, but Kusuko's heart was hammering wildly in her chest. She turned to lock eyes with her father's, just as he opened his mouth to speak once more.

"There are two of them, after all. Which means that we hardly need this healer."

Kusuko moved before she could think. She moved before she saw her father's hand twitch. She moved before the light had a chance to glint off of the oil coated shuriken that left her father's hand, once she'd already made her leap. She moved with the lightning reflexes she had honed for cycles, and she worried that it was still too late. She barely felt the blade impact her chest, but she smiled, even as she collapsed on the floor in front of Taka-san.

She could hear the room dissolve into chaos around her. Part of her mind even registered that Mishi and Mitsu seemed to be stirring from the feigned sleep they'd assumed before letting her truss them up and throw them into the barn. She ignored all of it. Taka's eyes appeared before her face, and the concern that shone from them was almost enough to take away the excruciating pain.

"Which poison is it?" she heard Taka ask, though her voice sounded distant.

"Henbane," Kusuko said, her voice a harsh whisper. She couldn't be certain, really, but that was the poison her father favored, and, judging by how painful the wound was, it seemed likely.

She saw Taka nod, then felt the healer's hand against her neck. Along with the kisō that she knew was flooding into her from Taka, Kusuko could feel warmth radiating out from the young woman's hand. She wondered if that was a side effect of Taka's healing, or if she was simply feeling the tingle that had always come from touching Taka, even through the pain of the poison. She watched Taka's determined face, trying to ignore the blackness that crept in around the sides of her vision.

"Beautiful," she murmured, as her vision continued to darken, against her will. She saw Taka turn and smile at her briefly, with tears streaming down her face, and the sight filled her chest with warmth, even though she didn't like the tears or what they probably signified. Her eyes slipped closed, then, and she thought that maybe the warmth in her chest had actually come from the poison, but before she could decide which it truly was, the blackness claimed her.

⇒ Mishi ⇐

Mishi still couldn't quite believe what she'd seen. Not only had Mamushi-san been willing to kill Taka, seemingly for no reason other than his own whim, but Kusuko, somehow anticipating the move, had flung herself in front of a poisoned shuriken to stop it from happening. Both actions mystified her, for entirely different reasons, but she didn't take the time to contemplate either one. Instead, cycles of training took over, and she pressed the advantage of the shocked silence that initially followed Kusuko's sacrifice by charging Mamushi-san before he could loose any more shuriken.

Speed was of the essence, and while Mishi wasn't fond of attacking opponents who weren't already attacking her, she and Mitsu were in an enclosed space, and greatly outnumbered, not just by soldiers, but by hishi. She needed whatever advantage she could get.

So she struck quickly, before Mamushi-san could gather himself for another attack. She winced, slightly, as she struck a shallow cut across his chest. The man still had his eyes locked on Kusuko, with an odd look of shock etched across his face. She moved away before he had time to register the blow, and hoped that the oil on her sword would do its job quickly.

Without waiting for him to react, she turned to the former Rōjū standing behind Mamushi-san, and saw that these men, at least, had drawn their swords. She'd fought them both before, and recalled that the taller one was an indifferent swordsman, while the shorter of the two was a worthy opponent. Luckily, Mitsu had already engaged the taller man with his dagger, which left Mishi facing a single opponent. Not that she expected that to last very long—the room was crawling with hishi, as were the woods outside, and Mishi wondered how long it would take before those men overwhelmed them. She had to hope that Tsuku and Yasuhiko could hold their own against the hishi who held them.

Mishi had just succeeded at breaking the skin on her opponent's forearm, a success that would hopefully lead to his losing consciousness soon, when a shrill whistle caught her attention. She didn't break her focus on her opponent, but she noted that Mitsu's opponent had already collapsed to the floor of the barn. She tensed, expanding her senses, expecting a pile of hishi to mob her at any moment.

Instead, she was shocked to find her senses telling her that the hishi surrounding the barn were moving away. Her peripheral vision confirmed that the hishi next to the door were already making their way outside. The hishi closest to her were in the act of picking up Mamushi-san's unconscious form, and that made even the Rōjū that she was battling pause in his swordplay.

Mishi didn't lower her guard, but she didn't attack, either. The man was already swaying on his feet, and she thought it likely that he would soon lose consciousness.

"What's the meaning of this?" he asked, even as his legs buckled.

One hishi, who had just checked Mamushi-san's pulse, and then loaded him into another hishi's arms, stepped forward.

"There has been enough death here today. I do not think that Mamushi-san will find himself attracted to your cause any longer. It is clear that you are on the wrong side of history."

Mishi was tempted to step forward and pull the dark grey mask from the man who stood before her, since she was fairly certain she recognized the voice, but she resisted the impulse.

"You'll pay for this betrayal," slurred the Rōjū that she had been fighting, even as he toppled sideways to the floor.

"I very much doubt that," replied the hishi.

Then the man shocked her even further. After sending all the remaining hishi, including the one carrying the prone form of Mamushi-san, out of the barn, he knelt beside Kusuko and Taka, removing his hood. Mishi was unsurprised to find that Inari-san was the man beneath it.

"Does she live?" he asked, his voice barely more than a whisper.

Taka nodded, but did not speak, and Mishi wondered how much longer that would hold true; Kusuko's form was quite still, her breathing so shallow that Mishi could barely make out the rise and fall of her chest from where she stood.

"Can you keep her alive?" he asked.

Taka didn't reply, but continued with whatever work she was doing.

"Inari-san, it may be best to leave her to her work," Mishi said, as kindly as she could. She was surprised to see that Inari seemed to hold some affection for Kusuko, though the evidence was clear enough on his face.

Inari nodded, and stood.

"I know that you've no reason to trust me, but I'd like to stay with you for as long as…" his voice trailed away as he looked at Kusuko once more. "I'd like to stay with Kusuko."

Mishi certainly didn't trust the man, but he'd just had ample opportunity to kill them all, and had chosen not to, so she didn't think it likely that this was a ploy to attack them singlehandedly. She nodded, then looked down at the two Rōjū collapsed at her feet.

"We'll have to tie them," she said to Mitsu, who had come to stand beside her. He nodded, making his way to Tsuku and Yasuhiko, who, though abandoned by the hishi who had been holding them, still had their arms bound with rope.

Mishi took another long look at Taka and Kusuko. With her heart hurting for her friend's pain, and Kusuko's sacrifice, she turned to do what little she could to help.

12日 4月 新議 1年

12th Day, 4th Moon, Cycle 1 of the New Council

~ Kusuko ~

KUSUKO BLINKED HEAVILY, wondering why her limbs felt as though they were filled with lead, instead of blood. Opening her eyes seemed like the most difficult task she had ever accomplished and, while her mind wished to raise her head once her eyes had regained their focus, her body suggested that it would be a very bad idea indeed to do anything of the sort.

She tried flexing her fingertips, instead.

Her fingers took so long to react that she worried, briefly, that she was paralyzed, and when they finally moved, it was but a twitch. She tried the same with her toes, and found the response similarly delayed and weak.

She tried to remember what had happened to her that might have caused this state, but a voice distracted her before she could get her mind to focus on the memories.

"Kusuko-san?" the voice asked.

Kusuko tried to reply, but a soft moan was all that came out. Damn it all, even her throat wouldn't move faster than a tortoise crawling uphill.

Suddenly, the white ceiling that she had been looking at was replaced by a more welcome sight. Her physical reactions might be slow, but her brain recognized Taka's deep brown eyes in a single heartbeat. She felt the corners of her mouth rise in a smile, and vaguely wondered why those muscles had been so much quicker to respond than all the others.

"Taka," she managed to croak, after a moment of trying.

Traitor's Hope

Taka smiled, her eyes shining brightly, and Kusuko wondered if she was crying, or if her eyes always shone like that. She couldn't quite remember.

"You had us very worried, Hifu-chan."

That was not Taka. That was another voice, and Kusuko wondered why on earth Inari-san was there with Taka.

Taka's face disappeared from Kusuko's limited line of sight for a moment, and then returned.

"You will be very tired for a long time, days and days yet, maybe a few tendays, maybe a moon, it's difficult to say. And it will take…time and effort to finish your healing. Please continue resting. I'll go get you some food, and leave you here with Inari-san for now."

Kusuko couldn't find her voice in time to object to Taka leaving before her face disappeared from view, and she heard a shoji slide open and closed somewhere close by. She wasn't sure she wanted to talk to Inari-san, while she knew for certain that she wished to spend more time with Taka.

"Why are you here?" she managed to croak, knowing that Inari remained close by, even though she couldn't see him.

The man's face appeared in her view, shortly after she asked the question.

"I couldn't bear the thought of your father killing you, even if by accident, and I wished to stay by your side until I was certain that you would recover. Besides, I thought you would like to know how everything played out."

It came back to her, then, all at once. Mamushi throwing the shuriken at Taka, and Kusuko just barely getting herself in front of it. She couldn't raise her arms to feel for a mark in her chest, but she was certain that she would find one if she could. What she didn't understand was how she had possibly survived. Mamushi favored only the most deadly poisons for his blades, and a poisoned wound to the chest should have made for a very quick death.

"How am I alive?" she asked, when she could force her throat to form the words.

Inari-san's face was deadly serious above her.

"I think the only credible explanation is that Gensokai's greatest healer happened to be immediately by your side, in the moment that you were injured. She also seemed particularly…invested in your survival. It was remarkable to witness, really, though I was sure that I was staying only to be able to collect your remains to return to your father. I have to say, I have never been so thankful to be wrong in my entire life. You owe that young woman everything, and no mistake."

Kusuko only nodded, or tried to. She thought she might have managed to get her chin to dip slightly, but she couldn't be sure.

"Will I be able to move soon?" she whispered.

Inari shook his head, as he spoke. "That is a question best directed at your healer. Judging by the fact that you can move your fingers and toes, I would say it's possible. In truth, I don't know if even Taka knows how much you'll recover."

Kusuko tried to nod again, and this time she thought she had a fraction more success at getting her chin to duck toward her toes.

She wanted to ask more questions: Why had Inari stayed with her? What had happened to her father? Why had Taka worked so hard to save her? But she couldn't find the energy to form the words, and her eyes were beginning to drift closed once more, against her will.

"Rest, Hifu-chan. You have earned it."

Kusuko didn't particularly wish to follow that command, but she found she had little choice. Sleep began to claim her, though she was vaguely aware of the sounds in the room around her. She thought she heard the shoji open and close once more, then she smelled broth, and felt Taka kneeling beside her.

"You should rest too, Taka-sama, you're barely in better condition than she is."

"You shouldn't call me Taka-sama. I by no means outrank you, let alone by so much that I would earn that honorific."

"Anyone who can do what you did, to save Kusuko-san, is worthy of that honorific."

"Hmph…well, in that case, you can't tell me what to do and use that honorific in the same breath. Either I am above your ability to coddle, or you should strike the -sama from my name."

Traitor's Hope

"Ha! Well played, Taka-sama. I retract my suggestion that you rest. As the most talented healer in the realm, and probably far beyond, I defer to your expertise in this matter."

Kusuko couldn't hear Taka's reply, but she doubted that it was a kind one. She was sure that Taka took much greater exception to being referred to as "sama" than to being coddled and told she should rest. She wanted to say as much, but she was long past having control over her voice, or even her eyes. She fell deeper into slumber, and the last thing she heard before sleep fully claimed her was Inari, saying, "I'm not sure where the hishi took Mamushi-san, but I will not be seeking him out anytime soon, unless it is to cut him down for what he did to Kusuko, and what he meant to do to you."

She could hear true anger in Inari's voice, and she wondered why he was being so obvious with his emotions, or if it was simply a very good act. She had never heard the man express himself so directly. He was a master of subterfuge...

Sleep took her, and dreams of her father fighting Inari with snakes and swords danced through her mind, while she lay cocooned in a shell of cool, protective water, watching the whole thing. Then she dreamt that Taka came to her, placing a hand on her face, the gentle touch spreading warmth through her, even as it covered her in a refreshing sensation like water from a fresh spring. After that, she did not dream.

22日 4月 新議 1年

22nd Day, 4th Moon, Cycle 1 of the New Council

⇌ Taka ⇌

TAKA SAT ACROSS from Tsuku-san, trying not to feel embarrassment at the state of her kimono. She really should forgo the pretense of wearing them, even when she was in civilization, since she could never keep the damnable things clean. She had only been wearing this one for a candle's burn, but already the hem was covered in dirt and she'd just managed to drag her sleeve through her tea cup. Impressive, considering how small a target it made.

"Are you getting enough sleep, Taka-san?" Tsuku-san asked, after carefully sipping her own tea and replacing the cup on the table, with all the grace of a young dancer. Taka tried not to let the older woman's elegance, poise, and ability to keep her kimono immaculate make her feel self-conscious, but it was a struggle.

"As much as I can. Kusuko-san still needs help healing. Her body is fighting the long-term effects of the poison and I fear that, if I do not help her, she will never recover fully."

"It is a miracle that she will recover at all, Taka-san. Be sure not to treat yourself too unkindly, if she cannot be all that she was before."

Taka repressed a shudder. It had been a full tenday since Kusuko had first regained consciousness, and it had taken a full tenday of healing and sleep before Kusuko had woken that first time. She could now move her hands and feet, and raise her arms for short periods of time, but her body was still struggling to repair all the damage that the poison had done to her system. Her lungs and heart had suffered the most damage, but all of her muscles seemed to be struggling to regain their capacity to move, and Taka wondered if there was some damage to the connection between her mind and body.

She sighed, as she thought about it.

"I know. However, I'm confident that she can regain much of her movement, possibly all of it, with more help. It's as though her body doesn't wish to reconnect with her mind's control. It's something that she can't do alone, but I can help her, and…"

Tsuku raised an eyebrow at the hesitation in Taka's speech.

"Yes, Taka-chan?"

"Tsuku-san, have you ever heard of a fire kisō doing healing work?"

Tsuku's eyebrows rose in a display of surprise, which Taka had rarely seen from her, and Taka waited for incredulous words to follow. Instead, the older woman was silent for a long time.

"I haven't…but that does not make it impossible," Tsuku-san said, at length. "To my knowledge, no healers have found a way for fire to connect with the inner workings of the body…but, Taka-san, if you have an idea about how to do it, you should look into it. You certainly have a capable fire kisō to work with."

Taka nodded, surprised at the encouragement from Tsuku-san. She had been expecting the older and wiser woman to tell her that she was crazy to even suggest the idea, that there was a reason that all the fire Kisōshi were senkisō and not yukisō. Still unsure, she asked the thing that had been bothering her most since the idea first occurred to her.

"If it *is* possible, why is it that trained healers are only ever water and earth kisō? Why not allow air and fire to train as yukisō as well?"

Tsuku-san shrugged.

"There is much that has been lost in the thousand cycles since the Yūwaku took power, and were then overthrown. Even so, not many scholars have done any research into the times before the Yūwaku, since the Rōjū discouraged anyone from looking too closely at a history that contained female Kisōshi who were equal in numbers and ability to their male counterparts. We're lucky that they only locked that history away, rather than destroying it, although who knows how much was lost in the initial rebellion. Either way, I would say that you should not limit yourself by what others deem "impossible." There is much we do not know about the healing arts anymore. And how much has been lost about Kisōshi in general? One of the committees that I'm attempting to establish within the New Council has the sole purpose of relearning our history, and spreading that information throughout Gensokai."

Something about Tsuku-san's tone of voice made Taka meet the elder woman's eyes at that point. Usually, when she looked at Tsuku-san, she saw only a graceful and well composed elderly woman, who always seemed to know what she was about. Now, for the first time, she got just the smallest hint of the Tsuku-san who was undertaking a huge effort, trying to restore an entire culture skewed and perverted by centuries of corruption and lies. She saw, although only for a moment, the weariness and weight in the woman's eyes, face, and jaw.

"What can I do to help?" Taka asked, without really thinking.

Tsuku-san smiled then, and the weariness and weight were hidden once more.

"Continue as you are. Work to learn as much as you can about healing, and the different ways it can be accomplished. Ask your tree-kami as many questions as you can think of, and search for your own answers as well. Go to the school where you've agreed to teach, and share your knowledge with as many others as possible. There is no better way to reverse what has been done to Gensokai than to educate its people."

Taka nodded, wondering if she would ever be content within the confines of a school again, even if that school was nothing like the Josankō that had scarred her so long ago.

The truth was, she missed her cave in Yanagi's woods, missed the simplicity of that life, and missed the ease with which she had been able to travel to and from that home to anywhere she liked. It made her sad to think that she would need to be away from Yanagi's woods for so long. It was the only place she'd ever truly felt at home.

"Do not mistake my words, Taka-san," Tsuku said, as though she had been reading the thoughts from Taka's face. "I do not mean to say that you should do nothing else, save work at that school. After all, how can one expect you to ask Yanagi-sama all the questions that you will surely have, if you spend all of your time away from him? I only ask that you spend some of your time sharing your knowledge with others. How and where you do that is entirely up to you. It seems like a school for healers would benefit from your knowledge, and would be eager to share it with others, but that does not mean that it is the only place you should spend your time. I imagine one could teach a small number of very exceptional students from just about anywhere in Gensokai...even a small cave in the woods..."

Taka smiled then, though she was unsure if Tsuku-san was simply saying that to make her feel better, or if she truly meant it. Taka didn't think there would be very many students who would want to learn from a hermit in a cave and her strange tree-spirit mentor...but Tsuku had said very special students, and Taka could think of a pair of yukisō who, while only five cycles old, might very much appreciate living in a place where no one would try to make them sleep in separate dormitories, or attend regular classes, but rather teach them through the experiences that the woods had to grant them, and allow them to take fighting lessons from a wandering female Kisōshi, every now and again, as well.

"I should ask Yanagi-sensei what he would think of me bringing more humans into his woods."

Tsuku-san nodded. "That seems wise."

⇒ Mishi ⇐

Mishi sat quietly, her face in the sun, a gentle breeze that smelled of cedar and far-off rain caressing her cheeks, her feet dangling from the deck above the garden, rubbing choji oil into the blade of her katana and listening to the almost inaudible sound of footsteps approaching.

She said nothing as Mitsu lowered himself to sit beside her, his legs mimicking her own, dangling from the raised deck.

"It's nice to see you treating your sword well," he said quietly.

She hadn't looked at him yet, but she thought that he was looking into the garden as he spoke, not inspecting her while she cleaned her blade. She appreciated that.

"Tools must be well kept, and weapons are the most finicky tools of all."

Mishi knew why Mitsu was mentioning it. She had always kept her katana and wakizashi in impeccable condition…until she had decided that spending time with her swords was a danger to the people around her. They hadn't sat unattended long enough to rust, but she had ignored them until she needed them to defend against the sanzoku, so this was the first time in many moons that she had cleaned them properly. Yet she knew it was her mindset that Mitsu was referring to, and not the availability of choji oil.

"If the past few moons have shown me anything, it's that it would be just as dangerous to the people I care about for me to wander around unarmed, as armed," she said, her attention still focused on the task of rubbing the fragrant oil into the blade.

Mitsu smiled, and she didn't have to see his face to know that was what he was doing. An odd sensation, but one that she'd become accustomed to in the past few tendays.

"Well, it's nice that you've finally come around to recognizing that. I, for one, have been terrified of being killed in my bed by hishi for tendays now, and knowing you're armed takes quite a bit of the stress away."

Mishi smirked.

"And what makes you think I'd be able to do anything in time to protect you, even if I slept with a katana beneath my pillow?" she asked.

"Well, I was rather hoping you might be lying next to me," Mitsu said quietly.

Mishi finally raised her eyes then, and when she met Mitsu's gaze, what she saw there filled her stomach with a tingling heat that briefly made her wonder if she'd called fire to her skin. In the moon since they had defeated the sanzoku in Shikazenji, they had shared many kisses and spent much time together, but they hadn't resumed their explorations of each other's bodies for a number of reasons, only one of which was lack of privacy.

"Oh?"

There was mischief in his eyes, but longing too, and Mishi wondered if he could sense all the conflicting emotions that ran through her at the mere suggestion of sharing his bed.

The mischief left Mitsu's eyes, then, though the longing stayed, and Mishi's breathing hitched as he spoke again.

"I don't...Mishi-san, you can say no...our friendship means so much more to me than anything else, but I can't pretend that your kisses don't set my body alight and...I often think of that one night in the woods. I don't wish to hold any claim on you, Mishi-san, but consider it an invitation...one you can accept or reject, at any time you like."

Mishi thought about that for a long moment. Had fear of some claim kept her from Mitsu's bed this long? No, Mitsu was just as prone to wandering as she seemed to have become, and she didn't sense anything in him that seemed to wish to hold her against her will. But she knew that he loved her; he had made that clear enough. She thought that she might love him too. Or, at the very least, she would be devastated to lose him, and she thought that might be the same thing. And he said he felt as though her kisses set him on fire. Didn't she feel the same way?

"You know, there's still a chance that I might accidentally kill you in my sleep..." she whispered, the heat suddenly leaving her body, as she realized the words might be true.

"You still have the nightmares?" he asked.

She nodded.

Mitsu was silent for a long time, and Mishi was sure that he would reply with a retraction of his earlier invitation.

"Well, one has to die somehow," he said at length. "I can think of far less pleasant ways to die."

Mishi's mouth dropped open, as she stared at him.

"I meant with a sword, you fool."

The mischief was back in his eyes.

"I know, Mishi-san, but perhaps if I've tired you out first, it'll lessen the risk."

And just like that, the heat returned to her body, and the tingling spread from her abdomen.

1日 6月 新議 1年

1st Day, 6th Moon, Cycle 1 of the New Council

⁓ Kusuko ⁓

KUSUKO CLUNG TO the shadows like a warm cloak in winter, and made certain not to let even the tiniest hint of her kisō escape her. Luckily, her perch in the rafters of the chamber was comfortable enough that she could be confident that she was remaining completely silent. She ignored the smell of mold and dust that permeated the thatched roof above her, and instead kept her attention on the conversation taking place below.

"You've taken much longer to report back to me than I had anticipated," Mamushi said, his back straight as he sat with his legs folded beneath him and poured the tea.

"It has taken me this long to decide whether or not I wished to kill you, brother."

Kusuko knew better than to allow any reaction to Inari-san's words, but the shock still radiated through her, and surprise was even evident on Mamushi-san's face.

"And what did you decide?" Mamushi asked, his voice as flat as if he were inquiring as to the health of the other man's horse.

"If I wished you dead, I wouldn't have come to speak with you first," Inari replied.

"Oh? I would have thought you would enjoy my knowing who had orchestrated my end."

"No, Mamushi-san. Even after all you've done, I would take no joy in taking your life, nor would I come to throw your mistakes in your face. If I ever choose to kill you, it will be because I've decided that you're well beyond salvage, and if that's the case, then it would do you no good at all to know the reasons for your death."

"And what are my mistakes, then, *brother*?"

"You killed your own daughter, Mamushi-san. Is that not sufficient?"

Mamushi-san's face paled at that, and Kusuko knew then that, whatever trick Inari had insisted he could use to convince Mamushi of their lie, it had worked. Until that moment, Mamushi-san had believed her alive.

"It cannot be," he whispered.

Inari snorted.

"You saw the deed yourself, Mamushi-san, the shuriken embedded in her chest. Why you chose to attack the healer I will never understand, but Kusuko sacrificed everything to save that young woman, and you of all people know how well your own poisons work."

"But my spies…I've had word from the Zōkame estate that a young woman matching Kusuko's description was being cared for."

"And did you not expect that the Zōkame family would go to great lengths to keep you from coming after their household, once more? What better way to protect themselves from harm than to pretend they were housing and healing your own daughter?"

"But no one knows that she is my…"

From where Kusuko was perched, she could clearly see the twist of Inari-san's face that marked his incredulity.

"You told them?" Mamushi asked, his voice disbelieving.

"There was no further reason to hide the secret from them. With your daughter dead, what could it possibly matter if they knew?"

Mamushi's face greyed further, and Inari let out a long sigh.

"It was anticipation of your reaction now that made me decide you did not deserve death, after all."

Mamushi's eyebrows rose in puzzlement at that.

"You knew what my reaction would be?"

"I had hoped," Inari clarified. "I didn't like to think that you had killed your daughter without remorse."

"I still cannot…why? Why would she do something so foolish, Inari-san? I trained her better than that."

"Is it so foolish to try to save the ones we love, Mamushi-san?"

Inari rose then, leaving his untouched tea cup on the low table before him.

"I am sorry that you have lost your daughter, Mamushi-san...but I hope that you recognize that her death was not a waste. She sacrificed everything for love, and I do think there was once a time when that was something you would have understood."

Inari turned and left the room then, and Kusuko waited in silence for her father to follow, so that she could exit without being seen. The man sat in silence for half a candle burn, and Kusuko began to wonder if he would ever leave.

"Did you think that I wouldn't know?" Mamushi-san asked the empty room. "Did you really think that Inari-san could fool me, after all of those reports?"

Kusuko's breath caught, as she realized that Mamushi was addressing her. Knowing that the man could easily send a signal that would fill the room with hishi, and not wishing to fight against overwhelming odds, Kusuko dropped from her position, moving to stand before Mamushi-san.

"He did fool you," she said, though she was less sure now than she had been only moments ago. "I saw it in your eyes."

"He told the truth..." Mamushi said. "Which doesn't make any sense, unless you claim to be a ghost."

Kusuko shrugged.

"I may as well be..." Kusuko paused for a moment, thinking about what Inari had done. The truth of the words she had just spoken sank in for her then, and she knew why the lie had worked. "Your daughter is dead, Mamushi-san. It turns out she was just another hifu among many, shed in the moment that you tried to kill the woman I love. The me that still lives is less...and more, than your daughter ever was. The loyalty I owed you is gone, and the affection too. I...I will no longer answer to you, Mamushi-san. I am my own master from now on."

She straightened as she said it, certain that it was true, all of it. Even if Mamushi-san struck her down right now, even if he called in a whole room full of hishi to end her life, she was not now, and never again would be, his creature. She saw the moment when the truth registered in his mind, and waited for the inevitable fury that would follow.

It didn't come.

"Then you should go, Kusuko-san," he said, calmly.

Kusuko worked to keep her expression neutral as she took in the look on his face, but his features were once more the mask they had always been. She nodded, still waiting for the blow to fall as she turned her back, but it never came.

She walked to the door of the receiving room, slid it open, and stepped out into the hallway. One step at a time, she walked away from what she had once thought was the core of her being, and she almost laughed. She had always thought of herself as a snake, shedding its skin with each identity she left behind, and growing into a new one, but now…now she felt rather more like a phoenix. She had burned through everything within her, emerging as something entirely new and unexplored.

She took a deep breath, and wondered if Taka would appreciate a visitor at her cave in the woods. Would she wish to see Kusuko at all? Would she ever be able to trust her? Kusuko didn't know, but decided she would like to find out.

5日 6月 新議 1年

5th Day, 6th Moon, Cycle 1 of the New Council

⇒ Mishi ⇐

MISHI HAD LEFT Mitsu in the woods outside the school, reluctantly, even though it had been her idea to do this on her own. She could hear the sounds of Kisōshi drilling, even from this side of the gate, and she waited for the sounds to conjure visions.

She closed her eyes, anticipating the bile that would rise in her throat, the tightness that would clench her chest…but it didn't come. Instead, her eyes pricked with tears, as images of Kuma-sensei shouting instructions at her and her sisters flooded her mind. She wiped at the corners of her eyes with her hands, and took a deep breath. Tears were all right, tears wouldn't harm her or any of the people on the other side of that fence.

She pushed the gate open, and the sight that greeted her surprised her, even though she'd been listening to the drilling for some time before she entered. What surprised her was the fact that she was looking at young boys and girls, *both* training together. A smile came to her lips then, as she thought of how Kuma-sensei would have reacted to that.

She was startled from the warm thoughts that that filled her, though, when a shout caused all the children in front of her to stand at attention, with their arms behind them. She realized belatedly that she was, as usual, dressed in her uwagi and hakama, and wearing both of her swords. Of course, the training would stop for an unknown Kisōshi of rank.

She bowed slightly to the group, and spoke with enough force to be heard over the twenty tiny heads arrayed before her.

"Please, continue your training," she said. "I did not mean to disturb."

"You heard Yamainu Ryūko-san. One hundred more side kicks on the right leg!"

Mishi schooled her face into neutrality at the groans she heard from a few of the youngest children, but she couldn't help but smile when Ami came around the crowd of students and wrapped her in a tight embrace.

"Ami-chan," she whispered, her throat suddenly tight with emotion.

"It's good to see you, Mishi-chan," Ami said, her own voice sounding just as affected. "Come, let's head to the kitchens. One hundred side-kicks should keep them busy for a while, and one of the senpai will take over when I don't come back immediately."

"You have them so well trained, already?" Mishi asked.

Ami nodded, pushing her back to arm's length, presumably to get a better look at Mishi's face.

"You look much better than when last I saw you," she said, unshed tears still in her eyes.

Mishi only nodded. She didn't think she could speak without shedding her own tears, and she preferred to wait until they were in the privacy of the kitchens before she did that.

"Come," Ami said again, taking her hand.

Everything looked different now, as Mishi had known it would, since everything was new. The old school had been razed to the ground by the fire that Kuma-sensei had asked her to light when they were abandoning the place to the Rōjū soldiers seven moons ago.

Ami, Katagi, and Tenshi had been forced to construct a new school, from nothing. Yet, Mishi was pleased to find the layout identical to the old school, her old home, and was delighted that the kitchens were exactly where she had expected them to be.

"I never thought I'd be able to return here," she said, without thinking, as they entered the kitchens and the smell of steaming rice filled her nostrils.

She was surprised to see that Ami only nodded.

"I had thought it might be that bad," she said.

"You knew what was wrong with me?" Mishi asked, awestruck.

Ami tilted her head to one side, in a manner that was so nostalgic to Mishi that she almost laughed, despite her surprise.

"Not exactly, no, but I could tell that I made you uncomfortable, and that Katagi-san did as well. Mishi-chan, we've been sisters for eight cycles now, and in all that time I've never made you uncomfortable, not even when I've pelted you with nosy questions, or spent a tenday without bathing. I knew something was wrong, and, well...you weren't the only one who was having nightmares. Mine likely weren't as troubling as yours, but...I could guess."

Mishi fought back tears at the thought that Ami had suffered any portion of the same nightmares that had been tormenting Mishi for all these moons. Unsure what to say, she reached forward, embracing her adopted sister and letting tears stream down her face.

"I'm so sorry I didn't talk to you about it," she said, still holding Ami close. "I don't know how I could have been so selfish as to think that I was the only one suffering..."

"It's all right, Mishi-chan," Ami said, her own voice also choked with tears. "I didn't say anything either, and...well, it was hard enough as it was, ne? I'm just glad that you came back. We've missed you, Mishi-chan."

Mishi couldn't think of anything else to say, so she simply held Ami tighter, and let the tears flow freely from her eyes.

"Any chance you've got one of those to spare?" an uncertain voice asked, from the doorway behind them.

Mishi released her sister and looked up. She had been too absorbed in the emotions of the moment with Ami to sense anyone approaching, and her stomach dropped slightly to see Katagi standing in the doorway, his eyes downcast like a kicked puppy's.

"Katagi-san," she muttered, unsure if she was pleased to see him or not. Still, when she saw the pain in his eyes, as he glanced at her once more, she knew that she didn't want to be responsible for that hurt any more than she already was. "Come here," she said, opening her arms and wrapping him in a hug that was only slightly less desperate than the one she had given Ami.

"It's good to see you, Mishi-san," Katagi said, returning her embrace.

Mishi nodded, not sure what she could say without her voice breaking.

Ami touched both their shoulders, then wiped at her eyes.

"I should go check on the students," she said. "You're staying for dinner, Mishi-chan?"

Mishi nodded, even as she and Katagi released each other.

"You look much better," Katagi said, as Ami made her way out of the kitchen.

Mishi chuckled, wiping at her eyes.

"So everyone tells me," she said dryly.

Katagi smiled then, and Mishi grinned to see the genuine happiness on his face. She had worried that she would see hurt in his eyes every time that she looked at him.

"You look better too," she said, only now remembering the brooding stares she had received from him moons ago, before she had taken off with Taka and Mitsu on their travels north.

Katagi laughed then, a full and earnest sound.

"Yes, well, I think I've finally learned that pining after a woman doesn't give you any right to her affections."

Mishi flinched at that statement, surprised by the brutal honesty behind it, but there was no malice in Katagi's tone, and he only laughed again when she cocked an eyebrow at him.

"I think I owe you an apology for...my assumptions about our friendship, Mishi-san."

Her puzzlement must have shown on her face.

"Let's just say that, after many hours of conversation with Tenshi-san and Ami-san, I've reassessed what all my confessions of love were really worth."

Now Mishi was sure that her eyes must be wide as tea cups.

"Mishi-san, you were the first person that I had ever had feelings for, and...well, you know everything that I said...and I meant it all, but...after you left I felt that you had betrayed me somehow. That I deserved your time and affection simply because I had offered you my own."

Mishi waited for Katagi to say more. She couldn't begin to guess what kind of a response she was expected to give.

"Thankfully, Tenshi-san and Ami-san made it very clear to me that I was...well, an ass, to put it simply. You had never made any kind of commitment to me, and it was ridiculous for me to expect anything from you."

Mishi was dumbfounded. She had come here dreading the conversation she would be forced to have with Katagi, worried that the hurt puppy face she'd seen at the beginning would only be the start of a long conversation, in which she would have to explain her feelings to him. Instead, he had flipped the whole thing on its head, and was telling her all the things that she'd thought she would have to explain to him.

"I do hope you'll still accept my friendship, though," Katagi said quietly, after a long silence.

Mishi looked into his eyes, and saw that the offer was sincere. She smiled then, and wrapped her arms around him once more.

"Katagi-san, I would be honored to continue to call you friend."

19日 9月 新議 3年

19th Day, 9th Moon, Cycle 3 of the New Council

~ Epilogue ~

TAKA LISTENED TO the rhythmic clack of Mizu and Tsuchi going through their forms together, then laughed as the choreographed play of wooden swords deteriorated into an unplanned wrestling match.

"Knock it off!" she called, from her place by the fire at the mouth of her small cave, without ceasing her careful scribbling on the scroll she had laid out on her small scribe's lap desk. The school of yukisō was expecting her latest report on the advantages of mixing kisō from various elements in healing soon, and she wasn't about to allow Mizu and Tsuchi's sibling squabbles to distract her from her writing.

The children continued their wrestling match, though, and she was about to stand, to break things up, when another voice called from the far side of the clearing in front of her cave.

"I can guarantee you that your weapons instructor will be furious, if she hears that you're ignoring your healing instructor."

Taka swallowed then, recognizing the voice, and took a moment to breathe and compose herself, before looking up at a face she hadn't seen in over two cycles.

"Mishi-san will be here in a day or two. She had business at the Zōkame estate, and she will not be pleased to learn that her pupils are ignoring their other instructor," Kusuko said to the children, who now stood with their gazes on the ground.

"Yes, Kusuko-san," they replied.

"Now, Yanagi-sensei has informed me that he is in need of some arrowroot for a salve, and I have some sweet bean mochi, fresh from the Zōkame's kitchen, for the first person who finds him some."

The two children were gone, almost before Kusuko had finished issuing her challenge.

"I have arrowroot stored in the cave," Taka said, not knowing what else to say to the woman who approached her, clad in a pristine red and black kimono, complete with an elaborately tied obi and shining hair combs.

"Then I suppose you win the mochi," Kusuko replied, smiling.

Taka laughed, though she wasn't sure what was funny.

"It's good to see you," she said.

"Is it?" Kusuko asked, the hope in her face almost painful for Taka to see. "I wasn't sure I'd ever be a welcome visitor here."

Taka sighed. She didn't know how to explain how she felt to Kusuko, or anyone else, for that matter, so she changed topics.

"Mishi-san told me that you'd been helping her look for female Kisōshi," she said.

"Yes. After she started helping me heal, after you talked to her about using fire kisō to heal another fire kisō...we've become friends, of a sort. And I find myself well suited to asking the kinds of questions needed to find people who might still be in hiding."

"I imagine so," Taka said. She felt the smile that had started to form on her lips fading, and realized that they had inadvertently come right back to the topic that she'd been trying to avoid.

"Do you think you could ever trust me again?" Kusuko asked.

"Was it you who told the hishi about the children running away? About how they could be used against us?"

Kusuko hesitated, but eventually nodded.

"It was. I went to report to Mamushi-san, as soon as you turned me away," she said.

Taka cringed, hating the reminder that she had been cruel to Kusuko that night. Could she blame her for acting against them, then?

That still didn't explain things.

"What made you change your mind? Inari-san said that you sent him to us, that day."

Kusuko smiled, then.

"Ah yes, Inari-san. Rather like the many-tailed fox he's named for, don't you think?"

Kusuko paused for a moment, but when Taka said nothing, she continued.

"He found me that day, right after I'd reported to Mamushi-san, and questioned me about everything I'd just done. I told him, as he was a colleague, if you will, and I had no reason to hide anything from him, anyway. And then he looked me in the eyes and asked me a question that I couldn't answer, for a moment. He asked me if I wished it undone. Of course, I told him that was preposterous, that it couldn't be undone. He admitted that was true, in the strictest sense, but that the outcome could be changed, if I wished it."

Kusuko stopped then, and Taka waited for her to continue, but she didn't.

"That still doesn't tell me why," she said, after a long while.

"Two reasons," Kusuko said, after pausing so long that Taka thought she wouldn't speak. "One of them was that none of it made sense anymore. I used to think that following my orders helped to preserve the ruling of Gensokai, helped to keep things running. But everything I was asked to do against the New Council was sowing disruption—it was the opposite of the purpose that I'd always thought my role was serving. I had just spent moons with you and your allies, learning how desperately the New Council was trying to establish order, an order that made way for women with power, and consequently those without it as well, and then my actions, my orders, were to help tear that all apart."

"And the other reason?" Taka asked, after a long moment.

"The other reason was you," Kusuko replied, her gaze suddenly flitting to the trees nearby. "I hated the idea of putting you, and those you cared for, in danger."

Taka was quiet for a long time, and Kusuko didn't disturb the silence.

"I wondered why you never joined Mishi-san when she came to visit and instruct the children," she said, at last.

"I thought I wouldn't be welcome, and…I was too much a coward to see the rejection in your eyes."

Taka appreciated the honesty of that reply.

"Kusuko-san, I can't say that I can trust you right now," she said, after careful thought.

She saw the disappointment in Kusuko's eyes, and quickly added the rest of what she wanted to say.

"But I would love to get to know you, the real you, whatever you've decided that is, and learn to trust you."

The smile that radiated from Kusuko brought a warmth to Taka that did much to help counter the chill fall air.

"I hear you need help keeping the two miscreants in line anyway," Kusuko said, her face full of too many emotions to name. Taka decided she preferred it to the cold mask that she was used to seeing on Kusuko.

"They do prefer their fighting lessons to their healing lessons, most days," she admitted. "And Mishi-san doesn't visit often enough."

"Perhaps I could help with that," Kusuko offered.

"Perhaps you could," she replied.

A Note to Readers

DEAR READER,

THANK YOU! Thank you for choosing to read *Traitor's Hope*, for staying with it to the end, for caring enough about what happens to Mishi, Taka, Kusuko et al to want to get to the last page. I'm honored that you have come this far with me.

Reviews are an author's lifeblood. Both good and bad reviews (as long as they are thoughtful) help a book find the right audience, so if you feel inclined to leave a review on Amazon or Goodreads it would be much appreciated!

If you haven't read *Blade's Edge* yet, but you would like to spend more time with Mishi and the gang, you can find it on Amazon, or ask for it by name at your local bookshop.

If you enjoy short stories, you might enjoy *Rain on a Summer's Afternoon*, which is a collection of short stories that are completely unrelated to the world of Gensokai.

If you want to say hi:

Get in touch with me via e-mail at virginialamcclain@gmail.com

Check out my blog at www.virginiamcclain.com

Acknowledgements

WRITING ALWAYS SEEMS like such a solitary job (and in many ways it is), but in truth there so many people who play a pivotal role in making a book come to life. If I miss anyone, it's the product of an addled brain and too many people to thank. I'll do my best though.

First, I have to thank my editor, Aurora. Not only is she a rockstar under normal circumstances, but for this book she powered through like a champion to finish up her edit before giving birth. She knocked it out while nine months pregnant. You know, no big deal. She's a total boss.

Next, I have to thank my husband and daughter. My husband is always supportive. He plies me with tea and coffee, takes care of more than his fair share of the housework, and encourages me at every turn. My daughter is miraculously patient for an almost one year old and lets me ignore her long enough each day to not only write books, but to get them ready for publication too.

Nonetheless, I wouldn't be nearly as productive if I didn't have some wonderful people in my life who are willing to distract the aforementioned almost one year old periodically so that I can get some more intense work done. Namely: Anne, Kirby, and Lee. Without you three… well, this book would still be sitting on my computer and no one would be reading this acknowledgements section.

A huge thank you also needs to go out to my Japanese language hero, Gavin Greene. Gavin is the magic behind all of the Japanese and pseudo-Japanese used in both *Blade's Edge* and *Traitor's Hope*. Of course, his volunteered wisdom can only go so far, and my user error is to blame for any and all mistakes you might find within the text. He is a professional translator, so if you ever need Japanese-English translation done, be sure to look him up.

The following people were kind enough to volunteer their time in helping to seek out and destroy comma splices, typos, and continuity errors (again, anything left over after these superheroes helped out is entirely my own responsibility): Angela, Brenda, Anthony, Corey, and Jill. Thank you all so much!

Finally, I would like to once again thank the Kickstarter backers for *Blade's Edge*. Had that first project not succeeded, this book would never have been written. In particular, I would like to thank my dear friend Johnny McDowell, whose name (thanks to a communication snafu) was left out of the print edition of *Blade's Edge*. Hopefully, this will make up for it a bit.

About the Author

VIRGINIA WRITES because when she stops the voices pile up, and it's more fun to share them anyway. When she isn't writing she'll take any excuse to go play outside. If there are no excuses to play outside, she will curl up with a good book and a warm beverage. She currently resides in Winnipeg with a dog named Artemis, her husband, and a tiny, new human that delights and mystifies her daily.

Made in the USA
Columbia, SC
18 September 2017